BLAZE of PASSION

Lisa Ann Verge

W0008739

POPULAR LIBRARY

An Imprint of Warner Books, Inc.

A Warner Communications Company

POPULAR LIBRARY EDITION

Popular Library® and the fanciful P design are registered trade-
marks of Warner Books, Inc.

Cover illustration by Gregg Gulbronson

Popular Library books are published by
Warner Books, Inc.
666 Fifth Avenue
New York, N.Y. 10103

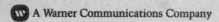 A Warner Communications Company

Printed in the United States of America

First Printing: July, 1989

10 9 8 7 6 5 4 3 2 1

"Kilian, please— You must stop, this must stop,"

♡

she heard herself whisper, at the same time lifting her head to kiss his hair.

"You do not mean what you say." He rubbed his unshaven chin against her bosom. "Come, sweet—look me in the eyes and tell me."

She felt weak with passion. Her gaze focused on his face, so close to hers, so open, so emblazoned with naked desire.

His gaze swept from her parted lips to the turmoil fermenting in the darkened depths of her gray eyes. "I want you, Aimee, but if you truly want me to leave, I shall."

Her throat was thick and she could not speak. You are a commoner. And I am a woman bound by a bargain to another man. What did it matter? The reasons sounded empty and meaningless. Why not succumb to this ecstasy?

"Come, Aimee," he whispered, his voice ragged against her ear. "Come, my ice maiden. Melt for me."

She slowly wrapped her arms around his neck. "I have already melted, Kilian," she murmured, tilting her head for his kiss. Whatever Kilian planned to do to her she welcomed it willingly, openly, with a full heart. Tomorrow she would let the shame and recriminations surface. For tonight, she was a woman.

CHAPTER

1

Aimee de Chacontier stood before the open door, her voluminous black skirts moving in the cold March wind. She reread the letter then crushed the thick parchment between her stiff fingers.

"I am sorry I had to be the bearer of bad tidings, Vicomtesse."

She started at the sound of her solicitor's voice and looked up at him. His pale skin was flushed from the battering of the wind as he stood on the threshold of her doorway. "What a terrible hostess I am," she murmured, suddenly remembering herself. She smoothed the parchment, folded it into neat quarters, and slipped it into the pocket of her quilted dress. "Come in from the cold and have some cider."

With a coolness that belied her inner turmoil, Aimee lifted the heavy wool cloak from the solicitor's shoulders and handed it to her maid, Manon, who stood nearby. She closed the carved oak door and threw the bolt decisively into place. The roar of the wind stopped and the Great Hall was encased in a strange, expectant silence.

"Manon, spread Monsieur Valerin's cloak over the grating to dry," Aimee said, her voice hoarse despite her efforts to control it. "And bring us some hot cider and *carré Norman*, would you? We shall be in the parlor."

Aimee glided soundlessly over the marbled floor as she led the solicitor across the main room of her castle. An apple tree log burned in the enormous fireplace, releasing its spicy scent along with blasts of heat. Normally, she would have entertained the solicitor in this Great Hall, among armor and ancient weapons, but she could not do so today. She glanced up at the portraits of her late husband's ancestors. Somehow, she could not let *them* hear what was soon to happen.

She entered the parlor and walked directly to the brandy. "Manon should be awhile with the cider. Will you share some calvados with me?"

"Of course."

Wordlessly she poured two glasses and handed one to the stout solicitor. Lifting hers briefly to his, she poured the rich gold contents down her throat. She closed her eyes as the burning liquid quelled the queasiness that had begun in her stomach.

"Feeling better?" he asked.

"No." She turned away and moved to look out the high, thin window at the newly ploughed fields. "I knew this would come, Monsieur Valerin. I've known it since my husband died, one year ago. Still, I was not prepared." She pulled upon the belled, weighted sleeves of her widow's weeds. "I don't think I will ever be prepared."

"I am afraid, Vicomtesse, that you have no choice." He reached up to push a few wispy gray hairs beneath his powdered wig. "You should prepare for what you will do when the king makes his decision."

Aimee's gray eyes narrowed. Reaching inside her

pocket, she unfolded the letter and scanned it carefully. "All the intendant of Normandy says in this note, monsieur, is that the search for an heir for my husband's estate is over. The fate of this estate is now in the king's hands." She tilted her head. "There is a chance the king may decide to leave the estate to me, the vicomte's widow."

The solicitor's gaze slid away from her penetrating stare, and he did not answer.

"In addition, my friend, the Comtesse de Vierzon, is in the French court, and she is an intimate of Madame de Pompadour," she continued, heedless of the solicitor's silence. "She may persuade the king's mistress to plead on my behalf."

The solicitor placed his glass on a table and shrugged his broad shoulders. "We have discussed this many times, madame—"

"Or, maybe now that the war with the Austrians is over, the king will no longer need as much money."

"It was not my choice to bring you this news, but I have warned you since your husband died that this was going to happen. You were, after all, the vicomte's wife for only two days."

Aimee stared at him in silence. Her thin fingers toyed with the sleek, black tresses that had escaped from her haphazard chignon. Her solicitor had never dared to say this to her; indeed, no one had dared say those words in her presence. Though the entire village talked about nothing else but the Vicomte de Bocage's hasty wedding and hastier death, no one had dared face her with suspicions and accusations.

She may have been the vicomte's wife for only two days, she thought, but she had been his ward for fourteen years. Since childhood she had played on these lands, worked on these lands, and finally, when the vicomte became too frail, she had run the entire estate. She had been mistress of this house long before the hasty marriage to the vicomte made her position official. The wedding was the vicomte's idea. He had wanted her to remain on the estate and take care of these beloved lands.

She frowned, unconsciously narrowing her gaze on the uncomfortable solicitor. The vicomte's will had stated that she, as his wife, would have a life estate in Château Bocage, but the workings of the monarch's ministers were slowly prying her fingers away from the title. Today's news brought her one day closer to the frigid poverty that awaited her when these lands were taken away.

"Please, Vicomtesse," Monsieur Valerin pleaded. "You know that Norman law does not allow a childless widow to stay on her husband's estate."

"It seems I do now," she replied tartly. "But I believe that it took more than those ancient laws to overturn my husband's will to the contrary. I think it took a war with the Austrians and the excesses of Madame de Pompadour to convince the intendant of Normandy to offer this estate to the crown."

"There is little doubt that the king of France's treasury is depleted."

"Yes," Aimee mused. "If it were before the war, rather than 1748, I might be able to stay on this estate. But because King Louis XV is in need of money he feels justified overturning the will of an aristocrat."

Manon entered the parlor bearing a wooden platter with two earthen mugs of cider and a large square of pastry. Aimee turned away brusquely, unable to stomach the sight of the rich food. Monsieur Valerin reached for a steaming cup and then lifted a slice of the *carré Norman* to his lips.

Aimee watched over her shoulder as her solicitor in his blue satin finery pressed the pastry between his thick fingers. He could eat so easily—it was not his life that was being torn into pieces. After she left Château Bocage he would undoubtedly become the solicitor of the next vicomte, whereas she. . . . Aimee closed her eyes. She would return to the poverty and hunger and misery of the days before the vicomte took her as his ward.

"Have you no more schemes, monsieur?" she asked abruptly. "Last year you managed a year's grace by forcing the intendant to perform the search for an heir, even though the entire province knew the vicomte left no survivors. Do you have any more tricks for me?"

The solicitor spread his hands, now sticky with pastry, in distress. "I'm sorry, Vicomtesse, but there is nothing more we can do, except wait for the word of the king."

"And how long will that take?"

"I don't know. Weeks. Perhaps only days."

Days. Aimee turned and leaned into the window, clutching the damp stones of her castle with cold hands. Days were not enough. She needed weeks—perhaps months— to implement her last plan, her most desperate plan, to keep Château Bocage. She could not begin until Palm Sunday, and though Palm Sunday was barely two weeks away it shimmered in the distance like an eternity.

Her clear gaze scanned the familiar, precious horizon of the Bocage estate through the ancient crystal panes. The northern fields had not yet been plowed, but the western fields already glistened with the swiftly melting remnants of the winter's ice. Soon the skies would clear and the sun would heat the land until it smelled like spring. It was her favorite time of the year. She would not let the king throw her out of her home now.

"Don't forget that the vicomte did leave you a small amount of money," the solicitor said.

"That money has already been spent, as you well know." Her gaze was arrested by the sight of a lone rider emerging from the forest. "The intendant would not allow me to touch any of the vicomte's assets except what was legally mine. What do you think I have been living on in the past year?"

"Certainly the king will leave you with a dower of some sort."

"The king has not been particularly sympathetic to this widow's woes," she said tightly. She recognized the rider as her overseer, Gustave, but his white blond hair was nearly obscured by mud and offal. He rode around to the side of the castle, toward the servants' entrance and out of her sight.

She turned away from the window and faced her solicitor. "The vicomte married me to save me from poverty, you know." She arched her long neck to stare at the vaulted ceiling. "He also married me to save this estate. What will happen to this, Monsieur Valerin?" she asked, caressing the castle wall with a graceful white hand. "Will the next Vicomte de Bocage tear it down and build in its stead some opulent, gilded château?"

"That, madame, will not be your concern—"

His answer was interrupted by a vigorous knock on the parlor door.

"Come in, Gustave," she called, staring at the burly, disheveled man as he entered. "What's happened? I saw you riding out of the forest. You look as if you've been fighting off a pack of wolves."

"Nearly, madame," Gustave said, running his hand through his filthy hair. "We were scouting the east end of the estate when we came upon another trespasser."

"Another!" She walked briskly to the cider and refilled her mug for Gustave. "Did you capture him? We'll put him in the fields—"

"We didn't capture him."

Her arched brows drew closer. "You didn't?"

"No. He had a horse, a fine one," Gustave explained. "We fought, but he rode toward the northwest before I could get to my pistols."

"I see you are still having problems with trespassers," Monsieur Valerin interjected. He wiped his fingers, one by one, on a ragged linen. "They will end when the king makes his decision."

"I suspect they will only get worse," she argued, her eyes narrowing. "After all, if the king sells these lands to a typical French courtier, the courtier will never be here. Who will my tenants turn to when these thieves and vagrants roam the lands?"

"But at least the estate will be settled, and it is my impression, Vicomtesse, that it is only since the vicomte's death that these vagrants have caused problems."

Aimee's chin tightened, for she knew the solicitor's words to be true. In the past year her cider house had been ransacked, dozens of bags of her grain stolen, as well as several goats and one horse. The sound of gunshots had become common in the forests as poachers killed her deer and wild grouse. These men thought that she, as a woman with a tenuous claim on wealthy lands, could not protect her own. She was determined to prove them wrong.

"Where are your men, Gustave?"

"Not far behind me. They followed the trespasser for a while, but their horses were tired and his stallion is strong. He was heading northwest, deeper into these lands."

"Send the men to the north, past the orchards," she ordered. "They may be able to cut him off before he reaches the border of the Duc de Montchamp's lands."

"Madame. . . ." Gustave turned his cap in his hands. "The men are exhausted. So are the horses."

Her lips tightened. Gustave and his men had captured four trespassers in the past week. She did not want this one to slip out unpunished. "Then tell Benoit to saddle my mare, Gustave," she said defiantly. "I'm going to scout the north side."

Gustave's blond beard quivered slightly. "Madame, with all due respect—"

"Gustave."

"The man had a musket, madame, and it seemed he knew how to use it."

"I have pistols, Gustave, and I *do* know how to use them." She turned to Monsieur Valerin. "You will understand, monsieur, if I leave you to find your own way out."

Aimee pulled her black, woolen cloak tightly across her chest as she slipped down the spiral staircase to the dank, ground floor of the castle. The gesture was useless—she knew that the quilting was a meager defense against the Norman wind—but somehow she felt safer swathed in the voluminous folds.

She pushed the rear door open and entered her gardens. The wind whirled restlessly through the dry boughs of the elms, scattering twigs across the unkept paths. She chose the darkest route and wandered briskly through the narrow turns. Her slippered feet gripped a loose cobblestone, and Aimee made a note to tell Gustave to fix it before the spring planting.

If I am here for the spring planting. The thought scattered through her mind, loud and lonely. She slowed her pace along the winding paths and lifted her face to the sky. The clouds loomed angrily above her, while their sooty black bellies rolled swiftly over the landscape.

So the time had come. After all she had been through—the vicomte's hasty wedding, the battles with the intendant of Normandy, the rejected will—it would all come to naught. She would be tossed out of her castle without a second thought by a king who valued the favor of a courtier more than the will of a country aristocrat.

Aimee shook her head, willing the dark thoughts away. The king's decision was tomorrow's problem— Today she needed to capture this errant trespasser before the rain hid his path. She lengthened her stride until she reached the stables, where Benoit, the stable boy, stood holding the reins of her mare. Absently Aimee tousled the boy's shining cap of blond hair before pulling herself upon the horse.

Kicking the mare into a gallop, she leaned over her neck. The horse raced down the slope of the courtyard and headed recklessly toward the dark edge of the forest. In places the ground was still hard from the winter's chill, but Aimee knew that soon the rains would turn it all into an endless bog. She lifted her head and let the hood of her cloak flap against her back.

Skillfully easing the horse onto the thin, winding path toward the apple orchards, Aimee glanced around warily. If the trespasser rode straight, she knew he would pass through this glade. The evening mists had already begun their slow, languid dance around the trunks of the oak trees. She glanced fretfully at the sky, gauging the proximity of the storm by the color of the clouds. Too many trespassers had escaped justice on her estate. She could only hope that this one would not find a break in the hedges that bordered her lands. If he did, he could run straight through to the Duc de Montchamp's estate where he would be safe from her own scouts.

Aimee lifted her head sharply. The sound wavered through the thickness of the charged air; but to a woman who knew the sounds of this forest like the sound of her own heart, it was undoubtedly the crack of a musket. The echo reverberated among the trees and she tilted her head to determine the direction. With silent care, she nudged her mare toward the east, pulling the ramrod from beneath the stock of her pistol.

The acrid scent of sulfur drifted to her, tart and sharp over the mellow odor of the budding earth. Aimee pulled the mare to a stop. Her gray eyes scanned the fencing of trees and were arrested by a movement in a clearing some distance ahead. Her slim back straightened beneath the light corset.

A man crouched there.

Her melancholy dissipated under a rush of anger. She despised the wiry, shifty-eyed men she and Gustave found roving her borders. They were sly, cowardly fools who cringed in fear when faced with punishment for their crimes. She primed and loaded her pistol, silently wishing that she had the stomach to enforce a more violent punishment on these detested vagrants.

She gently urged the mare toward the small clearing where the man squatted with his back toward her. The litter that covered the earth was soft from the melting snow and the mare made little noise as they approached. Deliberately, Aimee raised her pistol from her thigh and cocked it.

A muscle in the intruder's back twitched slightly. In one glance, Aimee noticed his musket, discarded beside his foot, and the sudden, almost imperceptible, tightening of his body. "I suggest you stand, monsieur. Very slowly," she said loudly. "And don't believe that because I am a woman I will not shoot. I have deadly aim."

The man hesitated for a moment, then lifted his empty hands above his head and straightened. He wore breeches of a rough weave and a dirty linen shirt, torn at the sleeve. Though Aimee was looking down at him from the height of her mare, she could tell he was a tall man—a very tall man. His unbound, tawny hair flew irreverently in the breeze.

"You are trespassing, monsieur, and that is a very serious offense."

He turned around and stared at her, suddenly, boldly, and Aimee stifled the surprised gasp that rose to her lips. His clear green eyes riveted her from beneath the striking darkness of his straight brows.

This was no ordinary trespasser. She knew in that one shared look that this was no ordinary man.

"Has the Vicomtesse de Bocage reduced herself to hiring women to guard her borders?" the man asked, one brow lifting in mockery. "Or have I already vanquished all the men?"

Aimee struggled with the strange gushing of her thoughts. The man had an unfamiliar accent, far different from the broad, nasal inflection of the Normans. Unnerved, she glanced at his steed and immediately recognized the quality of the Arabian. "So you are the wolf that attacked Gustave," she mused aloud. She forced her voice to be stern. "You have gathered a litany of offenses, monsieur: assault, trespassing, poaching. And for your information, I *am* the Vicomtesse de Bocage."

The surprise flickered in his eyes. His gaze traveled slowly, insolently, over her swaddled frame. A slow smile began beneath the short scruff of his beard and mustache. "So you are the infamous Vicomtesse de Bocage. I have heard much about you in the village."

She bridled instinctively and lifted her pistol higher. "What is your name?"

"Kilian Laclos." He bowed shortly, like a courtier, extending one coarsely stockinged leg before him. "At your service."

"Indeed you are at my service, monsieur, since you killed one of my stags."

"Fortunate for me, for the incident has led me to your acquaintance." His gaze probed the folds of her cloak. "It is not often a common man gets to meet a woman of your notoriety."

Her lips tightened. She had expected to find a wild-eyed peasant clutching a bag of grain on a stolen horse, not this tall, straight-backed man with eyes like the devil. He spoke well—far too well for her tastes, and she wondered what such a finely built man was doing poaching on her estate. "This is one acquaintance, Monsieur Laclos, that could well lead to your death. You *do* know the punishment for your crimes?"

"Aye."

"Have you nothing to say in your defense?"

A light glittered in his intense green eyes and he crossed his arms across the width of his broad chest. The wind toyed in his hair, tossing the tawny waves in playful, wayward disarray. He looked as calm as a man at market evaluating a horse, rather than a poacher facing his judge. His fearlessness irked her.

"I was merely passing through these lands, madame. I meant no harm."

"You are trespassing. If you were merely passing through these lands you would have used the roads. Do you usually blaze your own path from one place to another?"

"Yes, in fact, I do," he said calmly. "I am a soldier by trade."

"You, a soldier?" She glanced at his rough clothes and unshaven face. "Surely the French army clothes its soldiers better than this."

He glanced down absently at his attire. One side of his lips lifted under the beard. "A beggar is less likely to be robbed than a soldier, madame." He straightened and captured her gaze with his own. "When not in battle, I prefer to stay out of danger."

Aimee frowned at his explanation. It was possible that he was a soldier; all the French troops were returning from the German states after the war with Austria. And despite the clothes and his unshaven face, he had the look of a soldier—tall, lean, as straight-backed as any aristocrat. She glanced at his steed. "And how does a 'simple soldier' get such a fine horse and musket?"

"Trophies of war. The English did not need them as much as I."

Aimee suddenly realized that he had killed the owner of the horse and musket, and he could very well do as much to acquire her pistol and mare. Her fingers tightened on the smooth wooden handle of her pistol. The wind whistled among the dry branches and the fresh, green scent of rain teased her. She knew the deluge would begin soon, and she did not relish leading this man back to the château while thunder cracked and rain dampened the priming of her pistol. There was danger in this man, in every lean line of his tall body.

"Move away from your horse, Laclos. You are coming back to the castle with me. I do not take kindly to men who trespass on my lands, still less to those who kill my stags."

"Still less to those who threaten to take away your estate," he murmured, watching with interest the slim woman's flashing eyes. "Your behavior has become legendary, madame."

Aimee chose to ignore his taunting, and instead kicked her mare over to his steed and reached down for the reins. The musket lay, gleaming, beside the stag.

"Certainly you will bring the stag back with us," Kilian said. "Night is falling. If it is left here, only the wolves will have a meal of it."

"If you step any closer to that musket, Laclos, you'll have a ball in your chest." She lifted her pistol higher. He shrugged and stepped back.

She glanced at the musket. She could not leave it here, unguarded, for any trespasser to pick up. She could bring Laclos back to the castle and direct Gustave to retrieve it, but night was falling and soon the wolves would smell the deer and swarm to this glade. Yet to get off her horse and pick it up herself was risking a battle with Laclos. She glanced at the breadth of his shoulders beneath the ragged linen. She knew who would lose such a battle.

She had no choice.

"Turn around and place your hands on that elm," she said sharply, gesturing to the tree behind him. The sky growled in response. Kilian turned and did as he was told, glancing briefly over his shoulder.

Her heart pounding in her chest, Aimee slipped out of

her saddle. Her booted feet touched the littered earth silently and she tightened her grip on the pistol. Her mare pranced as the first flash of lightning lit the clearing. Aimee whispered quietly in her ear, her gaze fixed on Laclos's back.

She walked away from the mare's warmth into the windy clearing. The branches rustled above her, sending a spray of nettles upon her hair. The breeze brought the scent of pine resin, then washed it away with the tartness of imminent rain. Aimee approached the musket, her eyes never leaving the tightness of Laclos's back. She kneeled beside the weapon and felt along the rug of dead leaves until she contacted the icy smoothness of the gun. Curling her cold fingers around the barrel, she slowly straightened.

The lightning flashed anew and Aimee started. Kilian unwound himself from the elm and leapt toward her. Lifting the pistol, she squeezed the tight trigger, but her arm was pressed away and it discharged uselessly in the air.

His hard body slammed against hers, pushing the air out of her lungs. His fingers formed a viselike grip around her wrist until she could no longer feel her hand and the pistol fell to the ground. He wrenched the musket from her and tossed it into the litter, then he captured her arms and forced them behind her.

Aghast, Aimee blinked up into Kilian's face. Her dark hair tumbled down her back. His gaze seemed to burn her skin as it swept from the top of her head to the pulse beating in her throat. There was something untamed in the rough stubble of his chin, the uncompromising slash of his brows, and for the first time Aimee felt terror.

He smiled as if he read her fear, and the smile swept up rakishly on one side, revealing strong, even teeth. "Now we see who has captured whom, Vicomtesse."

She struggled briefly, but his grip was too sure and her efforts only increased his amusement. Her throat dried to hoarseness as she struggled to speak. "You shall find yourself on the wheel by sunrise, Laclos, if you multiply your offenses."

"And who is going to send me there, madame, if you are in *my* custody?"

"My overseer will find me—"

He laughed, and his entire body rumbled with the sound. Aimee's cloak had fallen open and she could feel—all too well—the vibrations of his body through the worn velvet of her riding habit. She looked away from his eyes.

"*Ach*, no, Vicomtesse," he murmured, locking both her arms with one hand and using the other to turn her face to his. "I will look at you. The villagers did not do you justice—they did not tell me you were so young and had eyes of silver."

"And am I such a common topic of conversation?" she snapped breathlessly.

Kilian's brows lifted. "Come, Vicomtesse. Certainly a woman who marries a dying vicomte two days before his death, then rides to the intendant of Normandy's offices to claim the vicomte's estate for her own—such a woman should not be bothered by gossip."

Anger eclipsed her fear and she struggled uselessly in his hold. He held her closer as her struggles became more violent until, finally, she collapsed in his arms. "And what will you do with me now, Laclos?" she hissed. "Take me hostage? Demand ransom? I assure you that I've not a *sou* to my name—"

"I want no ransom, madame."

"Then what do you want?" She glared at him, willing herself to meet the brightness of his eyes. She had to arch her neck to stare at him—an unusual position for a woman who stood a hand taller than most men. His gaze wandered unfettered over her face, her neck, and still lower. When his eyes met hers, she saw in them the raw, unhindered light of desire.

"No!" Dredging the depths of her strength, she struggled

anew in his arms, but his embrace stiffened until she could do nothing but wave her head against his chest.

"Easy, Vicomtesse," he whispered into her ear. "I have no quarrel with you."

"Then leave me alone—let me go!"

His breath brushed her nape as he laughed softly. "Aye, I'll let you go, *cailín deas,* but not without regret."

Suddenly, he released her. The coolness of the breeze swept between them, and she rushed away, but Kilian caught her arm. "Not yet." Still holding her, Kilian walked to where the pistol lay on the ground. Shoving the barrel beneath his roped waistband, he led her to where the musket lay and took it firmly in hand. Then he released her.

Aimee scampered away, rubbing her wrist. She pulled her cloak tight around her body and warmed her icy fingers in the rough wool. She glanced frantically into the thickness of the woods as the thunder boomed harder overhead.

"Mount your horse, madame," he said, his fingers curling over the musket.

"Am I free to go?"

"Free?!" he barked, his brows lifting. "Nay, madame. You're not free. Not for many a league." His smile twitched. "It's been a long time since I've enjoyed the company of a beautiful woman. I intend to take advantage of my luck."

CHAPTER

2

Kilian Laclos saw the fear in the vicomtesse's eyes clearly across the distance
that separated them. Her eyes were like
the stormy Norman sky—wide and open and tumultuous
—and he wondered how a woman known for her courage
could look so incredibly vulnerable.

The lightning flashed again, brighter, and a few drops of
rain splattered through the dark, budding branches to the
forest floor. "Come, Vicomtesse. Don't make me raise this
musket against you."

Aimee tightened the cloak around her tall, willowy body
and tilted her chin as she walked toward her mare. With a
grace that belied her fear, she lifted herself upon the horse
and settled in the saddle.

Kilian tied the mare's reins firmly around the narrow
trunk of a young tree. Pulling a length of hemp out of his
saddlebag, he approached the stag. He had not eaten in two
days, and he'd be damned if he'd leave these woods without venison, whether it be stolen or not. His plans had been

delayed already by the advent of that overseer, and now, the vicomtesse herself.

He glanced at the vicomtesse, ramrod-straight on the mare. She had come upon him with the stealth of a Mughal warrior—he had not heard the step of her mare until she was well within firing range. She probably would have succeeded in capturing him if he weren't so much stronger than she. He must be losing his skill as a scout, he thought wryly, to be caught in such woods by a woman.

It seemed years, not months, since he had scouted through the lush jungles of India, searching the thick underbrush for signs of British soldiers or native warriors. With the end of the War of the Austrian Succession and the subsequent treaty negotiations, his skills were no longer needed in French India. How quickly he had forgotten all the lessons of his Indian teacher, Mafauz, in the misery that greeted him when he had returned to Paris.

The anger began again, deep in his belly. He tried in vain to quell it, but it rose, demanding, to the surface. It had been only a week since his sister lay, cold as the winter snow, in communal burial grounds. Her anguish and her shame still rose to haunt him in the nights, as fresh and sharp as the day he walked into her town house and found her lying in state, the swaddled form of the Duc de Montchamp's bastard babe in her cold arms.

He tied the stag's legs together with violence. He must control his anger, for it blinded him and dulled the sharp edge of his instincts. The fact that he had nearly been captured once by the vicomtesse's scouts, and then again by the vicomtesse herself, proved that. He must muffle the fury of his vengeance until he was face-to-face with the Duc de Montchamp. Then, and only then, could he allow the blinding hatred to surface and guide his hand.

Kilian heaved the dead stag upon his shoulders and balanced the weight. *Patience*, he cautioned himself, the anger still boiling his blood. *Patience and determination. The duke will pay for his sins.*

"Where are we going, that you have to bring the entire beast with us?" Aimee asked, her eyes widening as she watched Kilian approach her with the heavy animal resting on his broad shoulders.

"I'm not about to leave carrion here so that your overseer can find us," he explained calmly. "And you'll be hungry before the night is over."

"The night. . . . Certainly you won't keep me for the entire night!"

"I can't risk your sending your hounds after me." He heaved the stag over his shoulders onto the back of her mare.

Aimee tightened her knees as her mare pranced beneath her and the belly of the stag rubbed against her back. Kilian saw the light of terror dance in the gray depths of her eyes and he felt a strange pang of sympathy. This unusual woman had unwittingly stepped in the way of his plans. Despite his words, he had no intention of keeping her hostage for more than a few hours. He simply needed her presence to make it safely onto the duke's lands.

Still, he wondered, staring at the smoothness of her cheek, how tempting it would be to play the brigand and sweep her away. It had been months since he'd enjoyed the company of a woman, and then it was the overfed, vacuous wife of an absent general. This woman, he thought, his gaze sweeping over the severe black velvet of her riding habit, would be far from vacuous. Though she was thin, he could tell she hid the subtle curves of a slim Venus beneath the dark clothes. Her eyes, as he met them, glowed with the energy of a restless spirit.

Fitting for a woman of her reputation, he mused. Most women would be faint with fear by now, but this was no courtly aristocrat. This was a woman who defied the law, who defied her fate, and who wielded a pistol with the skill of a soldier.

"You're looking at me as if you will eat me for dinner," she snapped, pulling her cloak around her.

"Nay, the stag's for dinner." His lips twitched. "You, however, may be for dessert."

The vicomtesse's lips opened in surprise, then closed into a tight line. She looked away from him, but not before he saw the flash of fear.

So she is a woman, after all. "You have no reason to fear, Vicomtesse," he said, securing the deer to the horse. "Though you think I'm nothing better than a vagrant, I assure you that I am a soldier. And I promise, on my honor, not to harm you."

"Honor!" she retorted. "You trespass on my lands, kill one of my deer, wrestle my pistol away from me and then promise me *on your honor* that you will not harm me." She tossed her head in defiance. "Why should I believe in your honor?"

"Because you have no choice." His lips twitched in a wry smile. "I wager that had the situation been reversed, you'd not have shown me as much leniency."

Her eyes flickered above his head, slightly, but enough to tighten Kilian's muscles into taut wires. His hand moved to the loaded musket beside him.

"Not a move, *salaud*." Gustave called from behind a web of bushes. "There's more than one musket aimed at your back." Kilian heard the rustle of several men as they settled in the undergrowth. Cursing beneath his breath, he lifted his hands. Two men rushed from the bushes and pulled his arms behind his back.

The vicomtesse slid off the mare and walked toward him. She brazenly pulled the pistol from the rope around his waist. "You are right, Laclos," she said, stepping away from his tall body. "I will not show you as much leniency."

"Are you all right, madame?" Gustave cried. "He did nothing to harm you?"

"I am quite well, Gustave," she answered, calmly replacing the pistol in the makeshift holster at her waist. She smoothed her disheveled hair with white hands.

Kilian's gaze slitted and focused on her. The ropes around his wrists bit into his toughened skin, and he felt the frustration and constriction of his sudden captivity. The thin veneer of his control snapped with a deafening crack and his anger rose like bile to his throat.

"Gustave! Secure him!"

He heard her cry through the blood-red haze of his fury. No one, *no one,* would hinder his vengeance, and certainly not a slip of a woman. Jolivette had died giving birth to the Duc de Montchamp's unwanted, illegitimate child, and Kilian had sworn at her grave that the aristocrat would not live to spread the tale. For seven days he had lived with this rage; for seven days he had waited restlessly for this opportunity, and now his plans were threatened because of the intervention of a country aristocrat. The laws of this province might sentence him to death, but he would not die alone.

"Gustave!"

Kilian saw the frightened eyes of the vicomtesse as if through a tunnel, and then arms like iron bands crossed his chest. He strained against their restraint; with all the force of his will he tried to rip the hemp that bound his hands. If he could get to the vicomtesse, hold her captive, then these men would release him and he could find his vengeance. He saw her raise his musket and aim over the barrel toward him.

And then all was blackness.

* * *

The room smelled like barley oats and the air was so moist it felt like a blanket against his bruised skin. A ray of dusty, unfiltered light illuminated the rushes of a simple chair and the cracked pitcher beside it. A gray mist obscured his vision, but Kilian could see the ripple of water beneath the lip of the pitcher.

He did not know how long he lay there, wavering between consciousness and a tormented sleep. His thirst cried louder than his pain now and the water tempted him like Tantalus's grapes. Licking his parched lips, Kilian lifted his head from the hardness of the cot and winced at the pain shooting from the back of his head to his shoulders. He supported his head with a roughened hand and slowly squeezed his abdominal muscles until he was sitting upright. Something jangled as he moved. Glancing down at his bare feet, he noticed the chains that linked his ankles.

The memory of the evening returned and with it, the echo of his fury. He cursed hoarsely and the imprecations bounced off the solid walls of his prison. He could not believe his carelessness. In his life he had eluded the most skilled of soldiers, the most thorough of native Indian warriors, yet within twenty-four hours of arriving in Normandy he had been captured by a woman and her bearish overseer.

Resisting the faintness that rushed over him, Kilian reached for the pitcher of water. The liquid cleansed his throat of dustiness and brought him new strength. He stopped for a moment to fill his lungs with air, then drained the pitcher of its contents. He tossed the empty vessel to the floor.

He glanced around his quarters. Each side of the room was piled high with sacks of grain, and the center of the hard-packed floor dipped from wear. The high window was nothing but a slit in the wall. Rising from the bed and clutching his head, Kilian stepped back as far as his chains would allow and tried to gauge the thickness of the wall. His brows lifted as he realized that he must be in the cellar of a castle because no prison would be this fortified. The presence of the stored grain supported his suspicion.

His dark brows lowered slightly. This must be the Vicomtesse de Bocage's castle, no doubt. Probably a room on the ground floor. Why would she keep him here and not hand him over to the intendant of Normandy? Was she waiting until he was conscious? Or did she plan her own brand of justice, and was merely waiting to inflict it upon him?

He would know soon enough, he mused, and for now there was no chance of escape. He sat down on the bed and rubbed his temples with callused fingers. Slowly, his head cleared of haziness. He forced the angry thoughts of the Duc de Montchamp out of his mind and concentrated on what had happened.

He had been foolish to pass through the vicomtesse's lands in order to gain access to the duke's estate. The villagers had told him that she guarded her lands jealously, but he had thought he could elude her country scouts easily. He had been reckless to stop within the perimeter of her estate after defeating her overseer and his men, but his instincts had been dulled by the blood-red haze of his vengeance. He knew that now, sitting in the dank ground floor of the vicomtesse's castle, with his anger lying under tight rein. But now was too late.

Now he would pay for the folly of his hastiness. He would lose his freedom, his vengeance, and perhaps, his life. He was fortunate that the vicomtesse had not killed him on the spot, as was her right. He was fortunate, so far, that she had not turned him over to the law where his real identity would be revealed and his plans thus permanently defeated.

A key scraped in the lock of the door and Kilian stiffened. With a high whine, the door swung open and Gustave's ruddy face peered around the splintered edge.

"You're awake now, are ye?" he said, his gaze traveling the length of Kilian's tall body. "I had hoped I'd put you out for more than an evening."

"I wouldn't want to keep the intendant of Normandy waiting," Kilian sneered, absently rubbing the back of his head. "And the vicomtesse must be itching to make an example of me."

"Indeed I am."

Kilian stilled the strange, unfitting urge to rise to his feet. Though the vicomtesse wore somber black with no jewelry and no *maquillage*, she had the bearing and the grace of the most elevated woman of the court. "Good morning, Vicomtesse. It seems, once again, that the tables have turned."

"Yes," she murmured absently, pushing past Gustave into the narrow room. Her gray gaze fell upon him coolly, assessing his worth in one all-encompassing sweep. He looked more ragged and disheveled than the night before, yet that violent light that had glowed in his eyes still lingered. "Are you feeling better?"

Kilian lifted a brow at this expression of concern. "Why do you ask, madame? Are you concerned that I may die too quickly and ruin your torture?"

"Torture!" she exclaimed. "Is that what you fear?"

"Fear is not a word I understand." He dropped his hand from his neck and met her gaze. "Torture is what I expect from a woman who has promised me 'no leniency,' and, further, has not yet handed me to the authorities."

Aimee's lips tightened and she plucked at her dark sleeves with white fingers. He looked like a chained animal, restless and agitated in the dim quarters. Disturbed by his volcanic presence, she turned away and graced him with her profile. "After last night, Monsieur Laclos, I am strongly tempted to get you off my lands and into the authority of the intendant—which, as you know, is a punishment far worse than torture."

Kilian shrugged but remained silent. In the dim light of the room her skin seemed as white and translucent as a pearl. He leaned back against the wall of the keep, forcing his body to relax. She had come to see him for a reason. He would wait, test his thin patience, until she revealed her purpose.

"Unfortunately," she continued, watching him warily, "I do not trust the intendant. Nor do I necessarily agree with his methods of punishment." The bridge of her nose wrinkled then smoothed. "Though in your case they may be fitting."

He lifted a brow but remained silent. So she had no plans to hand him over to the intendant. His blood coursed hotly through his veins.

"What, no confession, no apology, Laclos?" she snapped suddenly. "This is the fate of your life I am determining."

"If I 'confessed' or 'apologized,' madame, would it make any difference?"

"No," she admitted. "It would make no difference at all."

"I thought not."

Aimee pressed her lips tightly together for a moment, then tried another tactic. "Where do you come from, Laclos? Your accent is unfamiliar to me."

Kilian lifted his brows at the abrupt change in conversation. He straightened on the bed and met the vicomtesse's eyes warily. "I am French by birth, madame. My mother, who brought me up, was Irish and therein lies my accent."

"Your mother is dead?"

His eyes hardened at his unwitting slip. "Yes. She died less than a year ago."

"Brothers, sisters?"

"Why this sudden interest in my family? Will you bring them in to witness my punishment?"

"Then you do have family alive?"

Another slip. He would never live to see vengeance if he continued to let his ire control him. His nostrils flared. "I have a brother, but he is somewhere in Italy, hiding from his debtors."

"Somehow, that does not surprise me." Aimee shrugged her thin shoulders beneath the coarse material of her widow's weeds. "I simply want to know, Laclos, whether you wanted me to contact anyone about your stay here."

"Why would I want to tell anyone of this?" Kilian asked, spreading a bare and bulging arm about him.

"They may worry," Aimee persisted. "Your stay will be quite long."

"Not if I can help it."

Aimee recoiled. For a brief moment, he looked as he did the night before—wild, raging, untamed—and she was afraid despite the iron chains that held him captive. "You have very little say in the matter, Monsieur Laclos."

Kilian suddenly turned his back to her and crossed his arms. He lifted his head to the shaft of light coming from the thin window and sighed deeply.

Gustave stiffened beside her and his face ruddied. "Don't turn your back to the vicomtesse, *salaud*—"

"Hush, Gustave. This is no gentleman."

A muscle in Kilian's back twitched. "I beg to differ, Vicomtesse." He looked at her over his shoulder. "I am a soldier, with a soldier's—"

"Honor," Aimee finished. "So you have told me, though you certainly have not behaved like a man of honor."

Kilian mulled over this for a moment, reining in his fury. He had not intended to let his rage control his words, or his actions, as he had so many times in the last twenty-four hours. He had to escape this place and his unlikely warden. He would not succeed by insulting her or making her afraid of him.

He turned back to face her. He met the coolness of her gaze. "Then let me prove my honor, madame."

"And how are you going to do that?"

He shrugged, glancing around his prison. "Don't leave me in here, to rot," he said, gesturing to the sacks of barley. A gleam entered his eye. "Let me work for you, on the estate."

"Precisely what I had in mind."

Kilian lifted a straight brow. "Indeed?"

"Yes. I can't allow a strong, healthy man to eat my grain and do nothing for me or my estate in return. And I am in need of men to work the fields, since most of the *journaliers* have already been hired by the neighboring estates."

"I see," Kilian mused. "So then, I am slave labor."

"Hardly. You will work, Monsieur Laclos, and I will accumulate your wages until you have paid the debt you owe me for stealing my stag."

"So I should trust your accounting?"

"Would you rather stay in here," Aimee said, imitating his gesture of disdain, "to rot?"

"No, but—"

"Good. You will work in my fields. There is much plowing to do before we seed. Gustave is my overseer and you shall regard his orders as binding as my own—"

"Though I appreciate your offer, madame," Kilian interrupted, watching with detached interest the flush of fury that stained her cheeks, "I must tell you that it will take a lifetime for me to pay off my debt that way."

Aimee crossed her arms tightly across her chest and stared at her prisoner with narrowed eyes. His lips had spread into a slow, languorous smile, and she wondered how a man whose life was in her own hands could so easily toy with his fate. All the other prisoners had thanked her for this lenient punishment, but Aimee knew that this man was no ordinary prisoner. The thought disturbed her. She did not know who he was, this strong, unbridled man who stared into his destiny with an arrogant grin. She wondered why he was here, on her lands, in her castle, in her thoughts.

The silence stretched between them, and so did Aimee's anger. "If it takes a lifetime for you to pay your debt, Laclos, then so be it." Her lips tightened. "Your life is now mine."

His eyes flared, but his smile did not dim. "I merely meant, madame, that I know nothing of plowing and scythes. I will be useless to you in the fields."

"Don't worry, we shall get our wages' worth from you," Aimee retorted as she walked toward the door. "You'll soon learn all you need to know about working my land."

"Wait, Vicomtesse."

It was a command, not a plea, and as terse as a general's order. Aimee stiffened instinctively. Grinding her teeth, she slowly turned to face him. "What is it, Laclos?"

"I will be a hindrance in the fields—"

"Only if you make yourself one, and if you do your punishment will be severe."

Kilian watched Aimee's narrowed eyes with speculation. An idea had begun to form in his mind, and he struggled to grasp it and wrestle it into a plan. "Certainly, Vicomtesse, with my experience as a soldier, you could find more suitable work." A gleam lit his eyes. "I fought with Bonnie Prince Charles in Scotland, I fought in the Netherlands, and I was once a scout in India—"

"There is no war in Normandy, Laclos."

"I hear there is," he murmured, watching her flushed face with interest. "I hear that a certain vicomtesse has been waging war on trespassers for quite a while."

"I'd hardly call it a war."

"Nonetheless, you do not deny that you need men to guard those borders?"

She opened her mouth in astonishment. "You cannot possibly be suggesting—"

"Make me a scout," he interrupted. "I promise you you'll have no more vagrants on this land."

"And no more prisoner, as well," she retorted. "Do you think I would really return your horse and musket and send you off to the borders? Do I look like such a fool?"

Kilian stepped closer to her, his chains jangling against the earthen floor. He blocked the ray of light coming from the high window and cast a long shadow over her form. Aimee blinked at this subtle assault but did not recoil. "You are no fool, Vicomtesse. Any man with eyes or ears knows that. You must be quite sharp, and quite shrewd, to accomplish what you have."

"How dare you!"

"I meant no insult, madame," he persisted, reading her elusive emotions in the changing shades of her gray eyes. "I am offering you a bargain, a bargain that shall profit us both. I will rid your land of vagrants, of thieves, of trespassers, and in exchange, you will shorten my stay."

She lifted a brow and crossed her arms before her. Her rage had reached intolerable heights, but she suppressed it for one minute longer. "Really? And how short would you want your stay to be, monsieur?"

"One month."

She laughed without humor. "Ridiculous. Completely absurd." She tossed her head and walked toward the door. "I don't bargain with thieves, Laclos, nor do I get rid of trespassers by releasing them."

"I was not asking to be released, madame," Kilian persisted, his anger breaking slowly through his control. "I was merely asking for you to accept my offer on my honor."

"Your honor, Monsieur Laclos, is so far nothing but a word. You will start in the fields tomorrow." Aimee turned briefly to her overseer. "And Gustave, keep him chained," she said, glancing toward him. "I don't want him to escape."

Kilian watched the door long after the vicomtesse's dark, twitching skirts had disappeared behind it. The idea that had struck him slowly took form and grew into a plan. Before the evening darkened the room into pitch, Kilian Laclos knew exactly how he was going to complete his revenge. There was only one major problem.

That problem was the inscrutable, blunt, ephemerally lovely Vicomtesse de Bocage.

CHAPTER

3

Aimee walked sedately down the center aisle of the church, ignoring the whispers that erupted at her arrival—they were as common to her as the beat of the rain or the crush of the earth beneath the plows. Today, in particular, she did not care, for Palm Sunday had come. The king's decision, fortunately, had not.

She settled in the Bocage pew and placed her small reticule on the seat beside her. Absently she reached up to toy with her hair, but then forced her hand down. Manon had spent a good half hour tugging her slick, black tresses into the soft coiffure that left tendrils brushing her temples and nape—Aimee swore she would not ruin it until after she returned from church, after the need for it was over.

She closed her eyes and rested her head against the hard back of the pew. It felt good to escape the estate for the morning. The plowing and planting was now in full force and the fields buzzed with activity. After two weeks of warm weather the earth burst in all its verdant finery, and it

took too many hands to control it. She was almost grateful
for the numbers of trespassers that Gustave had captured in
the past weeks—they eased the workload considerably.

A frown creased her brow. She grudgingly admitted that
one of the most valuable additions to her estate had been
Kilian Laclos. Though he knew little about husbandry, he
compensated with his sheer, Herculean strength. Aimee
squeezed her eyes shut, trying to force away the image of
that half-Irish stranger straining, bare-chested, beneath the
weight of a broken plow. His body was lean and tautly cut,
and in the brilliance of the sun his skin had darkened to a
rich gold. Though he was only one of dozens of workers,
he seemed to stand out among them like a king among
peasants.

Her frown deepened. She wondered why his presence
plagued her so. He had done the work of three men in the
past two weeks, but she still was uneasy. She knew that he
had charmed all of her workers, for she could hear their
banter clear to her garden in the afternoons. He strode
about the fields as if he did not have iron chains on his
ankles. Though he had not tried to escape, his very presence made a mockery of imprisonment.

Aimee opened her eyes to stare at the altar. She thought
far too much about that curious trespasser—far too much.
At least he kept her mind off the constant fear of the arrival
of the king's messenger. The two weeks had passed
quickly and without incident, except for the advent of Kilian Laclos. She could only hope that her luck would last a
little longer.

A flurry of gasps rippled over the congregation. Aimee
shook out of her reverie, but she did not have to look over
her shoulder to determine the cause of the excitement. Unlike the other villagers, she had known the Duc de Montchamp would attend the late morning mass. In fact, she
had arranged to come to this mass for that very reason.

The duke had arrived in Normandy two days ago, bringing with him a fleet of carriages the likes of which the province had not seen since King Louis visited several years ago. The peasants had lined up for miles along the pitted road to watch the glittering array. She had watched the parade from the safety of her castle. Later, she had scanned the Comtesse de Vierzon's letters for details of courtly life. Aimee had guessed that the duke, like most courtiers, would go to a late morning mass.

She had guessed correctly.

Leaning slightly forward, she peered toward the arched portal. The doors were still open and the duke was framed in the morning light. His light green satin waistcoat and matching breeches shimmered with gold embroidery. His buttons were pure, polished nuggets and the buckles of his shoes held the clearest rubies. Aimee had seen the Comtesse de Vierzon several times dressed in her court dresses, but never had she seen a man so bedecked. The duke paused in the portal and lifted a handkerchief to his face. He glanced about the church and a frown creased the powder on his forehead.

Aimee did not need to look around the church to know the source of the frown. The church was small and meant for the peasantry—there was no place for a man of the duke's stature to sit. The curé, standing at the foot of the altar in preparation for mass, looked stricken at having such a wealthy patron present and no place to seat him. His face grew florid above the frayed black collar of his robes.

Aimee squeezed her eyes shut. She had only this chance, only this last chance, and no faintheartedness would stop her.

Her cold fingers smoothed the voluminous folds of her black dress over her side-hoops. Her slippered feet stepped silently out of her pew and she ascended the steps of the altar. The curé did not see her until she touched his trembling arm.

"Monsieur le curé, I think it would be best if we welcomed this gentleman to our church."

The curé glanced at her, unseeing for a moment, then his gaze slowly focused. "Yes, yes. I think that would be best, but—"

"And be so kind to introduce me to the gentleman, as well," Aimee continued evenly. "I shall invite him to share my pew."

"Madame!" The curé's dark eyes widened. "I don't think that would be appropriate."

Several members of the church turned away from the spectacle of the duke to stare at the curé and the tall, thin form of the vicomtesse. "I know it may not be appropriate, monsieur, but I will make the sacrifice."

"I can't allow it, madame—"

"Where else will you place such a wealthy patron?" she interrupted, lifting a brow. "Shall you make him stand in the back, with the day-workers?"

The curé struggled with his conscience for a moment, and his dark gaze grew disapproving. Aimee knew what he was thinking—she was brash, bold to invite a stranger to her pew, but what more could he expect from the notorious vicomtesse? She also knew he could not deny her request without losing the duke's patronage. She glanced down the aisle. "The gentleman awaits, monsieur le curé."

"Come with me, madame."

Aimee followed the curé's robes down the narrow aisle. The congregation seemed to hold its breath and a dozen fans snapped open and fluttered. The duke awaited them, a small, tolerant smile on his pale, powdered face.

"Monsieur, I would like to welcome you to our humble church." The curé bowed briefly. "I am the curé Vernier."

The duke inclined his head a fraction. "I am the Duc de Montchamp." His dark, quick gaze moved to Aimee, who sank into a deep curtsy before him. "And who is this lovely widow who enticed you to greet me?"

The curé flushed at the subtle insult and extended a hand to Aimee. "This is Madame la Vicomtesse de Bocage."

The duke took her hand as she rose from the cramped curtsy. To her utter dismay, he lifted it to his lips. "I have you to thank, madame, for this greeting. It is comforting to know that *politesse* exists even in the wilds of France."

The scent of his potent cologne washed over her. His face was fleshy and slightly wrinkled, and Aimee estimated he could be no older than forty. His hands were as smooth as a lady's—certainly much smoother than her own. Suddenly self-conscious, she snatched her hand from his.

Stepping away from him, she inclined her head. "You must forgive us, monsieur. We are not often honored with such a noble presence as yours."

"Yes, I see." The duke glanced around the congregation, a bored smile on his otherwise immobile face. "Had I known I would have caused such a fuss I would have forewarned the curé."

"Perhaps then we would have reserved a seat of honor for you," she said slowly, her gray eyes level to his. "As it is, we have no suitable seat. You would do me great honor if you would share my pew."

The churchgoers released a collective gasp of surprise. The duke glanced over her head to the shocked congregation. He lifted one gray-streaked brow. When he met her serious gaze again he saw no hesitation in her eyes. He took her hand and tucked it inside his elbow. "It is quite obvious that it is I, madame, who shall have the honor."

Aimee and the duke walked down the aisle toward the Bocage pew amid the hiss of muted disapproval. She ignored the maliciously gleeful stares of the bewigged bourgeois. She concentrated instead on the mundane—the swish of the duke's satin as he walked, the rich scent of his cologne, the tightness of her hand in his elbow. The curé turned at the altar and stood stiffly in disapproval as the

duke gallantly allowed Aimee to enter her pew first. The
duke's footman reverently placed a square, silk pillow on
the floor of the pew, then retreated to the rear of the
church.

The curé started the Mass immediately, hushing the bub-
bling fervor of the new gossip. Aimee released the duke's
arm. It felt strange to have another man in the seat where
the Vicomte de Bocage used to sit, every Sunday, for as
long as she had known him. She could feel a hundred
gazes on them. The entire congregation ignored the dron-
ing Latin of the curé in favor of the spectacle of the widowed Vicomtesse de Bocage sitting next to the wealthy
Duc de Montchamp. Aimee could almost hear the gossip
hatching in their fertile minds.

The Mass seemed interminable. The middle of her back
ached. The heavy corset she had forced herself to wear bit
into the softness of her sides. She became suddenly conscious of the dreariness of her widow's weeds beside the
splendor of the duke's satin. This first meeting she had
planned as carefully as a seductress, but now that she had
the duke beside her she wondered how she was ever going
to bring the plan to completion.

She wished this could just be a simple business transaction devoid of flirtation and seduction. She wished it were
no more complicated than the purchase of a horse or the
settling of a marriage contract, but she knew, in her heart,
that this affair would entail much more detail and much
more subtlety.

She knew nothing of flirtation. In all her twenty-four
years she had never been courted. Though the vicomte had
lifted her from poverty and given her a home, she hovered
in a strange limbo between the aristocracy and the bour-
geoisie, a limbo markedly devoid of suitable men. Aimee
had never cared, but as she sat hesitant beside the Duc de
Montchamp she fervently wished she had some experience,

any experience, with men. All she had now was the memory of the Comtesse de Vierzon's brief and frequent affairs.

When the mass finally ended, the curé led the procession down the aisle and out into the bright sunshine of the early afternoon. The duke offered her his arm with a flourish, and she had no choice but to take it. They walked down the aisle of the church behind the flowing robes of the curé and under the intense scrutiny of the entire population of the village. As soon as she felt the sunshine on her face, Aimee released the duke's arm and stepped away.

"I thank you, madame, for allowing me to share your pew," the duke said suddenly, forcing her to turn and face him. "It seems that you may have sacrificed your reputation for my comfort."

"My reputation, monsieur, was sacrificed long ago." She toyed with the folds of her skirts. "You may regret sharing my pew after you hear the gossip that will arise from it."

"*Non*," he insisted, reaching for her hand. He lifted it to his lips and Aimee fought the urge to yank it out of his icy-smooth grasp. "Gossip is common and often vicious at court. Any gossip that shall arise from your invitation this morning could not possibly hurt me anymore." He released her hand and pulled on the beribboned edge of his waistcoat. "The only thing I shall regret is if you refuse to see me because of it."

"It would be quite bold for me to see you at all, monsieur." She gestured to her skirts. "I am a widow."

"Yes, it would be bold, wouldn't it?" The duke's dark gaze roamed discreetly over her black sack-backed dress. "It was also quite bold for you to invite me to share your pew this morning, yet that did not stop you."

"I was merely being polite."

"Were you indeed?" A light entered the flat, black eyes and one of his brows twitched. "Then may I, in politeness, offer you the comfort of my carriage for the ride back to your château?"

"I already have a . . ." She hesitated over the word cart. "I already have a conveyance."

"Tell your servants to bring it back without you." A note of insistence entered his otherwise monotone, lisping voice. "You have intrigued me, madame, and I would very much like to speak with you without a hundred ears listening."

Aimee studied his immobile face and wondered why he was taking so much interest in her, when she had truly done nothing to deserve it. She had heard so much from the Comtesse de Vierzon about the arrogance of French courtiers, but she had said nothing about their secrecy. This man held himself aloof from the people around him, she thought, but it was as if he were wearing a mask.

She took a deep breath.

"I, too, would very much like to speak with you," she said beneath her breath. She slowly lifted her gaze to meet his in the way that the comtesse had taught her, so many years ago. She knew her fear shone in her eyes. "But not now, not here. Not with so many people listening."

"When, then, my mysterious Vicomtesse?"

"Soon, monsieur." Unwittingly, her voice broke. "I think I have surprised enough people for one day."

"Indeed," he murmured. "You have surprised me, madame. Had I known I'd find such a lovely wild rose among the briars, I may have returned to Normandy long ago."

"You flatter me."

"Yes, I do." The duke extended one leg and bowed regally before her. "*Au revoir,* madame. I shan't give these fishmongers any more fodder for their tongues today. I assure you, however, that I shall see you again. Soon."

Aimee managed a short curtsy and watched as the duke retreated toward his carriage. She saw Madame Valerin intercept him and smile widely into his face, but she did not stay to watch. Her stomach still churned.

She had succeeded, at least in part. He had promised to seek her out again.

Manon waited calmly in the cart. Her gaze followed the bright satin-clad form of the Duc de Montchamp with a mixture of curiosity and awe. Aimee climbed into the creaking cart and lifted the riding whip from the back. She heard the sound of a carriage and turned to see a powder blue phaeton stopping just behind her cart. The robust form of the tax collector's wife, Madame Androit, leaned out of the carriage.

"Madame la Vicomtesse," she called loudly, lisping her words like a courtier. "I just wanted to tell you that I thought you were wonderful to share your pew with the Duc de Montchamp this morning."

Aimee's brows drew together. Madame Androit had spoken few words to her in the past year, and those rare words were far from complimentary. Aimee wondered what brought on this sudden bout of suspicious amity.

Unwilling to continue a conversation, Aimee murmured a stiff thank you and turned back to her horses. She heard the bourgeoise yell a command to her driver and the phaeton lurched forward, leaving clods of mud in its wake. As Aimee leaned forward, she saw the gaze of the Duc de Montchamp fixed upon her. He stared at the cart in horror.

Aimee's eyes narrowed and she looked away. Madame Androit was clever. She had wanted the duke to see Aimee's cart, and compare it with the shiny newness of her phaeton. Cracking the whip with unnecessary vigor over the horse's back, Aimee urged it on to the pockmarked road. Her heart sank, but she held her head high. If the duke were concerned with her financial status, then she would never succeed in her plans; and it would be better if he knew now rather than later.

Moments after the cart rumbled onto the main road, Manon glanced behind her. "It's a dark day, madame, when a woman as low as Madame Androit drives a carriage and you, a vicomtesse, goes to church in a cart."

" 'Tis not the conveyance that makes nobility, Manon," Aimee said as she lifted her face to the wavering warmth of the sun.

"Nonetheless, you should be driven to church in the carriage, madame. As the vicomte did, when he was alive."

"The vicomte is no longer alive."

"*Oui*, but if he were you know he'd not abide this," Manon said, clutching her splintered seat as the cart bumped over a rut in the muddied road.

Aimee glanced at her servant. Manon often forgot that Aimee was no longer the gangly, awkward child who used to help bake pastries in the kitchen, and was now her mistress, the Vicomtesse de Bocage. "The fact that I go to church at all is considered flamboyant—nearly sinful, Manon. I need not frame my notoriety with gilt and white horses. I seem to be able to cause enough gossip without it." She shrugged. "Besides, the vicomte's carriage is ancient and would never compare to the tax collector's phaeton. Collecting the king's taxes is a far more profitable occupation than being a landed country aristocrat."

Manon made a small *humph* and glanced over the fertile fields. Aimee turned her attention back to maneuvering the horses. She, too, wished that she had brought the ornate, ancient carriage rather than the rickety cart. She could not have possibly shocked the villagers any more than she already had, and the duke might have been a bit more impressed with her position.

Mentally, she shrugged. Her rise to the aristocracy had been too sudden for the pious residents of Beny-Bocage. No one believed that the dying Vicomte de Bocage had willingly wed his twenty-three-year-old ward. They assumed that she had coerced him into the union for the wealth and prestige it would bring her. Ironically, the marriage had been the vicomte's idea. He had tried to protect her—to save her from the misery in which he had discovered her, fourteen years earlier.

She glanced over toward the start of her apple orchards. She still remembered the day the vicomte found her hiding in the Bocage woods, half-starved. She had been scared to tears that he would send her to an orphanage. She was nine years old and her father, a St. Simon, had just died. Although the name of St. Simon was once revered in this part of Normandy, her branch of the family had long fallen into poverty. But the vicomte was an old man, even then. He remembered the St. Simons, and was appalled at the state of the last living member. In one of his spontaneous gestures, he took her as his ward.

Fourteen years later, just as spontaneously, he took her as his bride.

"Madame, what is that noise?"

Aimee blinked and turned to Manon, struggling out of her thoughts. "What?"

"Listen."

Aimee glanced toward the apple orchard. Over the creaking of the cart and the slap-slap of the horse's hooves, she could hear a high, raucous whine. She pulled upon the reins and urged the horse to stop. She peered through the fencing of gnarled trunks toward the cider house in the distance.

"Voices," Manon said, sniffing loudly. "I'd wager that Gustave is in there now, drinking all the apple cider."

"It's a holy day," Aimee said, tilting her ear toward the building. Another voice, a deeper one, rose above Gustave's. Her stomach tightened.

"Gustave sings like a wounded goat!" Manon exclaimed. "Who's that other man singing?"

"I don't know." Aimee dropped to the ground, reached into the back of the cart, and pulled out the tangled riding whip. "I am going to find out."

"Wait for me, madame, I'd not miss this for a week's wages—"

"*Non,* wait here, Manon. I shan't be long."

Aimee marched through the evenly spaced rows of apple trees toward the half-timbered cider house. The moistness of the soil seeped through her thin slippers, but she barely felt the dampness. The voices grew louder as she approached and she became more and more certain of the owner of the second voice.

The song stopped abruptly when Aimee swung open the door. She peered into the dimness of the room. Gustave's ice blond head was clearly visible, and as her eyes adjusted to the darkness she made out the tall, unmistakable frame of Kilian Laclos. A smile spread white and arrogant across his shaven face.

"*Bonjour,* madame," he said, gesturing to a cask. "Sit down and share some cider with us."

She ignored the offer and glanced at his unbound feet. Her gaze moved to her overseer. "Gustave, I told you to keep him chained."

Gustave lowered his light blue eyes from her insistent gaze and fumbled with his earthenware mug. "I did, for a while, madame. But it soon seemed unnecessary."

Kilian pushed away from the cider keg. "Don't be harsh with Gustave, madame—"

"I shall be harsh with *my* overseer, Laclos, if I please."

"But I am afraid it was my fault—I coerced him to take off the chains."

"No doubt," she retorted, glaring at him. She could not believe he stood before her, unbound. She remembered all too vividly the blaze of his hatred and anger the night he was captured, yet here he stood, only two weeks later, as free as any Frenchman. She turned her fear and fury onto Gustave. "I have never known you to be so easily coerced, Gustave."

Gustave's face, already ruddy with drink, flushed a

deeper and alarming red. He glanced at Aimee, then at Kilian, and lowered his gaze to his hands.

"Madame, please," Kilian said, leaning on the copper hood of the cider pump. "I made a promise to Gustave, weeks ago, that I would not leave the Bocage estate until my debt to you was fulfilled. On the merits of that promise, Gustave agreed to take the chains off my ankles."

"That promise should have been made to me, not to Gustave," she said slowly, her eyes narrowing on Kilian. "And then I would have decided whether it was appropriate to take off the chains."

"You, madame, are far more elusive than Gustave." His green eyes, bright in the dimness of the room, roamed over her body. "I have only seen you as a dark flash on a horse in the distance, or as a lovely face staring out a window. Gustave was available."

Aimee flushed at Kilian's evocative description. "Nonetheless," she said slowly, struggling to regain her argument. "Gustave should have told me."

"I did not want to bother you with such details, madame," Gustave said, speaking up finally. "You have enough to think about, with the king's decision—"

"My foremost concern, Gustave, is the safety of this estate. Not even the words of the king of France surpass that. By releasing Monsieur Laclos you have threatened the tenants and everyone else who works on this land."

She knew the irony of her words as soon as she said them, for Kilian stood not ten paces away, calmly sipping from his mug, watching her with steady eyes. Unarmed, relaxed, he posed no threat to anything except, perhaps, her stock of cider.

And her peace of mind, she admitted reluctantly. She did not trust this man. He was hiding something from her, from all of her people. The thought tightened her stomach into a knot. There was something about him, something extremely dangerous, that frightened her in a way that no one had frightened her before.

Aimee suddenly realized that she did not fear for her estate or her people—she feared for herself.

"Meaning no offense, madame," Gustave began, "but Kil—Monsieur Laclos will harm no one."

"And you believe this promise?" she asked, crossing her arms before her.

"Yes, madame," Gustave said quietly. "He has not tried to escape yet."

"Will you risk your position here for a thief's promise?"

"'Twas a gentleman's promise. Yes, I'd risk my position."

Aimee lifted a hand to her neck and rubbed the stiff muscles. Her gaze traveled reluctantly to Kilian. His smile had widened and he shrugged his shoulders at her perusal. His arrogance was unbearable. He was no prisoner—he never was. A man like this could never be kept captive. She wondered why he lingered at Château Bocage.

"Very well." She turned and headed for the door. "Gustave, since you've seen fit to release Laclos, I shall make you responsible for him. If he escapes, it shall be on your conscience."

"Then he has nothing to fear, madame, for I have no intention of leaving the Bocage estate until you have determined that my debt is paid."

Aimee ignored Kilian's statement and left the cider house. The air was cool and fresh and she walked briskly toward the road. She noticed through the haze of her confusion and anger that many of the trees had begun to bud. If the rain continued, the crop of apples would be fine this year.

"Madame!"

Kilian's voice echoed around her and destroyed all thoughts of husbandry. "What is it, Laclos?"

"Let me walk with you to the carriage." His long stride carried him quickly to her side. "These woods are full of thieves and trespassers, you know."

"That will not be necessary," she murmured. Clean-shaven, Kilian was far more handsome than she remembered. His chin was square and strong, and his hair, streaked with light from the days in the fields, was pulled away from his face. The dark brows slashed across a wide forehead until they nearly met above the bridge of his nose. His lucid eyes held no malice, yet she moved away when he came too close.

"You still fear me, don't you?"

"Fear is not a word I understand," she mimicked, hiding her surprise at the abrupt question.

"Then trust me."

"Trust you!?" she exclaimed, stopping in her tracks. "You can't be serious."

Kilian stared at her, for the first time, in the brightness of the day. Her skin was flawless—fair and tinted peach on her cheekbones where the sun had kissed her. Her midnight black hair, drawn smoothly away from her face, formed a perfect frame for her delicate features. Her brows arched.

"I am quite serious, Vicomtesse."

His voice rumbled over the title like a caress, and his roving gaze wreaked havoc with her pulse. Unlike the duke, Kilian wore no mask. She could read his emotions clearly on his face and they frightened her. She stepped back instinctively, drawing the thickness of her skirts before her like a shield.

"You may be able to charm my overseer, Laclos, but I am not as easily coerced. I don't make promises over apple cider."

"I am not asking you to make any promises," he said quietly. "I'm simply asking you to allow me to prove my trustworthiness." He smiled suddenly, and Aimee's heart jumped. His smile could melt the ice from the winter's eaves.

"You have ample opportunity," she murmured as she turned and walked toward the cart. "My overseer has seen to that."

"Don't be harsh with Gustave," Kilian said, quickly reaching her side. "He is a good, honest man and was hesitant to the last to set me free. He had to choose between your orders and what he came to know of me."

"He chose incorrectly." She was far too conscious of his rolling, athletic gait beside her. She wished he would move away. He seemed to hover over her. Everything about him was disconcerting—his eyes, his smile, his height.

"Vicomtesse." He reached for her arm and pulled her to a gentle stop. Her gaze fluttered to his large, callused hand on the thinness of her arm, but he did not release her. He willed her gaze back to his face. "I know you fear me because of the night I was captured—"

"I don't fear you. Unhand me."

"You're lying," he said, ignoring her order. "Your eyes cannot hide your emotions, Vicomtesse. Your strength is like a coat of armor, but your eyes give you away. Beneath that armor is a woman, soft and vulnerable."

Aimee caught her breath. Anger and confusion and some other emotion she dared not name rushed through her body. "You overstep your bounds, Laclos. Remember to whom you speak."

"I speak to a woman," he explained quietly. "You may be an aristocrat, madame, and myself a commoner, but we are also man and woman."

Whatever or whoever Kilian Laclos was, he was foremost a man, she thought suddenly. She shook the thought from her mind. "We are noblewoman and commoner, warden and prisoner," she insisted huskily. "It would behoove you to remember that."

Kilian ignored her words and continued staring at her. His gaze deepened on her face, then slipped to her lips. For one brief, quivering moment, she thought he would kiss her.

She wanted him to kiss her.

"I meant you no harm that night," he said softly. "I was angry, frustrated, for reasons that are not important. I meant no harm to you or your estate."

"I find that hard to believe."

"I know." Kilian was surprised to feel disappointment at her withdrawal. "That is why I want you to trust me—at least, I want the opportunity to prove to you that I can be trusted."

She gathered her skirts and turned away. "You have your opportunity, Laclos, by default. Gustave has given you that opportunity." Her gaze touched his briefly. "But remember, you have only one chance for I will not allow another breach of my orders."

"One chance is all I will need."

She whirled and walked toward the cart. She felt Kilian's gaze on her back until the cart rounded a curve in the road, out of his sight. Manon barraged her with questions as they rode, but Aimee's curt and distracted responses soon discouraged her. As they approached the castle, Aimee could not admire its straight walls and crenellated roof against the gray blue of the sky. Her mind was busy trying to figure out the mystery of a certain Kilian Laclos.

She urged the horse up the rise to the castle. They passed through the opening of the crumbling chemise wall that once surrounded and protected the castle from foreign invaders. Pulling the cart to a stop in the small courtyard, she tossed the reins to a stable boy and ascended the well-worn stairs. A blast of heat greeted her when she opened the heavy oak doors. Someone had built the fire in the Great Hall so high that it disappeared up the chute, nearly six feet off the ground. The reddish glow reflected off the ancient tapestries lining the opposite wall, and put color into the alabaster skin of the portraits of her husband's ancestors. Aimee pouted. *Her* ancestors, too. Her own ancestors had once owned this château, three hundred years ago. Unfortunately, the familial link was too distant to qualify her as a potential heir to the vicomte's estate.

Stretching, she walked to the spiral staircase in the northeast tower and climbed the stairs to the second floor of the château. She pulled a candle from the gilt-bronze candelabrum at the head of the stairs, lifted her skirts, and walked past the empty, musty guest rooms to her own bedroom at the very end of the hall. She placed the candle in a holder on her dresser and sank into an embroidered armchair by the hearth.

A slip of white paper at the edge of her writing desk caught her eye. Her forehead furrowed. Curiosity overcame her weariness and she rose to pick it up.

Her fingers caressed the rich gold writing.

> The Duc de Montchamp requests the joy of your presence at an Easter Ball to be held at Montchamp at 10 P.M., Easter Day.

Aimee's heart fluttered. The duke had wasted no time. His messenger must have passed her on the road.

She knew she should refuse to go on the basis of her mourning. One year had passed, but her tenants were pious and would frown upon her emerging from mourning so suddenly. She also should demur because she would go unescorted. She was widowed and had never been *formally* introduced to the duke. She should demur because the fête was being held on a holy day—the holiest day of the year. There were a dozen reasons why she should not attend the Duc de Montchamp's Easter Ball.

As Aimee sat down at her writing desk and pulled out a piece of parchment embossed with the coat of arms of the Vicomte de Bocage, she knew she would go. She was determined to keep her estate.

Even if she had to become the Duc de Montchamp's mistress.

CHAPTER

4

Kilian eased the carriage up the slight incline to the courtyard of Château Bocage. The ancient carriage creaked and squealed in annoyance, as if, after so many years of rest, it resisted waking and being put to use. He winced as he passed over a pothole and the entire conveyance bumped in response. The coach obviously lacked the leather straps that cushioned the ride of more modern carriages, and he mused that it would be a long and painful ride to Château Montchamp.

The tenants who had gathered to view the departure of the Vicomtesse de Bocage parted at his arrival. The torches attached to each gargoyle on the banister of the castle's wide, sweeping staircase blazed high and hot. The wavering light flickered over the rough stones and set the narrow *meurtrière* windows in stark relief. He had rarely seen a castle this old in France—most had been torn down by their owners and replaced by comfortable, gilt châteaux. This castle, he knew, dated from at least the fourteenth century; and in the darkness of the early spring evening it looked as cold and foreboding as a medieval fortress.

He pulled the horses to a stop and climbed down from the carriage. A strange, restless silence permeated the courtyard. A small child darted toward the coach, but his mother snatched him by the shirt before he could escape. She pulled him close to her calico skirts and turned her face expectantly toward the high oak doors. Her lips tightened in a dark, disapproving line.

Kilian leaned back on his booted heels and waited. He might be the only one in the grim circle who did not completely disapprove of the vicomtesse's decision. Her announcement last week that she was to attend the Duc de Montchamp's ball had shocked her tenants. She had been widowed for only a year and to these provincial folk it was unseemly that she attend a social function. For Kilian, however, the vicomtesse's announcement was a ripe, golden opportunity.

After three weeks of forced patience, he would finally have a chance to further his plans. No one would look at him twice when he arrived at Château Montchamp dressed in the Bocage livery. After his duties as carriage driver were complete, he would be free to prowl about the estate. The Vicomtesse, in her defiant way, had unwittingly given him the very tools of his vengeance.

Kilian frowned. Though it was fortuitous that the vicomtesse had accepted the duke's invitation, he wondered why she had done so. She had once again defied tradition; and though one part of him admired her rebelliousness, another part of him wondered at the cause.

What would entice a woman of her character, of her earthiness, to attend a ball of a French courtier? He could not believe it was for the joy of the dance—a woman who worked in her garden on holy days was not prone to frivolity. There was another reason, he was sure of it. Her decision was out of character, and he wondered with a dark

sense of déjà vu what schemes were hatching in the vicomtesse's fertile, intelligent mind.

The memory of his sister rose sharply to his thoughts.
She had gone to the Duc de Montchamp once, long ago,
for aid. The duke had given her a home and protection in
his town house in Saint-Germain. From all appearances,
the duke had behaved as a generous gentleman taking care
of an innocent woman. Yet within a year, the duke had
shamed his sister, and killed her with his unbridled lusts.

Kilian's gaze narrowed and focused on the oak doors.
He knew the vicomtesse was about to lose her estate. He
knew she had no living relatives. He suspected that she
was attending this ball for the same reasons that his sister
went to the duke over a year ago; to ask for the duke's aid.
Kilian's nostrils flared. Whatever the vicomtesse's plans
for the duke, they would all be smashed, for after Kilian's
vengeance was done the blackguard would not have the
opportunity to repeat his depravity on the vicomtesse, or
anyone else.

He quickly suppressed his growing fury. He would not
let rage control him anymore. The last three weeks spent
pushing a heavy plow through the rich, dark loam of the
Bocage fields had restored his strength. He had regained
control. His anger burned steady and hot, but his instincts,
honed once again to battle sharpness, tended the flame
carefully. He would have his vengeance against the duke,
but it would be on his own, carefully planned terms.

Then, when it was done, he would return to Paris, and
the business that awaited him there.

The heavy oak door of the castle opened suddenly and
Gustave, looking uncomfortable in his frayed livery,
stepped out. A murmur rippled over the crowd as they
pressed closer to the stairs. Kilian could see the vicomtesse's white skirts shimmering in the shadows of the doorway as she hesitated. Then she stepped out into the night
air.

Kilian stood straighter, at attention, his own soldier's instincts reacting to the elegant woman. He did not know what it was about her that made him want to bow in reverence. She had the carriage of a queen as she glanced around the assembled tenants. The gold embroidered threads on her white satin gown shimmered in the light of the torches.

He had thought she would look awkward in the stiff, unyielding clothes of the aristocracy. He had only seen her in her common widow's weeds, often corsetless and without side-hoops. He liked her that way. He liked watching her toil over her garden with nothing restricting the softness of her smooth sides, with no side-hoops distorting the curve of her hips. Her body was long and sinuous and it was a shame she hid it beneath somber black dresses.

She descended the worn stairs, moving gracefully, managing the wide side-hoops with an uncanny ease. As she came closer Kilian noticed the small strand of pearls that rested against her throat. The translucence of her skin rivaled their iridescence, and he watched the battle between the two with a small smile on his face. Her décolletage was so wide that his gaze quickly slipped lower, to the tempting mounds of flesh that rose behind her stiff, embroidered stomacher.

The vicomtesse was an unusually beautiful woman.

"I see, Monsieur Laclos, that you have managed a giant leap in stature on my estate."

Her voice broke into his musing and his gaze slipped to her eyes. They were narrowed and silvery in the darkness. Kilian could barely conceal his smile of admiration as he bowed before her.

"I am continually searching for ways to best serve you, madame."

"I wish that you would stop searching and stay put," she whispered in a low voice. "All this jumping from day-worker to stable master to carriage driver is unnerving."

Kilian smiled but did not answer. She wore a wig of the purest white, shimmering with the glitter of rice powder, and the color brought out the gray of her eyes. With the exception of a touch of rouge on either cheek, she looked as pale and ethereal as a winter spirit.

"Where's Old Lucien?" she asked abruptly, caressing the ivory of her fan with a less than steady hand.

"Old Lucien is arthritic, madame. It has been over a year since he has driven this carriage."

"Is he sick?"

"He is well, but stiff. Gustave thought it best that someone else drove the carriage. Since I have some experience. . . ."

"I see." Her tone of voice indicated quite clearly that she did not approve.

"Gustave will be riding ahead a bit," he reminded her, a slow smile spreading over his face. "For safety."

Aimee flushed at the innuendo and she drew herself up to her full height. She tilted her chin and realized with dismay that the motion that usually cowed most men would do nothing for the towering Kilian Laclos. By the amusement growing in his green eyes, she knew that he had recognized her futile gesture for what it was—a vain attempt to intimidate him. His gaze slipped to her bosom and her cheeks heated.

Refusing to deflate, she turned away and gathered her skirts to enter the carriage. Kilian opened the door and reached for her hand. She considered snubbing his offer, but she knew she'd never ease her skirts into the coach without his assistance. His fingers curled around her hand.

Kilian's nostrils flared as he breathed in the sweet scent of apple blossoms that clung to her skin. He closed the door firmly and took advantage of the opportunity to wink at her through the open window. Not waiting to see the look of angry shock on her face, he ascended to the box and urged the horses out of the courtyard toward the road.

Though the Duc de Montchamp's lands bordered the vicomtesse's estate, the duke's château was several leagues
away. It took an unbearably uncomfortable hour on the
potted, uneven roads to travel from one estate to the other.
As Kilian neared the duke's lands he noticed the thinning
of the forests, the leveling of the land and the planned,
symmetrical layout of the bushes. The duke had spared no
expense to bring the comfort and structured luxury of the
French court to his duchy, Kilian mused as he eased the
carriage on the pebbled drive to the château.

The château shimmered with the glow of a thousand jas-
mine-scented candles. He could feel their heat as he pulled
the carriage to a stop.

Two liveried servants, their expressions disdainful, approached the ancient vehicle. Their maroon and gold livery
formed a sharp, tailored contrast to Kilian's ill-fitting cotton and Gustave's unembroidered wear. Aimee glanced
briefly at Kilian before the footmen hustled her toward the
gaping doors of the château. His gaze lingered on her stiff
back as she disappeared inside the building.

"Come on, Kilian," Gustave called, drawing Kilian's attention away from the vicomtesse. He led the way down a
wide path toward the carriage house. "It will be a long
night, I suspect, and my thirst is deep."

Kilian stopped the carriage beside a shiny berline and
descended to unhook the horses. Leading the two horses
and Gustave's mount to the stables, he glanced around the
courtyard.

At least a hundred carriages littered the grounds. He had
not expected the duke to draw so many guests to his provincial estate—after all, Montchamp was easily a half
day's ride from Paris. Kilian knew that all these carriages
could not have come from Norman nobles, for there were
few Norman country aristocrats with any wealth. By the
size and luxury of the vehicles, he could tell they were the
carriages of French courtiers. He frowned. He could not

risk being recognized by anyone—particularly a member of Louis XV's court. He would have to be very careful in his wanderings.

They unsaddled the horses, watered them, and left them with oats in the stables. Gustave grinned and pulled a bottle of calvados out from beneath his waistcoat and took a healthy draught. Wiping his lips with the back of his sleeve, he handed the bottle to Kilian. "I've got a mind to avoid the others," he said, glancing toward the back of the stables at a gathering of well-liveried servants. "There's hardly enough for the two of us."

Kilian smiled wryly. Gustave's appetite for liquor was as well known as his intolerance. Within an hour he'd be asleep, Kilian wagered as he took a deep sip of the apple distillate. "Then let's find a place by the château to watch the festivities." He opened his own waistcoat to show a bottle he had secreted from the boot of the carriage. "When we run out, we'll return and drink what's left of the duke's wine."

Gustave slapped Kilian on the back as they walked out of the humid warmth of the stables into the coolness of the night. The rain had not yet started, but a mist rose from the earth and seeped through their thin livery. Gustave handed him the calvados again and he drank until the chill left his bones.

"The vicomtesse was an eyeful tonight, eh, Kilian?" Gustave's bright eyes glimmered with mischief.

"The vicomtesse is always an eyeful. This night, however, she was exceptional."

"She looked like a princess," Gustave said boisterously. "And I don't care what her damned ungrateful tenants say, she did right by coming here tonight. A girl that young shouldn't have to stay in mourning for so long—*Sacré bleu*, I don't think I've seen her smile since before the vicomte died."

Kilian's brows knitted over the bridge of his nose. He,

too, could not remember ever seeing the vicomtesse smile.
He could not picture her without the wistful light of sadness in her eyes. "She's not had much to smile about."

"Mayhap the Duc de Montchamp will put the roses back
in her cheeks."

"The duke is married," Kilian snapped. "He'd best not
be putting false hopes in her head."

"You need not worry about the vicomtesse. She's not
one to fall for the manners of a fancy courtier. If the duke's
married, she'll not give him the time. Aimee's one of us at
heart—she can see through pretty words and shiny clothes
to the heart and soul of a man."

"If that's so, then why does she still despise me?"

Kilian regretted the words as soon as they left his lips.
The calvados had begun to buzz in his head. He had nothing to fear, for Gustave was discreet in his way; but still he
did not want anyone to know about his strange, growing
obsession with the willowy widow.

Gustave laughed. "You are a man caught poaching on
her estate. You are her prisoner. Why shouldn't she despise
you?" Gustave settled down on the ground by the trunk of
a huge oak. His gaze moved to the couples swirling behind
the tall French window, only a few paces ahead. "She also
suspects you, Kilian. You are not one of us. Perhaps if you
were honest with her, she would trust you more."

"You know no more about me than she does, Gustave.
Yet you trust me."

"I have drunk apple cider with you, Kilian. If you had
meant me or the vicomtesse harm, I would have known
then."

"Perhaps I should abduct her and force her to trust me
with a mug of calvados."

Gustave's ruddy face broke into a grin. "Such rituals are
for men, *mon ami*. A lady like Aimee must be treated more
gently." He reached for the bottle. "But I should not be
telling you what you already know."

"Aye." Kilian's gaze slipped to the window and he watched the myriad colors of satin whirl by the leaded crystal panes. Though he recognized several of the dancers, he passed over their faces without comment. He was looking for white satin, embroidered with gold threads, but when he realized what he was doing he turned away and drank some more calvados.

He caught sight of her skirts anyway, and despite his efforts he found himself watching as she neared the windows. He straightened against the rough bark of the oak as he realized with whom she was dancing.

The anger throbbed in his blood, harder, hotter, mixing with the fire of the calvados until his ears were singing with fury. The duke had not changed since Kilian had last seen him. No trace of remorse marred the autocratic stiffness of his face. His dark, shifty eyes were fixed on Aimee.

She was smiling. Kilian's gaze narrowed on her. Even in the brilliance of the ballroom, she looked stunning. The gold threads of her dress caught and toyed with the light of the tapers burning in the chandeliers. Caught up with ivory bows, her dress revealed a multitude of stiff lace petticoats that could not hide the graceful turn of her ankle. Her waist seemed a hand's span wide, her bosom rounded beneath the graceful line of her collarbone. Her teeth were small and perfectly formed, and it angered him to madness to see her smiling at *him*.

"It seems he's got her smilin'," Gustave remarked, his gaze drifting sleepily to Kilian. "She should know better."

"Aye."

"She's probably just enjoying herself," Gustave continued, yawning widely and closing his eyes. "Can't fault her for that."

Kilian watched as the duke led Aimee back into the mass of whirling couples. Gustave reached for the bottle, but Kilian was holding it as tight as a musket.

"Come, Kilian, give me the bottle. You're going to break it and waste good calvados."

Kilian released the bottle wordlessly, his gaze still fixed to the panes. Her smile seemed to linger in his memory.

"I don't know what she will do when she leaves Château Bocage," Gustave said, his words thick and slurred. "I once considered asking her to come and live with my family—my mother always had a soft spot for Aimee—but that was before she married the vicomte. Now that she's the vicomtesse she can't live as a peasant."

"Of course not."

"Before the vicomte took her as his ward she was poorer than the poorest tenant on the Bocage estate, you know. She was orphaned when she was barely nine."

Kilian's brows drew together. Aimee de Chacontier, Vicomtesse de Bocage, was becoming a more intriguing woman with each passing day. "Why did the vicomte take her as his ward?"

"She was born a St. Simon, and the St. Simons were once a great family in this part of Normandy. The vicomte was an old man, and he remembered them." Gustave sighed heavily. "He was a good man, the vicomte. But he could not save Aimee, not then, and I fear, not now."

Aimee. Gustave often forgot in his drunkenness that he was calling his mistress by her Christian name. It was a wondrous name, Kilian thought. Aimee. *Beloved. Muirnín.*

"Now, she's no longer a peasant, and soon she won't be a vicomtesse. What will she be then, I wonder?" Gustave's head tilted to one side as his words wavered. "Not good enough for her own world, and too good for ours, *mon ami.*"

Kilian mulled over Gustave's words as he watched the dancers. He did not glimpse Aimee or the duke in several sets, and strange thoughts wandered through his mind. As the third minuet began, he rose to his feet and glanced at

Gustave. The overseer lay, mouth open, his fingers curled around the second half-empty bottle of calvados.

"Sleep well, *mon ami*."

Kilian slipped off into the darkness and made his way back to the courtyard of the carriage house. Silently he searched for the Bocage carriage among the multitude, his keen eyes seeking any trace of movement in the forest of wide, spoked wheels and gleaming coaches. He avoided a small cluster of liveried servants and veered off until he found the carriage.

He opened the door and pulled up the creaking seat. The faint scent of apple blossoms teased him, but he did not linger to breathe more deeply of her fragrance. Pulling a pair of black breeches, hose, and a dark linen shirt from beneath the seat, Kilian glanced about and quickly changed. He tossed his white and blue livery and boots back beneath the seat and closed the door.

The evening closed over him like a living thing. He felt it descend upon him, swathing him in its night black folds. Mafauz's teachings, repressed beneath the fury of his vengeance for so long, rose hot and vivid in his mind as he slipped like a shadow through the courtyard. His unshod feet made no noise as he passed the liveried servants. He melted into the darkness as he approached the brilliance of the château.

Avoiding the well-lit areas just outside the windows, Kilian skirted the château until he reached the darkened north wing. He merged with the shadow of the wall and felt the cold stones with dry hands. This earth beneath his feet was different from that of Pondicherry, India. It was boggy and clinging but bereft of the myriad vines and roots and underbrush that hindered silent travel. He must be careful not to leave muddied footsteps in his wake.

With quick fingers Kilian checked the bolts on each darkened window, clinging to the side of the building like a vine. The servants had done their job well; the north wall was secure, and Kilian crouched down to circle to the inner side of the wing. A grand garden stretched out between the two wings of the castle, lit in places by the orange glow of oil lamps. He could see the bright, wide silk and satin skirts moving in some of the paths, but he did not fear detection. Behind the high fence of bushes no one would discern his figure.

The night was moonless, mercifully, and only the glimmer of stars pierced the sky. Kilian flattened against the wall and lodged his toes into the slight indentations between the stones of the château. With practiced ease he sidled up the sheer face until he could reach the lower window bolts. He began his search anew, checking periodically over his shoulder into the perfumed maze of the garden.

He reached the second to last window before a bolt gave. Smiling in satisfaction, he eased the window open. He waited a moment for voices, then lifted his head level to check the darkened room with accustomed eyes. Satisfied, he rolled over the sill into the room and waited, crouched behind a large desk, searching the corners for any signs of life.

Satisfied that it was empty, he rose to his full height and closed the window behind him. He straightened a paper on the desk that had been pushed askew by the wind, then slipped across the high-piled rug to the closed door. A dim shaft of light shone beneath it.

How easy this is, he thought as he slowly pushed open the door. How easy it will be to kill the duke. If it were not for the hundreds of guests who danced downstairs, he would kill the vile aristocrat now and return to the unfinished business in Paris. What Kilian had planned as a one-week strategy had already stretched to three, and he knew it would be at least two more weeks before he could complete his plans. He had already wasted too much time here in Normandy. Aimee's face rose to his mind and he smiled slightly. The time had not been totally wasted, he mused. He had met the lovely vicomtesse.

He pushed the wayward thoughts out of his mind and stepped out of the room. The halls were empty but for an occasional, hushed laugh. He saw a couple embracing in a darkened alcove and walked by without their notice. He entered each room and categorized it, then searched the walls and the bookshelves for secret passages. In one large bedroom he found a small door behind a red lacquer partition and he hesitantly opened it. It led to a narrow flight of stairs to a lower room, a servant's room, and then out into the darkness. Retracing his steps, Kilian returned to the north wing.

A hall of mirrors linked the north wing to the south, and though it was far from the noise and glitter of the ballroom, several couples had found their way here. Kilian hid halfway behind heavy velvet draperies while the last, lingering couples finished their oft-interrupted promenade through the hall. Then he moved swiftly toward the south wing.

Voices stopped him still. He crouched low and blended in the shadows. He saw a shimmering white skirt in the darkness of the south wing and his brows drew together. Leaning precariously to one side, he attempted to identify the owner of the skirt.

Her voice rose softly, and Kilian knew it was Aimee. His body tightened as he recognized the deeper, male voice that accompanied hers.

Despite the warnings ringing in his head, Kilian stretched to his full height and eased his way along the mirrored wall. Her perfume teased him, even from this distance, and his nostrils flared like a hunting hound's. He could see the graceful curve of her cheek and the duke's straight back. He strained to hear their conversation, but they spoke in whispers.

He watched, his anger mounting, as the duke took her arm and led her to a portal. Pulling a key from his breeches, he opened it and waited for her to enter. He glanced up and down the hall as he closed the door firmly behind him.

Kilian stood, stock-still, his fury burning in his ears like a fever, as the lock clicked loudly in the hall.

Aimee tried not to stiffen as the duke turned the lock. Though he had been polite, attentive, and discreet all evening, she wondered if he would continue that behavior now that they were away from the curious gazes of the other guests.

"Wait here, madame. There are tapers just by the hearth."

His fingers brushed her elbow as he stepped in front of her and entered the darkness. She could hear him fumbling as he searched for the taper. Aimee folded her hands and closed her eyes.

Had she known that the duke's ball would be so full of French courtiers, she would never have dared to come. Her amended wedding dress looked coarse and time-worn beside the embroidered brocades, the rich satins, the plentitude of stiff laces, and the jewels the size of bird's eggs. She had thought she was daring to wear rouge and powder, but most of the women painted themselves as thick as the traveling actors and actresses she had once seen in the village. They wore small black patches scattered about their faces and stared at her with distasteful curiosity.

Part of the curiosity, Aimee admitted, was due to the duke's incessant attentions. Since the moment she had arrived at Château Montchamp he had stayed by her side. She had ample opportunity to ask him for a private audience, and he had willingly agreed. As she stood in the darkness she wondered where she would get the courage to make him this offer.

The duke made a small sound of success as the taper took flame. Placing the candle in a brass holder, he walked toward a small desk and lit another. Aimee glanced around the room and breathed a sigh of relief. He had brought her to a library. Not a bedroom—a library.

"Are we alone?" she asked quietly.

"Yes, madame. We are quite alone." The duke lit one more candle, then put the brass holder down on the desk. He crossed his arms over the rich scarlet velvet of his waistcoat. The rubies that decorated his cuffed sleeves glittered in the dim light. "We should not stay long. My absence will be noticed quickly, and so, I fear, will yours."

"I shan't take but a few moments." She walked hesitantly into the room, her gaze scanning the tall bookshelves filled with shiny tomes. Though the room was damp and cool, her skin flushed with heat. She wrung her hands before her and wondered how she was going to start.

"Would you like some brandy, madame?"

She nodded. He walked to the far end of the room, his high-heeled red velvet shoes making no sound on the rug. Aimee heard the clink of crystal against crystal and the splash of liquid before he returned, two goblets of the amber brandy in hand.

"You are very kind," she murmured as she took a goblet. His cologne still overpowered her and she tried not to sneeze. Instead, she lifted the glass to her lips and took a healthy sip of the fine, smooth brandy. She had eaten little that afternoon and the liquor warmed her blood.

"Come now, Vicomtesse. Tell me what plagues you so much that you entered a darkened room with a strange man."

Her fingers tightened on the goblet. "Am I so transparent?"

"Your eyes are. They cannot hide your feelings." He shrugged. "You are also quite daring, madame. I admire that in a woman. Or a man."

"I fear this is more desperation than daring, monsieur. I have come to you this night because I have nowhere else to turn."

"Really?" He lifted his brows and placed his hands on his pure white breeches. "What can I do to help you?"

She licked her lips and took a deep breath, knowing that the motion made her breasts press precariously against the tautness of her embroidered stomacher. "I don't know how much you know about me, monsieur, but I am in a very unsteady position. Some people say I should not be using the title of Vicomtesse de Bocage—"

"If you are talking about your marriage and the events that ensued, I should tell you that I am well aware of them."

"You are?"

"Of course." He crossed his feet at the ankle. "After Palm Sunday I made sure I found out everything I could about you. You intrigued me. I had never known a vicomtesse, especially one with such grace, who rode a cart to church. I made a few inquiries, and soon heard all the rumors and all the sordid opinions of the villagers and the bourgeois. You are a much talked about woman, madame."

"Then your opinion of me must be quite low."

"Quite the contrary. I put little value on the opinions of small minds, and from what I have seen so far of this village, it is full of small minds."

"You are being kind—"

"No, not kind. You should not judge me before you know me. What I did find out was that you are an exceptionally brave woman. Quite daring, and quite willing to fight for something you want. Am I right?"

Aimee searched for some sign of mockery. No one had ever described her quite like that, and she wondered if it were to her advantage to agree. "There is one thing that I would fight for," she agreed hesitantly. "One thing above all others."

"Château Bocage?"

"Yes."

"It is as I expected then."

Aimee put the goblet down on the desk and stepped away from the duke. "I have to admit that I have done a little research on you, too, monsieur. As you know, my estate is adjacent to yours. I also know that you own some land on the southern side of my lands."

"Yes, that's true," he noted with the slightest hint of amusement in his voice.

"If our estates were merged, you would become the largest landowner in Normandy, and nearly as wealthy as a Prince of the Blood."

The duke digested this slowly, then lifted his hands. "Interesting, and probably true, but I don't understand what you are proposing."

Aimee wandered farther away from the duke, unable to meet his direct, shadowed gaze. She lifted her hand to the loaded shelves, absently fingering the rich morocco binding of his books. "I am proposing a bargain, monsieur, a bargain that will be . . . beneficial for both of us."

"Please go on, Vicomtesse. I am intrigued."

Aimee took a deep breath, dropped her hand from the bookshelves, and grasped the delicate ivory handle of her fan that hung from her wrist. "As you probably know, the king currently holds the fate of my estate in his hands. It is generally thought that he will sell it to one of his courtiers."

"That is the most logical decision. His tiresome ministers are screaming for money to pay for the war."

"Unfortunately, yes." Aimee tapped her fan against her skirts as she wandered deeper into the room. "When he sells it, the new owner will evict me from the castle and, well, I shall be set adrift." She turned to him and suddenly rued the lack of light, for she could not read the subtleties of his expressions. "What I am proposing, monsieur, is that *you* buy my estate."

"I do not understand." The duke shifted his weight to face her better. "If I buy your estate, you will still lose your title, and in effect, your estate."

"I care naught for the title, and there is nothing I can do, as a woman, to keep my estate," she explained. "You, however, have the means to buy it. Possession of the Bocage estate will make you a wealthier man. All I ask is the opportunity to live in Château Bocage and care for the lands and the people." She tilted her chin. "And that, monsieur, is my proposal."

"I see." The duke stood and paced to the fireside. His heavy brows lowered slightly over his quick, dark eyes. "I am afraid that what you ask is more difficult than you think."

She bit her lower lip as her heart lurched in her chest. She struggled to keep her voice as cool and even as it had been since she had dared to walk into this dark library. "Is it . . . is it a matter of money?"

"Hardly. The situation is far more delicate than that." The duke toyed with his watch chain. "Aristocrats—true *noblesse d'épée*—don't go about buying estates. We are given estates by the king and thus are further ennobled. Only the bourgeois dare to rise into gentle society so crassly."

She flushed pink to the roots of her hair. How subtle the details of court and how utterly gauche and common she felt. "I . . . I did not know."

"Further, madame, I have no need to enlarge my estate, for it supports me quite well. Nor do I have need to rise higher in court through wealth, for I am already a favorite of King Louis XV."

She straightened her shoulders above the bite of her corset. "Then there is no chance that you will consider my proposal?"

"I did not say that." The duke's lips twisted into a smile
—a strange, cavernous smile. "Indeed, I did not say that.
All I have said is that the additional land and wealth means
little to me. It is, in effect, not enough return for a rather
large investment."

He slipped his arm off the mantelpiece as he walked
slowly toward her. She breathed deeply and watched him
with widening eyes. "I don't understand, monsieur."

"Jean-Jacques, madame. I think our acquaintance has
matured enough for such intimacies."

Intimacies. The word rang loudly in her head. The duke
stopped before her and took both her trembling hands in
his. His quick, piercing gaze flickered over her face.

"And you are Aimee." She nodded silently, her throat
too thick for words. The duke's breath, scented with cologne, fell upon her cheek. "There are things a man will do
for a woman that he would not normally do, especially if
the woman promises certain favors."

She knew what he was suggesting, she had expected it
all along. If he had not suggested it, she would have done
so herself. She had a sudden urge to run from this place
and the ties that were binding around her, but she knew she
couldn't. She had to stay for the sake of Château Bocage
and all the tenants that depended on her.

"I know little of coquetry, monsieur—Jean." The duke's
grip was warm and moist. "I dare not think that you would
favor me."

"You underestimate your charms."

"Then, monsieur," she began quietly as she lifted her
gaze to his, "are they worth the price of my estate?"

"There is only one way to estimate that."

His grip was strong on her hands, surprising for a man
of his age. She became acutely aware of his body only
inches in front of her. Heat seemed to emanate from the
rich folds of his waistcoat and burn her own skin. In her
desperation she had nearly forgotten that what she was

proposing to do would bring her body in intimacy with another man's, and the physical reality made her stomach churn. His gaze slipped to her lips, and she knew with sudden clarity that he would kiss her.

"No!" She twisted out of his grasp and turned her back to him. She lifted her hand to her stomach to quell her nausea. "If indeed, my favors are going to be the payment for my side of the bargain, then I am afraid I must withhold them until. . . ." She took a deep breath. "Until you fulfill *your* side of the bargain."

There was a moment of tense silence as she waited for his response. The duke sighed heavily behind her. "You have missed your calling in life, madame. You should have been born a diplomat. If you were negotiating the Treaty of Aix-la-Chapelle I'd wager France would not be giving so much away." His hands fell upon her shoulders, and their warmth scorched her skin.

"Then . . . then we have a bargain?"

"Indeed, madame. We have a bargain."

CHAPTER

5

Aimee's carriage was the last to pull out of the courtyard of Château Montchamp. Inside the warm, dry vehicle, she pulled the thick fur rug against her chin and buried her face in the pelt. The warmth of the duke's good-night kiss lingered on her fingers.

She closed her eyes. She should be triumphant now, for she had accomplished exactly what she had set out to do. The Duc de Montchamp had promised to buy her estate from the king. She would be able to stay on at Château Bocage, care for her lands and her people, for the rest of her life. All she had to do in return. . . .

Abruptly, she opened the window of the coach. The night had grown cold, but she needed the brisk wind and the early morning mists whipping through her hair. She pulled off her wig and several pins scattered onto the shaking carriage floor. Running her fingers through her dark tresses, she removed the remaining pins and placed them neatly inside the lining of the wig.

To be the Duc de Montchamp's mistress. Not a terrible fate for a woman who would otherwise be living off the generosity of her ex-tenants, or begging in the streets of Beny-Bocage, or, worse, living a sterile life in a convent. As his mistress she would never have to worry about food or warmth or shelter. She would have jewels, a new carriage, and the right to live on her estate. All for the price of her untried charms.

She closed her eyes and the heat of her shame suffused her cheeks. She mouthed silent prayers for forgiveness to the mother she never knew, and the father who had died when she was nine but had abandoned her long before. She was almost relieved that she had no family left to witness her infamy. The only person she degraded in this sordid affair was herself, and she was nothing but a commoner in aristocratic clothes. To be branded an adulteress was not so high a price to pay, she argued weakly, for the welfare of her people and the protection of the estate.

The carriage jolted to the right and Aimee clutched her wig as it tumbled off the seat. She braced herself against the chair as the coach rumbled through rough terrain.

Suddenly, the carriage stopped.

Aimee sat, wide-eyed, in the darkness, images of highwaymen and pistols flashing through her mind. The carriage lurched to one side as Kilian stepped off the box. She strained to hear voices—but she heard only the snorting of the horses and the sound of Kilian's footsteps.

The door opened and she squinted against the light of the lanterns on either side of the frame.

"Why are we stopped?" she blurted, her throat tightening with fear. "Is there . . . are there thieves?"

"No, no thieves, madame," Kilian answered as he reached for her hand. "Come out for a moment."

"Why? Is there something wrong with the carriage?"

"Nothing of the sort. I want to speak to you." He low-

ered his voice to a dangerous pitch. "Come out of your
own free will, Vicomtesse, or I shall pull you out myself."

Aimee's gaze focused on him and her heart skipped a
beat. She had forgotten that danger held the reins of her
horses. She cursed her own foolishness. Kilian had never
fit into the mold of a prisoner and she wondered why she
had trusted him to be her carriage driver. She wondered,
with a tremor, what he wanted.

She forced her voice to be stern. "I can hear what you
have to say very well from inside—"

He clutched her bare shoulders with both hands. He
lifted her off the seat, twisted her to the side and pulled
her, skirts and all, out of the narrow carriage door.

"What are you doing!?"

"I am taking you out of the carriage, madame, since you
were so unwilling to come out yourself."

"Well put me down!"

"In the mud?"

She quieted. She glanced over his shoulder to the
ground, which was wet and muddy from the week's rain.
Unconsciously, she pressed closer to his chest. With a triumphant smile, he heaved her higher in his arms and
turned toward the darkness of the forest.

"Where are you taking me?" She twisted to stare at his
profile, and her gaze rested in fury on his arrogant smile.
"What have you done to Gustave?"

"Gustave is well. He had too much to drink tonight so he
rode on the box with me."

Aimee glanced toward the carriage and saw Gustave
lying awkwardly on the velvet-covered driver's box. Panic
touched her with cold fingers. Despite the mud that pulled
noisily upon Kilian's boots, Aimee began her struggles
anew.

"Don't fight me, madame, else you will find yourself in
the mud."

"Isn't that where you are taking me anyway?"

He laughed and the low rumble vibrated in his chest. "Though the thought of us in the mud gives me great pleasure, Vicomtesse, I must disappoint you. I have never taken a woman against her will and I do not plan to start now."

"Then why are you dragging me out into the darkness?" she snapped, piqued at his words. "You certainly can't be planning a kidnapping, you know I have no relatives—"

"You truly believe I am an outlaw, don't you?"

"What else do you call a man who tosses women around with such utter disregard for their wishes?"

"A rogue, a rake perhaps." He looked at her.. "But certainly not an outlaw."

Her throat dried as their gazes locked. "You're dismissed," she said, hiding her fear with haughtiness. "I have had quite enough of you and your antics."

"'Twould be prudent to wait until I have driven you home before you relieve me of my services." He suddenly released her knees.

"At least bring me back to the carriage! Don't leave me here in the mud! This is the only ball gown I own!"

He flashed a wide, white smile. "There's a rock beneath you. Though your touch is heady, madame, your arms are choking me."

She looked down and saw the shiny surface of an uncovered boulder. Tentatively, she placed one slippered foot on the smooth surface, then the other. She released her grip around his neck immediately. The night air rushed between them.

He stepped back and leaned against the trunk of an elm. She glanced around for escape but found herself on a dry island in a sea of mud. Emphatically, she cursed the rain that had watered her fields for the past weeks. Because of it, she could not escape without ruining her mended wedding dress. She glanced toward her captor. She suspected he would be far more agile than she in such a bog, and all attempts at escape would be futile.

"Very well, Laclos," she said, crossing her arms in front of her. "What is it that you want? Certainly you have humiliated me for a reason—or do men like you enjoy treating a woman like this?"

"I don't usually have to resort to such rough tactics, but you are an extremely stubborn woman." He shrugged one broad shoulder and glanced at the extent of her bosom exposed above the embroidered stomacher. "I will not deny that I enjoyed it. You are usually dressed in those staid black dresses—I had no idea you were quite so well made."

Her eyes widened. His words, spoken so casually, so quiet and low, sent her blood coursing through her veins. Yet it was not terror alone that coursed through her blood. Another emotion joined it. An emotion she could not name.

She lifted her chin and stared into his lean face. "So much for your promise to earn my trust. This act tonight has done nothing to endear you to me."

"I think you may trust me more before the evening is through," he said, pushing away from the elm and walking toward her. "Believe it or not, madame, my intentions are for the best."

Her gaze wandered over his face. He was close, too close, and his proximity was making her dizzy. She clutched her fan and lifted it to her chest. Why couldn't she think when he was so near?

"You expect a lot from me," she said casually, coldly, not meeting his eyes. "You toss me about like a doll, drag me out into the woods in the middle of the night, threaten to ruin my clothes, then tell me your intentions are good."

"Perhaps I do ask for too much." He reached for her chin and pushed it up until she could not avoid meeting his gaze. "Nonetheless, will you trust me?"

She felt vulnerable, weak, and bared beneath the unflinching intensity of his gaze. She tried to twist her head, but his fingers tightened gently on her chin. He rubbed her cheek with his forefinger, which was roughened from weeks in the fields.

"Is it so very hard for you to trust, *cailín deas?*"

Aimee's brows lowered at the unfamiliar words. She started to ask him what they meant but bit back the question. She was not sure she wanted to know. "Trust . . ." She closed her eyes and lowered them, anything to break the contact with his intense gaze. "If I say no, you shall toss me into the mud. If I say yes, I shall be lying—trust is something earned, Laclos. Not promised."

"Perhaps if we were to become more familiar you would trust me more." He ran a finger over her bottom lip. "Perhaps if I called you Aimee—"

"No!" Her name, on his lips, was a dangerous, disturbing thing. "You forget your place—"

"'Tis your name, and I am partial to it." He shrugged and released her chin. "If you would call me Kilian, instead of Laclos, perhaps you would sooner trust me."

"Unlikely."

"You don't know the Duc de Montchamp very well, do you?"

She blinked, surprised at the sudden change in topic. "No. No, I don't."

"Then you would no more easily trust him than you would me?"

"The duke is far more trustworthy than an arrogant poacher."

His mood changed. Aimee felt as if a breeze had come by and snuffed out the meager starlight. His brows lowered and veiled his eyes with shadows.

"Don't you wonder why the duke is in Normandy, and not in the French court?"

"No."

"You should. For a French courtier, leaving Versailles is a fate worse than death."

"Are you telling me that the duke is exiled?" Her heart began to beat hard in her chest. If the duke was in exile, then he had toyed with her this evening, and all her hopes were dashed.

"No, not officially." Kilian forced his voice even for the next sentences. "He debauched a young, innocent aristocrat without claiming her as his mistress. The woman died giving birth to his illegitimate child a month ago, and she was denied a Christian burial."

She stared at him with rounded eyes, speechless.

"Yes, horrible, isn't it?" he continued. "But the king did not exile the duke—the duke left on his own, to 'recover.' That is why he is here, in Normandy."

Aimee reeled. *He debauched a young, innocent aristocrat.* Could the duke possibly be doing the same to her? Would he keep his bargain with her? Or was Kilian just telling her gossip culled from the streets of Paris? Certainly, the rumors that the duke heard about her were no more shocking.

"What does this have to do with me?" She shook her head vigorously. "I'll not listen to vicious gossip. What you've told me tonight, it's just poison—"

"Why did you go to the duke's ball, Aimee?"

She shrugged a shoulder and her cream silk sleeve slipped a fraction down her arm. "I have been a widow for a year and a month. What harm was there in seeking solace in the duke's ball?"

"Is that what you were seeking? Solace?"

Anger prickled up her back. "Who are you to question me? You are my *prisoner!*"

"It seems to me, madame, that you are now *my* prisoner." His gaze raked her face. "A situation I enjoyed once before, I remember. Until Gustave interrupted."

"Fortunately."

"Nay, quite unfortunately." He stepped closer. "I never look fate in the eye twice, Aimee."

She felt his hands first. Each callused finger dug into the indentation of her waist. The cold buttons of his frayed waistcoat pressed into her naked bosom as he pulled her flat against him. He muffled her terrified protests with his lips.

For the love of God . . .

All rational thought whirled, exploded, and fled. For a moment she fell against him, stunned, as his rough lips pressed against her own. He released her waist and wrapped his arms around her, cradling her head on his arm. She could not move, she could not struggle, and as his kisses deepened Aimee knew that if he did not hold her up she would faint in a puddle of white satin.

His breath tasted of calvados and heat. His hands did not move over her, but she was conscious of their touch, of their warmth, and of their potential. His lips parted her own and her heart fluttered. She felt her soul move like a flower opening to the caress of the warm spring sun.

She knew, suddenly, what she had feared these past weeks. She feared his power. He seemed to reach into her spirit and probe all that she hid from the world. Kilian of the emerald eyes, flecked with sunshine—those eyes saw right through to her spirit. She feared this joining of the lips, of the bodies, of the souls.

He lifted his head from hers. He breathed hard and fast upon her flushed cheek, and she could feel his gaze upon her face. She twisted away.

"I brought you out here only to warn you about the duke," he whispered. "I suppose you don't believe that now."

"Please let me go." It was her own voice, but she barely recognized it.

"Aye, I'll let you go. I should say I'm sorry, but I'm not. You are a very distracting woman, Aimee." He ran a hand over her hair. "And that's not the first time you've been kissed." Kilian pulled her body close to his and wrapped his arm around her knees. She struggled briefly. "Don't—I'm taking you back to the carriage."

He carried her through the mud to the coach. His body was hot, hard, and intensely vibrant against her own. She did not meet his eyes, even as he placed her carefully upon the steps of the carriage. He closed the door on her averted face.

She sat in the darkness, stunned. Her heart still raced beneath her stiff stomacher. Kilian was wrong—that was her first kiss, and she feared she would never be the same again.

She clutched her cold skirts as the carriage rumbled over the uneven terrain onto the road. In that one brief moment Aimee suddenly understood the forces that drove the Comtesse de Vierzon into the arms of her lovers. She had felt it herself—she had felt her insides melt to liquid, her thoughts mingle and separate until they were meaningless words, her body throb with some unfamiliar, urgent passion. She had *wanted* Kilian Laclos, and she feared he knew it.

She moaned in the darkness. *Wanton fool!* She took a deep breath to calm her rampant heartbeat. He was a handsome man, a masterful man—an arrogant commoner, a thief. Her body sparked with the heat of her embarrassment. How could she have succumbed to his kiss so easily? She struggled through the memory and realized that she had not even tried. She had melted in his arms like butter on a summer day.

Kilian Laclos must leave Château Bocage, she concluded hotly. He must never spread this tale, and moreover, he must never try this anew. She would make sure he would have no more opportunity.

By the time the carriage drove up the pebbled drive of Château Bocage, Aimee had gathered her scattered wits and settled into the unemotional mien that had kept her calm during the months after her husband's death. Kilian Laclos, she swore, would never know how much he had truly unnerved her.

The carriage stopped before the castle. Through the thin walls she heard the voices of her tenants. Not waiting for Kilian to climb down from the box and open the door, she pushed it open herself and kicked the stairs down.

"What has happened?" Her voice rang discordant over the huddled group as she collected her skirts and walked to their sides. They looked at her with work-weary eyes.

"I'm afraid there's been thieves, madame," Monsieur Enver said, holding his cap in his hand. "The Bouches were robbed of two goats and several bags of grain."

She swore to herself, closed her eyes, and lifted a hand to her forehead. "Was anyone hurt, Robert?"

"*Oui,* madame. Monsieur Bouche was beaten when he caught them in the goat's pen."

Aimee sighed, long and heavily. She felt rather than saw Kilian's presence beside her, but she did not turn to him.

"How long have these thieves been gone?" Kilian asked.

"Hours now," Monsieur Enver answered. "They struck not long after madame left for the ball."

Aimee heard the accusation clearly, but chose to ignore it. "Has Monsieur Bouche been tended?"

"*Oui,* Manon has tended him, but his family is still awake and about."

"Kilian, have my mare saddled." She lifted her skirts and headed toward the worn steps. "I must see the Bouches."

"Madame," Kilian interrupted, "there is still some chance that these men may be found."

Aimee took a deep breath and turned to him. "These men have been gone for hours. They are far from here, enjoying their stolen goods."

"If they stole some goats and grain, their escape would be slow."

"They also stole some of the Bouches' best calvados," Monsieur Enver added, glancing with hope at Kilian, "and several bags of dried apples."

"Let me saddle my stallion, madame." Kilian watched her with steady eyes. "I may be able to capture these thieves for you."

"I should send a thief off to catch thieves?"

"No." A muscle twitched in his lean cheek. "You should send an experienced French soldier to hunt them down."

Aimee's tenants stared at her and waited for her reply. She was trapped, and Kilian knew it. She could not refuse his request, not without earning the enmity of her tenants. But if she agreed, she would lose Kilian, for he would certainly escape as soon as he sat upon his powerful steed.

Aimee tilted her head. Yes, she would lose Kilian, but was that so terrible a fate? She would be rid of him without ever having to face him across her study. He would escape, and she would be free of him and his disturbing attentions.

She wondered why the words were so difficult to say.

"Very well, Laclos. Mount both our horses. I wish you luck . . . in capturing those thieves."

Kilian bent low over his stallion's back, reveling for a moment in the steed's movement beneath his thighs. It had been too long since he had ridden. He felt his muscles stretch and bunch in rhythm with the beast's.

The farmer had directed Kilian toward the north, where the thieves had escaped after the beating. The trail was still fresh with broken branches and hoofprints. The thieves were amateurs. No professionals would leave such a clearly marked trail. He gauged their speed by the depth of the hoofprints and realized that they had slowed to a walk only a league away from the thatched hut. If he kept up his pace, he might catch them before they left the hedged perimeter of Aimee's land.

Aimee.... Her eyes had grown so smoky gray after he had kissed her. She had wanted him. Kilian had known enough women to recognize desire, but this time the knowledge did not give him strength. It made him weak and he did not understand why.

It made him foolish, as well, he thought ruefully as he rose to the top of a small hill. He wanted to win her trust so badly he had offered to hunt down these bold, and probably drunken, thieves. What he should do was ride straight through to the Duc de Montchamp's lands and kill that insidious nobleman. Then, after he had hidden for a time, return to Normandy to court Aimee de Chacontier in a far more proper manner.

Court? He wondered why he had suddenly thought of courting her. He slowed his stallion in surprise. She was not the most beautiful woman he had known—the ladies of Versailles, though frivolous, had the money and the time to make the best of their charms. Yet Aimee's simple, direct, uncomplicated honesty made her far more attractive than the wealthiest duchess. There was something vulnerable and elusive in her clear gray eyes. There was something in the tilt of her head, the curve of her delicate throat, the thinness of her collarbone and the creamy texture of her skin. She was grace, strength—and he wanted more of her.

He wanted all of her.

His body responded and he kicked the stallion into a run. His lusts had led him into folly this evening. He should not have kissed her. For the taste of her lips he had risked three weeks of planning. He knew now that Aimee would never trust him again unless he proved himself. These thieves were somewhere in the forest, and Kilian sensed that only if he caught them and dragged them to her door would she consider his next proposal—the next step in his plan of vengeance.

His vengeance. His anger still burned hot in his heart. He was mad to consider making love to Aimee when so much had to be done. After he killed the Duc de Montchamp, after this hatred and anger was purged from his soul, only then could he consider the lovely vicomtesse. First, and foremost, he had his sister's shame to avenge. Until he succeeded he could think of nothing else.

The trail led to a thicker part of the forest. Kilian followed it to the hedges that ringed Aimee's estate. He hesitated only for a moment, then followed the hoofprints into the next holding.

If these thieves were typical of the trespassers who had plagued the Bocage lands, Kilian knew he could purge her estate of them in a matter of weeks. He wondered if he could talk her into allowing him to try. He sensed she had permitted him to ride tonight because she was too weary to argue. She was too young to have so much worry. Part of him wanted to take her in his arms and make her forget. . . .

Dangerous thoughts, these. He shook his head free of the fog of passion and reined his stallion to a stop. Suddenly, he heard the rhythmic loping of several horses—not far ahead. Stiffening to absolute stillness, he searched the black forest for signs of the thieves.

He counted the number by the rhythm of the hooves. Three, maybe four. His muscles tensed and his body sizzled with the anticipation of the imminent battle. He'd brought down more than four men with stealth and strength in battle. This should be no more difficult.

Still, he wished Aimee had given him his musket. It would have made his task all the easier.

* * *

Aimee rocked the child in her arms, running her fingers through the thin, wispy blond hair. She closed her eyes and rested her head against the oak back of the chair. The eastern sky had already begun to lighten, for she could see the bluish glow diffusing through the uneven slats of the wooden shutters. Madame Bouche bustled about the room and piled more tinder upon the dwindling fire.

Madame Bouche glanced at her child in Aimee's arms. "François is finally sleeping. It must be your singing, madame."

Aimee nodded silently and toyed with his wayward bangs. "He was just weary," she whispered. "And afraid."

Madame Bouche reached for her son and gathered him to her ample bosom. Aimee released his weight reluctantly and wrapped her arms around her midriff. The child had kept her warm, in more than one way, and she regretted the loss.

"François must sleep in his own bed," she murmured, cocking a brow at Aimee. "And perhaps it is time, madame, that you slept in yours."

Aimee watched Madame Bouche's retreating back. Her eyelids drooped over her eyes. She was tired, but it was a weariness that went deeper than that of the body. She was weary in spirit. Monsieur Bouche was resting comfortably now, but Aimee had seen the extent of his beating. Had the thieves not been interrupted, they would have killed him and left a widow and three fatherless children.

She glanced into the sputtering fire and ran her hands over the rumpled skirts of her oldest riding habit. The rice powder she had patted on her face the evening before stained her fingers and left a thin dust on her dress. Her hair fell in a long, ragged mass over one shoulder. She did not look like a vicomtesse, and she did not feel like one either. She felt completely and utterly powerless.

"Would you like some apple cider, madame?" Madame

Bouche offered as she closed the door to the children's room behind her.

"No, thank you, Marie. I should return to the castle." She rose from the seat by the hearth. "I'll send Gustave and some of the men over this afternoon to help you with the chores. And don't worry about the fields—I'll have my own day-workers tend them until your husband is well—"

"I know, madame," Madame Bouche interrupted. "There's no need to tell me this. I know you'll care for us."

Aimee swallowed the lump that had suddenly risen in her throat. There was so much she wanted to say: how sorry she was, how guilty she felt, how impotent she was in trying to rid these lands of danger. Madame Bouche watched her with kindly eyes well cushioned in wrinkles. A strand of half gray, half blond hair peeped out of her simple cotton bonnet.

"I'll send Manon, too, to look at your husband."

"Merci."

Aimee squeezed the older woman's hand, then wrapped her cloak around her shoulders. Before she could open the door, it opened in front of her. A pair of broad shoulders filled the portal.

"Kilian!"

His green gaze focused on her. Aimee blinked in shock. She had thought she would never see him again. Her heart leapt with an irrational joy.

"Madame." Kilian bowed before her. The motion did not seem out of place despite his disheveled state and the thatched roof cottage in which they stood. "I've brought you your thieves."

"My thieves?"

"Yes." One brow quirked on his dirt-streaked face. "Remember? The men that beat Monsieur Bouche? I have captured them, and"—he glanced inside to the woman who stood, stunned, near the hearth—"I've got the goats and the bags of grain, as well."

"Are the thieves outside?"

"Nay. I left them under Gustave's care. I brought them to the castle. When I was told you were here, I came immediately." He hesitated. "I wanted you to know that the men were caught."

He had caught the thieves. Aimee stared at him in disbelief. After all that had happened after the ball, after all her threats to dismiss him, he had returned. *To me*, she thought, irrationally. They watched one another from across an arm's span. She could smell him—all earth and April rain and salt. She wanted to hug him in thanks, and his warm green eyes promised that he would not object. Tearing her gaze from his, she glanced at his livery. The rough wool was streaked liberally with the rich Norman soil and torn in tatters at the chest.

She sucked in her breath at the sight of the blood. "You're hurt!"

"'Tis nothing but a scratch."

"Come, sit by the fire." Breaking the spell that bound them, Aimee turned to Madame Bouche. "Madame, I need the medicines that Manon left for your husband. Kil— Monsieur Laclos needs tending."

Madame Bouche bustled out of the room without a word. Kilian entered the cottage, carefully wiping the caked mud off his knee-high boots. Aimee pushed her cloak off her shoulders and tossed it on the heavy table. She watched him as he settled, stiffly, in the hard wooden chair.

Gathering her riding skirts around her knees, she sat down by his side. The blood that stained his waistcoat was fresh and red and she knew that he had been bleeding for some time, yet his lean cheeks still glowed with color.

"Are you surprised?"

His voice startled her as she reached to pull open his coat. "Surprised? At what?"

"Surprised that I came back. With the thieves."

She was surprised he had come back at all, but for some unknown reason she was reluctant to tell him. His gaze tethered hers, and he searched her eyes for his answer.

"You were surprised," he said.

"Of course I was."

"Here're the linens," Madame Bouche said as she bustled back into the room. "Manon's got a whole sack full of evil-smelling herbs, but I don't know—"

"It's all right, Marie," Aimee interrupted, her nerves tense. "I know what is needed." Her gaze flickered over Kilian anew. "You'll need to take off your waistcoat and shirt."

"With pleasure." He glanced past Aimee to Madame Bouche. "Madame, your goats are tied up outside. I did not know where to pen them. They have had a long walk. Perhaps it would be wise to feed them."

"Yes, yes," she said quickly. She untied her white apron. "They must be cared for, poor dears."

Madame Bouche left the room. As Aimee's gaze strayed to where Kilian was stripping his bloodied linen shirt off his chest, she suddenly realized that they were alone.

CHAPTER

6

Aimee tried not to stare. Kilian's shoulder blades spanned the great length of his shoulders, strong and firm above the musculature of his chest. The sight of the long, thin wound running the length of his ribs spurred her to stop her wayward thoughts and start her work.

She bent down beside him and leaned over his lap. Her fingers gently probed the edge of the wound. "You are wrong. This is not a scratch."

"I did not want to alarm you."

Her winged brows flew up on her brow. "Since when? I thought you enjoyed alarming me."

"Not like this," he said, glancing at the long knot of dark hair that spilled over his lap. He winced slightly as she probed the sorest part of the wound.

"This will be painful."

"It *is* painful," he murmured. "But I have felt far worse."

She did not doubt it. His chest was nicked with a dozen

scars, some darker and deeper than others. He hardly moved beneath her ministrations and the only sign of pain was the tenseness of his muscles in the flat, rippled abdomen. His skin felt hot to her fingertips. A spray of light hair covered his upper chest and whirled around his dark nipples. Aimee flushed when she realized where her gaze had strayed.

She could not look into his eyes, though she felt the searing heat of his gaze on her head. With learned efficiency she rifled through Manon's sack of herbs and searched for the oils necessary for a poultice. Soaking a linen in the pungent brew, she lifted it to his chest and pressed it hard against the open wound.

"Calvados would be nice," he said huskily as the astringent mixture burned through the ragged edges of the cut.

"Here. If you promise to hold this in place I shall pour you some."

He placed his hand over hers but did not release her. She stumbled as she tried to rise. Her gaze fluttered, surprised, to his. His eyes were the color of unripe apples and his gaze grew warm on her face.

"I can wait for the calvados."

"The pain will get worse." She silently cursed her wavering voice. "It would be best if you had something to stop it."

"You haven't slept all night, have you?"

"Is it that obvious?"

"Ah, the defenses have cracked." His lips curled in a small smile. "It took a sleepless night, an attack by a rogue, and a raid on your estate to weaken your defenses, but you are, indeed, a woman."

She yanked her hand away from beneath his but felt guilty as soon as she saw the spasm of pain flutter over his features. She whirled away and walked toward the heavy oak table, which held several bottles of Château Bocage's best calvados. Her throat itched for a tumbler of her own, but she knew if she drank any calvados she'd fall asleep on the hard-packed earthen floor.

Or in his arms.

"Why did you stay up all night?"

"I had to," she said, pouring a glass of the gold liquid. "The Bouches are my people. After all that has happened. . . ."

"It was not your fault."

She handed him the mug. Kilian had an uncanny way of reading her own thoughts. "They are my responsibility. Perhaps if I had not gone to the ball—"

"If you had not gone to the ball then you simply would have found out sooner," he argued. "You could not have stopped them."

"Gustave was with me. If he had been scouting, instead of opening doors for me in his livery, then perhaps this would not have happened."

"With all due respect to Gustave, Aimee, he is not the best of scouts." He winced as she applied a fresh linen damp with the herb mixture. "He sings loud enough to warn thieves for two leagues around."

She pressed the linen against his chest. She could feel the slow, even beat of his heart. His skin, so close to her face, emanated the earthy scent of musk. She leaned on his long, strong legs. As she pressed the linen more tightly over the ridge of his muscles, he lifted the mug of calvados and finished it in one draught.

Her hand trembled against his body. She did not know where to look but found her gaze drawn to his face. A bristle of a beard drew a shadow along his chin, but the darkness only emphasized his lean cheeks and his short cheekbones. His hair, usually bright with blond streaks, lay dirty and matted against his head. He was a handsome man. Never had she been so aware of it as now.

"How . . . how did you catch the thieves?" she asked,

pressing the linen against the bottom half of the cut. "I thought there were two of them."

"Four."

"Four! How did you capture four?"

"It was not easy," he admitted, gesturing to the slash. "One of them had a dagger and nearly carved out one of my ribs."

"Did they have pistols, or muskets?"

"Aye, both."

Aimee's incredulity grew. "But—"

"I told you I was a soldier in the French army." His eyes sparkled behind a thick netting of gold-tipped lashes. "Didn't you believe me?"

"No." She tossed the dirty linen in a growing pile by the hearth. "Frankly, I thought you were lying."

"Do you believe me now?"

She reached for a fresh linen and dipped it in the herbs. One man, unarmed, against four. Her gaze wandered over his chest as she wiped the cut for the final time. His body was spare but undeniably strong. She realized just how strong when he reached for her hand and lifted it to his lips.

"Come, Aimee. Answer me."

His lips found the shallow valley of her palm. "Yes," she murmured. "I believe you now. After your capturing four thieves, I can't help but believe you."

She tried to pull her hand away as his hot lips settled on the pulse that beat in her wrist, but his grip was too sure. Sensing her unease, he twined his fingers in hers and held their joined hands between them.

"Will you let me help you now?"

Her winged brows drew together, leaving a slight wrinkle between them. "Let you help me?"

"Yes. Let me be a scout on your lands. Don't waste my talents in the fields."

Her face closed. "Kilian, I—"

"Think of your tenants, Aimee. I can stop these raids. I can prevent the beatings. I can ease this worry from your brow."

He rubbed a callused finger against her forehead. Despite the roughness of his fingertips, his touch was infinitely gentle. She closed her eyes. She was exhausted, and in no shape to battle with him.

"Don't fall asleep, *a stor*," he whispered. "Not until you give me an answer."

His gaze searched her face. She realized that he was still holding her hand. She felt the inevitability of her decision. Not four hours earlier she had sworn to expel Kilian from her lands, and now she knew that she would hire him on as a guard. He had wanted this from the start, and fighting him was like battling the March storms. He said nothing as he watched her and she had the uneasy feeling that he could read her every thought.

She met his gaze. "Very well, Kilian," she said, rising from her cramped position and pulling her hand from his warm grasp. "You are now a scout in the employ of the Bocage estate." She glanced at his wound and forced severity into her voice. "As soon as you are healed, I expect you to start work."

Aimee pulled on the jacket of her long-waisted riding dress and smoothed the worsted wool pleats of the split skirt. She carried her short riding crop beneath her arm as she walked over the long grass to the stables, some distance beyond the château. Her silver buttons gleamed in the sunlight, and with the matching tricorn on her head she felt exceedingly English, exceptionally fashionable, and extremely smart.

She had not ridden in the past week because of the heavy rains. The bogs had thickened so much that she knew it

would be too dangerous to venture into the woods. Though
the sun had been out for only a day, she judged it would be
safe to ride in some parts of the estate if she were careful.
She needed to ride. She needed to get away from her study
and the ledgers and the constant fear of a messenger—either from the king, or from the Duc de Montchamp.

She also had to get away from her own thoughts. She
had not seen Kilian at all since the night he captured the
thieves. True to his word, he had stopped all attacks on her
estate. Her tenants spoke of him in glowing, heroic terms,
as if he were a miracle bestowed upon the region. At last
Sunday's Mass she had even heard Madame Bouche pray-
ing for him.

Though Kilian scouted the black Norman forests in the
evenings, he had never been far away from her thoughts.
Or her dreams. He had convinced her that he was the answer to her trespasser problems, and it seemed he was correct. But now that he had succeeded in his goals he seemed
to have lost all interest in her. She wondered why the
thought bothered her so much.

It was a single kiss, she thought, lifting her face to the
sun. A single, meaningless, angry kiss. She was foolish to
read any more into it.

"I assume this is the horse you requested?"

Aimee started. Lost in thought, she didn't realize she
had walked so far. She stood in the middle of the stable
courtyard. Kilian stood in front of her, the reins of her
favorite mare in his hands. Dressed in simple ratteen
breeches and an open linen shirt, with his face as tanned as
a deer hide, he looked every bit the part of an avenging
hero.

"Where's Gustave?" she asked. "I thought he would be
here."

"I overheard your orders to Gustave, and, since he was
busy, I decided to saddle your horse myself." He caressed
the horse's side. "This is your horse?"

"Yes."

"I thought as much. I can always pick a horse by its owner." His eyes twinkled. "This mare is lean, sleek, and spirited, so I knew at once it must be yours."

"If that is the case, Laclos, then your horse must be stubborn and arrogant." *And handsome*. She struggled between a smile and a frown. She really shouldn't let him be so intimate. He was, after all, in her employ.

"Temper, Vicomtesse." The corners of his eyes crinkled as he looked at her. "Has Gustave been dipping into the apple cider again? Or is it Manon this time, messing up the papers in your study?"

She lifted a brow. "And how have you heard about Manon? Surely my voice doesn't carry to the day-workers' quarters."

"No, but it carries to the buttery, Aimee. Distinctly."

"You shouldn't call me that."

"What? Lean, sleek, and spirited?"

"No." She flushed. "Aimee."

"But that is your name."

"It's Madame Chacontier to you, I'm afraid."

"Afraid?" Kilian bent slightly, and Aimee found her back against the warmth of her mare, and her bosom dangerously close to Kilian's very broad and slightly familiar chest. "I didn't think you were afraid of anything."

"I am, actually. I'm afraid of many things."

"Like?" He did not move though they were close—too close for propriety's sake.

"Lightning. Floods. Drought." She lowered her gaze. "And poverty."

"Simple things, I see."

The mare shifted and Aimee took advantage of the opening to reach for the saddle horn. "Please, Kil—Laclos. Help me mount."

"Nay. I'm afraid it must be Kilian—at least when we're alone." He lifted a hand to touch a black tress that had fallen out of her chignon. "I like the way my name rolls off your Norman tongue."

"Very well, then . . . Kilian."

He held out a hand to assist her. His fingers closed around the soft leather of her boot far too tightly as he hoisted her on the mare. Aimee settled quickly in the saddle and held out her hand for the reins.

"You will be back before sundown."

Aimee's winged brows flared slightly. She recognized that tone of voice from the day he was captured. Though he worded the phrase like a question, it was a command, a very sharp and distinct command. "Perhaps." She shrugged a shoulder beneath the wool of her riding jacket. "Perhaps not. Don't wait for my return."

His smile disappeared and with it, all levity. Kilian's dark, straight brows lowered and his nostrils flared. He held the mare's reins tightly.

"I suggest you do come back before sundown, Vicomtesse, or I will find it necessary to send someone to look for you."

Aimee felt a seed of anger blossom in her chest. "That will not be necessary, Laclos. I have been riding these lands since I was a child. I know them better than any man, better than any soldier. And I shall ride them whenever I wish."

"Not while I guard your borders."

"I beg your pardon?"

"You have hired me to protect this estate and the tenants of this estate, Aimee." He turned and led the mare to a post where he tied the reins. "You are one of the tenants, and I do not intend to allow you to ride in the dark of night."

"You forget that *I* am the one that hired you." In his week-long absence Aimee had forgotten how infuriating he could be. "I can just as easily dismiss you."

"For what? Protecting your pretty hide?" The sunlight

shimmered in the gold flecks in his eyes. "For doing precisely what you hired me to do?"

"I can dismiss you without any reason at all," she said tautly, pulling on her skirts. "And if you do not immediately untie this horse and hand me the reins, I will do so now."

"Your tenants would not like that."

"To hell with my tenants," she snapped. "I have not been known to worry about the opinions of my tenants."

Kilian's lips drew taut over his teeth. The dimple had disappeared, and nothing marred the lean line of his cheeks. A breeze tossed his hair in a blaze of sunlight.

"I will escort you."

"No. I wish to be alone."

His emerald eyes flashed fire. "For an intelligent woman, you can be as bullish and stubborn as a fishmonger's wife."

"Now you insult me."

Kilian shook his head and walked angrily to the post. Untying the reins, he tossed them over the mare's head. Aimee managed a small, triumphant smile as she caught them in her gloved hands. She whirled the mare around toward the forest.

"Wait a moment," he yelled. "I'll be mounting mine."

"You are not following me."

He paused in the doorway of the stables. His hands rested on his lean hips. "There is a point where pride becomes foolishness, Aimee. There were poachers out there last night. Do you have any idea what they would do if they saw an unescorted woman?"

"They'd have to outrun me, and that, indeed, would be a difficult task," she retorted. "Don't follow me, Laclos, else you'll have to find another estate to guard."

She kicked the mare into a gallop and headed full speed toward the forests. She did not turn to see if he followed her—she did not want to know. Her insides churned in

anger and confusion. No one had ever questioned the
safety or propriety of her rides. No one had ever paid quite
so much attention.

She did not slow down until the mare entered the border
of the forests, where the air was cool with mists. She
pulled her tricorn off her head and let it hang behind her.
Loosened by the gallop, her hair fell in inky tresses down
the length of her back. The mare cantered to a field spread
with the violet and pink flowers of heather. Aimee dared to
look over her shoulder but discovered with a strange sense
of disappointment that no one had followed.

She let her mare wander aimlessly through the swells
and valleys of the forests. She passed a spring whose banks
were covered with cowslips, buttercups, wild jacinths, and
daffodils, but she did not stop to gather the bright flowers.
Kicking the mare into a canter, Aimee urged her toward a
higher hill in the distance. Pine needles, twigs, and shreds
of bark covered the forest floor.

Aimee urged the horse up a hill, watching the last glorious rays of sun linger on the walls of her castle. The deep-
set *meurtrière* windows seemed purple in the shadows.
Wider at the base than at the top, the castle seemed rooted
to the earth, as if it were growing straight from the rich
Norman soil.

She lowered her head and let her hair shadow her face.
The summons from the Duc de Montchamp could arrive
any day. Part of her could not wait for the news, but another part of her dreaded its arrival. She wished she could
don the heavy armor and sword that stood by her hearth
and guard her castle from siege, but such was the way of a
far more barbaric people. Instead, she must wrap her body
in silk and lace and wield a more subtle weapon. The duke
was her last, lingering chance to keep this estate. Her
stomach tightened. His loyalty depended fully on how well
she could fuel his lusts.

If it were Kilian's lusts. . . . The thought entered her head uninvited and she sternly pushed it out. He had over-stepped his bounds this evening, again. Kilian Laclos seemed to have a very difficult time staying in his place, no matter how many times she attempted to put him there.

She stood on the hill until dusk fell and the first stars twinkled in the clear sky. Finally, she led the mare down the slope into the depths of the forest. She did not return to the stables, not yet, for Kilian's words still rang in her head. Besides, she needed to feel the brisk night air against her skin. Aimee recklessly kicked the mare into a gallop and they raced in the dark woods. With a vision born of familiarity, she led her around the muddy bogs, the thick roots rising from the ground, the sudden drops, and the low-hanging branches. She rode the length of her estate, first along the crumbling stone wall that marked the northern edge, then back inside again, past the orchards rich and heady with the fruity scent, back into the thickness of the forest.

She dismounted near a stream whose banks seemed dry enough for walking. The mare lapped the cold, clear water greedily. Aimee kneeled near the edge to caress a fern whose leaves dipped into the stream. She rested her chin on her knees, enjoying, for the moment, the peace of the silent land.

"Fool!"

She gasped as a strong arm gripped her around the waist and pulled her back from the stream. Turbid green eyes, fiery with anger, assaulted her.

"Kilian!"

"Fortunate for you, Vicomtesse, that it is I." Still holding her with one arm, he loosened his manteau and tossed it on the ground. Without ceremony, he threw Aimee on it, and then followed to lie fully on top of her.

He drowned her words with his kiss. She struggled beneath him, but the weight of his long, hard body prevented movement.

"Stop!"

"Stop? Is that how you would have warded off thieves, Aimee?" He clutched her face and forced her to look at him. His fingers, roughened from working in the fields, scraped the softness of her cheek. "I'd wager they'd not listen to that."

Aimee glared at him. Her breath came short and fast—just the shock, she told herself; it is just the shock. She tried not to think of the fascinating, unfamiliar ridges of his body pressing against her; she tried not to breathe the rich, musky male scent that rose from the folds of his linen shirt. She wished he would roll off of her, for his nearness was making her pulse pound furiously. As she stared at his shadowed eyes, she knew he had no intention of leaving her alone.

"Speechless, Vicomtesse?" The anger slipped out of his eyes in favor of a more disturbing emotion. "I don't believe I have ever seen you speechless."

"I'm not. . . ." she said breathlessly, struggling for her senses. "Please get off me, Kilian. You're heavy."

"Is that better?" He rose on his elbows. His lips twisted in a smile and the dimple seemed cavernous in the shadows.

"I'd rather you got off of me."

"Nay, I like it here." His breath fell upon her cheek as she turned away. "I like it here very much."

Aimee's breath hissed through her teeth as Kilian's warm lips descended on her throat. His hair—could a man's hair be so soft?—brushed her jaw. Shivers swept her body as he tasted the length of her neck to rest, finally, in the slight hollow behind her ear. She hated herself for her own response to this arrogant commoner, even as she melted against him.

"Come, Aimee. Don't fight me."

"Fight you?" She was fighting herself. Herself and her treacherous body's response to this thief's skillful touch.

She closed her eyes. His lips were working magic on her nape, making her dizzy though she lay flat on the ground.

"You fight me, Aimee, always, though your eyes and your body say you want me as much as I want you."

"I don't want you."

He laughed and his breath cooled his kisses on her throat. He turned her head with one finger and forced her to look at him through half-closed eyes.

"I can read your eyes, Aimee, as I have learned to read your capricious Norman weather." He tilted her chin higher. "Why deceive yourself so?"

"Stop, Kilian." She turned away, her cheeks flaming with shame. She felt wanton, dirty—she did want him, whatever that meant. She wanted him to continue, to touch her, to make love to her.

He ran a finger down the length of her neck. "Sometimes I think you are an innocent, you seem so afraid of me and of this."

"I am not afraid," she said halfheartedly. *And I am an innocent.* His finger wandered from her throat to the rim of her high bodice.

"You are afraid." He stopped his ministrations to turn her head toward him again. He framed her face with his hands. "I'll have to add lovemaking to the list of your fears. Right next to floods and poverty."

"I forgot rakes and rogues."

"Touché." He shook his head. "I may be a rogue, but I mean you no harm—"

"You only say those words when you've got me trapped."

"Seems that way," he admitted. "It's the only way I can get you to listen to me."

"Why don't you just—" She gasped as he kissed the tip of her nose. "Just leave me alone!"

"You are far too beautiful to be left alone. Far too beautiful and far too brave." His gaze grew more serious as he looked at her face bathed in the dim starlight. "I have been watching you these past weeks. I have watched you walk through the fields in all your tall, lithe grace, staring off into the forests or gazing mournfully up at your castle. There is a sadness in your eyes, Aimee. A loneliness—"

"I will soon lose my estate, Kilian." She tried to look away from him, but his hands were her prison. "Isn't that enough of a reason to be sad?"

"Yes. But it is no reason to be lonely." He brushed a strand of night black hair off her cheek with one wandering finger. "I keep waiting for a man to appear at your side."

"There is no man in all of France interested in this impoverished widow."

"There is at least one."

His hands tightened on either side of her head and she could do nothing—nothing—to escape him, yet she knew she would not escape even if she could. His lips caressed hers with insistent gentleness, coaxing her response, willing her to kiss him back. He tasted of spring, of fresh air, and his cheek, rough with stubble, grazed her own. He released her lips briefly, hovered over them, teased them, then captured them anew.

"Kiss me, Aimee."

"Kilian, please . . ."

"Kiss me."

She could no longer resist. His demands echoed in her body, and her limbs responded. He moaned above her as her lips parted. The sound, so unfamiliar yet so natural, encouraged her. His chest radiated heat like the stone bread oven that glowed outside the castle. He released her head slowly. His hands found the hollows of her ribs, her abdomen, and wandered still lower to trace the outline of her thigh beneath her skirts.

She would die, she knew she would die if this continued. Her body throbbed with each touch. He drew her deeper into mindlessness. His kisses scorched her skin from her chin to the rise of her bosom. Aimee buried her fingers in the warm silk of his hair.

"You taste like the mists." A click rent the air as Kilian opened the clasp beneath the first silver button of her waistcoat. He folded the velvet open and moistened the rise of her breast with his lips.

Aimee took a deep breath as she felt the second clasp release. Her lashes fluttered against her cheeks. His fingers teased her skin, but Aimee could not help drawing away as the third fell open.

"Nay, *a stor*. Don't draw away from me." Kilian lifted himself up against her, the coarse linen of his shirt brushing against her nearly bared bosom. He captured the corner of her mouth, her upper lip, her lower lip, then teased her tongue into his mouth.

The earth was cold, but Aimee felt only warmth as his kisses deepened. Though they lay on the uneven ground, sprigs of gorse sticking up against his manteau, she knew only the touch of his hand as it caressed her neck, her shoulder, her arm to finally entwine in her own trembling hand.

He lowered his head to her bosom anew, taunting the edges of her chemise with his tongue. Every warm touch made Aimee quiver and she squeezed her eyes shut against the intensity of her own response. He pushed away the lace edge, probing deeper beneath the silk until the heat of his mouth captured the stiff peak of her breast.

Aimee arched. She gasped and then moaned as her body sang with this wicked, unfamiliar pleasure. She mouthed the word "stop" more out of fear than reason, but she could not say the word. Kilian continued, persistent, unaware of anything but the passionate undulations of her body beneath the weight of his own. He released her hand and caressed the arched curve of her other breast.

She no longer pretended to escape his touch. She entwined her fingers in his hair and dared to massage the bunched muscles of his shoulders. His tongue caressed the rigid bed of her nipple and his teeth carefully nipped the engorged peak. Aimee heard her own cries of passion slip from her throat. One part of her mind held to sanity, but its cries were growing weaker and weaker with each touch of his skilled hands.

"Kilian, please—you must stop, this must stop," she heard herself whisper, at the same time lifting her head to kiss his hair.

"You do not mean what you say." He rubbed his unshaven chin against her bosom. "Come, sweet—look me in the eyes and tell me."

She felt sotted with passion. Her head felt heavy and weighted. Her gaze focused on his face, so close to hers, so open, so emblazoned with naked desire.

"Why do you draw away?" he whispered, once again lifting himself so his face was level with hers. His gaze swept from her parted lips to the turmoil fermenting in the darkened depths of her gray eyes. "I want you, Aimee, but if you truly want me to leave you, I shall."

Her throat was thick and she could not speak. Her lower body seemed to have dissolved, yet her abdomen quivered beneath his weight and she longed to arch against him. Her reasons rang in her ears. *You are a commoner. And I am a woman bound by a bargain to another man.* What did it matter? The reasons sounded empty and meaningless. Why not succumb to this ecstasy?

"Come, Aimee," he whispered, his voice ragged against her ear. "Come, my ice maiden. Melt for me."

She slowly wrapped her arms around his neck. "I have already melted, Kilian," she murmured, tilting her head for his kiss. He groaned and clung to her lips. Swept up in the heat and ferocity of his passion, she matched his desire with a skill born purely out of instinct.

He released her from the riding jacket, and her body

trembled in the night air. She reached for his linen shirt and pulled it from his breeches. Tentatively, she reached beneath it to caress the wall of muscles in his sides. Her fingers moved lower, but Kilian stopped her straying touch and lifted her hand to his lips. "Nay, *a stor*," he whispered. "I've wanted you too long. If you touch me, I'll not be able to bring you pleasure this night."

She bit her lower lip and shivered in the chill of the night air. *Bring me pleasure this night . . .* She sought pleasure in the caress of a thief in the darkness of the woods, and suddenly she no longer cared. Whatever Kilian planned to do to her she welcomed it willingly, openly, with a full heart. Tomorrow she would let the shame and recriminations surface. For tonight, she was a woman. If only for tonight.

As if sensing her thoughts, Kilian pulled her against his chest. His fingers toyed with the lace-edged sleeve of her chemise until it fell off the roundness of her shoulder and drooped by her elbow. The other soon fell and Aimee knew only her breasts held the material against her body.

Gently, he released her and searched her eyes. She could not hold his stare—she could hardly breathe in his presence. The sultry green gaze soon fell to the delicate material and its tenuous hold upon her breasts.

"You are lovely, Aimee, perfect and beautiful." His fingers touched her chest and the material melted away. She flushed as her chest was bared to the night sky. He pressed her back on his manteau again and his fingers began a skillful dance upon the sensitive arcs of her breasts.

Suddenly, he lifted his head from hers. She blinked, dazed, and stared at him. He lifted himself on his elbows and stared intensely over her head.

"Kilian?" Her hesitant voice drew his attention. He caressed her cheek.

"I hear something, my sweet."

She frowned and listened. Her heart, pounding hard and fast in her chest, drowned all other sound. But as the minutes passed and the heat of her blood cooled, she, too, heard the cries.

Fire!

CHAPTER

7

Kilian rose to his feet and pulled Aimee after him. He kissed her quickly on the lips. "The fates are not with us, Aimee." He cocked his head and listened as the cries continued. "To the north—come, we must help."

Pulling on her riding jacket, she clutched the reins of her mare and lifted herself into the saddle. Kilian had already disappeared into the darkness, but she followed the sound of his mount's hooves as he thundered through the thick of the forest. As her passion ebbed, she felt the first touch of dread. Though the earth was damp from the recent rains, a fire in the depths of the woods could clear the land for leagues and, worse, destroy the year's crops if it burned through the wheat fields.

She smelled the burning thatch long before she charged into the clearing in front of the house. Kilian's horse stood, riderless, near the edge of the clearing. Her eyes widened as she saw his bare shoulders fade into the smoke pouring through the doorway.

"Kilian!" Her heart leapt. She dismounted and ran toward the door but stepped back as the thick smoke stung her. She lifted a hand to ward off the scent, coughing as it dried out her throat. She stumbled back and turned to find the tenant of the house, Madame Bonchamp, clutching the singed wings of her bonnet.

"My husband— My husband! He is still in there!"

"*Sacré bleu!*" Aimee crouched by her side and squinted at the flaming house. The barley that thatched the roof burned quickly, though it, too, was damp from the rains. She pulled on Madame Bonchamp's arms. "You cannot stay here, Marguerite, it's too close to the house—"

"My husband!"

"You'll be hurt here!" A shower of flaming timbers fell at their feet and lit the bottom of Aimee's split skirt. She frantically shook out the flame, staring in growing desperation at the empty doorway.

She was crazy, mad, to crouch here in the path of falling thatch and smoking timbers. Madame Bonchamp refused to budge from her vigil. The roof fully blazed now, and the fire helped to dry the dampness. Where was Kilian in this inferno and what was taking him so long?

The spiral stairs that clung to the outside of the house creaked loudly beside them. The fire devoured the spindly supports and the stairs sagged away from the wall.

"Come—the stairs!"

Madame Bonchamp finally noticed the flaming timbers. Aimee pulled her away from the house, breathing deeply the crisp, dry night air as they moved farther and farther away from the fire. Marguerite sobbed and repeated her husband's name amid her tears. A crash reverberated through the night and Aimee swung around as the stairs fell far out into the courtyard, sending slivers of flaming wood over the flattened earth.

Aimee gasped as she watched a block of fresh thatching catch fire near the edge of the clearing. Glancing around, she saw Kilian's dark manteau spread across the ground. She scooped it up, ran toward the thatching, and smothered it with the thick, damp wool. Frantically she rushed around the yard, staunching the threatening embers until her hands were pink with burns.

Madame Bonchamp screeched. A form emerged from the smoke-filled doorway. Aimee breathed a deep, haggard sigh of relief as she recognized Kilian carrying Madame Bonchamp's husband over his shoulder. He fell to his knees near the flickering splinters of the staircase. Several tenants who had heard the cries of fire took Monsieur Bonchamp from Kilian's shoulders and carried him into the fresh air. Aimee rushed into the searing heat to take Kilian's hands. He followed her blindly, his eyes closed against the smarting heat of the smoke, then fell to his knees and breathed deep gulps of air as they reached the perimeter of the clearing.

"You idiot! Rushing in there like a fool!" Aimee, unabashed, checked his body for cuts and burns. His chest, heaving from the exertion, gleamed in the golden light of the blaze. The scar that traced his rib threatened to break open anew. His body was covered with soot, his breeches were torn at the knee, and a thin patina of sweat covered his skin.

"I knew 'twas you who called my name with such concern," he said huskily, his throat raw and parched. "Would you have missed me if I had not come out of there?"

"What in God's name tempted you to rush into that fire?" she snapped, ignoring his question.

"There was a man in there. I am a soldier. Heroics are part of my line of work." He opened his eyes tentatively, and they twinkled in teary pain as they traveled over her disheveled attire. "Part of the reward is supposed to be the gratitude of a woman. Won't you kiss me for my bravery?"

"More likely I'll slap you for your foolishness," she retorted. She glanced at the house. Peasants filled the courtyard now, and a man began yelling orders. Several men gathered behind the house and formed a line that led down to the pump at the foot of the slope.

"I'm afraid I'll have to collect my reward later." He rose to his feet and held out a hand for her. She stood without his help.

"What are you going to do?"

One sooty eyebrow rose in the lean, sweaty face. "I, my dear Vicomtesse, am going to help these men put out the fire before it spreads to other parts of your estate."

"What can I do?"

He glanced at her worsted wool skirts and silver-buttoned riding jacket. "Unless you want to ruin your finery, you should probably go back to the castle."

"I am *not* going back to the castle." Without hesitation, she took off her riding jacket and tossed it near the foot of a tree. His straight brows rose as he stared at her bare arms and shoulders and the thinness of her chemise. "Well, don't stand there leering at me," she snapped, wrapping her hair up away from her face. "Tell me how I can help."

"Very well, madame. . . ."

Beside her tenants, Aimee clutched pails filled heavy with water and thrust their contents onto the burning wood. After only an hour, her arms and back ached and her arms were dotted with burns from flying tinder. Kilian, noticing the pallor of her face, ordered her to stop, and she did not argue the point. Yet while she and others in the line fell out to rest, she noticed that Kilian continued. She watched him as she rested, watched his arms bulge with the weight of the filled pails, watched his back flex as he flung the liquid on the skeleton of the house. *He fights the fire with the same ferocity as he would fight an enemy*, she thought. Then she glanced at the sky and prayed for rain.

A young girl ran to her and fell into the sooty and seared wool of her skirts. Aimee started and held her close, recognizing her as the only child of the Bonchamps.

"Caroline is still in there," she cried. "Caroline is still there!"

"Oh, Helene, I will get you—"

"There is someone in there?!" Kilian yelled as he rushed to their sides. Aimee glanced up at him in surprise, her gaze engulfing his gleaming, half-naked body outlined against the fire.

"No—it is just her doll, Caroline," Aimee corrected, yelling above the din of the blaze and the men around it. Relief washed over his features and she stared in surprise. For a common thief, Kilian Laclos showed an inordinate amount of concern for a child. She tore her gaze away from him and her dangerous thoughts, and hugged the girl close to her. "I will get you another doll, Helene, and you can call her Caroline."

She cooed into the girl's ear, rocking her in her thin arms. Kilian crouched beside them to rest and ran a hand through his dirty hair.

"Helene!" A voice sounded over the din. Aimee glanced up to see Madame Bonchamp.

Aimee rose achingly to her feet and walked Helene to Madame Bonchamp's side. "You must come and stay at the castle until we rebuild your house. There is plenty of room and you are more than welcome."

"The Souliers have offered hospitality, Vicomtesse," she said quietly.

"Very well then. I shall send Manon over to care for your husband. And I promise I shall have your house rebuilt before the season ends."

"Madame?" The woman clutched Helene close to her skirts. "When will the king make his decision? What will happen to us when . . . when you are gone?"

"I don't know, Marguerite."

Madame Bonchamp took Helene by the hand and led her up the rise to where her husband lay under the care of a

local healer. Aimee watched them until she became aware
of Kilian's presence behind her.

"Have food, clothing, and blankets brought to them at
the Souliers'," she commanded, cursing her breaking
voice. He turned to one of the men and issued the orders.
She clutched her riding jacket tight around her body, and
shivered despite the heat of the blaze in front of her. Kilian
stepped between her and the blaze, and his shadow fell
dark and cool over her frame.

"You should go back to the castle. It looks as if the fire
is under control and there is nothing left for you to do
here."

She glanced at him, distracted. Her hair tossed in the
wind and she pushed a strand out of her face. "No, I must
stay here until the fire is out." Lowering her gaze, she
turned and headed away from him, down the slope, toward
a small copse of spruce trees.

She stopped in the darkness as she sensed his presence.
"I would rather be alone, Kilian."

"I don't think so."

He took her in his arms. She pressed her face against his
hard chest, her body against his strength and warmth. She
knew this should be the last man upon whose shoulder she
should cry; this should be the last man to trust with her
agony, but she could not help the comfort she felt in his
embrace. She wanted to be held closer than this, though
her cheek was molded between the muscles of his chest.
She wanted him to sweep her up and engulf her in his
comfort.

"Aimee. . . ." He rocked her in his arms. He ran a hand
down the length of her hair, stopping to rest at the base of
her back. She moved against him, burrowing in his chest.
Kilian pressed his lips against her head. "Don't worry,
Aimee, everything will be all right," he whispered. "I
promise."

Oh, sweet promise! she thought, running her hands over

his back. *I could almost believe you, Kilian. I want to believe you, now, here in the semidarkness of the forest.*

He touched her chin and urged her face to his. She lowered her lids, not wanting him to see her tears. His lips clung to hers for a moment, then clung again.

"Rogue, I am," he said softly, "for stealing a kiss in your sorrow. Come, let me see you to the castle."

"No," she whispered. "No, hold me for a little longer."

"If I hold you any longer, *a stor*, I will not let you go this night." He gently lifted her chin. "And I don't think that is quite what you want, at least not tonight."

She stared at him. The wavering light of the fire cast strange shadows on his lean face. She wanted to touch his cheek and feel the bristle of his unshaven jaw, but she resisted. She did not want to set fires she could not easily extinguish, either in herself, or in the intense man who watched her.

"Let me get your horse. It is late and you are tired." He released her to brush his hand against her cheek. "There is plenty of time for us, my sweet. For now, wait here."

"But . . . but the fire," she said, confused. "No, I must stay until the fire is out."

"It is under control, and there's rain coming."

She watched, mute, as he walked away from the copse of trees into the clearing before the fire. She waited patiently, leaning against the trunk of a spruce, willing for the first time to allow someone else to make the decisions.

Decisions. First the thieves had stolen only farm animals and cider, then they beat Monsieur Bouche, and now they set fire to the Bonchamp house. How long would it be before they killed one of her tenants?

The estate must be settled, Aimee thought. Soon.

"It seems one of the men took your horse to get blankets and food from the castle," Kilian said quietly as he rode his horse through the copse to her. "We can ride on mine."

She made no protest as he lifted her up in front of him.

The saddle was not made for two and she found herself nestled tightly between his thighs. He wrapped a strong arm around her waist.

As they rode away from the dying fire the air became misty and crisp. The breeze toyed with the hem of her skirts to show teasing glances of graceful ankles. She touched his bare chest.

"You must be cold."

"No. Your hair shelters me." She twisted to face him so her hair would blow around both sides of his body. Her nose pressed between the plates of his chest, and she breathed in the unique mixture of charred wood, fresh barley, and male sweat. A tear slipped from beneath her lashes and fell on his chest.

Kilian reined in his horse.

"I think you are melting, ice maiden." He lifted her face and wiped the wet trail from her cheek. "'Twas passion I wanted before, not tears."

"I am being foolish," she said, mustering as cold and distant a voice as she could. "It is just . . ."

"It is good to see you soften." He tilted his head and a dimple, soft and shallow, hovered on his cheek. "Now that I know you can cry I also know you can laugh."

"There is little to laugh about lately."

"Ah, then we will have to find something to make you smile." He kicked the horse into a walk and wrapped his arm around her shoulder. Despite herself, she leaned heavily against him. There was so much warmth, so much comfort in his arms. What harm was there in drinking it in for the evening? Soon enough she would be alone in her castle, alone with her thoughts and her fears.

The first droplets of rain had begun by the time Kilian's horse stopped in front of the castle. He dismounted and reached up to lift her down by the waist. Her hands fell on his shoulders.

Aimee, half-asleep already, blinked up at him as her

boots touched the pebbled courtyard. His disheveled hair fell over his forehead and shaded his eyes, but Aimee could well read the lights that glowed in them.

"This has been an interesting evening, *a stor.*"

That strange word again. She blinked and lowered her gaze, and he kissed her forehead. She stilled the urge to chastise him for being so bold with her. Somehow, it didn't matter.

"Thank you, Kilian, for your help this evening." She tilted her chin. "You saved a man's life and may have saved my estate from disaster."

He smiled irreverently and tipped a nonexistent hat. "All in a soldier's day, madame."

Her lips quivered in a half smile. "Nonetheless, you shall be rewarded."

"The only reward I want is the gift of your laughter." He dipped his head and stole a kiss from her. As he straightened her brows lowered crossly.

"Kilian, please—"

"But I see that is a hard-won gift," he interrupted, stepping away. "Perhaps, then, you will allow me to escort you to the festivities in the village on May Day, Saturday next?"

Aimee's mouth opened in surprise. "Escort me?"

"Yes. I understand that it is the custom for the local lords—and ladies—to attend?"

"Why, yes, but . . . ."

"Then let me be your guard on the long and arduous trip into the village."

"Kilian, I don't think—"

"Don't deny me, Aimee." He reached for her hand and lifted it to his lips. The smile had dissolved into seriousness. He watched her closely. "Say you will come, even if it is just with me among your entourage."

Aimee stared at him and her heart fluttered lightly. *He is courting me,* she thought with a thrill. As she watched, his lips stretched into that heart-rending smile.

"Yes," she said breathlessly. "Yes, I will go."

Aimee sipped the musky May-milk from the clay urn as she walked through the sarrasin fields back to her château. She wiped the foam from her upper lip and nodded in greeting as she passed another of her tenants making the early morning pilgrimage to the barn. The first of May was just breaking over the eastern hills, but by the brilliance of the sunrise it would prove to be warm and dry. Aimee smiled. She would wear her green silk. Granted, it was rather bold for a widow of a year and some months to dress so opulently during a trip to the village, but she felt like a maiden this morning—young and naive and deliciously daring.

After a quick check to make sure no one was about, she fell to her knees in the damp grass and placed the urn carefully beside her. Small drops of dew clung to the tips of the grass and she ran her hand over them, collecting the wetness on her fingers. The first dew of May was said to be a powerful protector of youth, and though Aimee did not believe in such old wives' tales, she still loved the feel of the cool droplets against her cheeks. She rubbed them in reverently and smiled as a single drop, like a tear, slipped over her chin and ran down her throat.

Two women emerged from the edge of the forest and Aimee hastily rose from the ground. Wiping her skirts with her hand, she turned and smiled at them. The wings of their high Sunday bonnets fluttered as they bowed their heads in greeting.

A dark thought slipped into her head and she closed her eyes to ward it away. She did not want to think of the fire, not this morning. She had hired four more men to work under Kilian to assure that such incidents would not recur.

She lifted her head to the sky, her skin chilling as the air dried the dew. A flock of sparrows flew above, then dipped down to skim over the bristling green fields. They were a harbinger of spring, of better things to come. As Aimee approached the stairs to her castle, she wished fervently on the freshness of the day that her estate would remain in her loving hands.

She stopped suddenly.

At the top of the stairs lay a garland of violets, with a note pinned to one side. Her eyes widened as she picked up the delicately knotted circle. The note was addressed to her.

Her hands trembled as she opened it.

> *It is May, my maiden.*
> *Time for the winter's ice*
> *To melt.*

It was unsigned, but she knew without doubt who had written it. It was from Kilian, Kilian whose gaze had rested far too warmly on her in the past week, whose smile suddenly took on a wealth of meaning. Realizing that she was crushing the violets in her grip, Aimee lifted the garland with both hands and fingered the bruised blossoms.

No one had ever given her a garland on May Day, not even her husband. And certainly no man had written her such an intimate note. She flushed and glanced around the courtyard. It would not do to be seen carrying such a maidenly gift. She looped the garland around her wrist and entered the castle.

She hurried up the stairs of the northwest tower before Manon could catch her. She did not know whether to be cross or in rapture for Kilian's boldness. Certainly, she should not encourage this; after all, he *worked* for her. A smile spread across her face—she would not think of it today, for today was May Day and she intended to enjoy the spring with a full, unfettered heart.

An hour later, she walked sedately down the worn stone steps and smoothed her hair. Manon had lifted it into a chignon, but she did it so the dark tresses formed a black cloud above her nape. Aimee was tempted to wind the violets around it but decided it was too bold. Instead, she pinned two blooms to the bodice of her green silk dress.

"Gustave and Kilian are waiting, madame," Manon said as she came from the parlor. "I've some bread warm from the oven if you'd like to break the fast."

"En route, Manon." She smoothed her dress, from the long waist over the short panniers. "We should be on our way if we want to watch the planting of the May-tree."

She stepped into the brilliant sunlight. The cart was hitched to two roans and Gustave sat upon it, waiting for her arrival. Aimee caught her breath as Kilian galloped into the courtyard, her mare in tow. Manon turned to her, twisting her hands in her apron.

"You'll be riding, madame?"

"Yes, Manon. I need the air." She could not take her eyes off Kilian's tawny hair, neatly clubbed back with a black ribbon. She had never seen him on a horse in the bright of day and now, staring at his straight seat and easy control, she wondered how she ever denied he was a soldier. He looked like a *maréchal*.

"There's only room for two in the cart, Manon," Gustave yelled from his seat. His ruddy face flushed as if he had already been drinking cider. "Come, now, you promised you'd come to the village."

"That I did, but mind you keep your eyes to the road and your fingers off the applejack," Manon said sharply as she descended the château stairs. "And off me."

"A tongue so sharp! On such a sunny day." Gustave held

out his hand to help her, but she ignored it. "Tch, Manon —I'll not be biting you."

Kilian laughed at them and dismounted in front of the stairs. As Aimee descended, his gaze fell upon the violets pinned to her bosom. His dimple deepened and she flushed despite all her valiant efforts to stay cool.

"You look as charming as a wildflower, Vicomtesse," he murmured, bending over her hand. She bit her lip and glanced over to Manon and Gustave, who, fortunately, were involved in a lively discussion. Self-conscious, she pulled her hand away from his warm lips.

"Will you help me mount?"

Kilian's eyes twinkled and he linked his fingers to take her booted foot. Aimee lifted herself on the steed, and started as she felt his fingers caress her ankle. She reached down and batted his hand away lightly with her riding crop.

"Mind you keep your hands in full view," she warned lightly. "Else I will have to relegate you to the cart and put Manon on your horse."

"Manon? On this steed? She'd be thrown in a minute. Besides, Gustave would never allow it. He's been looking forward to this trip for a week."

"Obviously," she mused. "How long has this been going on? I never noticed he was interested in her before."

"It often takes a woman a long time to notice the advances of a man." His bright eyes twinkled at her as he mounted his horse. "Even when he is quite obvious."

"Perhaps a woman prefers to keep that knowledge to herself." Aimee pulled her horse toward the path to the road. "Or . . . perhaps she does not want to encourage his advances too boldly."

One of Kilian's straight brows lifted and his smile spread across his face. Aimee's heart trilled; it was a glorious day, an unparalleled day, and she could attribute it to nothing more than the spring. Her mare pranced beneath her as if

she, too, could feel the richness of the scented air, the
warmth of the pure sunlight, the wondrous taste of youth.

"Vicomtesse, please—mind you do not travel too far
from the cart." Manon frowned at Gustave. "He'll get lost,
I am sure, and then we won't have salt or coffee for a
month."

"There's only one road, Manon," Gustave interrupted. "I
could hardly get lost, even if I wanted to."

"We shan't ride too far ahead," Aimee said, watching
Manon's tight face ease in gratitude. Kilian's horse nudged
hers and she turned to face the brilliance of his eyes.

"I wouldn't make such a promise, Vicomtesse, for if I
have my way we shall find several moments to be out of
sight of that cart."

She flushed, but a smile hovered about her lips. She
kicked her mare into a canter and pulled past Kilian. The
sleeves of his stark white linen shirt fluttered as he caught
up with her. He laughed, throwing his head back until his
Adam's apple protruded from the muscular strength of his
throat.

"You and Gustave are in league, I suppose."

"Gustave and I? In league?" Kilian sat easily on the
horse and seemed to take in her whole body with one easy
gaze. "Certainly not—not officially, in any case. I suppose
an unwitting agreement has sprung between us, since we
both seem to be dealing with extremely reticent women."

"Not reticent, but wary."

"Wary?" He clicked his tongue. "And why do you need
to be wary of me? Haven't I wooed you by the banks of a
river in the moonlight? Haven't I saved your estate from
disaster? I'd find a dragon to slay, but I don't believe they
exist anymore."

"You would, too." She allowed herself the luxury of
gazing fully at his long, lean, well-muscled body. "You
would go out and kill a dragon for me, for nothing else
than to win my undying gratitude?"

"Certainly for more than your gratitude." He reached over and brushed a finger against her cheek. "I'd do it if I knew I would win your heart."

"My heart!" She smiled and glanced away. "You'd then take my heart, eat it, and throw the rest away. That is the way of men like you."

"Men like me?"

"Yes." She glanced at him sideways, then returned her gaze to the road. "Soldiers—charming, brash, brave military men. You sweep into a woman's life, charm her, woo her, and finally seduce her. Then you go off to another battle." She shrugged her shoulders. "That is what you like best—the battle, not the ultimate victory."

Kilian's eyes widened and he kicked his steed closer to hers. She turned and looked back at the cart to avoid his gaze. She had said too much. She did not know what possessed her to be so honest, but now she regretted it and wished to return to the lightness of the morning.

"You know little about me, don't you, Aimee?"

"I know nothing about you, Kilian Laclos." She pressed her lips together, reluctant to say more. "I only know that you are a soldier, that you are foolishly brave sometimes, and"—she glanced at him then hid her eyes behind a netting of lashes—"you are extremely persuasive."

"Obviously not persuasive enough, or I would have won this battle weeks ago." He reached beneath her averted chin and turned it to him. She smiled hesitantly. "If I tell you something of myself, will it ease your mind?"

"No, but 'twill pass the time of day."

Kilian laughed loudly. Gustave and Manon's bickering, which had followed them from the foot of the château, stopped suddenly. Aimee flushed.

"You can be brutally honest when you wish to be, Aimee. 'Tis a quality of which I would like to see more."

"And when have I ever lied to you?"

"Never, directly. But you get that elusive look in those clear gray eyes, and I know you are planning something."

"You, my dear Monsieur Laclos, have a vivid imagination."

"Kilian, Aimee. My name is Kilian."

Her cheeks pinkened and she smiled in defeat. "Very well. Kilian. You have a very vivid imagination, Kilian."

"'Tis the way of the Irish. We believe in sprites and elves and all sorts of strange, mischievous creatures." He shrugged a shoulder. "My mother had a vivid imagination, too. She used to tell us stories about her native Ireland when we were children until we begged to go there ourselves."

"Did you? Ever go to Ireland?"

"Once." He lifted his chin and blew his hair off his forehead. "We went for a while and I saw more leprechauns than ever there were leprechaun stories, but then I was no more than ten. My older brother soon became sick in the cold winter and we came home after a few months."

"Ah, yes, I'd forgotten that there's another of you," she moaned. "Beware the women of France."

Kilian smiled his rakish grin and his dimple deepened. "Nay, my brother's a different breed. You'd never know we were siblings. He takes after my father."

"Who is French, I assume?"

"Yes. Quite."

She watched him as he talked. He cut a fine figure on the horse—straight and lean and upright. The wind toyed with his hair and the sun darkened his skin to a deep tan. His gold-flecked green eyes glowed in his face. He was a man in his full, energetic prime and she could not seem to keep her eyes off him today. She shrugged mentally. Why fight it? Today she felt as free as a peasant woman.

". . . but they are both dead now."

"What?" she asked. "Who's dead?"

"My parents," he explained, turning the full power of his gaze upon her. "Haven't you been listening?"

"I was for a while." She flushed and looked down at her fingers, which were clutching the leather reins.

"Tell me you were totally distracted and you will be forgiven," he teased, bending to try to catch her eye. She urged her mare forward, and Kilian followed in kind.

Not far behind them, Gustave broke out into a rustic May Day song and sang it in a growling, gritty voice.

> *The first day of the month of May,*
> *What will I give my love?*
> *une perdriole . . .*

Manon rapped him on the arm then gripped her conical bonnet as the horses surged forward. Gustave, laughing, continued his singing.

Her mare danced beneath her, and Aimee decided it was time to give her her head. Loosening the reins, she urged the mare down the road in a healthy gallop while she valiantly tried to stay steady. Her voluminous silk skirts battered the mare's side, but the horse did not seem to mind. It did not take long for Kilian's horse to catch up and pass them.

She watched as Kilian soared past and frowned. He would not beat her, certainly not in a race past her own estate! Glancing behind her, she swung her leg around and spread her skirts over the horse's back. She had done this all the time when she was a child, but then it did not matter if her skirts flew above her knees. Now, it seemed more important to show Kilian that she was not a lame rider.

Kicking the mare into a frenzy, Aimee bent low over her slim back. The mare flattened out and raced over the uneven ground, the stallion's black tail flying not far in front of her. Kilian turned around and his eyes widened in surprise as Aimee, a smile spread wickedly across her face,

sped past him. He kicked the stallion into a full gallop, but
it was too late. Aimee and her mare were far past them by
the time they reached the turn in the road. She reined in,
triumphant, watching as his steed rushed up the rise.

"Your horse must be quite winded from the heat," she
teased as he stopped before her. "Else the rider is less than
expert."

"Had we started at the same point there'd be a different
ending." His gaze drifted to her legs, bare to the knee, and
her white lace petticoats upturned on her thighs. "Still, I'd
say, overall, that I got the best of that race."

Flushing, Aimee lowered her skirts over her legs. The
cart came into view and she slipped her leg over the horn.
His brash, unfettered smile widened at her sudden return to
propriety.

"Stop grinning so," she warned halfheartedly. "If Gustave sees you there'll be more gossip for the village ears."

"I doubt it," he retorted, glancing over his shoulder. "It
was, after all, Gustave who taught you to ride like that. I
should congratulate him."

Aimee was suddenly embarrassed at her own behavior.
She headed toward the cart. "I'd better save Manon," she
murmured as she passed him. "There is no telling what
Gustave will do when there is no chaperon."

"He'd do precisely what I would do." Kilian clutched
the reins of her horse as she tried to pass. Aimee was facing the opposite direction and she glanced over her
shoulder at him. The cart had disappeared, temporarily,
behind a small clump of apple trees. Kilian wrapped his
arm around her waist and pulled her back against him.

"Kilian, the cart—"

"They're beyond the first rise," he murmured in her ear.
Her reins, still in his hands, rubbed against the flatness of
her stomach. Her eyes fluttered closed as her cheek fell
against his chest.

"Is Gustave beyond the first rise doing the same to Manon?"

"For his sake, I hope so," he murmured, his lips caressing her hair. He twisted her toward him until she was forced to gaze up at his shaven, sculpted face. "I can think of no better way to while away a spring day."

The dimple disappeared as his lips claimed her own. Aimee closed her eyes against the glare of the sun behind his tousled tawny hair. He tasted of salt and freshness and his lips were gentle and firm at the same time. His hand spread over her stomach, his fingers curling against her in restraint. Aimee touched his arm, hardened and warm from the exertion of the ride. Her fingers sought the texture of his skin beneath the linen.

She breathed deeply, smelling the musk of his skin, the warm fragrance of his hair. His tongue probed her lips and with a hazy hesitation she opened her own. His other arm curled around her shoulders and pulled her closer against him. Unwittingly, she twisted so their chests touched, fully, and she was engulfed in his warmth.

"Aimee . . ." His tongue rolled over her name softly. She buried her face in the nook between his neck and his shoulder. He toyed with a few tresses that had escaped from the soft chignon and blew upon her damp nape. "You are not fighting me this day, Aimee. You are as soft and pliant as a woman in love."

"The cart." She pulled away suddenly, hearing the rumbling of the ancient cart's wheels. Struggling to regain her equilibrium, she glanced toward the road. Though Gustave and Manon were in full view, they seemed too completely absorbed in their own discussion to notice what had just occurred on the hill. Nonetheless, Aimee glanced at Kilian sharply and whirled her mare around.

"I must be feverish," she murmured. "Kissing you like that in the bright of day."

"If it is a fever, then I am stricken, as well," he teased relentlessly. "A fine disease, this."

She smiled despite herself. His smile was far too fine to resist, and if the truth be known, she had little will to resist it.

She made sure he had no more opportunity to caress her in the two-hour trip to the village. She pointed out the features of her estate—the stream that eventually merged with the Orne, the hills, and the rows of poplars and forests once full of wolves. Kilian amused her with stories of Ireland and tales of lovely gray-eyed maidens and their lovers. She could not mistake the innuendo, and she flirted like a courtesan.

The four arrived in the village just when the ceremony had begun. A poplar was being planted in the village square, next to the one that had been planted the previous year. Several young girls of the village, dressed in their best dresses with garlands around their heads, danced around the tree to the singing of a local bard. Unabashed and infected with the unusual brilliance of the warm day, they kicked their bare feet up, showing long, supple legs unfettered by stockings. Aimee glanced at Kilian as one of the maids danced toward him. An alien sense of jealousy pierced her heart.

"Come, Manon. We have much to buy before this day is through."

"Let me come with you," Kilian said, dismounting then rounding his horse to help her. His hands felt warm and far too strong on her waist. She could not meet his eyes.

"No, that is not necessary—you go with Gustave, to the alehouse. But mind you don't drink so much that you cannot ride back this evening."

"I would much rather spend the afternoon following you," he whispered.

Gustave jumped down from the cart and moved to help Manon, as Kilian had helped Aimee, but Manon scrambled down before he could do so. "Yes, Vicomtesse, let us shop and leave the men to their devices," Manon agreed. "My legs are sore from such a long, tortuous ride."

"No, no," Gustave said, hoisting an empty pack over his shoulder. "I know you both will buy hoards of supplies—Kilian and I, we will follow and help you carry."

Aimee winked at Manon. "I would say that we have no choice."

She could not help feeling a touch of pride having Kilian, tall and lean, walking beside her like a husband. She knew by the way the village women were looking at him that he was an attractive man, but she had known that long before she had ever come to the village. He did not seem to pay them any mind, yet he opened doors for her and watched for holes in the unevenly cobbled streets and held her hand gently as he led her across a muddy puddle. His gaze fell on her so warmly that there were times when all she wanted to do was throw herself in his arms.

Instead, she tossed slabs of cheese into his arms, and oranges, and gold and silver embroideries, and a bolt of cotton from the West Indies. Weighed down by the bulky items, Kilian rolled his eyes as Aimee gazed lovingly at the cream-colored English earthenware. Finally he tossed his bundles at Gustave and told him to take them back to the cart. Aimee, absorbed, did not notice that they were alone until Kilian suddenly clutched her hand and dragged her into the cool darkness of a narrow alleyway.

"Kilian!"

"Hush, Aimee, and they will never notice." He kissed her, swiftly, on the lips, then pulled her deeper into the alley, where the air was cool and dank—a welcome relief from the blaze of the midday sun.

"You're mad!"

"I am mad for you—" He pulled her into his arms, and captured her lips unequivocally. Her heart trilled, sang, leapt in her chest and she wrapped her own arms around him. She could no longer resist him, she no longer wanted to resist someone who could make her feel like this, make her feel happy; happy for the first time in her life.

Wanton, drunk with the joy of the spring, she pressed herself against him; silk against ratteen, lace against coarse linen. He leaned against the stone wall, pulling her up until her body could not be any closer to his own. Their lips parted simultaneously and he clutched her head with his hand.

"I want you, Aimee. Tell me you want me, too," he whispered, forcing himself apart from her for a moment to say the words, then capturing her lips again, gently, taking the lower one between his own, then kidnapping the upper, then taking them both in his kiss. Aimee gasped as he released her to nuzzle her neck.

"This is dangerous, Kilian. What if one of the villagers saw me—the Vicomtesse de Bocage—kissing in the alley like a wanton?"

"They'd gossip, as busybodies always gossip about beautiful women," he murmured. "But you still have not done what I have asked you."

She started as a shadow passed the alley and she pulled away from him. "Not here, not now."

"Then when, and where?"

Her heart pounded as her gaze met his. Desire shone in his gold-flecked eyes, and it shone bright and full and promising. He wanted her. He wanted her. She did not truly know what that meant, but she knew with the fullness of a woman in love that she wanted him, too.

"Later," she whispered, scuttling toward the open end of the alleyway. A plan began to form in her mind. "Later, when we are alone. . . ."

Gustave and Manon stood in the middle of the square, looking around. Aimee smoothed her skirts and ran a hand over her mussed hair before stepping out of the darkened alley. Manon saw her immediately and approached in relief.

"We couldn't find you, madame," she said. "We were worried for a moment."

"You have nothing to fear for the vicomtesse while she is under my protection," Kilian said from behind her. Aimee knew she was flushing but hoped Manon would attribute it to the heat and the excitement of the village.

"Indeed." Aimee glanced briefly over her shoulder. "Why don't you and Gustave look at the horses for a while —Manon and I are going to wander through the milliner's."

Kilian's brows lowered in annoyance. He nodded reluctantly and winked before turning to join Gustave. Manon breathed a deep sigh of relief as she came to Aimee's side.

"I thought I'd never get rid of him," she whispered beneath her breath. "He's a nuisance, that Gustave."

Aimee turned as she heard the distinctive clip-clop of a horse and the rumble of carriage wheels over the cobblestones. Manon pulled on her arm to get her out of the way. She caught a glimpse of Kilian, who stood where she had left him. He was watching her. She smiled mischievously at him.

"Why, Vicomtesse. I did not expect to see you here."

Aimee started, realizing that the carriage had stopped right beside her. As she glanced into the window she found herself face-to-face with the dark, intense eyes of the Duc de Montchamp.

"Monsieur de Montchamp!" She dropped a hasty curtsy. "I . . . I did not expect to see you, either."

"It is a pleasant surprise."

The village quieted. The hawkers stopped their incessant yelling, the children picked up their toys and watched, even the chickens that roamed around the poulterer's stifled their clucking for a brief moment. Aimee was intensely aware of Kilian's fervent stare.

"Yes . . . a pleasant surprise." The duke's face, powdered and lightly rouged, glowed absurdly white in the bright light. His cravat dripped with lace and the gold-threaded embroidery of his peach satin waistcoat glittered. His hand rested on the head of a carved ivory cane, which he twisted in his hands.

"I have already sent you an invitation, madame, but I wish to take this opportunity to invite you personally to an afternoon of cards at Château Montchamp, three days hence." The duke's gaze roamed over her green silk, her tousled black hair—nearly chestnut in the sun—and rested on the crushed, wilting violets pinned to her bodice. One of his pale brows lifted slightly.

Aimee folded her hands in front of her. In the glory of the day she had forgotten her troubles, had forgotten that she had an estate that she would soon lose. She had forgotten that the only hope she had to keep it was in this man, the Duc de Montchamp. She stilled the urge to turn to Kilian, to stare once again at his fine, sculpted face and the warmth of his eyes. Such happiness was not for her.

"Yes, monsieur." She tilted her chin. "Yes, I would love to come."

"Splendid. How did you get here, madame? I did not see your coach."

"I rode the way, monsieur."

"All the way? Perhaps that is why your color is so high. It is becoming, quite becoming. I did not realize you were such a sturdy horsewoman."

"Quite, monsieur. I ride daily, if I can."

"Then sometime soon I shall invite you to a hunt."

"I would be honored."

"Have you finished your shopping? If so, I would like the honor of your presence in my carriage. I was just on my way back to Château Montchamp and your estate is on the way—"

"I could not impose." Her heart lurched. The afternoon

had already lost its wonder, as surely as if a thunderstorm had come and blocked out the sunlight.

"I insist."

What choice did she have? What choice did she ever have?

"Very well, monsieur." Aimee mustered a wide, stiff smile. "It would be my honor."

CHAPTER

8

Aimee stepped out of the wrought-iron tub and reached for a cotton towel. The small room smelled like the wild thyme, laurel, and marjoram that still steeped in the bathwater, but she did not linger to enjoy the scent. Though the oriel's myriad windows were obscured by steam, she feared that someone might see her from the ground.

Pulling the towel tight around her, Aimee left the oriel and entered her bedroom. She settled down on the rich red spread and began to dry her scented skin. The blue black glow of twilight suffused through the leaded windows, and her gaze was drawn to the rolling, hedged lands behind her castle. She heard Manon enter the oriel and fuss with the bath, but Aimee did not call out. She wanted to be alone tonight. Alone and lonely.

She closed her eyes. She could not remember a morning more glorious. For the span of a few hours she had forgotten that she was the Vicomtesse de Bocage. For the morning of May Day she was nothing more than a woman—a woman free to choose her own destiny. Had the duke not arrived to cast a pall over the day, Aimee knew she would have given herself to Kilian freely.

She sighed and ran the towel over her head, wrapping the long swath of black hair in its damp folds. The duke had reminded her of her responsibilities and of her obligations to her tenants and to this land. She had made a bargain with him. Although he talked little about it during the ride back to her castle, she knew from his hints that he had made some progress with the king of France. She suspected he would have news at the card party, three days hence. Then she would be forced to complete her end of the bargain. Or else lose her estate.

When she had first made the bargain she knew she would be sacrificing herself for the sake of the estate. She knew her reputation, already tarnished, would be crushed completely. She knew she would be shunned by the church —perhaps even excommunicated—for committing open adultery. She would be ridiculed by the rich bourgeois and scorned by the peasantry.

What she had not known was that she would be giving up love.

Damn you, Kilian. She rose from the bed and lifted her cotton chemise to her face. She had thought love was for the Comtesse de Vierzons of the world—the lovely, rich, voluptous women. Not for bony, impoverished vicomtesses. Few men had looked at her twice except to gossip about her notoriety or scorn her for her tenacious efforts to stay on the estate. She had not cared—at least, not until Kilian. Kilian and his eyes, his gentle hands, his arrogance, his insistence, and his courage. Kilian could see through all her strength to the pain beneath. Why now, why now had she found love when she was bound by honor and loyalty to bargain herself to the devil?

She tossed the worn cotton chemise on the bed and walked to the chest that stood at its foot. Running her hand

over the carved mahogany, Aimee found the catch and
lifted the cover. The rich odor of gardenias rose from the
interior—a quick and brutal reminder of her hasty wedding
day. Searching through the neatly packed folds, she pulled
out a slip of white satin and pressed it to her face. She had
worn this peignoir on her wedding night.

Unwrapping her hair from the towel, Aimee pulled the
white satin over her head. The material slipped softly over
her damp skin. The material clung to her breasts and hips
and was held up by two thin satin ribbons. Riffling through
the chest anew, she pulled out a matching robe and
wrapped it around her. She threw her head back and let the
weight of her damp hair lie against her buttocks.

I would have worn this for you, sweet Kilian. . . . If the
world were different. If *I* were different.

"Dreaming, *a stor?*"

She started and searched the shadows. Had she only
imagined his voice? Her gaze plumbed the depths of the
darkened room until she saw him—a dark swath near the
window. His hair, lit by the last dying rays of twilight,
gave him away.

"Kilian?" Her voice came out far too husky.

"Expecting anyone else?"

"No."

He stepped away from the hangings until his lean body
was outlined against the window. He was angry. She could
tell by the set of his shoulders.

"How . . . how did you get in here?"

"I can be resourceful when need be." His gaze flickered
over her body. "Why the white satin, Aimee? It looks like
a bride's peignoir."

"It is."

"Indeed." He crossed his arms. "Should I be congratu-
lating the duke for winning you over?"

"Winning me over what?"

"Over me."

Aimee sucked in her breath. He had struck too close to the truth. "There never was a battle, Kilian."

"Yes there was. And is." A muscle moved in his cheek as he walked more deeply into the room. He wore black breeches and a dark linen shirt—clothes she had never seen. His stockings were worn at the knees and he wore no shoes. She realized with a shock that he had climbed the outside of the castle and come in through a window.

"Did you scale the castle wall?"

"It doesn't matter how I got here."

"It's two stories high!"

"Would you care if I had fallen to my death? Or would you have consoled yourself in the duke's arms?"

"Stop."

"Nay. I stopped once before without getting an answer from you. I'm not letting you go tonight until I know the truth about the duke."

"What does the duke have to do with us?"

Kilian crossed the space that separated them. He clutched her shoulders and held her at arm's length.

"You tell me."

She smelled sweet and damp and it took all of Kilian's will not to sweep her up in his arms and make love to her. Her gray eyes watched him warily, but in their depths he saw the elusive glimmer of trust. A tress of her wet hair brushed over his fingers. Her body swayed toward him.

"Tell me, Aimee."

Her scent drove him to insanity. He knew she was naked beneath the robe and peignoir for the sleek white satin molded to her curves intimately. She had been as soft and willing as a bride this morning as they rode to the village, but when the duke arrived all light left her face. The duke controlled her in some demented way—perhaps in the same way he had held Jolivette. This woman, he thought, staring into the softening light of her gray eyes, this woman he would save.

"It is nothing—"

"Don't lie to me." He pulled her closer and knew as soon as he felt her breasts against him that he was lost. He could not resist her. Her lips yielded. Unbearably soft, all of her, from her thick swath of hair to her long, sinuous body pliant against his. Her tongue sought his own and the fires that roared in his blood exploded. She weighed nothing as he lifted her up in his arms. She folded in his embrace like a child, wrapping one arm trustingly around his neck.

He tasted tears. Through the fog of his passion he lifted his head from hers. Her dark lashes were spiky and wet. He forced her to look at him.

"Tell me, *a stor*," he whispered, setting her down on the bed. Taking a deep breath, he walked away from her and sat on a chair near the hearth. Her scent clung to his skin.

"How did you know?" Her voice was small and trembling and he fought off a pang of guilt.

"Whenever I mention his name you become evasive. And this afternoon, I could tell that you did not want to leave with him. All the color left your face."

"He's not forcing me into anything."

He felt his stomach tighten. "Has he touched you?"

"No. Not yet."

"He never shall then. I shall see to it."

"No, no, you can't." She bent her head and her hair screened her face. "You can't stop it. I won't allow you. I've made a bargain with the Duc de Montchamp."

"Bargaining with the devil," he snapped, watching her. "He'll not honor his bargains. He didn't with—with the young aristocrat he debauched."

She flinched at his choice of words. "It can't be changed, Kilian, for it is I who initiated the bargain."

Silence fell over the room, as thick as the darkness. Kilian reached for a log by the side of the hearth and tossed it on the fire. The embers sparked and crackled and soon the log began to burn. He struggled with his anger. He knew if he were not careful she would draw within herself and make him leave. If he were not careful his anger would boil over and he would give himself, and his vengeance, away.

"The duke has promised to buy Château Bocage," she began slowly, "from the king. He has also promised to let me live on these lands. I will be able to take care of my people and protect the castle."

"For what price?"

"I . . . I would become his mistress."

"I'd kill the duke before I'd ever let him touch you."

Her eyes widened at his vehemence. He had blood and murder in his eyes—and she drew back in fear. She had seen that look once before, long ago, when she had first captured him in the forests. When only moments ago she was weak and soft beneath him, willing him to make love to her on this great bed, now she feared him and his anger.

"Ach, *a stor*, don't fear me." He buried his head in his hands, running his fingers through his blond-streaked hair. "I would never harm you—it is the duke I hate."

"I . . . I don't understand."

He lifted his head sharply. He had almost given himself away. No one—least of all this woman—must know why he lingered in Normandy. Not until after the Duc de Montchamp was dead.

"Kilian?" Aimee whispered as she wrapped her arms around herself. The castle's ancient, weighty stones cooled in the nighttime breezes and chilled the air. She had told Kilian her darkest secret, and though it would not be a secret for much longer she feared his reaction the most.

"How can you make love to him?"

"How can any woman make love to a man she does not love?" She sighed. "How can a woman make love to a man she hates? For food, for shelter, Kilian. For many reasons." She hesitated. "Why do you hate the duke so much?"

"For taking you from me," he whispered, rising from his seat by the hearth. Her eyes widened as he walked toward her. "For letting you sell your body for something he could easily give to you."

"Don't—"

"Yes, Aimee. I'm going to make love to you." He reached for her. "When we're through you'll remember what it was like to be loved—and give up this dangerous bargain with the duke."

He kissed her. The sweet pungency of his breath mingled with hers as his tongue boldly parted her lips. Aimee's eyes fluttered closed and her lashes brushed his unshaven cheeks. He seemed to draw the strength out of her until she leaned feebly against his tall, indomitable body. His strong arms lifted her up and spread her across the bed, then he covered her body with the full length of his own. She gasped as his chest crushed her breasts, as his legs moved sinuously between hers, as his arms captured her and held her prisoner. He kissed her and then he worshiped the tender flesh of her throat.

So this was making love, she thought as she closed her eyes under his caresses. He slipped off her and ran his hand over her body. Her skin sizzled wherever he touched and her breasts swelled to fill his hands.

"*Ar ghrá Dé*, Aimee," he murmured in strangled Gaelic as his hand captured her breast. She saw the glimmer of his green gold eyes as he kissed her anew, harder, his tongue probing her mouth. She reached for him and ran her fingers over the hard, long muscles of his back. They twitched beneath her caress. Her body softened beneath his and she felt her soul opening to him like a wildflower to the morning sun.

He pulled away from her abruptly and captured her face

with his hands. "You promised me something this afternoon, Aimee. Do you remember?"

She remembered. She remembered everything about the morning. "I promised to tell you that I wanted you." Aimee felt as if she were teetering on the edge of a precipice. The winds of her passion pressed against her, urging her over, and only the wavering voice of reason kept her rooted to the earth. She blinked, dazed, and stared into the depths of his eyes, darkened by passion. "I hardly know you," she whispered. "I know nothing about you."

"You, too, have secrets."

The winds blew harder. "Kilian . . . I can't think."

"Don't, then," he said huskily as his lips descended to her own. "Don't think, my heart. Just feel."

She was lost. His hands sought the burning, aching parts of her body, but his touch did not soothe her. He increased the ache until she thought she could no longer bear it. He murmured to her as he peeled the satin from her body. The white peignoir fell to a gleaming heap on the worn rug and she lay bared to the musty castle air. Just when she thought she could bear no more torment his lips claimed the taut peak of her breast.

Her moan rent the silence and her nails dug into the dark linen shirt on his back. She did not recognize her own voice, she did not recognize her own body and the passions that swirled within it. Kilian's words eased her though she hardly heard them—she heard only their gentleness. He was friend and enemy at the same time. She loved him and feared him. She wanted him.

"Kilian. . . ." His name slipped off her tongue as he suckled on her breast. He lifted his head and kissed her into silence.

"Such passion, *a stor*." He lifted himself off her and pressed her lips as she moaned in protest. With one smooth motion he stripped the dark linen shirt from his back and tossed it to the far corner of the room. His eyes feasted on

her and Aimee suddenly, sharply, became aware of her nakedness.

"Nay, don't cover yourself. You've the body of a god-
dess." He reached out and traced the curve of her breast,
pushing her arms away from the dark nipple. His finger
rubbed the hardening peak softly, then slipped beneath her
breast. "Your breast fits in my hand," he murmured,
warming her bosom, "where it belongs."

She flushed and watched his face as his gaze traveled
over her naked body. The light of the fire played in the
tawny streaks of his hair and his eyes seemed to glow gold
in the dimness of the room. His finger reluctantly left her
breast to travel over the curve of her waist, lingering for a
moment in the indentation of her navel. Aimee pressed her
legs together instinctively, knowing by the direction of his
gaze where his fingers would next be.

He did not tease her. He lay beside her and gathered her
in his arms. His rough hands caressed the length of her
back. "Such soft skin. Such hair. . . ." He lifted the damp
mass of black tresses and buried his face in them, breathing
deeply the scent of wild thyme and marjoram. She felt his
arousal pressing on her thigh and the heat of her passion
rushed to her cheeks. Her fingers curled into his back.

His hands trembled on her and she knew, of a sudden,
that he wanted her as much as she wanted him.

Wantonly, she lifted her face to his and met his gaze. His
nostrils flared. "I want you, Kilian." His eyes flashed with
desire. "I want you now."

A groan caught in his throat. He rolled atop her and
claimed her lips as his prize. His passion, unleashed, had
no boundaries and she felt herself drowning in it. With
frantic urgency he loosened the ties to his breeches and
yanked them, and the hose, off his long legs. The garments
fell like dark shadows over the white satin peignoir.

The last shreds of her modesty fled as his fingers gently
parted her legs. She arched against him as he touched her.

Shamelessly she reached for his body and explored the scarred surface of his chest, the furred expanse of his abdomen, and still lower. His sharp intake of breath rewarded her as she touched him as he was touching her.

"Sweet Aimee." He took her hand and lifted it to his lips as he rose over her body. Mindlessly, she responded. She did not realize until he lay poised over her that he did not know she was a virgin.

His gaze captured hers as he pressed against her. His face was only inches away. The gold streaks in his eyes glowed. He pressed again and Aimee moaned as he entered her, full and warm, slipping deep inside her. Touching her soul.

There was pain, a twinge, a tearing of flesh. The pain had passed almost before she was conscious of it. Then all she knew was the joy of this joining.

"Aimee. . . ." His green eyes widened in surprise. He searched her face for answers. "*Sacré bleu*, Aimee. My love."

He kissed her—a sweet, gentle kiss. She could feel him inside her and the sensation made her tremble. He pushed her hair off her cheek and rubbed his bristled chin against her.

Time stopped. She knew nothing of her world except the coarse coverlet beneath her, and the rough texture of Kilian's heated skin against her own. He stroked her, deeper, and she thought she would die with the glory of this. He stopped, suddenly, as if remembering her pain, but she murmured in his ear and he began again, again, again, this time moving in her, his body in rhythm with her own. She lifted her arms above her head and clawed the coverlet as his touch sent her spinning higher, higher until she cried out, her body pulsing beneath his, throbbing in the culmination of their passion.

She lay, stunned, as he pressed one last time upon her. His body gleamed with sweat and she wrapped her arms around him. His breath seemed loud in the room, but so did her heart. She could not seem to get close enough.

He lay atop her for a long time, nuzzling the length of her neck. Slowly, he slipped to her side and wrapped his arms around her body. He rubbed his lips in her hair.

"I did not know you were innocent, *a stor*," he whispered. "I would have been gentler."

"It did not hurt." Her voice was muffled in his chest. She snuggled closer, reveling in this strange, peaceful feeling, pushing away all the fears and doubts that crowded just behind the peace.

"Aimee, I thought. . . ." He hesitated as he ran a hand over her hair. "I thought you and the vicomte had. . . . You were married, after all."

"To an eighty-five-year-old, very sick man. For two days."

"Yes, but. . . ."

She lifted her face from his chest and gazed up the strong column of his throat. "What is it, Kilian?"

He searched her gaze. She lifted her brows as he looked away and a light flush suffused his cheeks. "What?" She pushed farther away and stared at him. "Tell me, Kilian."

"I thought he had died in the throes of passion."

She stared at him, surprised, then struggled with laughter. "In the throes of passion?! *Dieu!* The vicomte was sick for months before our marriage—"

"Nonetheless, the rumor is that he died in the marriage bed." His lips quirked. "And if it weren't for your virginity, I wouldn't wonder. I can imagine what you would do to someone with less energy than I."

She sat up, forgetting for a moment her nakedness. "Are you telling me that you heard a rumor that the vicomte died while. . . ." She shook her head. "You must be joking."

"I'm not."

"You are."

He spread his hands before him, then folded them beneath his head. "I'm afraid I'm not, *a stor*. The rumor came from a very reliable source."

"Who?"

"Gustave."

She covered her mouth with her hands. A crease appeared between her arched brows. Rumors had abounded after her wedding and the vicomte's death, but this rumor she had *not* heard. For it to come from Gustave meant that either he believed it himself, or the vicomte had told him to spread it. The more she thought about it, however, the more it made sense.

"That's why the intendant never ordered me to be examined by a doctor," she murmured as the realization set in. "He, too, believed the vicomte and I had consummated our marriage."

"So here I am, expecting an experienced tigress in bed, and what I find is a very innocent, very passionate woman." Kilian jolted her from her reverie and pulled her down beside him. His dimple deepened. "I can't say I'm disappointed."

"You'd better not be!" She sucked in her breath as he lowered his head.

"I'm not. I'm flattered." His face was a breath above hers. The dimple softened and all levity disappeared. He was suddenly very, very serious. "I had wondered why you seemed so innocent, and why you resisted me so much. Why did you make love to me tonight, Aimee?"

Because I love you. The words stuck in her throat. His gaze probed hers and she knew he could read her thoughts as easily as she could see the small lines that fanned out around his eyes. She lowered her gaze to his lips. "You really did not give me much of a choice, Kilian."

"If you had said no, even once, I would have left you alone."

"It's hard to say no when you're . . ."

He laughed quietly. "So, then, you were simply swept away by passion?"

"No!" She answered too vehemently. He brushed her hair off her cheek. "No . . . It was more than passion." Unable to meet his omniscient gaze, she turned her head into his shoulder.

"I suppose I'll have to settle for that for now." He slipped to her side and caressed her head. "Though I can see my answer in your eyes, *a stor,* I will want to hear the words someday. Someday soon."

"What does that word mean?"

"What?"

"*A stor.*"

His hand slipped around her waist and he pulled her full against his body. His lips slipped to her ear. "It means 'my treasure' in Gaelic."

Aimee's heart fluttered at the husky sound of his voice in her ear. *My treasure.* Too sweet an endearment for a man who wanted only a night's pleasure. She felt her heart melt against his warmth and tears welled in her eyes. His long, strong body moved against hers and she felt the glorious roughness of his skin. She gasped as she felt him, hard and aroused against her thigh.

"It is early yet, *a stor.* Let me touch you again."

"Ah, Kilian." She lay pliant beneath him, her blood roaring in her ears. She felt a draft as Kilian moved off her but thought, at first, it was only her passion. A voice broke into their languid lovemaking.

"Madame, will you be wanting dinner?"

Aimee stiffened. Pushing against Kilian, she half rose from the bed and stared at the open door of the solar. Manon's eyes and lips rounded in shock as she noticed that Aimee was naked from the waist up. She clutched her apron and lifted it over her face when her gaze strayed to the undeniably male leg lodged firmly over Aimee's knees.

"Manon!"

"Madame!" Manon struggled with words as she pressed the apron against her face. *"Pardon! Pardon!"* Not waiting for dismissal, she whirled around and slammed the heavy oak door shut behind her. Aimee heard the rapid click of her *sabots* all the way to the stairs on the far side of the castle.

"Oh, no." Aimee covered her burning cheeks with her hands and stared at the closed door. "Oh, my God."

Kilian laughed softly beside her. "Your reputation is surely ruined, madame."

"It's not funny." She struggled from under his leg and searched for the peignoir. Finding her simple cotton chemise first, she shrugged her shivering body into it.

"What are you going to do? Go down and explain to her?"

"Yes!"

"What are you going to say?"

"Well . . ." She frowned as she stared at him, unabashedly naked on her bed. The bed linens twisted and turned in the oddest directions. Her color heightened. Manon could not help but guess the truth and nothing would convince her otherwise. "It would help if you didn't just lie there with that nasty grin."

"I can't help it."

"I could scream and claim you attacked me."

"But you won't." Kilian sat up on the bed. "You won't bring scandal down on yourself unless there's a reason for it."

"You're quite sure of yourself."

"No." He held out a hand to her. "I'm not sure of myself. But I am sure of you. Come to me."

She stepped toward the bed then stopped. She curled her fingers in the rough cotton of her chemise. The air blew chilly around her bare legs and arms and she hugged herself for warmth. The mussed bed tempted her, as did Kilian

who lay warm and patient atop it. She knew that she could
revel in his embrace no longer.

"Aimee?"

"You should go, Kilian."

He lowered his outstretched hand. "You shouldn't worry
about Manon. Though she was shocked to see us together
tonight, I assure you she'll say nothing. Nor will she
bother us. She told Gustave just this afternoon that she
thought you needed—"

"It's not Manon I'm worried about," she interrupted as
she turned away from him and walked toward the hearth.
She stood close enough to the flames to feel the heat singe
the skin of her shins. "This . . . this should not have happened."

"But it did. And I think neither you nor I regret it."

He approached her and stood behind her. He did not
touch her, but he stood close enough so she could feel the
heat of his body. Aimee lifted her chin and willed away the
tears that welled in her eyes.

He wrapped his arms around her body. Unable to resist,
she leaned back against his chest. He rubbed his cheek
against her temple. "Wait for me, Aimee. Don't give yourself to the duke. Wait for me and trust me."

"It is not a matter of trust, Kilian."

"Yes, it is," he insisted, holding her tighter. "If you
would trust me, just this one time, then everything shall
work out."

"Can you give me this estate, Kilian?"

He hesitated. "Perhaps."

She smiled and turned her cheek to his chest. "And how
are you, a soldier in the French army, going to get a titled
estate from the king of France? Some things cannot be
taken by pure prowess, Kilian. This land is one of them."

"Just trust me."

"I cannot."

He stiffened. "Cannot or will not?"

"I cannot." She left his embrace and sat down on one of the embroidered hearth chairs. She dared not look into his eyes, but she could sense his withdrawal. The air seemed to chill to below freezing. "For three years, since the vicomte first fell ill, I have been the master of these lands. I have supervised the planting, I have filled out the ledgers, I have tended the garden and harvested the turnips and fed the chickens and chosen the horses and stored the grain. I have pressed the cider and drunk the bounty of my own efforts." She met his gaze. She needed to make him understand, but his eyes were as hard and flat as ice on a pond. "I have seventy tenants, Kilian. Over twenty-five families depend on me and my efforts—"

"Your lands will be cared for by whoever owns this estate."

"You know what happens to estates owned by absentee landlords. My lands will become as unproductive and useless as the Duc de Montchamp's. He may even tear down this four-hundred-year-old castle and put up some gilded monstrosity for a 'summer home.'" She shook her head and her hair flew before her face. "Whatever courtier upon whom King Louis XV decides to bestow Château Bocage is sure to be a devoted man of the court. Not the type to live in obscurity in a Norman castle."

"So then it is for the good of your people that you will become the duke's mistress." A muscle twitched in his cheek. "Not for his money? Not for the jewels he can give you?"

"Kilian!" A flash of anger lit her eyes. "How dare you."

"I dare, madame, because I cannot bear to see you lie."

"I am not lying."

"After what just happened—" he gestured angrily toward the rumpled bed "—you can sit there and tell me you are going to sell your body to the Duc de Montchamp?"

The tears came anew. She did not have time to staunch

them and one fell over her cheek. She brushed it away
angrily, but another joined it.

"Aimee—" He pulled her into his arms and held her
tight against his chest. Her heart thumped painfully against
him and she could feel his, too.

*Oh, Dieu, I love you, Kilian. But I am bound, by honor
and by obligation, to leave you.*

"Leave me alone, Kilian," she sobbed. "Please."

"You don't understand," he said, as much to convince
himself as to convince her. He held her tighter as she
struggled weakly for freedom. "I did not come to you tonight to slake my lusts, Aimee. I came to make love to
you."

"Don't, Kilian. Don't make this harder than it is."

He clutched her arms and held her away from him. His
eyes, only moments ago burning with desire, now burned
with a far darker flame. Anger. Murderous, unrelenting
anger.

"And if I offered you marriage, Aimee. Would you come
to me?"

Marriage.... She gaped, searching beneath the anger in
his eyes for truth. *Marriage....* How sweet the word
sounded, how wondrous the possibilities. In a brief moment a lifetime with Kilian flashed before her eyes—years
of lovemaking, of children bright-haired and gray-eyed, of
warmth and love and joy, of nights spent in a small home
cuddled on a pelt before the fire.

"Give me an answer."

She was too shocked to move or to think, only to stare at
Kilian's lean face, the brows that slashed so straight above
his eyes, the nose that leaned so slightly to the left. *Marriage.* Such dreams were too precious and too fantastic to
be believed. They were not meant for her. Yet here a man
stood, a man she loved, tall and proud and demanding her
hand in marriage.

"Aimee."

He shook her as reality intruded into her dream. She remembered the trust of Madame Bouche, the concern of Marguerite, the sweetness and innocence of Helene. *What will we do when you are gone?* The words of her tenants rang in her head and as the voices grew Aimee knew in her heart that she could not leave them. She could not leave them, she could not leave Château Bocage. And she could not rescind on her bargain with the duke.

Kilian released her as he read her answer in her eyes. He stepped back and stared at her wildly. The anger had grown until it eclipsed all light. His brows drew together and cast shadows over the emerald of his eyes.

"After tonight, after all that has passed between us, you will whore yourself to the duke."

She swallowed and lowered her head. *The anger is good,* she thought to herself even as her heart broke. *The anger will purge me of him and his love.*

He dressed in black. She could not watch. She closed her eyes, wishing that the night had ended when Manon had interrupted them, wishing that this was over and she could try, try until her dying day, to forget the man she had grown to love. She held on to the thought of Helene as her heart weakened and called for her to run into his arms.

She saw him out of the corner of her eye. He gripped the back of one of the hearth chairs and his fingers dug deep holes in the petit point. She wondered if he would throw it, if he would release his volcanic anger on the frail cherry wood legs. The air sang with his rage.

"Mark my words, madame." He tossed the chair to the floor and walked before her. With an unyielding hand he thrust her chin up until she was forced to stare at him. "The Duc de Montchamp will never—*never*—have you. I swear it."

As the tears rolled down her cheeks, Kilian Laclos left her room, her castle, and her life.

CHAPTER

9

The rain returned full force two days later, drenching the thirsty land. Aimee peered through a slit in the carriage window and wrinkled her nose. The roads, in terrible condition in the best of weather, were boggy from the deluge. She could hear Gustave's shouts just ahead of the carriage, warning the carriage driver away from the deepest ruts.

The weather fit her mood too well. Everything in her life had taken on a certain shade of gray, especially her future. Aimee clutched the edge of the seat as the carriage lurched to one side then righted itself. Old Lucien was not nearly as good a carriage driver as Kilian.

Kilian.

She pulled her manteau close around her shoulders. Kilian had left Château Bocage after their shared evening, taking his horse and gun with him. He had left nothing behind except memories, but those memories haunted her. Her skin flushed beneath the blue velvet of her dress as images of their evening flashed through her mind. He had touched her as no man had ever touched her—and his mark still lay, imprinted, on her heart. She wondered if she could ever forget him.

I must not think like this.

She shook her head and her wig lurched in protest. Puffs of white rice powder hovered in the damp air. Aimee glanced out the window again, trying to determine how much farther they had to travel. The crisp, rich scent of rain masked all the subtle fragrances that usually marked the passage. Her stomach tightened in protest. The sooner she finished this business with the Duc de Montchamp, the sooner she could try and forget the man who had so boldly stolen her heart.

An agonizing, jarring hour later the carriage came to an uneasy stop in front of the rain-washed stones of Château Montchamp. The carriage door opened and the rain blasted against her skirts. Aimee pulled her voluminous hood over her wig and held it against her face as she stepped down into the swirling rain. She noticed a fleet of guards standing, armed, by either side of the door as she followed the liveried servant up the slippery stairs into the warmth and dryness of the château. As she entered, the roar of the storm subsided to the patter of rain against the wide crystal panes.

"Vicomtesse! I feared you would not hazard the trip in such weather."

Aimee pulled her drenched hood off her head and glanced at the duke. A footman took her dripping manteau from her shoulders, another took her wet gloves, and a third handed her a scented towel to dry her hands.

"I promised I would come, monsieur." Her gaze drifted over the taut lines of his powder blue satin waistcoat and breeches decked with silver embroidery. Diamond buttons graced the front of his waistcoat. She suddenly felt dowdy in her simple blue velvet: She had no jewels to hang about her neck or ears.

"Many people make promises, Vicomtesse." The duke took her hand and led her toward the long, curving staircase. "Not everyone keeps them."

She glanced at the two guards that stood at the foot of the curved stairway. "Why the guards? I noticed you had some outside, as well."

"We had a rather uncomfortable incident several nights ago," he explained. "A thief broke into the château. Since we will have so many guests here, I decided it would be best to post a few men."

"I see." She felt a glimmer of fear. "Have any other guests arrived?"

"A few. They have already started playing cards."

"And are we playing upstairs?" She hesitated in front of the stairs and clutched the gilt bronze baluster held up by golden cherubs.

"No, there is a card room on the far side of the château. I am leading you to a place where you can refresh yourself before meeting the guests."

"You are very kind."

The duke did not release her hand even after they reached the top of the stairs. Bereft of the chandeliers that lit the lower floors, the halls were shadowed and dark. Aimee stiffened, suddenly realizing that no one but the servants had seen her arrive.

"I wished to show you this room in particular." The duke stepped in front of her and opened a carved door in the dim light of a single candelabrum. She squinted as the door swung open and sent a flood of hazy gray light into the hall.

"Mon Dieu!"

The bedroom—the woman's bedroom—shimmered in the light that poured through the high windows. She stepped in, stunned, her gaze roaming over the gray *boiseries* that lined the walls, the rich silver curtains that hung in long, deep folds beside the crystal panes drenched with rain. The canopied bed dominated the center of the room, draped in the whitest watered silks tied back with braided gold ribbons, and a dozen white fur pillows lay upon the embroidered bedspread. Her damp, slippered feet sank in the thick white carpet and she gasped as she caught sight of her reflection in the gilded dresser mirror.

She fit here as if the room were tailored to her. No milliner could have dressed it better—the mahogany dresser and matching armoire mirrored the color of her hair, the *boiseries* and drapes, the color of her eyes.

"I shall leave you for a while, madame, while you refresh yourself. I shall return in a quarter hour."

She stood motionless in the center of the room as he closed the door behind her. There was no doubt in her mind—the duke had decorated this room specifically for her. Her gaze fell on the bed. This was the bed upon which he hoped to consummate their unholy bargain.

She padded across the room and sat heavily in the cushioned chair of the dresser. She glanced at her face in the undistorted mirror. With her cheeks flushed from the storm and her eyes wide with shock, she looked like a maiden of sixteen, not a widow of twenty-four. She tucked a dark tress back under the wig.

Her gaze fell upon the small crystal decanters scattered on the lacquered table. A tub of the finest powder stood next to two graceful urns of a thick, pinkish liquid. She pulled the delicate cork from one and lifted the bottle to her nose. She closed her eyes. The rich essence of apple blossoms rose to tease her.

My favorite scent. Her stomach twisted beneath the tight corset. She rose restlessly and lifted a hand to her head. She supposed it was the way of French courtiers to woo their prospective mistresses with such grandeur, but this was alien to her. She felt nervous in this setting, as if her favors were being bought.

Aimee shook her head. Why should she be so offended

by this, this manifestation of their contract? She noticed a closet on the far wall and approached it.

She pushed it open. It was full from one end to the other. She ran a finger over an ermine collar, the textured embroidery of a stomacher, the smoothness of a brocade skirt. The satin felt icy against her hand. She closed the door firmly and returned to the dresser.

She noted with distress that a gossamer peignoir was draped over one of the chairs adjacent to the bed.

Perhaps he expects me to put it on.

She lifted her hands to her flaming cheeks and stared at her own reflection. Gathering her wits, she methodically pressed a warm towel against her face, wiping the traces of powder that had fallen on her bodice. She reached for a pot of rouge on the dresser and applied the mixture to each cheek. She needed the paint to face the ordeal to come.

And so soon after Kilian. She closed her eyes, her heart lurching in her breast. She had known all along that this would happen. She had arranged it herself to keep her estate. Why, suddenly, was she regretting her actions? And why couldn't she wipe the image of Kilian out of her mind?

"I assume everything is to your satisfaction?"

She started and stared at the duke's reflection.

"I did not mean to startle you, my dear, but you did not seem to hear my scratching."

"No, no. I did not." She put the pot of rouge down on the dresser, loudly.

"Do you like this room?"

"It's lovely."

"I had it decorated with you in mind."

"I thought as much."

The duke crossed the room, regally, his dark gaze avid on her. His hands fell upon her shoulders.

"I wanted you to know that I have given much thought

to our agreement." His thin lips twisted into a smile. "In fact, I have thought of little else in the past weeks."

"You flatter me."

"I have not yet begun to flatter, Aimee." The duke placed his lips on her shoulder. She closed her eyes and tried to staunch the nausea that rose in her throat.

"Then you have made some progress?" she asked as the duke toyed with her sleeves.

"I have made some initial inquiries."

"And?"

He twisted her seat around with unexpected strength. His thin lips curved into a smile and she glanced at his yellowed teeth.

"Come, Aimee, don't be so persistent. Surely we can discuss details at a later date."

His lips descended on hers. She squeezed her eyes shut as he touched her mouth. She did not feel revulsion—the nausea had passed. She felt nothing, absolutely nothing, as his lips pressed more urgently on her own.

His jeweled fingers skimmed the edge of her bodice, then roamed over the velvet to cup her breast. She started and broke the kiss. "Please, monsieur."

"Reluctant, *ma cherie?* Certainly this is what you wanted."

His chest was firm beneath the frothy layers of his cravat. She pressed against it. *"Bien sûr,* monsieur—Jean-Jacques, but before we become more involved I wish to know the progress you have made on Château Bocage."

"Ah, such bothersome details." The duke reached for her bare shoulder and rubbed his fingers against her smooth skin. "Later, *ma cherie,* later."

"No," she said firmly as the duke moved to kiss her again. She rose unsteadily from her seat and stepped away from him. She clutched her skirts. "Please understand that I am anxious about my estate: I yearn to hear your good news."

"These affairs will take time, Aimee. The king is involved in negotiating the peace and has little time for other affairs of state." His gaze lingered on the dark valley of her cleavage. "And, the affair is rather delicate. The purchase must be discreet. The king, however, has made me assurances that the estate will be mine . . . in time."

"Truly?"

The duke reached for her hands. "My dear vicomtesse. I am a man of honor."

To question him further would be the biggest folly. She took a deep breath, noting in a distracted fashion that the movement caught and held the duke's attention. He moved closer. She realized she was looking down at him. Bereft of the heels he had worn at the ball, the duke was a thumb shorter than she. She had a strange urge to laugh and then, quickly, to cry.

He drew her to the edge of the bed. Their difference in height dissolved as they sat side by side; it disappeared entirely as he pressed her down on the silken covers. The virgin white pelt of one of the pillows brushed Aimee's cheek. As the duke's kisses descended over her throat and toward her bosom she pressed her face in it to dry her tears.

How ironic, she thought as the duke's hands began kneading her breasts. *Within three days I learn to love, I learn to make love, and I learn . . .* She squeezed her eyes shut. She could not put a name to this. The duke's breathing grew ragged in her ear and she turned her head away from his lips.

She opened her eyes. The white and gray hues of the boudoir shimmered beyond her tears. As she watched, the door to the boudoir opened. She stared in bewilderment as the shape of a man came into her vision.

I must be mad, she thought, her heart lurching in pain. *I surely have lost my mind.*

"I regret to interrupt your pleasure, Monsieur le Duc, but I have some news which will interest you."

The duke lifted his head from her bosom and stared at Kilian. Aimee blinked. Shame roused her from her drugged state. Kilian's eyes settled on her for a brief, murderous moment, then turned again to the duke.

"Guards!" The duke leapt from the bed with surprising agility and sought the room for a weapon. "How did you get in here, de Laclos? Did you kill my guards—"

"No need." His lips whitened against his teeth. "They let me in without a murmur. That is the difference between a man dressed in rough wool and one in satin."

Aimee sat upright on the bed, clutching her wig as it threatened to tumble off. Her gaze widened on Kilian—not the Kilian she knew, but a new man. A man dressed in rich chocolate satin carrying a gold-handled walking stick with cascades of point d'anglaise lace dripping from his wrists and throat. This was not the Kilian Laclos she knew, yet as she stared into the gold-flecked eyes, now narrow with fury, she knew that it was. Guards appeared at the door and pointed their muskets at his back, but he took no notice of them. Or of her.

"Fool you are to come into my château," the duke spat, straightening at the sight of his guards. "You tried two nights ago to kill me, Laclos, and failed."

"Aye, I failed. But for a richer vengeance."

"Is this then the vengeance you seek for your sister? You seek a fate for me that she never sought, and you shall be exiled from court for trying to kill me—"

"I did not come to kill you, Montchamp, though there will be a day when I will do just that." His nostrils flared. "One day, Jolivette's death will be countered with your own."

"Jolivette herself would defy you," the duke countered. "You knew less about her—"

"How dare you defile her name when she lies dead by your hand!"

"Not my hand—"

"Damn your soul to hell, Montchamp!"

The guards lifted their primed muskets and pressed the ends against Kilian's back. He stood as if they had never moved, as if no threat existed. His eyes flared with fury and his face whitened to ash. He flexed his hands into tight fists and held them taut by his side.

"The king has seen fit to give me an estate for my victories in the war, Montchamp," Kilian said from between clenched teeth. "Do you know what estate I have chosen?"

"No. Nor do I care."

"You will." Kilian glanced at Aimee once, and his eyes held the murderous light of rage. "You will, for it will abort another of your plans to debauch a woman, though I vow this one is not so innocent."

"Insult me, de Laclos, but leave her alone."

"How very noble for a man who allows a woman to sell her body for the price of a room in Versailles." Kilian drew his gaze away from Aimee and settled it, full force, on the duke. "But your pleasure is over, Montchamp, for I have been given the Bocage estate."

Aimee stood and clutched her bosom. Her eyes widened in shock.

"That's correct, Vicomtesse," Kilian persisted, his eyes narrowing. "I am now the Vicomte de Bocage."

Through the haze of his fury, Kilian watched Aimee's luminous gray eyes fill with tears before she rushed mindlessly out of the room. The duke—the bastard duke—called her name and it took all of Kilian's will not to leap on the aristocrat and choke his voice and his life from his body.

"Don't bother calling her, Montchamp, for all she ever wanted from you was her estate."

"Don't be so sure, de Laclos."

"I am quite sure," Kilian retorted. "And by the end of the day she shall be *my* mistress."

The duke straightened and a fire flickered in his dark eyes. There was pleasure in stealing the fruit of the duke's passion from his very arms, Kilian thought as he watched him. The only thing that would make this moment sweeter would be to shoot the bastard for what he did to Jolivette, and for what he tried to do to Aimee, and watch him bleed to death on the white rug.

There would be time for that, later, when a dozen witnesses were not around to watch. Kilian turned away from the impotent aristocrat and pushed the barrels of the muskets away from his chest. He walked down the hall, amid the fearful gazes of a dozen liveried servants. Kilian knew the duke would not dare arrest him. The aristocrat had risked exile once by debauching Jolivette; he would guarantee it by arresting her brother. And if word of the duke's plans with Aimee reached the king's ears the duke would not be long on French soil. Kilian would make sure of it.

For it was the duke's fault—everything was the duke's fault. From Jolivette's death to his family's shame to the corruption of Aimee. Two nights ago Kilian had brazenly scaled the Montchamp château walls and entered the building with the intent to kill the duke, knowing that the duke had guests, knowing that he himself would be discovered and decapitated for killing a nobleman. But nothing had mattered then—all that mattered was killing the duke, not only to avenge his own sister's death, but also to rip Aimee from his greedy hands. He had failed, but his failure had made him only more determined. If he could not kill the duke, then he would destroy him with cunning.

Then the idea had come.

Kilian climbed into his carriage, vaguely aware of the

guards that watched his every move. His manteau dripped with rainwater though he did not remember walking through the downpour. The carriage lurched forward toward Château Bocage. *His* estate.

He fingered the head of his gold-handled cane. King Louis XV had been surprised and embarrassed to see Kilian de Laclos, the Chevalier de Bourg-en-Bresse, at his apartments in the early morning levée yesterday, but he granted him a private audience anyway. Kilian had entered the carved and painted door a mere chevalier, and had left a vicomte. The king could deny him nothing, for after the death of Kilian's sister and the subsequent shame of the de Lacloses, the king had hesitated to exile the Duc de Montchamp despite his promise to the chevalier. The monarch had tempted Kilian with a marquisate in Champagne and another in Brittany, but Kilian would not be dissuaded. He wanted the Bocage estate, a meager title and lands—the same estate that the king had already promised to the Duc de Montchamp. And Kilian wanted it immediately.

How subtle, he thought, leaning back on the plush leather upholstery of the carriage. With one simple request he had received an estate and vengeance. Granted, the vengeance was not complete, for the duke must die, but it was vengeance nonetheless. There was sweetness in aborting the duke's well-made plans. There was sweetness in catching him in his own lust, and staunching it.

He closed his eyes. He knew the image of the duke lying atop Aimee would never leave his mind. There was some triumph in proving his own power to the vicomtesse, but even now that taste turned sour. She had not trusted him— she had categorically rejected him and his offers—and because of that, she, too, must pay a price. He wondered as he fingered the knotted top of his cane whether he would pay that same price.

He had never proposed to a woman. He had offered Aimee everything: his name, his heart, his protection, and she had rejected it all with one wave of her hand. She had rejected it for the coldness of her castle and the chance at being the mistress of the duke. He wondered if her answer would have been different had she known that he was of noble blood. He could not tell her then, for that would have ruined all chances of his vengeance by revealing his identity. Part of him wished he had told her nonetheless, if for no other reason than to determine whether it was money or her estate that she wanted.

The fervor boiled in his heart as the carriage drove over the near flooded roads toward Château Bocage. Now she would have nothing—not her castle, not her mistress-ship, and certainly not marriage. Not yet. His face settled in a frown. He would not marry her until she learned that love was not something to be idly tossed to the winds. Before he ever proposed to her again, she would melt in his arms and love him as much as he loved her.

Kilian did not glance at his castle as he climbed out of the carriage and ascended the worn steps. He pushed the door open and stood a moment in the portal. Manon rushed from the buttery and lifted her apron to her face. Her worried glance directed Kilian to the staircase in the northwest tower.

He took the steps two at a time. He knew Aimee's bedroom was in the southeast corner, for only a few nights earlier he had scaled the castle wall to be with her. It seemed like months, not days, since he had held her gently in his arms. Now he had no tenderness. He walked heavily through the hall and opened the last door on the right.

She looked up. She was not surprised to see him. A flimsy wicker case lay full and open on the bed beside her. She held a letter in her hands.

"Packing, Aimee?" he snapped, gesturing to the valise. "Where are you going?"

"Does it matter?"

"Yes."

"Don't worry, Kilian. I'll not run back to the duke."

"No, you won't."

Her chin tilted, as it always did when he spoke to her like that. Her gray eyes narrowed and her fingers tightened on the letter. Kilian saw traces of tears on her pale skin, but her eyes were now dry. "You should be grateful to me, Aimee. I've saved you from selling yourself to the duke."

"Grateful!" She breathed heavily and tossed the papers on the bed. "I should be grateful for this? For your betrayal? For destroying everything I have worked for?"

"I have not destroyed anything," he said quietly. "I have merely transferred the bargain."

"What are you saying?"

"I am saying that you no longer have to whore yourself to the duke. Now you must give yourself to me."

Silence grew taut and furious between them. Aimee's eyes widened then darkened to the color of sooty black clouds. "So now that the barbarian has slain the abductor I should give myself to the barbarian?"

His lips tightened. "If I am the barbarian, then the answer is yes."

"How dare you." She gestured to the letter. "You have lied to me, seduced me, stolen my virginity, then betrayed me. The Comtesse de Vierzon has written and told me that it was your *sister* that the duke debauched. Now I understand everything. I understand that the only reason you were ever on this estate was to wreak your vengeance on the Duc de Montchamp. I understand that all your seduction, all your flattery, all your pretty words and useless warnings—they were all done in an attempt to steal me away from the duke. You wanted to snatch the apple from his grasp and when your words and your looks and your seduction failed, you went to the king." Her eyes grew bright with tears and her throat became hoarse as she struggled with her anger.

"That's not true," Kilian argued, shaking his head. "I wanted to kill the duke for what he did, but I failed—"

"So you bought my estate instead, after I, in my passionate folly, told you about the bargain between the duke and myself. All the weeks you spent here, you knew that I agonized over losing Château Bocage. But that did not matter to you. You bought the estate only after you discovered that the duke wanted it, and me, as well." Her chest heaved in anger. "You have your vengeance against the duke, Kilian de Laclos. You also have it against me, though only you and God know why you wanted to hurt me so much."

Kilian reeled with her vehemence and pain. Her words, her story—they were not true. He had never planned this vengeance. He had thought of it only after her rejection. He had wanted her. *Dieu,* he had loved her—but she had rejected his love. "You rejected my offer of marriage. You ignored my warnings. I planned to kill the duke, but when you told me you'd never give up in your efforts to keep the estate I had no choice but to act in the quickest way possible. You did not trust me."

"Trust you! Why should I ever trust a man who would not tell me his real name? Who hid his identity? Who knew all along he could solve my problems with one word to the king—yet chose instead to *use* me in his twisted plans of vengeance?" The tears fell freely now, but they were hot, angry tears. Her hands and body trembled uncontrollably, but the steady light of fury held her high. "You betrayed me, Kilian de Laclos. I knew from the moment I set eyes on you that you were not to be trusted. I knew, as the weeks passed, that your charm would be my folly. I let a wolf in with the sheep, but I never dreamed he would destroy the shepherdess."

He stood speechless. The lies wove a web around him and tightened. He had *not* known he could acquire her estate with one word to the king—he had not thought of it until his frustrated efforts to kill the duke left him no options. He felt his vengeance twist and turn upon himself. In the face of such anger, in the face of such indisputable evidence, how could he ever explain to Aimee that he had done it to save her from the duke, he had done it because he could not bear the thought of her in another man's arms?

He knew his words would fall on deaf ears. But he could bind her to him in other ways.

"Whatever you think of me, Aimee, you must now deal with this. I am the Vicomte de Bocage. I own your estate." He took a step toward her. "If you want to live here and care for your tenants, you must now bargain with me."

"You are no better than the duke. You have just asked me to do exactly what the duke asked Jolivette. It's a pity I don't have a brother to seek my vengeance."

Each word hit him like a blow from a mallet. He searched her eyes but could see nothing beneath her tears and her rage. Her entire body shook and a pulse beat wildly in her throat. The color drained from her face. He knew that nothing would ease her hatred now.

Except time.

"What is your answer, Aimee?" He took a deep breath as he stepped closer. Her anger radiated from her tall, thin body like heat from a burning yule log. Her silver eyes cut into him. "Be my mistress and you can stay here, in Château Bocage."

"I'd rather sleep with the devil."

"You nearly did this afternoon."

She slapped him hard, and the sound reverberated through the room. "The duke never betrayed me."

"I never gave him a chance. I saved you before he could touch you." His cheek stung with her anger, but he did not touch it. He searched her eyes relentlessly, almost desperately, for some sign of softening.

He almost saw it. In the moment before she whirled away he thought he saw the dark clouds of her rage part and a glimmer of pain and love shine through. He stepped toward her, but she lifted her arms to ward him off. "Leave me alone, Laclos. You are exactly what I thought you always were—a thief. You've stolen my estate and you've stolen . . ." She pulled the straps on the wicker case closed. "You've stolen my pride."

"Where are you going?"

"Away. Far away. And, God will it, you will never find me."

CHAPTER
10

Aimee scratched on the carved door and turned her head to the wood. She heard a rustle of bedclothes and the low, husky laugh of the Comtesse de Vierzon.

The comtesse's voice rose in question. "Is that you, Aimee?"

"*Oui, c'est moi*, Marie." Aimee stepped away from the portal as she heard the servant's door within the bedroom close decisively.

"Come in and have some chocolate with me."

She opened the door and peered around its edge. Marie-Celeste, the Comtesse de Vierzon, lay back on a cloud of pillows, the seashell-colored silk of her peignoir stretching across her unbound breasts. She smiled as Aimee entered, and her saucy blue eyes arced in humor.

"It's quite all right, he has gone now." The comtesse gestured to the servant's door. "He feared my husband would be by in the morning and he fled at your first scratch. He's now running through the streets of Paris with his garters undone."

Aimee turned away so Marie would not see her blush. After four weeks in the comtesse's Parisian town house she still had not become accustomed to the licentious life-style. Paris was very far from Normandy, she thought, and not only in distance. But she, of all people, was not one to judge.

She opened the curtains and the midday sunshine spilled across the thick satin bedclothes. She sat down on a small chair by *le déjeuné,* where a silver pot of chocolate steamed next to a number of porcelain cups. She poured a demitasse of the thick liquid and settled back in the well-upholstered chair.

"You look pale, Aimee. Didn't you sleep well?"

"Not nearly as well as you."

The comtesse laughed her deep, throaty laugh and ran her fingers through her blond, pomade-stiffened curls. "You'd be sleeping just as well if you'd accompanied me to some of these salons. You'd have a husband within a year —a lover much sooner, if you wished."

"Marie—"

"Come, now, Aimee. It's been nearly a month since you arrived in Paris. I assure you that the company of an attentive nobleman will put more roses in your cheeks than that infernal embroidery." The comtesse gestured to the material that now lay in her lap.

"Marie, please. You're not dressed yet and you're already arguing with me. Drink your chocolate and speak to me of all that happened last night."

Her eyes sparkled. "I won't tell you all, of course, for that will only heighten the color in your cheeks, *mon amie.*" The comtesse laughed as she flushed anew. "Ah! You would be such a success in a salon, if you would only—"

"Marie."

"Very well." The comtesse settled her cup on the silver tray and poured a new one. Some of the chocolate spilled on the linen cloth, but Marie paid no heed. Aimee stilled her own urge to clean it up. This was not her house and the comtesse had servants who would tidy such messes. Her house—her beloved castle—was forever lost to her.

"The gambling continued in the salon until far after three. The respectable company left early." Marie sipped the chocolate and the froth rested on her upper lip. "The Comte de Coigney lost a considerable amount to the Prince de Dombes and the Comte d'Eu. He dared to suggest that the prince and the others had cheated. They threatened to meet at dawn."

Aimee shivered. "Did they?"

"I don't know. I wager we shall find out soon, though, for the duel, if it took place, is long decided. You should have been there, Aimee. You, rather than the prince, would have won the drunken Comte de Coigney's money and thus prevented the duel. He wouldn't dare challenge a woman."

"You overestimate my abilities at cards."

"Hardly." Her blue eyes narrowed. "You'd make a year's *rentes* from Château Bocage with one night at the card table. I have not yet been able to beat you at *brélau* or *comète*."

Aimee recognized the aim of the conversation and determined to turn it around. "Were any of the royal family present?"

"No. They, I believe, spent the night at the Comédie Française. A place I intend to bring you, and soon."

Aimee brightened despite herself. She had long wanted to attend the theater, but she knew doing so was tantamount to going out in society—and she certainly had no plans for that. If there were only some way she could go incognito, and staunch Marie-Celeste's plans to find her a lover.

"We could get a box at the Française, Aimee. A private

one, with only the two of us." Marie leaned forward in the
bed, sensing her advantage. "No one would have to see us,
except when we arrive and depart—"

"And you, my old friend, would take advantage of those
opportunities to introduce me to every leering, available
courtier you could find."

"I'll not deny it." The comtesse settled back in the cloud
of pillows and glanced mischievously over the porcelain
rim of her cup. "You're only increasing your intrigue by
keeping your presence secret, Aimee. It would be best just
to come out in the open."

"And be forced to face the false flattering attentions of
those men you find so irresistible?" She shook her head.
"I'd rather stay mysterious and secluded—though you,
with your constant gossiping, are making that a difficult
task." She tilted her head and glanced at Marie through
dark lashes. "If, however, my presence is intrusive
here—"

"Stop." Marie-Celeste shook her head and lifted her
dimpled arms in the air. "You know that is not what I
meant. There's plenty of room here since my husband
moved into that little town house in Versailles, and I adore
having you. It has been years since we've been together—
not since the vicomte was alive and holding those glorious
hunting parties at Bocage. And you, my faithful friend,
were looking out while I became more intimate with the
stable boy. Besides, none of my milliners can sew quite as
well as you, though I don't like you mending my clothes
like some common peasant."

"If you weren't having your clothes torn off you so
much I wouldn't have to mend them."

Marie-Celeste laughed. "Touché, *mon amie*."

Aimee smiled and sipped her chocolate. These morning
toilettes with the comtesse had become very special to her
in the month since she arrived from Normandy. They were
a balm to her bruised and battered spirit.

She bent her head over her embroidery as Marie continued her stories of the salon. Only a month had passed
under the comtesse's care, and her life had fallen into a
predictable pattern. After spending the breakfast hour with
the comtesse and helping her with her toilette, she would
slip downstairs to the garden and work in the dark Parisian
soil for a few hours, arguing with the hired gardener as to
the correct way of raising roses. Then, chided by the comtesse's continual pleas for her to stop working like a servant, she would join Marie in a game of cards or would
read to her if the June day was too warm for exertion. Soon
dinner would be served, then the evening would be spent in
minor chores as the comtesse dressed for her soirees.

Every night, the comtesse left her alone in the great
town house while she whirled through the glittering Parisian society. Those evenings were the most dangerous time
of the day for Aimee. In the unguarded moments before
she slept, Kilian's face would rise in her mind. She would
remember his kisses, his words, and the pain of his betrayal. Then she would drench her pillow with tears.

When she had come to the comtesse a month ago, she
had sought a refuge for only a few days. The comtesse,
Aimee's dearest friend from childhood, had taken her in
without a murmur and allowed her to stay long after the
initial shock of her loss had passed. Unfortunately, Aimee
knew that she could not stay in Paris forever. The only
place she could go was a convent, if she could ever find
one willing to take in a completely impoverished ex-noble-
woman.

The comtesse had different ideas. Marie-Celeste's incessant efforts to introduce her to "eligible" noblemen had
been frustrated by Aimee's insistence to be left alone. She
had recently discovered that the Comtesse de Vierzon took
pains to let all of Paris know that a "hidden beauty" was
installed in her own town house. Aimee did not approve of
this new notoriety, but she could do nothing to banish it.

Marie only had her best interests at heart. What the comtesse did not seem to understand was that Aimee wanted only to rest and plan a quiet future. After Kilian's betrayal, she felt as if she had no heart at all.

The pain still rested, heavy and aching, in her chest. Four weeks had not dulled it, but time had added a touch of fury. Kilian had betrayed her. He had never loved her. That gentle night they had shared was naught but lies; flowery, flattering, base lies. She could not think about it anymore.

"The Comédie Française is playing *Sémiramis* tomorrow," Marie said carefully, interrupting her melancholy. "Madame de Pompadour should be there to support Voltaire's piece."

"All the more reason for me to avoid the theater," she argued, bending her head over her embroidery. "I will only make her and the king, if he chooses to attend, very uncomfortable."

"*Au contraire*, the marquise is very sympathetic to your position."

Aimee stiffened and stared at the comtesse, who, realizing her error, quickly settled her chocolate on the silver tray. "Marie, you didn't."

"I didn't tell her anything that wasn't already common knowledge. It was several nights ago, at one of her suppers." Marie's lips puckered in annoyance. "She knows that de Laclos snatched your estate from Montchamp's hands. All I added was that there was a woman in between."

"Marie."

"Aimee, you know I have your best interests in mind."

She placed her cup on the service and it clattered loudly. "I know you mean well, but this time you have gone too far. I have already decided that it's best that I leave Paris. I never wanted all this attention. I'm going to enter a convent." She shrugged her shoulders. "Perhaps in Normandy."

Marie's eyes widened into large blue spheres. "You can't be serious. A *convent! Sacré bleu*, Aimee!"

"It is not so bad a fate."

"Yes, it is!" She pushed the sheets aside and swung her bare legs over the edge of the bed. "I'd rather plunge a sword in my heart than consign myself to a convent."

Aimee glanced meaningfully at the servant door. "You and I are made of different stuff."

"Not that different, I'd wager. You have had at least one lover." She planted her hands on her ample hips. "Why do you insist on living in hell because of that man?"

Aimee started at Marie's vehemence. "I . . . I'm not living in hell."

"Not yet. If you go to a convent you will be. Why shut yourself away from life because one man was too much of a fool to see what he had lost?"

Tears pricked the back of her lids. She blinked them back instinctively and shook her head.

"Listen to me, Aimee. Although you've lost your title to that *man*, you still have a respectable lineage." The comtesse rose from the bed and kneeled before her chair. "You can't go to a convent—you can't wallow in self-pity like this anymore!"

"It's not self-pity!" she exclaimed. "I simply don't want to spend the rest of my life wandering from friend to friend, like an unwanted spinster. A convent is the only practical option." Aimee frowned as she stared at Marie. "And what do you mean I have a respectable lineage? My father was not exactly the Order of Saint-Esprit."

"Granted, your father's branch of the St.-Simons long fell into destitution, but you are still nonetheless a St.-Simon. The bloodlines of that family easily go back four hundred years." Marie surged ahead. "You also still have the right to call yourself by your husband's family name, de Chacontier. You are still an aristocrat, at the very least by marriage. There are bourgeois with less noble blood than you being introduced to court every week. Madame de Pompadour herself is a bourgeoise."

"Court!"

"Yes!" The comtesse brightened with enthusiam. "Don't you see? If we moved carefully, if you let me use a little of my influence, I could get you introduced to court. Madame de Pompadour has already expressed some sympathy for your plight. Granted, you are impoverished, but you are lovely. At the very least you could become the mistress of a very wealthy, influential aristocrat—perhaps you'll receive a pension from the crown."

"Marie, you talk foolishness. I am nothing but a country aristocrat. The king has never paid attention to me in the year I spent fighting for my estate." She stood and wrapped her arms around her middle. Her fingers dug into the worn velvet. "Besides, I don't have the funds to dress myself properly for these functions—"

"Aimee—"

"And I won't accept them from you," she finished. "Your generosity has extended far beyond kindness. I have overstayed my welcome."

"You have not." The comtesse sighed in exasperation, stood up, and walked to her closet. She swung open the doors. "I have more dresses than I could wear in a year, Aimee. A few adjustments, and you could have a dozen, two—"

"It would take more than a few adjustments," she warned, staring at Marie's voluptuous figure and comparing it to her own. The month since Normandy had only made her thinner.

"Very well, then, I could buy new ones and send the bill to my husband. The comte signs off my bills without looking at them—my mother made sure that that was in the marriage contract. He would never know the difference."

"We are talking foolishness, for I will not be invited to

court," she concluded, staring out the window to the rush-strewn street. "And if I were, I could not possibly accept."

"You could not refuse. No one refuses the order of the king."

"The king has not yet sent that order, has he, Marie?"

Her pink lips puckered in annoyance. "No, not yet."

"I trust you will make no efforts toward that end?"

The comtesse turned away and reached for a matching silk robe that lay on the carpeted floor. She wrapped it around her body and tied the silken cord beneath her breasts. Aimee watched her, waiting for an answer.

"You used to be a very practical, clear-thinking woman, Aimee. That *man* has addled you. I will make no such promises, unless. . . ." The comtesse's eyes narrowed as she turned to her friend. "Come to the Comédie Française with me tomorrow."

"Marie, I am not a fool."

"I never said you were, *mon amie*. Listen. I am proposing a bargain. Come to the Française with me tomorrow night and I promise to make no further efforts of my own toward having you introduced at court."

Aimee's winged brows lifted in surprise. This was not at all like Marie-Celeste. "If I attend the theater with you tomorrow night, you will no longer try to push me into society?"

"Precisely. Come, Aimee, have you ever known me to go back on my word?"

"No." She frowned. "But you are far too clever for your own good."

"What? Aimee de Chacontier, frightened? I have known you to forge ahead in the most terrifying circumstances."

"I'm not nine years old. I don't ride unbroken horses anymore. Nor do I enter a wolf's lair unarmed."

"You will not be unarmed," she assured her. "You'll be among groups of Parisians of all classes, and you'll have me by your side."

Aimee's eyes narrowed. "Why would you make such a bargain?"

"Ever distrustful, are we? I simply believe that as soon as you see the glory of Parisian society you will want to come out yourself, and you will ask me for my services. There. Now you know that my motives are untrue. Will you come?"

She pursed her lips. The comtesse's bargain seemed too simple to be true. Aimee sensed with the familiarity of years of friendship that Marie-Celeste would attempt some ruse to convince her to stay in Parisian society. But, truly, what could the comtesse do? Introduce her to some charming nobleman? Aimee knew with cold certainty that no m..n could entice her into anything, not after Kilian. And a night at the theater would be exciting after the quiet monotony of her days. "I will probably regret it," Aimee sighed, staring into the comtesse's bright blue eyes. "But yes, Marie. I will go."

Aimee frowned as the comtesse fluttered around her, directing two milliners in their efforts to make her look like a duchesse rather than an impoverished, untitled, country aristocrat.

"Marie, it is not going to matter whether I have eight or ten inches of lace falling from my elbows. Nor does it matter if one or two of the bows on this bodice are crooked."

"It makes all the difference in the world, *mon amie.* There, trim the edge with this crimson ribbon. No, not so thinly, come—" Marie hitched her skirts around her knees and knelt by the milliner. "There. And be quick about it, we've less than an hour. Now, Aimee, if you expect me to keep my end of this bargain you are just going to have to endure my fussing. Look at you! Not a trace of rouge on your face."

"I feel like an actress with that paint on."

"You're undressed without it in this world, my friend." The comtesse, resplendent in pale pink silk scattered with tiny rosebuds, picked up the pot of rouge and pulled a small stool next to Aimee. "Besides, after all the time you spent altering this old dress of mine, I am certainly not going to let you go looking like a poor relation." She slabbed some of the cream on Aimee's cheek until she protested. "Very well." She wiped off some of the mixture. "But I warn you, there will still be some on." The comtesse's gaze dipped to Aimee's bosom, which pressed upward from the pressure of her whalebone corset.

"Don't think of it, Marie," she warned, seeing the direction of her stare. "I'll not paint my chest—absolutely not."

"It will enhance—"

"I don't want any enhancement!" The milliners at her feet giggled. "Now stop fussing. It must be near nine and we should be on our way."

"Not just yet, *mon amie*. . . ."

It was nine to the minute when Aimee finally climbed down from the stool and adjusted her skirts around her panniers. The milliners had done an exceptional job on the remade dress, considering the few hours they were allotted to sew on ribbons, lace, and bows. It looked as fresh as if it came right from the dressmaker's. The comtesse presented her with a fan of scented wood painted with large pink roses. The addition of a silk rose in the scaffolding of her wig completed the picture, and finally they descended the stairs of the town house and entered the waiting carriage.

The comtesse's perfume nearly stifled her in the small confines of the coach. Aimee had worn a few precious drops of her favorite scent—apple blossoms—and she suddenly realized that the delicate aroma would be lost in the wash of strong perfumes that would fill the theater. Not that it mattered. She was going simply to enjoy the production. Whatever plans the comtesse had Aimee was determined to destroy.

She pulled away the curtains to the carriage window and gazed out into Paris. The tallow candles that were lit and suspended high above the roads gave little light to the streets. Half of them had already sputtered out. Shapeless forms moved in the darkness and the carriage sprayed water on the wooden storefronts. The theater stood out like a beacon in the darkened city. The carriages lined up before the entrance while several footmen helped the aristocrats down onto the wet, cobbled streets. Though the early summer rain had subsided, the ground remained sticky from the shower.

As their carriage drew closer to the front, Aimee's stomach tightened. There seemed to be hundreds of people inside the large foyer. She could see the glimmer of jewels and powder and the obvious wealth of silks and satins. As their carriage stopped, she wondered if she had made a terrible mistake.

"Come, on, Aimee. It won't be so bad." Marie reached for the footman's gloved hand and descended to the ground, carelessly holding her skirts high. Sighing, Aimee followed, making sure nothing but her ankles showed as she held her skirts above the muck. Clutching her arm, the comtesse pulled her into the scented, swirling mass of theatergoers. It was too late now.

"Marie, I don't know why I agreed to this."

"Ah, Madame de Sassenage!" Marie pulled her bodily to a woman dressed in vivid green brocade with a fan working furiously in her hand. "Are you here, perhaps, taking notes for Madame de Pompadour's next production?"

Madame de Sassenage laughed, reveling in the attention this brought her. "*Bien sûr,* Comtesse," she murmured, her gaze skimming quickly over Aimee. "I am also going to see if Mademoiselle Dumesnil can play as good an Assyrian Queen as Madame de Pompadour."

"For her sake, we hope not," the comtesse said below her breath. "Madame, I would like to introduce you to a friend of mine from the country, Madame de Chacontier. Madame, this is the Marquise de Sassenage."

The marquise barely nodded as Aimee curtsied. "Is this the woman you have been hiding in your town house, Comtesse?"

"You make her sound like a fugitive!"

"I would not call it hiding, madame," Aimee interjected, meeting the aristocrat's gaze. "I would call it preparing. I am a simple woman from the country, and this"—she gestured to the sea of aristocrats—"is quite overwhelming."

"Indeed," Madame de Sassenage said as her well-powdered brow wrinkled. Her gaze slipped over Aimee's attire and returned to her face. "You've done well to bring her out tonight, Comtesse. You must know that half the court is here. Including all the men whose lusts you have fueled with hints of this lovely *amie*."

Aimee glanced at Marie sharply, but she simply smiled. "I had hoped as much."

"Mind that the king doesn't see her. Madame de Pompadour will not be pleased if she turns his head."

"How silly an idea," Aimee retorted, laughing. Madame de Sassenage was beginning to irritate her because of her refusal to address her directly. "I know of Madame de Pompadour's beauty. A simple country aristocrat could not possibly turn the king's head from such a flame. Nor do I have any intention of doing so."

"Indeed," Madame de Sassenage murmured. "You are unique among women, then, madame."

"Come, Comtesse." Aimee took Marie's arm. "We should find our way to the box. I don't want to miss one moment of the performance."

Curtsying briefly to the marquise, they headed toward
the well-worn staircase that led to the *loges hautes*.

"Really, Aimee, sometimes you can be so provincial."
Marie giggled as they reached the *premier étage*. "No one
actually comes to the Française to watch the performance."

"I do."

"Then there are other times when you can be quite
shrewd," Marie continued. "Madame de Sassenage was
trying to find out whether I was putting you forth as a rival
to Madame de Pompadour."

"She was?"

"Yes. You did quite well answering with such blunt-
ness." Marie stopped at a box and peered in. "Ah, Comtesse d'Estrades. . . ."

Aimee suffered through a dozen interviews as they made
their way along the hall toward their own box. The du-
chesses and comtesses and marquises behaved as if she did
not exist, even after Marie directly introduced them to her.
Some of the men did kiss her hand and gazed, without
artifice, at her un-rouged bosom. They turned away at her
direct stare.

Three warning thumps from behind the stage signaled
the imminent beginning of the performance. The comtesse
frowned in annoyance and they hurried to their box. Aimee
was relieved to find it empty.

"I expected you to foist some courtier on me," she muttered as they settled in the straight-backed chairs. "I'm surprised you did not invite anyone to join us."

Marie toyed with a blond curl that had fallen on her
nape. She traced her square, low-cut bodice with her fan as
she scanned the boxes opposite. "I considered it," she
murmured, distracted. "But I thought it would be best if
you were seen alone. You will attract more attention that
way."

"You are incorrigible, you know," she said, suddenly
aware of the gazes of a dozen aristocrats in the boxes di-

rectly opposite. Her skin began to crawl. "But when they raise the chandeliers at least these people won't be able to stare."

The comtesse laughed, and the sound drew the attention of more theatergoers. "My dear, they won't raise the chandeliers so high that everyone cannot get a good look at who is present." She tapped her fan on Aimee's forearm. "Really, Aimee. You have been in Normandy far too long."

Not long enough. Never long enough. She glanced down at her hands. Despite the work she had done in the comtesse's garden, they still were far whiter and far smoother than in the days when she worked at Château Bocage. Paris was changing her. The comtesse was changing her. She never wanted to be changed.

"Look!" The comtesse leaned over. "The king is here!"

Every eye in the theater turned to the middle box, hidden somewhat behind a grill. Everyone stood as Madame de Pompadour, resplendent in cream satin, entered and took her seat. The king, dressed in rich blue brocade, followed. A roar of approval greeted him and he inclined his head slightly, his hand over his blue ribbon.

So this was the *Bien-aimé*, she thought as she gazed at the dark eyes and the handsome features of the monarch. This man had controlled her life from afar for a year, and destroyed her happiness less than four weeks earlier. Yet he did not know her as Kilian knew her, and she felt no betrayal. The chandeliers immediately began their upward ascent.

The play began. Aimee's attention riveted on the stage as the plot unfolded, but hers was the only attentive gaze. All of Paris and most of the court was at the Française tonight and they came not to watch the stage, but to watch the boxes. The comtesse flirted outrageously with a young man directly opposite and the silence of their well-upholstered loge was frequently interrupted by a guest.

After the third interruption, Aimee gazed with exasperation at the comtesse. "You did not tell me this was as open as a salon."

"You never asked, *mon amie*," she retorted. "Here, have an orange and don't look so forbidding. Remember, I have made a promise, too. After this night, I will make no more efforts on your behalf, if that is what you wish."

Aimee dug her fingers into the skin of the orange and glared toward the stage. She had completely lost track of the plot and was determined to pay attention, despite the frequent visitors. She glanced at the other boxes and found most of the guests turned away from the stage. She wondered why they bothered to have a play at all. Only the crowd in the pit seemed to take any interest in *Sémiramis*.

"Madame de Chacontier, I have someone here who would like to meet you." Marie's voice broke into her concentration. She managed a stiff smile and turned to the curtained door. A young aristocrat, neatly dressed and not much older than her, smiled hesitantly as their gazes met. "Monsieur de Saint-Veran, this is Madame de Chacontier."

"*Enchanté*," he murmured as he bent over her hand. Aimee noticed that beneath his wig his hair seemed dark and luxurious. He had the black eyes of a Spaniard or an Italian. In a detached way she found him handsome, but she only answered him with a nod.

"You should not hide away in the comtesse's town house," he said, taking the liberty to sit in the extra chair provided by the door. "You deny society the benefits of your beauty."

Aimee struggled not to laugh and she looked to the comtesse for support. Marie was staring at the young man with speculation in her eyes.

"How long have you been back from the Netherlands?" Marie asked. She turned to Aimee. "Monsieur is a lieutenant in the army, under Marechal de Saxe."

"We've only been back a few months, since the majority

of the warring nations signed the Treaty of Aix-la-Chapelle. If Austria does not sign soon, we'll have to return."

"That will, indeed, be a pity."

"Not if we can take back Flanders and capture Holland,"
he began excitedly, "and not be bound to the peace."

He's so young, Aimee thought, as he continued to argue
about military maneuvers, and I am so very old.

A shadow fell over the box. The young man stopped
talking abruptly and stood up. The comtesse rose, and
Aimee, who had imitated Marie the entire night, soon followed suit.

"Monsieur!" the comtesse exclaimed as a gentleman entered the box. He wore the Order of Saint-Esprit over his
heart. "I . . . I did not expect you until later."

"I am a duke, not a king, Comtesse. You need not stand
in my presence." The duke's dark eyes riveted on Aimee's
pale face. "Hello, Madame de Chacontier. I don't think
formal introductions are necessary."

She felt the eyes of the theater turn away from the stage
and focus on the drama unfolding in the loge. Her face
heated with shame.

"Monsieur de Montchamp." She swallowed and tried
valiantly to regain her equilibrium. "When did you come
back from Normandy?"

CHAPTER

11

The chevalier made his excuses and left, and the comtesse followed him out. The duke gestured to the comtesse's vacated chair, and Aimee, still numb, nodded her assent.

He sat across from her. His dark eyes searched her face carefully, but she avoided his gaze. "I have returned to court only in the past week," he explained. "There was nothing left in Normandy to interest me."

"Don't insult me with flattery, monsieur." She folded her restless hands in her lap. "I am ashamed enough at all that has happened."

"You have no reason to be ashamed." His dark brows lowered on his well-powdered face. "It is I, not you, madame, who should be ashamed."

"Of what?"

"Of my own weakness. I took advantage of you in Normandy. It is my fault that de Laclos had the opportunity to use you as an instrument of his vengeance."

Aimee bridled. There had been so many lies, so much

deceit, that she could not help but suspect these sudden, unexpected words of apology. Especially when those words came from a man who was known to take advantage of young women; Jolivette and she were both fateful examples. "The feud between you and Monsieur de Laclos is none of my affair. I simply was in the way of his vengeance. I am trying my best to put it behind me, monsieur. I would appreciate no more discussion of the matter. In fact"—she looked at him pointedly—"I had hoped, by coming to Paris, to dissociate myself completely from that sordid affair and all those involved."

"And you are now dismayed to find that the Duc de Montchamp has followed you here."

She did not deny his words. She wished he would rise and leave. Was he planning a twisted form of his own vengeance? Was he here in her loge to "win her back" and thus wreak vengeance on Kilian? She wondered if she would now be forever caught in this strange circle of revenge.

"I am sorry, madame. But I cannot simply walk away."

"Indeed?" She reached for her fan and began to rise. "Then I shall."

"Please, Vicomtesse—"

"I am not a vicomtesse anymore," she snapped as she rose from her chair. "And I would prefer to be left alone."

"It is in part my fault, madame, that you lost your estate. And though you may think ill of me because of all that has happened and all that you have heard, grant me the opportunity to explain myself." He lowered his voice. "You once knew the viciousness of rumors and gossip. Give me the benefit of a doubt."

His grip was sure, but it was more than his insistence that made her keep her seat. The scene in their loge had received a lot of attention. She suddenly became aware of the stares of the king and his mistress from their grated box. She sat and shook off the duke's grip. "I have little choice. We are attracting more attention than the stage. I shall listen to whatever you feel you must say, but I warn you—you have only a few moments."

"A few moments should be all that I need." Sighing, he leaned back in the comtesse's chair and gazed over the pit toward the theater. Miraculously, the play continued despite all the furor they had created.

"I suppose I should begin at the beginning." The duke ran a finger idly over his gold watch chain. "You must know, by now, of Jolivette."

Aimee straightened in her chair. "Yes."

"The story is not as depraved as you think. Since you must understand what happened between Jolivette and me to understand Kilian de Laclos's anger, I feel obliged to tell you about her."

"You are not obliged to tell me anything."

"*Au contraire.* I am obliged to tell you everything. I sensed that Laclos was in Normandy long before he ever invaded my château. My own guards had sighted a tall trespasser on a fine horse several times in the weeks before our meeting, and Kilian himself had tried to kill me in my bed a few nights before." He shook his head. "I had no idea that he was employed as a scout on your estate, or that you had knowledge of him. I should have actively sought him out and made sure that he harmed no one but himself."

"That probably would have been difficult," Aimee conceded, lowering her voice. "He was very determined to hurt you, in one way or another, for what you did to his sister."

"Yes. His sister." The duke leaned back in his chair and released a long, ragged sigh. "Jolivette came to me a year ago, seeking protection after her mother died." He tilted his head to one side. "Kilian, at that time, was in India fighting in Pondicherry and her other brother, Patrick, was hiding in Italy from men whose honor he had besmirched. She had no other refuge, and I, as a friend of her late father, was the only person to whom she could turn."

Aimee had heard none of these details, nor did she wish
to. She nodded nonetheless.

"I took her in. I set her up in a small town house on the
edge of the Marais. I promised her protection until Kilian
returned from India."

She stared at the duke in surprise. She had not known
that the duke was supposed to be Jolivette's protector. That
made his role in this affair all the more disgusting.

Her gaze wandered over his pale blue satin breeches and
waistcoat liberally embroidered in silver and gold threads.
The diamonds that winked on the waistcoat matched those
on his shoe buckles. The ribbon of the Order of Saint-Esprit marked him as a nobleman of the highest rank, but the
haughty, shuttered expression that she had come to know in
Normandy had disappeared from his face. It must be the
light, she thought. His skin sank sallow and wrinkled beneath the thin sheen of rice powder.

"I spent some time visiting Jolivette, checking to make
sure she wanted for nothing. She had changed the decor of
the town house. She always had fresh-cut flowers on the
table, and she had draped the kitchen windows with brilliant yellow curtains." A slight smile fluttered across his
lips. "She was so afraid I would disapprove that she almost
tore them down one afternoon. That's when . . ."

"This is not necessary."

"Yes, I am afraid it is," he insisted, reaching for his
cane. "I have told no one of this, but you deserve to be
told. I'll not have you thinking that I am some amoral man
who had nothing in mind but getting you in my bed."

She flushed wildly and wondered if the aristocrats in the
neighboring boxes heard any of the duke's last, vigorous
statement. He began kneading the head of his polished
cane.

"Jolivette was very different from the women of *cepays-
ci*," the duke continued, gesturing to the members of the
court that populated the boxes. "She was fresh, a true inge-

nue. She had eyes the purest, most brilliant shade of green—"

"Monsieur." She closed her eyes, remembering all too vividly the same shade of green of Kilian's eyes.

"I was in love with her, Aimee. I swear that to you." He straightened a bit in his chair, using his cane as a lever. "I never wanted to harm her. I never expected that, at the ripe age of forty and a cynical courtier of Versailles, I would fall hopelessly in love with a penniless daughter of a country aristocrat.

"But I did. I spent more and more time at that town-house. I forsook my duties at court. I gave up the little actress of the Française, the salon in my hotel, almost all that linked me to the life-style of a courtier. The only thing I could not give up easily was my eight-year marriage to one of the queen's ladies-in-waiting.

"Six months passed. My peers encouraged me to claim Jolivette as my mistress, but I could not do so. Such a claim would honor her, they told me, but I could not bear to have her branded in such a way. She filled me with such... well, bourgeois sentiments. So I chose not to claim her as my mistress. Instead, I went to Italy, in secret, to confer with the Pope about annulling my marriage, and, if my efforts were successful, to seek her brother and ask for her hand in marriage."

The duke closed his eyes. "I received word of her death several months later. She had not told me she was with child, but I should have known. I should have guessed. She died, and the babe, long before term. By the time I arrived in Paris she had already been buried. She was denied extreme unction and a Christian burial. It was a fait accompli. There was nothing I could do."

The flickering lights of the raised chandeliers made shadows on his face. He lifted a hand in defeat. "I should never have kept our relationship secret, but I thought I was protecting her for something better." The duke shook his head. "Kilian arrived back from India soon after her death. He, understandably, was inconsolable. He swore on her grave to avenge her death." He looked wearily at Aimee. "But the king prevented him from challenging me to a duel."

Aimee sat stiffly in silence, trying to digest the story. It was too detailed, and his grief too raw, to be denied. Either that, or he was a better actor than Monsieur Roselli who now strutted upon the little stage.

"There was a stipulation to the king's orders to Kilian. He told me he had forced Kilian de Laclos to promise not to seek my death if the king exiled me from court. The king did not exile me, but he suggested I spend some time at my estate in Normandy until Kilian's hot blood cooled.

"I did not argue. I needed to get away from the rumors and intrigue and hate that seemed to ooze in and around the court at Versailles. I no longer had the stomach for the powdered, painted faces of the women hoping to take Jolivette's place. I went to Normandy willingly." He turned to her. "There, I found a woman. An intelligent woman, brave and graceful. You reminded me of Jolivette and her quiet, strong, simple ways. I began to feel again—"

"Monsieur."

"I took advantage of your situation—wrongful advantage. I swear to you that I never meant any harm."

"Please, Jean-Jacques." She flushed. "I don't want such apologies."

"You were simply trying to make a legitimate business transaction and I wanted more. In my grief, I twisted it into something illicit. You were desperate and had no choice but to agree with me."

She could not argue, but her cheeks flamed in shame. "I understand your need to confess to me, but your confession only makes the situation worse. It is over. All is done. I just want to leave it behind me."

"I fear that may be difficult," he said. "And that is one reason why I felt I must see you and speak to you no matter how repugnant you find me. De Laclos felt that the king did not hold to his end of the agreement. He swore to get his vengeance, and he succeeded, with you as the instrument." The duke sighed. "But his vengeance, I fear, is not finished, Aimee. Before de Laclos left my château that day, he swore to try to make you his mistress."

"He tried," she said dryly. "He tried that very day, and failed. He shall never succeed in that goal."

"Don't underestimate de Laclos, madame. What do you intend to do to avoid him? Enter a convent and hide away from the world?"

"You have been talking to the comtesse."

"The comtesse and I hardly know each other," he said, surprised. "She told me nothing. She treated me as if I were an insistent merchant when I first approached her concerning you. Only in the past few days has she agreed to let me speak to you, and that she did with great reluctance."

"Very well." Aimee straightened in her chair, vowing to chastise the comtesse thoroughly. "You have said your piece, monsieur. I would appreciate being left alone."

"Madame..." He shifted in his chair until his body faced hers. "I have done you much wrong since our first acquaintance. I must make all this up to you."

"There is no need, Jean-Jacques," she said wearily, the emotions of the evening tumbling in her breast. She lifted a hand to her forehead. "It is all over. I must get on with my life."

"In that I can help you." The duke captured her hand and held it in his own and Aimee did not have the strength to pull it away. "Through my influence, I could get you a pension from the king. Enough so you can live quite well in Paris, in Versailles, or anyplace else you choose."

"Except Château Bocage."

The duke dropped her hand. "That, I am afraid, is beyond my powers."

"That is the only place I wish to be, monsieur. Since that is lost to me, I see no other refuge but a convent."

"Which is no life at all for you."

"You don't know me."

"I don't know you well enough, unfortunately. But I do know that any woman with your spirit would die a slow, agonizing death in a convent."

She wavered between anger and confusion. She knew the truth of his words and struggled, nonetheless, to deny them.

"If it is truly Château Bocage you want, madame, then you must fight for it." The duke leaned forward. "I may not be able to help directly, but I can have you introduced at court. There are many powerful people there who may be able to help you."

"Château Bocage belongs to Kilian de Laclos."

"For now. Estates have been known to be taken away from their owners."

"Not very often."

"In a sense, it happened to you, madame. It could happen again."

Aimee watched the duke with speculation in her eyes as he rose slowly and bowed.

"Think about it. My only caution to you is that you make a decision soon. The interest of the court changes as quickly as your Norman weather."

"This court has no interest in me."

"*Au contraire,* the Marquise de Pompadour has taken an interest in you. The comtesse has made sure of that." He walked toward the curtained doorway. He stopped in the portal and turned to her. "You have nothing to lose, madame, except a few years in a convent. And he who leaves the field of battle first most definitely loses the war."

Aimee and Marie-Celeste descended from the comtesse's carriage and waited patiently while her footmen unhooked the two mares that they had chosen for the king's hunt. The forest of Rambouillet stretched before them, thick with oaks and beeches and a lush, green carpet of grass. The midday June sun beat upon the land and the hunters stood still beneath the shade to avoid the heat.

Hundreds of people—peasants, bourgeois, and aristocrats alike—came to watch the hunt. The phaetons and cabriolets littered the outer edge of the party, while other countrymen, mounted and unmounted, watched above a small knoll. Because of the comtesse's rank, her own carriage had pulled far past those of the tax collectors into the outer ring of the aristocrats. Through the circle of spectators Aimee saw the distinctive blue hunting dress of the royal party.

A liveried footman offered her his assistance as she mounted her pure white mare. The comtesse had offered her this, her finest horse, for the king's hunt. She knew that such an outstanding beast would help in Aimee's efforts to gain the attention of King Louis XV and his mistress. Aimee smoothed her emerald green satin skirts over the beast's back and straightened in the saddle.

"Help me with this tricorn, would you, Marie?" She struggled with the three-cornered hat and the long, sharp pins. "I can't seem to set it on my hair correctly."

"Don't, then. Most women don't wear them. They carry them or let them fall against their backs." Marie-Celeste regarded her critically. "You don't have nearly enough rouge on—"

"Marie, please." She frowned and pulled the hat off her head. She gathered the pins and put them in the pocket of her riding skirt. "It's bad enough I'm trussed up so tight I can barely breathe and this lace at my wrists is constantly getting in the way of the reins. How can I possibly ride with the hunters in such clothes?"

"You aren't supposed to ride with the hunters, my dear. You are just supposed to look decorative on the outskirts of the party." The comtesse kicked her mare and cantered toward the tight group of aristocrats gathered a small distance from the royal party. "Remember, when we see the royal party, don't be too bold. Don't stare—"

"Marie, I have been lectured on this too many times. I promise, I will cause the king no embarrassment by my presence. I suspect the Duc de Montchamp will be by my side for most of the hunt."

"I know." Marie frowned. "Are you sure you know what you are doing? That man has a reputation as corrupt as Richelieu's."

"You should have thought of that before you forced him on me at the Française," Aimee teased. "His reputation doesn't matter to me now. What does matter is that he wishes to bestow favor upon me—although his reasons are still suspect."

"He wants you as his mistress. When does a man want anything else from a woman?"

She tilted her head and raised it to the wavering sun of the late morning. "I don't think so. If he does, he's keeping quiet about his designs. He, truly, has been nothing but a gentleman the past two evenings."

"Yes, but I noticed he lost quite a bit of money to you at Madame d'Alençon's salon."

"Enough to buy this riding habit." She tilted her head and glared at the comtesse. "You don't think he lost on purpose?"

"I doubt it. You are uncommonly lucky at the card table.

I think that if you had been a man, the Baron de Wagneaux would have called you out last night for winning six thousand *livres* from him at piquet."

Aimee flushed. She still could not understand how in one evening she made one-third of a year's *rentes* at Château Bocage. The court was truly a different country; a country that had no real sense of the value of a gold *louis*. Her dress had been bought from her winnings, as had the services of a local hairdresser who had teased her straight hair into a semblance of fullness and piled the mass atop her head.

"You're pensive today, Aimee. Are you nervous?"

"Not nervous. It is just that things have changed so fast. A week ago I was determined to go into a convent, and now I'm planning my introduction at court."

"I have been trying to change your mind for a month! I'd like to know what the Duc de Montchamp said to finally convince you."

"He basically called me a coward."

"I should have thought of that."

She leaned over and tapped Marie playfully with her gloves. "I would have pulled your hair out if you had dared."

"I suppose you couldn't do that to the duke at the Comédie Française," the comtesse added, smiling. "It would have created such a scene that the actors and actresses would have stopped to watch."

"You mean they didn't?" Aimee groaned. "I felt as though every eye was upon me."

They eased their way through the outer circle of aristocrats until they found a spot not far from the royal hunting party. Several grooms struggled with the leashes of a dozen great red and white hounds who bayed in annoyance at their restraint. The hunting dogs leapt and wagged their tails for the attention of the monarch. Aimee gazed at the king of France with more than a little curiosity. Tall and

well built, the monarch cut a fine figure in his blue hunting
dress and tricorn, a large hunting knife at his belt. The
ubiquitous blue ribbon on his chest fluttered in the breeze.
Madame de Pompadour, dressed impeccably in a green
riding habit, watched him with as much admiration.

One hunter separated from the royal party and headed in
their direction. Aimee felt a hundred eyes follow his path
until he stopped directly before her.

The Duc de Montchamp looked different on a horse. The
elevation gave his short but powerful body an element of
grace. He handled the steed with skill. In the shade of his
tricorn his dark eyes gleamed with something other than
excitement at the hunt.

"You look absolutely breathtaking, Madame de Chacontier."

She nodded and suppressed the smile that always rose to
her lips in the face of outrageous compliments. "You, too,
look quite dashing in your hunting dress."

"Devilish costume," he said suddenly. "The knife keeps
ripping into my leg. Each time I hunt I limp for a week
until the cut heals."

"You should get a scabbard for it."

"That, my dear, would be flouting tradition."

"Indeed."

His gaze wandered over her slim body encased in the
rich satin and she lowered her eyes. "I am glad you decided to attend this hunting party, madame. This forest is
graced with your beauty."

"I am flattered more by your attention. It is not often a
woman of my low rank is honored with attention from a
duke," she said as she gazed meaningfully toward the king,
"especially in the royal presence."

"I hope, someday soon, that you will be a part of this
magnificent court, with my help." He lifted his tricorn to
her. "But for now, I must return. The Master of the Hounds

is giving me frightful looks for separating from the party.
Au revoir."

Aimee bowed her head as the duke left. As she raised
her gaze, she noticed the stares of both the king and Madame de Pompadour. Mindful of the comtesse's advice,
she turned away from the king and bestowed a respectful
nod on the marquise. She did not wait to see if it was
returned.

The horns sounded and the dogs were released. Flying
by in a red and white streak, the hounds headed toward the
edge of the forest with the cries of the royal hunting party
rising in their wake. When the party had passed, the rest of
the aristocrats followed at a safe distance. Aimee felt the
heat of her horse beneath her and had to suppress the urge
to fly after the hunters.

"Madame de Pompadour nodded to you, Aimee," the
comtesse whispered, catching up to her. "That's a good
sign."

"Why isn't she riding with the hunters?"

"Her health, she claims." The comtesse wrinkled her
nose. "I'd not want to ride with them, though—they ride
quite roughly."

Not since Normandy had she felt the power of a horse
beneath her, and Aimee wanted more than anything to ride
onward. She could feel the restlessness of some other
equestrians, but they reined their horses in carefully. She
wondered if she could ride off the track and race awhile,
then meet the party later.

"What are you thinking of?"

"This is a wonderful beast," she murmured. "I'd like to
give her her head."

"You'll get lost. It's dangerous, with those hunters
around."

"I'd ride in the opposite direction."

"Aimee, you'll attract attention."

"Isn't that what I came here to do?"

"Not in that way." The comtesse pulled up and forced her to do the same. "Come, Aimee. Don't be foolish."

"No one will ever know." She waited until the bulk of the aristocrats had passed, then glanced behind her at the row of carriages following. "Don't worry, Marie. I'll just give her her head for a while. Then I'll meet you. If anyone asks for me, simply say that I . . . Oh, I don't know. I had to powder."

Marie called her name as she kicked the mare out of the line of aristocrats. She plunged into the coolness of the forest and leaned low over the horse's neck. Her riding skirts flapped wildly on the horse's back, but the mare did not seem to mind. She rode recklessly through the thickening forest, reveling in the feel of the mare stretched beneath her. It had been so long since she'd ridden. It had been so long since she'd felt the fresh air against her skin. For the first time since she had left Normandy, she felt a little bit alive.

She discovered a stream and the mare slowed and walked along its banks. Aimee lifted her face to the sky and let the mare roam where it would. The horse stopped and lowered her great white head to the clear water and drank her fill. When she finished, she tasted some of the greenery that covered the lush banks. Aimee loosened her grip on the reins and gazed around the stream.

She could still hear the baying of the hounds in the distance and the occasional yell of a hunter. The hunt was still on. Marie-Celeste told her that it sometimes took hours for the royal party to capture and kill a stag, and that they would stop at two in the afternoon to indulge in dinner, before finishing the hunt. She knew she should not linger by the stream, but it was peaceful there.

She heard a rustling in the bushes. Tightening her grip on the reins, Aimee turned toward the darkness of the forest. She scanned the underbrush for signs of movement.

She did not fear a deer or a fox, but if the intruder were a boar or some other more dangerous beast, then she must leave before it endangered her and her mount.

Silence fell over the area. The birds stopped their singing. The gurgling of the stream seemed loud in the small clearing as Aimee once again heard the snap of a twig.

"Who's there?" she cried, hoping the sound would scare off any beasts hiding in the bushes. She squinted into the darkness and felt her first twinge of fear as the distinctive form of a horseman appeared between the trees.

Could it be the duke? Surely he wouldn't separate himself from the royal party?

"Monsieur de Montchamp, is that you?"

The rider stiffened, then moved out into the sunshine.

"It's not the duke, *a stor*."

Her blood froze to ice in her veins. The word echoed discordantly in her ears. She stared at the intruder with rounded eyes, wondering if she had truly lost her senses.

"Surprised to see me, Aimee?" His lips parted in an all-too-familiar smile. The light played among the tawny streaks of his hair. "Were you expecting the duke?"

He was dressed in a scarlet riding habit, gleaming with gold embroidery. The Order of Saint-Esprit fluttered on his shoulder. They were worlds away from Normandy, worlds away from the forest where they first met, yet Aimee felt as much fear as she had when she had first come upon Kilian de Laclos on the Bocage estate. He was still, despite his birth, a brigand and a thief.

Finding her senses again, Aimee pulled up on the reins and reared the mare around. Digging the heels of her boots into her sides, she urged the horse into a run. She heard the answering hooves of Kilian's mount and she lowered her body against the mare's neck. Kilian de Laclos would not harm her here, in the king's woods, not if she could prevent it. He would not touch her, he would not speak to her, he would not torment her. She concentrated on returning to the safety of the hunting party. Terror coursed through her veins and she wondered why the duke and Kilian had both returned to Paris. Would they always haunt her? Would they spend the rest of her life tossing her shame and her pain and her fear in her face?

He closed in behind her. She heard the heaving breath of his horse. Tightening her grip on her riding whip she rose in the saddle and lifted the whip high above her head. Staring straight into his green eyes, she snapped the whip down upon his outstretched arm.

"Leave me be!" she cried as he drew back. Aimee took advantage of the break to veer her mare off in another direction, but Kilian was too quick and blocked her path.

Breathless, she stopped and faced him. He nursed his arm as he watched her. A slight smile fluttered across his lips. "I see you are still angry at me."

The rage boiled over. "Why did you come here?"

"My aim was not to frighten you, Aimee." He sidestepped and prevented her from escaping. "I simply wanted to talk to you. I would have made my presence known sooner, but you looked so lovely seated on that white horse, staring into the waters, that I did not want to interrupt."

"Stop." She flung her riding whip at him and he caught it easily in one hand. "Leave me alone, Kilian de Laclos. I want nothing to do with you."

"Obviously." He tossed the whip back to her. "Aren't you even going to ask about Château Bocage?"

Her eyes narrowed. "Château Bocage is none of my concern anymore. You made quite sure of that."

"That was not my goal, *a stor*."

She could not listen anymore. Pulling her horse away, Aimee glared at him with anger. She felt a strange urge to cry in frustration as he prevented her from passing him anew. She tossed her riding whip at him again, but this time she aimed for his horse.

As his horse whinnied and pranced back, she broke through and passed him at a gallop. "Leave me alone, Laclos," she yelled. "You've done enough harm."

CHAPTER

12

"You're not two hours into Paris and already you've sent me on some job," Eamon O'Sullivan said loudly, his Irish brogue thickening his French into muddled, almost unintelligible sounds. He pounded his mug on the uneven boards of the tavern's table. "What happened to the man who used to greet his friends with a mug, eh? Now that you've got another title to your name, are you too good to be drinking with your mates?"

Kilian sat across from the florid-faced Irishman and smiled wryly. "All I asked, Eamon, is if you bought the costume."

He waved his burly arms in theatrical circles. "Aye, I've got the damned costume, may the devil take it, and you, to hell!"

Kilian gestured to the innkeeper as Eamon finished the last of his ale. The man brought a second mug without a murmur and placed it before him. "Come, O'Sullivan. I've promised you I would help Bonnie Prince Charles in the

French court. Haven't I done enough for you to warrant a small favor?"

The Irishman sobered behind his flaming red beard and settled down across the table. "Ach, of course you have, Laclos. But to send me off without a proper greeting—"

"If I had given you a proper greeting, you'd never be in shape to do what I asked."

A light entered Eamon's blue eyes. "I've done more than one favor with my fire lit, Laclos. You know that well."

"Aye, but this is a matter I wish to keep quiet, for now," he added. "No one suspected you?"

"I paid them all quite grandly to keep their mouths shut."

"Not too grandly, I hope."

Eamon's face flamed nearly as red as the beard that obscured his cheekbones. "You be doubting me, Laclos." He broke into a smile. "This must be about that woman, that 'ristocrat that I told you about to lure you back to Paris."

Kilian's eyes flared, and Eamon shook his great lion's mane and laughed heartily, drawing the disapproving attention of most of the tavern. "I knew it. After all the prince's bribes and promises of glory, I manage to lure you here with one word about that fine lass. I'll have to tell him that it's women, not battle glory, that strikes your fancy now."

Eamon O'Sullivan knew him too well, Kilian thought ruefully. They had spent too much time on the battlefield in Scotland, fighting with the Stuart prince. After having crawled half-naked through heather past enemy lines and having stitched each other's wounds by the light of dimmed, smokeless fires, there was nothing Kilian could hide from the Irishman. In such a war men's souls were forced close to their skins. Eamon knew every twitch of his face.

"Ah," he said in satisfaction. "I am right. All's forgiven then, though you'd best greet me proper with a pint of ale next time."

"Only if you swear to keep your damned voice down,"

he admonished. He took a deep draught of the bitter brew. "This is quite serious. I'll not have it ruined by your drunken rantings."

"You know me better." Eamon sobered a bit and slammed his cup down on the table. The innkeeper replaced it with a full one. Once the man had left, he lowered his voice. "I approached one of the Duc de Montchamp's servants in the market this afternoon. He told me the duke planned to attend the king's costume party dressed as a laurel tree—"

"A laurel tree?"

"Yes. The king has something planned, so half the dukes in his court are dressing alike." He shrugged. "Don't ask me to figure out the whims of the court. I bought you an identical costume, and it's now waiting in your town house."

"You've done well."

"'Twas a simple task, for all the trouble you're making of it."

"There'll be more trouble before the thing is done, Eamon." He leaned back in his chair. "The lady ran away from me like a fury this afternoon. If I fail tonight, then I shall be asking you for more such favors."

Eamon's bushy red brows lifted high on his forehead. "What? Is this woman not falling over you? I thought there wasn't a lass on God's green earth who wasn't willing to hitch her skirts for the likes of you."

Kilian frowned. "This is a lady. And I haven't treated her right, I'm afraid."

"A woman's anger is nothing but a bee buzzing around a jar of honey. You'll sweeten her."

"This woman's anger is far more serious. She's more likely to stab me in my own bed."

Eamon stared at him in incredulity. "I believe you're in love."

"Keep your voice down."

"And she's not in love with you."

"Not yet." Shrugging his wide shoulders, he leaned back in the chair. "But winning a woman's heart can't be any more difficult than winning a battle, eh, Eamon?"

"I think not," he mumbled, a smile twitching around his lips. "Especially for such a soldier as you, *mo cara.*"

"Then you shall help me if I fail tonight?"

"With pleasure, but"—he lifted his mug—"only if you learn proper manners."

Kilian signaled to the tavern keeper. "I'll keep your damned mug full of ale. But mind you, I'm quite serious. I'm going to win this woman back if it means selling my soul."

"I won't let it come to that. *Ar ghrá Dé,* I never thought I'd hear you speak about a lass like this."

"And you never will again." Kilian sobered and lifted his own mug. "Now, tell me of Prince Charles. I have heard things at court, and none of them are complimentary."

"And they are all true, I fear." His lips curled in disgust. "The prince has turned on us, Laclos. He is becoming more and more a 'ristocrat and less a prince fighting for his rightful English throne. You'd hardly recognize him now. He never wears his tartan and all he does is buy gold plate and dance. He's got all the women of Paris lusting after him."

"No talk of returning to Scotland?"

"Aye, there's plenty of talk. But it's just talk. The prince whines like a babe that King Louis refuses to subsidize the invasion and then, in the same breath, refuses the pension the king has promised him. He's grown fat and soft and sotted."

"He never was quite the same after his defeat at Culloden."

"He was at his best when he was hiding out after Culloden," Eamon said. "It was after he returned to Paris and received all this damned adulation. He listens to those stubborn Scots and no one else. He has set up his own little court, complete with a titled mistress, but I don't see how he's ever going to win back the English crown for his family if he doesn't start doing more than dancing with the French ladies." He sneered. "And all the work of our fathers and our grandfathers, Kilian—it is all for naught. If the prince continues like this, there'll never be a Stuart on the English throne and all their promises for freedom of religion in Ireland will crumble to dust."

Kilian sat back and watched his friend. The disgust was evident on his face. Eamon O'Sullivan had once been a close adviser to the prince when they had invaded Scotland.

"The talk at court was quite sour against the prince," Kilian agreed, "at least in the mouths of the ministers. I am afraid I have bad news, Eamon. The peace treaty France has signed requires that the king remove the prince from French soil."

"They wouldn't dare!"

"I'm afraid, old friend, that they would. Now that the war is over between us and England, France no longer needs to stir up trouble in Scotland. It seems that King Louis didn't care as much about returning the English throne to the Stuart family as he did about splitting English armies between Scotland and the war in Europe." He shook his head. "Now England is demanding we exile the young pretender and recognize their own Hanoverian throne."

"Blasphemy! How could this happen?"

"It is very simple, my friend. The Comte de Saint-Severin took my place at the bargaining table in Aix-la-Chapelle when I left for Normandy, and unlike me, he is no friend of the prince. He and the king have bargained for peace above all else."

Eamon's eyes blazed. "Blasted coward, Louis XV!"

"Keep your voice down."

"He's stabbing the prince in the back with a royal dagger!"

"Yes, it does seem so." Kilian finished the last of his ale. "If the prince had not been so arrogant after the Scottish campaign, in refusing King Louis's pension, perhaps this would *not* have happened. For a young prince, he is surprisingly ignorant in the ways of diplomacy."

"You'd not know it, looking at him now. When did you discover this information?"

"Only this afternoon, at the king's hunt. You should tell him. He should know what forces are working against him. Maybe he will listen to you instead of those Scots."

"Are you absolutely sure of this?"

Kilian lifted a brow. "Now who is being suspicious, O'Sullivan?"

"Aye, you've got me there. I just find it hard to believe that King Louis would do such a thing."

"It is not the king, it's his advisers."

"As always."

Kilian rose. "We shall talk at length later, Eamon. The king's ball will be starting soon and I must try on the costume you bought for me."

Eamon's lips curled as Kilian walked away. "You should look good in green hose, Laclos. Like an oversized leprechaun hiding in a tree stump."

Eamon's words rang in his head as Kilian stepped out of his carriage and entered Versailles. The bulky costume covered his body from his head down to mid-thigh, and though Kilian knew Aimee could not possibly tell the difference between him and the Duc de Montchamp, he did wish the king had chosen more comfortable costumes for his ball. The two slits that served for his eyes scarcely gave enough light to see.

The ball had started hours ago, and the effect of the generous quantities of champagne already showed. Young women scurried over the floor away from noblemen whose identities were barely concealed by the decorative masks. The king, he was told, had arrived earlier with seven or eight other laurel trees. The court women who vied for Madame de Pompadour's position rushed around trying to guess which laurel tree was the monarch.

Kilian reached for a glass of champagne as he entered the well-lit ballroom. The heat of thousands of tapers, combined with the crush of guests, made the mirrored room unbearably stifling. The music rose in melodious strings above the laughter of the courtiers, but few people danced in the heat. Liveried servants raced in and out of the ballroom carrying glasses of champagne. A table full of hors d'oeuvres had already been decimated. He wondered, as he pushed through the masses into the interior room, if he would even be able to find Aimee in the crush.

But he did. Immediately. How could he miss her? With her long, sleek hair and graceful body she stood above the rows of voluptuous, bewigged aristocrats like a queen among peasants. She was dressed as Diana, the hunter, and the graceful draping of ivory silk trimmed with gold ribbon did justice to the subtle curves of her lean body.

His heart lurched with love. She was breathtaking. The gleam of pain that lingered in her eyes seemed to make her more beautiful. No wonder she had been described as being as cold as a princess of the blood, he thought. Her sadness made her seem aloof and ephemeral. He could tell she did not want to be here. It was his fault she struggled to enter the teeming nest of intrigues called the court of Versailles. She had no other choice in life except a convent. For her, that was no choice at all.

He wanted to approach her, take off his mask, pull her into his arms and whisper that he loved her until she forgave him for his folly. He wanted to fall to his knees and beg her forgiveness, and he would do so if he thought it would win back her heart.

He knew from their brief encounter this afternoon that the five weeks that had separated them had done nothing to cool her anger, or ease her pain. He was not surprised. In her eyes, he had debauched her, stolen her château, betrayed her trust, and shamed her before an aristocrat of France. He knew that now. He had spent five weeks trying to understand what had happened. He also knew it would take more than time to heal those wounds.

But heal they would. He had sworn to it. The four lonely weeks he had spent in *her* house, filling out *her* ledgers, watching over *her* fields, sleeping in *her* bed, had been torture—enough to last a lifetime. Her spirit haunted the ancient castle. Many an evening he had risen from bed at the sound of her voice, many an afternoon he had looked up from his work, thinking he had seen the twitch of her long, black hair. It was Aimee de Chacontier who ruled in that castle, still, long after she had left it. He was an intruder. And as though to punctuate her loss, the capricious Norman weather had released storms so brutal that half the spring crops were ruined.

Kilian watched as she leaned toward her escort. He knew immediately that the laurel tree that stood beside her was the Duc de Montchamp.

He scowled behind the silk screen of the costume. The vision of Aimee and the duke, embracing, rose to his mind, as it had a hundred times before. As he watched them, he wondered if they were as intimate as he feared. Kilian knew the Duc de Montchamp was working to have Aimee introduced at court, and he swore that he would kill the aristocrat if he dared elicit another bargain from Aimee.

He would kill the aristocrat anyway. Jolivette's death still hung heavy on his mind, but if the duke dared touch Aimee. . . . Aye, he would kill the duke. But not yet. He had one other goal to reach before the duke received his

just punishment. He had to win back the trust and love of
Aimee de Chacontier.

That, he thought, remembering the cut of her silver gray
eyes, would be no mean feat.

Kilian waved away the attentions of several young
women who approached him, wondering if he were the
king. He watched with growing anger as the Duc de Montchamp took Aimee's hand and led her in a minuet.

The anger burned higher, but he forced himself to remain calm. Aimee seemed to think that the Duc de Montchamp was innocent of all crimes—yet didn't she know
about Jolivette? Perhaps she chose to deny that tale when
she discovered Kilian's true identity. Kilian watched as a
footman approached the duke and whispered in his ear. The
duke then led Aimee off the floor and bowed awkwardly in
the costume. He left her side.

Kilian moved behind a cluster of aristocrats as the duke
exited through the ballroom doors. Aimee looked around
the room and headed toward one of the windows. He
waited for two minutes to tick off on a nearby brass clock,
then walked in her direction.

She stood just outside the doors and lifted her face to the
sky. The air had cooled and her nostrils flared as she
breathed in the lingering scent of wisteria. Seductive
laughter rose in the well-pruned length of the enormous
garden. Kilian stopped in the doorway and watched her. A
breeze moved the folds of her tunic about her legs.

"Ah, monsieur!" she said suddenly, noticing him. "Back
so soon?" Her smile disappeared. "Did the interview with
the marquise not go well?"

Kilian sucked in his breath as she looked at him. He had
forgotten how lovely her face was in repose. He had seen it
so often distorted in fury. Her arched brows drew together
over her clear eyes as she waited for his response.

"What is it, monsieur? Has the marquise asked me to
leave?" She lifted a hand to her cheek. "I knew I should

not have accepted her hasty invitation. She was so angry that Kil—Monsieur de Laclos had arrived at the hunting party unexpected, that she extended the invitation to me in pity and without thought."

Kilian, remembering that the duke was trying to get Aimee introduced to court, suddenly understood. "*Au contraire*, madame," he murmured, imitating the duke's baritone as closely as possible. "She wishes to see you now. Come."

"Now?!"

He took her arm and led her back into the ballroom. He eased her through the crowds until they reached the foyer, then he turned down a hall into the first of several successive private apartments.

"But . . . but the marquise's apartments are in the other direction," she said as he dragged her through a carved door into yet another apartment. He closed the door behind her. "Really, you are being all too mysterious."

"The marquise wanted to see you alone. She's going to take the secret stairway to one of the king's rooms. Come." Kilian, knowing that the king and his courtiers were well involved in the ball, pushed open one of the doors that led to the king's private apartments. Glancing around, he made sure that they were alone. Then he closed the door firmly behind them.

"There are no candles here!" she exclaimed, stepping back. The moonlight illuminated the room and she sighed as she realized it was only a sitting room. "Really, Monsieur le Duc. Such secrecy. Is this truly necessary?"

"I'm afraid so." He no longer bothered to mask his voice. Pulling one arm, then the other from the silk and wire "tree," he lifted the contraption over his head and placed it beside a short-armed chair. He smoothed his tousled hair and faced her.

"No." She lifted a hand to her chest and whirled around.

Racing in the dark, she tripped over a small table and fell
to the hardwood floor. He fell on her.

"Are you hurt?"

"Get off me!" she cried. "I swear I'll scream."

"Don't, Aimee. Screaming will start a scene and at this
point in your rise to the court you don't need any scandal."

"Since when am I afraid of scandal?"

"I know you too well, *a stor*. You won't cause a scandal
unless there's a purpose for it." Rising from the floor, he
brushed off his breeches and then reached down to assist
her. She slapped away his hands.

"Leave me alone!"

"That seems to be your battle call lately."

"Then why don't you heed it?"

"Because I don't want to, *a stor*."

"Don't call me that."

" 'Tis your name, and I am partial to it," he said, bringing back a rush of memories of another time and place.
How little things changed, whether in the woods of Normandy or an anteroom in Versailles. He still battled with
this woman for her heart.

She shook him off and he did not try to overwhelm her.
How easy it would be, to just sweep her up into his arms
and make love to her. He was so much stronger than she.
He could control her body but, in the process, he would
lose her soul. In the end, it was her soul he wanted the
most.

He stepped away. She glanced behind him to the closed
door.

"Don't try to leave. You won't escape, and you'll only
find yourself on the floor again."

"I managed to avoid you this afternoon."

"But you didn't escape, my sweet. I chose to let you go.
There were too many people in the king's royal hunting
party, and I needed to speak to you alone."

She crossed her arms in front of her and the quiver of

arrows that lay strapped to her back jiggled. She tilted her chin and stared Kilian in the eye. "I see nothing has changed, Laclos."

"*Au contraire.* Many things have changed. I am now the Vicomte de Bocage, and I own your estate."

"Do you think I need to be reminded?"

The guilt again. "No," he said softly. He resisted the urge to trace the smooth line of her cheek. "I'm afraid I reminded you a bit too brutally in Normandy."

"Indeed you did." She turned away and walked toward one of the curtained windows. The moonlight spilled through the gossamer hangings and shimmered on her pale skin. "You've gone to great lengths to get me alone. Should I ask why?"

The words *I'm sorry, forgive me, a stor* lingered in Kilian's head, but somehow, faced with her anger, they sounded hollow. "I wanted to see if there was a way for you to forgive me."

She whirled toward him, her eyes wide and incredulous. She searched his gaze as if she could not believe what she had just heard. Then, she laughed.

He had not expected this. He had not expected such frigid, controlled anger. Her eyes were as hard as chips of ice. The laughter lingered in the painted ceiling. Her face, bathed in the moonlight, was as cold and white as alabaster.

"First the duke, and now you," she said in disbelief. "You tear my life apart and then expect me to accept an apology. What is it, Kilian? Why this sudden remorse? Are you upset because your plan to separate the duke and me has failed?"

"I will not lie to you. It does not please me to see you with the duke."

"How dare you come to me, after all you have done, and try once again to trick me."

"This is no trick."

"And I suppose the ruse at Château Bocage was no trick as well? Pretending you were a mere foot soldier when actually you were an officer of the French army? Pretending you were a commoner when you were a courtier of Versailles?"

Kilian sighed. "I needed to keep my identity secret."

"In order to wreak your vengeance on the Duc de Montchamp."

"The duke shamed and killed my sister."

"Are you so sure of that?"

Kilian's eyes flickered in anger. The duke and Aimee had obviously talked about Jolivette, and Aimee had listened to the duke's deceptive lies. He tightened his fists and lowered his voice. "Yes. My sister lies in unconsecrated ground, Aimee. The duke deserved all that I have done to him."

"And me, Kilian?" she asked softly. "Did I deserve what you did to me? You shamed me. And raped me of the one thing I held dear—Château Bocage." She shook her head vigorously in angry bewilderment. "The answer to your question, Laclos, is no. I won't ever forgive you for what you've done."

He had underestimated the depths of her pain and anger. He wondered, with a lingering sense of hopelessness, if the anger obliterated all those tender feelings that had burgeoned in Normandy. He could see no trace of them in her eyes. As he watched her, a seed of his own fury grew in his belly. Her damned Château Bocage. He had nearly forgotten that she had chosen that castle over him, right before he had obtained it. It was the one thing she valued above all others.

"Ah yes, Château Bocage," he murmured. "I remember quite well that you chose *that*, and the Duc de Montchamp, over me."

"I chose the welfare of my people and the continuance of my estate over you—it is you, with your twisted ideas of vengeance, who made it a matter between you and the Duc de Montchamp."

He closed the distance between them. "And if I proposed marriage to you now, would you accept?"

"Marriage?!" She lifted her chin defiantly. "Yes, Kilian. I would accept, for one reason. Château Bocage. It is the only reason I would ever marry a man as despicable as you."

"Not for love?"

She stepped back as if struck. "Love?" Her eyes narrowed. "I never loved you."

"Didn't you?" He approached her until her back was against the silk wallpaper. "Didn't you love me that night, when we made love in your bed—"

"That was not love," she interrupted. "Love is when two people trust each other. That night, Kilian, you did not trust me."

Her words, though spoken softly, held the force of daggers. Kilian wondered if she had learned all this quiet hatred from him. He had received the answer to his question—she did not love him anymore. Her love had twisted and metamorphosed to hate. He watched her face, tight and shut in the moonlight. At least she was not indifferent. Hate he could battle. Indifference he could not.

"You did not trust me either." He reached out and touched her cheek though she cringed and turned away. "Did you ever wonder what would have happened, Aimee, if you had trusted me that night instead of insisting on keeping the bargain with the Duc de Montchamp?"

She lifted her arms and whirled away from his touch. "How could I trust a man who would not tell me his true identity?"

"If you had listened to your heart you might not be in the same situation as you are now."

"What would I be, then? Your mistress receiving, for her

services, room and board in Château Bocage? Until you tired of me?"

He followed her, whirled her around, and clutched her arms. "That was the duke's bargain. I offered you marriage."

"That was *before* I discovered who you are. You told me to trust you, but you never told me why. How could I expect that the man I found poaching on my estate was a war hero and a beloved member of Louis XV's court? You asked me to give up everything for you, and you did not even tell me your true name."

"I offered you my protection, my name, and my love." He shook her gently. "Remember? Yet you chose the duke."

"The duke had my estate. I had no other choice."

"If I had told you who I was, would you have chosen differently?"

Aimee hesitated and Kilian saw the flicker of doubt in her eyes. Her brows lowered. "That was a long time ago, Kilian. A lifetime ago. The fact is that you did *not* trust me with that information, and that changed everything."

"And if I had?"

"Don't do this," she snapped. "You are trying to force me to say things I don't want to say."

He released her and she wandered away. He watched her as she approached the window and clutched the gossamer curtains. A curl tumbled down her back and brushed the curve of her hips. He tightened his hands. He wanted so much to reach for it and wind it around his fingers.

He wanted so much to erase all the pain and have her love him as he loved her.

"So what happens now, Laclos?" she asked. "I suppose you shall stay here, in court?"

"Yes."

"Then I shall leave it." She folded her arms in front of her. "I came to Paris to avoid you. I knew you were a member of court, but I assumed you would go off and fight in another war."

"I am already fighting a war, *a stor*."

Her chin tightened, but she ignored his statement. "The duke is here, as well. I suppose you shall continue to wreak your vengeance against him? Or did you do enough harm in Normandy?"

"The duke shall die for what he did to Jolivette. That I promise you." His voice lowered. "And if he touches you again, I shall take that as a personal insult."

"The duke and I are friends."

"I see." The anger surged to his skin. "Is he receiving the benefit of your charms?"

"How dare you!" She whirled on him. "You, of all people, have no right to ask me that question."

He knew she was right and he flexed his tightened fists. Her eyes cut him with anger. Straightening his waistcoat, he stepped away from her quivering body.

"You are right. I have no right to ask that question." He sighed and shook his head. "I hope you decide to stay in Paris and pursue an introduction to court, Aimee. I . . ." He hesitated as he looked at her face. "I will no longer bother you with my attentions, if that is what you wish."

She stood, dazed, for a moment. "You have not been known to keep your promises."

"This one, I swear, I shall keep."

"On your honor?"

Her words cut him. "Yes. On my honor."

In a fluid flash of ivory silk, Aimee de Chacontier left the dimness of the king's antechamber and slammed the door behind her.

He had lost her. As surely as he had lost Jolivette. If there were no embers left burning in the ashes he could not hope to stoke them into a fire; how could he expect to revive a love that no longer existed in her heart? He ran his fingers through his hair.

He had failed tonight, but he never entered a battle without a second strategy. He wagered that this war would be long and difficult. He could not wield patience and control as well as he could wield a sword, and his enemy was hidden behind Aimee de Chacontier's lovely gray eyes. He knew that in a single week in the French court she had garnered a few powerful friends, as well. The Marquise de Pompadour was not pleased with him, he was told, and the Duc de Montchamp was a visible, and powerful, enemy.

Kilian sank down in a hardwood chair near the windows. Before he tried to win her love, he must save her again from the Duc de Montchamp. Kilian knew he could marry her. But to marry her now would be to give up the one thing he owned that she wanted. He had learned, in the years and years of warring, never to retreat until the treaty was signed; never to give up the gold until the feat was accomplished. Someday he would marry Aimee, aye, and it would be a lovely thing. But it would be a thing of love and not of money.

He had a single advantage. He had Château Bocage.

He would use it as bait.

CHAPTER

13

"In God's name, what are you doing, Marie?" Aimee asked as she entered one of the dressing rooms on the second floor of the Princesse de Talmond's Parisian town house. She watched in incredulity as the comtesse, covered from neck to foot with several sheets, ran back and forth in front of an oak dressing table. Two of the princess's servants waved feather dusters full of rice powder in the air.

"I'm powdering," she wheezed.

Aimee coughed as she breathed in some of the residue. She lifted a perfumed, lace-edged linen to her nose. "Really, Marie-Celeste. Why don't you just brush it on like everyone else?" Powder hung in the air and coated most of the room like a dusting of early winter snow. "Look at this room! We asked for this room to refreshen ourselves before going downstairs, not to dress! Didn't you already powder before we left?"

"Yes." She stared at her reflection in her dresser mirror. "But I wanted to look my best, and this way I'll only catch the finest particles of powder on my skin. You *do* know who is to be at this salon tonight?"

Aimee rolled her eyes as the comtesse pulled off the sheet that covered her golden silk dress and brushed some powder from the bodice. "Of course I know. How could I not? You've been talking of nothing but him for weeks."

"Wait until you see him, Aimee, and you, too, will be tossing your linen at him." Reaching for her silk fan, the comtesse took Aimee's arm and walked out of the dressing room. The hall was wide and empty and Marie's whispers reverberated off the silk-papered walls. "He's tall and young and sharp-eyed with the bearing of a true king. And the stories I have heard! Of the battles in Scotland, where he himself rode into the fray, of his adventures as he hid from the English army in the isles, of dressing as a lady's maid to pass through—"

"I have heard them all, Marie. At least twice."

Marie pulled her to a stop near the head of the curving staircase. The murmur of conversation rose from the lower floor. "You seem prepared to dislike the prince on sight."

"He reminds me a little too much of someone else."

Marie pursed her lips. "I tell you—he's nothing like that blackguard of yours."

"That blackguard is not mine."

"Bonnie Prince Charles is a fine prince and a fine man. I wager he shall turn your head."

"I doubt it."

Marie-Celeste frowned. She glanced at Aimee's silver gray satin dress trimmed with ivory ribbon. A strand of small pearls encircled her neck and made her skin all the more translucent. "When *are* you going to take a lover, my friend?"

"You shouldn't get your hopes up." She clutched her reticule. "It will be a long time before I take a lover, especially now that I've been introduced to court."

"Being introduced to court has only given you all the

more reason to take a lover. Everyone else in court has one. What about the Duc de Montchamp?" Marie drew Aimee toward the stairs. "Now, I know I didn't approve of him, at first, but he has been such a gentleman, especially after arranging your introduction. I wonder. . . ." She glanced at Aimee through thick lashes. "I wonder if he will also arrange a pension for you."

"I don't know. Nor does it matter, for I have no plans of taking anyone as a lover. You'll just have to get used to it."

"You don't know what you're missing."

"Yes, I do."

They descended to the first floor where a footman, dressed in the red and gold livery of the house, announced their arrival. Aimee and Marie walked between the two rows of card tables toward the Princesse de Talmond. After extending their greetings, they retreated to a far end of the salon where the comtesse settled down with a glass of champagne and began to survey the guests.

"There he is," she hissed, elbowing Aimee and gesturing to one of the far tables. "I knew he'd be here. He's the one with the St. Andrew's cross hanging by a green ribbon. He's wearing his own hair."

Aimee glanced in the direction that the comtesse indicated. The prince played cards with great concentration, but her gaze did not linger on him. The tall man who sat across from him immediately caught her attention.

The comtesse saw him at the same time. "*Sacré bleu!* That man haunts us, *ma cherie.*"

Aimee swallowed the lump that lodged in her throat. She had seen Kilian twice since the night of the king's costume ball. She kept hoping he would return to Normandy, but she knew the Chevalier de Bourg-en-Bresse too well. Though he promised not to force his attentions on her, she knew that he would do all he could to torment her. "It's quite all right, Marie," she whispered. "He is a member of the court and belongs here, probably more than I do."

"If he dares to come near you—"

"He won't. He ignored me at the Comédie Française, and he ignored me at court. I suspect he will do the same here."

Her words were a half lie. Though he had not spoken a word to her since the night of the costume ball, Aimee had felt his gaze on her many times. Once, he had nodded in greeting. Kilian did not ignore but neither did he press. The fact that he seemed to be keeping his promise surprised her and she wondered, with a touch of anxiety, when he would finally break it.

She wished he would just stop appearing at the same functions. She could bear the endless, regimented, ritualized court activities if she were not forced to gaze upon the man who had once held her in lovemaking. In the past week, she had watched him flirt with Madame de Sassenage and she had watched him dance around the marbled floors of Versailles. He was a handsome man, and she had begun to realize that she was not immune to his charm.

She looked at him from beneath her lashes. He did not wear a wig. His fair hair was held with a black ribbon at the nape. Bereft of the locks that normally obscured it, his forehead was wide and broad and his slashing brows seemed more severe over his clear green eyes. The chandelier above him threw light on his cheekbones and left his cheeks in the shadow. As she watched, he turned and met her gaze.

She started and turned away. The comtesse stiffened beside her and glared at him, but Aimee could still feel the heat of his gaze on her body.

"He's not looking anymore, Aimee." Marie clicked her tongue. "He's got the eyes of the devil."

"And the soul of one," she agreed as her gaze slipped back to him. He wore a dark green satin waistcoat and breeches and rich boots that reached to his knees. She wondered why she had never suspected that he was an aristocrat when he was in Normandy. He fit into this background better than he had ever fit at her castle.

"Aimee, you really mustn't stare," the comtesse warned. "Perhaps we should find a table for you to watch."

She flushed. "Am I that obvious?"

"Yes." The comtesse looked at her curiously. "Though, from a distance, one would not know whether you were staring at the chevalier or the prince." She lifted a brow. "Did the prince turn your head, *mon amie?*"

"Indeed not. Don't worry, I shan't compete with you for the attentions of the notorious prince. You do your best, but be careful that the Princesse de Talmond doesn't see you and cross you off her list of guests." She rose and smoothed the satin of her skirt over her panniers. "Let's watch a game of *brélau*. I'm not yet completely familiar with the rules."

"Ah yes, another game for you to use to relieve all of us innocent aristocrats of our money." Marie knocked Aimee on the arm with her fan. "Even if the king doesn't give you a pension you will still be able to make your fortune at the card table."

"Only if these aristocrats continue to play with me," Aimee murmured. "I have won so much I fear that I shall soon be shunned from card parties."

"Your own fault, my dear, for being so devilishly lucky." The comtesse noticed an empty seat near a table three down from the prince's. "Come, let's watch here. I insist you sit." She lowered her voice. "You'll be less obvious sitting, and I want to capture the prince's attention."

"Who will be more obvious, Marie?" Aimee settled in the vacant chair and twisted it so she could not see the last table. The Princesse de Conti, who was at her court presentation yesterday afternoon, sat beside her. Aimee nodded a greeting and began the light, bantering conversation that filled every social occasion.

A game of *brélau* continued on the table. A pile of

painted wooden chips grew in the center. Aimee watched the Baron de Belleval as he carelessly tossed down his cards, and shook her head. It was no wonder she could win so much money at these games: Half the aristocrats played as if they did not care if they lost.

The comtesse's hands tightened on her shoulders and Aimee turned around. A large crowd of aristocrats had gathered at the rear table. The prince stood up and tossed a pile of wooden chips into the air.

"The game doesn't please you, Your Excellency?"

Aimee recognized Kilian's smooth voice and for a moment her blood pounded hard and loud in her ears. Clutching her bodice she took a deep breath.

"It lacks excitement, Chevalier." The prince fingered a token. "Perhaps if we played for something more significant than money it would have more interest for me."

Kilian laughed. "I can't play you for England and Scotland, *mon ami*."

"Not yet, at least." The prince's young face broke into a grin. "I do, however, have a set of gold plate made by King Louis's goldsmith, worth well over a hundred thousand of these tokens." The prince leaned over the table. "What do you have, Chevalier, that could match that?"

The hairs on the back of Aimee's neck prickled. She straightened in her chair. Conversation stopped, as did all sound in the smoky salon, as she waited in dread for Kilian's response.

"I have a small estate in Normandy," he said quietly. "It may match that sum, if the title goes with it."

The comtesse's hands held her down into the chair. All eyes suddenly turned in her direction. All of Paris knew that Kilian's Norman estate was once hers. The entire sickening relationship between her, the Duc de Montchamp, and the Chevalier de Bourg-en-Bresse had been served up as public gossip for weeks. How ruthless of Kilian to thrust it back into the light. It took every ounce of Aimee's will not to curse. *Château Bocage is mine! It is not yours! You have no right to barter my land!*

But he did, for Château Bocage was his. Indeed, what did it matter whether he kept it or sold it? It was forever lost to her. Somehow, the thought of its being in anyone else's hands—other than Kilian's—pushed it that much farther away. Aimee squared her shoulders beneath the comtesse's firm grip. She could not do anything about this wager, but neither could she ignore its existence.

She sat stubbornly facing their direction. The prince accepted the wager.

They began to play piquet. The crowds thickened around the last table. The salon silenced. The men called their hands aloud. Kilian called a point and a *tierce* major, but the prince claimed a *quatorze*. Kilian led the play, the prince got the point, then Kilian the next. Aimee closed her eyes and added up the scores in her head.

Kilian won the first hand. The men bantered as if a title, a parcel of land, and a hundred thousand *livres* of gold plate were not at stake. Aimee's heart pounded in her chest as Kilian dealt the second hand.

The prince called carte blanche, and Aimee's heart leapt in joy. Though carte blanche gave him ten points, it did not lend itself to winning tricks or points—and therefore the game. True to her thoughts, Kilian won the points and sequences again, plus a majority of tricks, and he easily topped one hundred points.

"You've won the first round only, Chevalier," the prince warned. "Three out of five for a *partie*."

"Indeed." Kilian handed the prince the other deck. "It is your deal, Your Excellency."

The comtesse leaned over Aimee's shoulder. "You don't have to stay here and listen to this," she whispered. "I will leave with you now."

"No. I'm going to stay. This was once my estate and I shall witness what that . . . blackguard . . . is doing with it."

Several aristocrats who sat nearby overheard Aimee's impassioned whisper and repeated it across the salon. If the situation weren't so sad, Aimee would have laughed at the murmurs that rippled through the room like so many waves in the sea.

"You can find out in the morning, Aimee."

"Marie."

"Very well," she said in exasperation. "I don't know why you insist on putting yourself through this."

Aimee tilted her head to better hear the calls, but the men had lowered their voices. The aristocrats, never able to stay silent for long, began to talk excitedly among themselves. She could hardly keep track of the game in the noise.

The prince won the second round. Aimee closed her eyes. She wondered how Kilian and the prince could remain so calm when the stakes were so high—or perhaps, to such aristocrats, these were not high stakes. She could scarcely sit still when there were a thousand *livres* on the table. What sangfroid! She could never risk so much.

The idea sprang into her head with the force of a blow. She opened her eyes and tightened her hands on her reticule. Why hadn't she thought of this before? What folly had prevented her from thinking of this from the first?

What, truly, did she have to lose? She had won nearly twenty thousand *livres* at cards in the past weeks. Perhaps it was not worth the prince's gold plate, and she knew it was not worth Château Bocage, but it was a considerable sum. She bit her lower lip. If she could excite the winner's gaming instincts, she could wrestle a chance at owning Château Bocage once again.

Aimee ticked off the risks in her mind. She was a woman, and there was a good chance that if the prince won this wager with Kilian, he would not accept her subsequent challenge. She was also known to be exceptionally skilled at cards. But they were playing piquet, and her skill in this game was not yet known to them. If Kilian won, he might laugh at her offer and shame her in front of the entire salon. Aimee's eyes narrowed on the back of his blond head. That was no matter, for she had felt shame before, at his hands. She would have to shame him into taking her challenge.

"The chevalier has won the third round, Aimee," the comtesse whispered in her ear. "Are you sure you don't want to leave?"

"I am not leaving."

The decision made, Aimee waited in serenity for the *partie* to end. She no longer cared who won, for the winner would receive yet another challenge. It was her right to challenge the owner of Château Bocage, for the estate was originally hers. Her heart beat harder in her chest. She would win at piquet, no matter who she played. She could almost smell the rich Norman earth.

She missed Château Bocage—more now than ever, now that she sat and watched it bartered for so casually. The past week's ennui suddenly left her, and her whole body seethed with excitement. She might leave this salon tonight a vicomtesse. She might leave this salon and travel straight to Château Bocage.

The comtesse began tapping the back of Aimee's chair with her sharp fingernails. Aimee reached up and stopped her. "It's all right, Marie-Celeste."

"That man should be drawn and quartered for doing this to you."

"Don't worry. The man will lose my estate one way or another."

She stopped her incessant tapping and stared down at her. Her wide, well-powdered cheeks rose in a smile. "What have you got in mind, *mon amie?*"

"You shall see."

A cheer went up among the aristocrats as Kilian won the fourth round, and thus the *partie*. The prince bore his loss well and rose from the card table. Excusing himself, he joined the Princesse de Talmond across the room.

Aimee stood up. The crowd, who had begun to disperse, stopped in its tracks and watched as she approached the last card table.

Kilian shuffled the cards idly. He glanced up and met her gaze, but there was no surprise in his eyes. Pushing himself away from the table, he stood and bowed to her.

"Madame de Chacontier. It is a pleasure to see you again."

She had forgotten how tall he was. She had forgotten how his eyes seemed to draw her soul from her body. His shoulders cast a shadow over her and she stepped back. To her complete surprise, Kilian reached for her hand and lifted it to his lips.

She drew her hand away and searched his eyes for mockery. "You've been playing for high stakes, Chevalier," she said, her voice far huskier than she liked.

"I always do, madame. It comes from being in battle. Once you have risked your life a few times, money is not so important."

"And land? Is that also not important?"

He hesitated and his gaze traveled over her bosom, exposed by the square-cut bodice. "It depends. Some people become quite attached to land. As for me—" He shrugged. "For me it is no more important than any other type of wealth."

"Good."

Kilian lifted his brows at Aimee's adamant answer. She moved away and caressed the back of the chair that the prince had just vacated. He stared at her in surprise. "Good?"

"Yes. Then you won't mind if I challenge you to another game of piquet."

He smiled slowly and she steeled her heart against its effect. "Your winnings must be quite large for you to chal-

lenge me for your former estate. I assume that it is Château
Bocage that you want?"

"Very astute of you."

"I have heard you are quite a cardplayer." He glanced
over her body. "It would be foolish of me to risk anything
in a game with you. What will you ante?"

"Twenty thousand *livres*. In cash."

The crowd quivered with excitement as Aimee and Kilian faced each other across the card table. Card playing
stopped at all the other tables and the entire party pressed
around to watch. Kilian shook his head.

"That is not enough, madame. Not enough for me to risk
a titled estate."

"Then name your price, Chevalier."

"I fear my price will be too high, even for you, *a stor*."

Aimee lifted her chin stubbornly. He watched her with
riveting green eyes. He owned her estate and she wanted it.
She would risk everything. "I said name your price."

He shifted his weight and crossed his arms in front of
him. The hilt of his sword glimmered in the light of the
candles. "If you win, Madame de Chacontier, you will receive Château Bocage and the title of Vicomtesse de Bocage. If I win. . . ." He leaned over the table to face her.
"You will become my titled mistress. Starting tonight."

The room erupted. The aristocrats pressed closer, aston-
ished at Kilian's wager. The gossip that had been put to
rest rose from its grave. Suddenly, the court wondered if
there had been a romantic liaison between Aimee de Chacontier and the war hero, the Chevalier de Bourg-en-
Bresse. The Princesse de Talmond stood near Kilian and
beamed, proud that such a juicy bit of gossip germinated in
her salon.

The guests waited with bated breath for her response.

Aimee pulled out the chair and calmly spread her skirts.
"Very well, Chevalier. It is done."

Marie-Celeste stared at Aimee in horror, but Aimee

avoided her glare. She had made a decision, and nothing was going to stop her now. She would beat Kilian at piquet, and win back all that he had stolen from her. The price she would pay would be scandal, notoriety. She had paid that price many times before.

She lifted her gaze to his. He watched her with his steady, gold-flecked eyes. The guests pressed so close that their powder and perfume mingled in the air between them. The noise grew deafening, but all the confusion served only to isolate them more. As Aimee stared at Kilian she felt as if they were alone.

He shuffled the deck absently and spread it in front of her. She chose the seven of spades, he, the jack of hearts. Having pulled the low card, she took the deck, which was warm from his handling, and began shuffling. Her fingers stiffened in excitement.

Suddenly, Kilian reached over and captured her hands in his. Startled, she stared at him.

"One round," he said. His fingers felt warm on her own. "The first to reach one hundred wins the bargain."

"But normally three out of five wins a *partie*—"

"I am well aware of the rules of play, madame." He still had not released her hand. "I don't want to wait so long to collect my reward. One round."

Aimee's eyes narrowed. He was confident—overly so. Defiantly, she nodded and pulled her hands from his grip. "Very well. One round. The first to reach one hundred wins."

She shuffled, cut, dealt twelve cards to each of them, and spread the remaining eight on the silk covering of the card table.

Kilian spread his cards in his hand. He did not rearrange them. He tossed one on the table and picked up the first card in the stack. As was his right, he looked at the following four. Aimee observed her hand carefully and rearranged by suit.

Her fingers grew cold. The hand was good, but not worth the fifty or more points she had hoped. She calculated and realized that his could not be, either. She tossed two cards out, of separate suits, and chose two of the untouched cards on the stack.

A good move, she thought as she chose two more spades. She quickly counted her points.

Kilian called out his hand. "Forty-six."

"No good," she replied, showing him her six diamonds. "I've got fifty-seven." Six points were added to her side of the tally.

"*Quint* major."

She frowned. All she had was a *tierce* to a knave. "Good." Kilian showed her a set of aces, a king, a queen, a knave, and one ten.

"I also have a *tierce* to a queen." Eighteen points were added to his side of the tally. "I've got a trio of kings."

"No good." She showed him her three aces, and three points were added to her side.

Someone placed a glass of champagne at her elbow. As Kilian tossed down his lead card, the ten of spades, Aimee drained the glass of its contents. Another point was added to Kilian's side for leading with a card ten or higher.

Aimee followed with the ace of spades, and, having won the point, followed with the nine of diamonds.

His hand was too good. He took the majority of the tricks with his kings and queens, and Aimee could kill only three of his leads with her aces. When the game ended, Kilian had thirty-eight points, and Aimee, fourteen.

She took a deep breath and handed the cards to Kilian. She was not worried. In piquet, the dealer must always be on the defensive. It was the non-dealer who usually collected the most points. Now, it was her turn. She watched Kilian as he methodically shuffled the cards. His gaze met hers, and held it.

"You do look lovely tonight," he murmured. The crowd

above and around them whispered the words into the multitude. "The gray of your dress shimmers in your eyes."

"Flattery won't help you win this game."

Kilian shrugged a wide shoulder beneath the green satin of his waistcoat. "I think it might."

"You should know, of all people, that I can't be distracted with pretty words."

"I'm not trying to distract you." Kilian's heavy-lidded eyes met hers and she knew that it was not his words, but his gaze, that was his most potent weapon.

"Then . . . then how can flattery help you win this round?"

"It won't help in piquet, but it may help me win another game." He cut the deck. "The game of hearts, madame. Our game of hearts."

"You lost that game long ago," she hissed beneath her breath, suddenly realizing what he meant. "And I am no longer playing."

"But I am, *a stor*."

He dealt another round and she set her mind to the task at hand. She could not think about his strange words, not now, when so much was at stake. She spread the cards and rearranged them. She smiled inwardly. This hand was excellent. Far better than the last. She set out to win the round.

She won the points and the sequences, but he won the trio. She led with the jack of spades and thus won another point. Already her score nearly matched his—at thirty-five. He took the trick but led with a nine of clubs, which she easily trumped. When the play was finished, Kilian had fifty points, Aimee, fifty-seven.

She took a new deck of cards. Her hands felt slippery. The game was too close—and the stakes were too high.

Someone freshened the glass of champagne by her elbow, but she did not reach for it. The first glass left her light-headed; a second would destroy her acumen. The smoke of the room closed in on her. She wished the aristocrats who leered over their game would step back and allow some air to circulate between them. She felt as if she were breathing Kilian's own breath.

The third round ended in a draw. She discovered that he had "sunk" some of his sequences in order to hide his cards from her. He had won the majority of trumps, though the points were nearly offset because she had won the trio. She narrowed her eyes as she handed him the deck of cards. The score was sixty-nine for Kilian, and seventy for her.

Kilian dealt the next round, and, if Aimee had her way, it would be the last. The scores were close, but as the non-dealer she would have this last advantage.

"This is it, *a stor*." His eyes twinkled. "You'll understand if I don't wish you luck."

She was tempted to pray. She had not expected the game to be so long. For the first time since she sat down to play Aimee began to wonder at the consequences of losing.

He dealt the cards. Kilian lifted them as if it were just another round, not the round that would determine her own fate. Aimee swallowed and picked up her own dozen.

She stared at her hand. She did not have a carte blanche because of a single king. Neither did she have any chance at points or sequences because her own cards were so low, which only meant. . . . She lifted her gaze to his. Which only meant that he held the majority of the high cards.

She tossed out the five lowest cards in her hand and picked up five from the stack. One ace, one knave, two low spades, and a low diamond. With a sigh she rearranged her hand. Kilian threw out nothing.

"Thirty-five," she said quietly.

"No good. I've got fifty." He showed her a fleet of spades. Five points were added to his score.

She examined her cards. They were low, but there were several sequences. She chose the highest. "I've got a *quint* minor."

"No good." He lifted his gaze to hers and lowered his voice. "I've a *quint* major, *a stor*. Plus a *tierce* major and a *tierce* to a king," he added, showing her the three sequences. She watched him as a slow smile spread across his face.

"Well, go on," she said quietly.

"A *quatorze* of queens, *a stor*." He laid his hand on the table. "I know you have nothing higher than that."

The murmuring began in the crowd again. Aimee let her hand fall, facedown, on the table. Kilian watched her as he settled his own, faceup, to show a fleet of royalty.

"That's one hundred and nine, Aimee."

"I suppose we need to go no farther."

"No." He rose from the gaming table and the crowd moved back. He walked around to her and picked up her limp hand. Lifting it to his lips, he urged her to her feet. "You've lost the round, Madame de Chacontier."

"It seems so." She kept her eyes lowered, too much in shock to stare into the face of the crowd. She felt the comtesse by her side but turned away. Kilian lifted her chin up with his finger.

His face was only inches away from hers. In a rush she saw the tiny lines around his mouth, the gold flecks in the deep green of his eyes, and remembered a dozen different expressions.

"Come, my mistress," he said, leading her through the crowd. "Let me show you your new home."

CHAPTER

14

Aimee pulled her wrapper around her shoulders as Kilian helped her into his carriage. He closed the door and sat directly across from her. She stiffened as his knees brushed her skirt.

She felt shame as she had never felt shame before. She had bargained her own body for a chance at Château Bocage—and lost. Again. This time, a whole room of aristocrats had witnessed her downfall.

"Your cheeks burn, *a stor*. I can see their color even in the darkness." He leaned back in the seat. "You have no reason to be ashamed."

"No reason?!" She wrapped her arms around her body. "I have just whored myself in front of half of the court."

"I wouldn't call becoming my mistress 'whoring.'"

"What would you call it, then?"

Kilian took off his hat and placed it on the seat beside him. The lantern outside the carriage cast gold light on his face. One lock of tawny hair fell over his forehead. "If you remember, the bargain was that you were to become my *titled* mistress. There is no shame in that."

"There is for me."

"I see you are still, in part, the country aristocrat. Good. I feared the court would change you into one of those vapid, insensitive women who care for nothing but their clothes and their positions in court."

"What difference would it make? You don't care about me, Laclos, you only care about how I can be used to get back at the Duc de Montchamp."

"Is that what you think?"

"What else would you have me think?"

"The Duc de Montchamp has nothing to do with this."

Aimee lifted a brow. "And I suppose he had nothing to do with Château Bocage, as well?"

His face darkened. "Come here."

She sucked in her breath. She should not have provoked him. His eyes, though shadowed, glimmered with anger. He picked up his hat and gestured to the seat beside him.

"Don't make me force you, Aimee."

She knew, instinctively, that he would force her if she did not come to his side willingly. She tilted her chin. Slipping off her wrap, she laid it and her reticule on the seat beside her. Then, clutching the wall of the carriage for support, she stood and stepped toward him. The swaying motion of the cabin unnerved her and she lost her balance. Kilian seized her waist and swung her into the seat beside him.

He did not release her. He twisted in his seat and pressed her body flat against his. His fingers curled in her hair.

"You forget that I wanted you long before the Duc de Montchamp wanted you." His gaze raked her face, from her forehead to her trembling lips. "You forget that I scaled your castle wall to be with you, to warn you away from the duke, and to make love to you. All you remember is that I took your damned estate."

"You used me, and lied to me—"

"I did not lie. I just did not tell you the full truth, and I did it for your own good."

He kissed her arched neck. His warm lips traced the pulse in her throat. Aimee strained against his grip, but he held her too firmly. He swung a leg over her skirts and stilled her entirely. His lips continued their relentless attack. She closed her eyes. She could not deny him her body—she had agreed to this—yet as he lifted his head to hers she wondered if she could find the strength to battle him in spirit.

"You underestimate your charms, Aimee," he said breathlessly. "I want you as my mistress because you are a beautiful woman. The duke has nothing to do with that."

He captured her lips. Though her mind railed against her, her body quivered in reluctant desire. She tasted the evening's champagne on his tongue and she smelled the smoke of the princess's salon on his skin. His bristled cheek scraped against her chin as his kiss deepened. Her fingers curled in silent restraint in the satin of his waistcoat.

He released her lips to kiss her temple, her cheek, her ear. She gasped for breath as his hands roamed over her back and sides. It is just a bargain, she thought, her control slipping quickly away. I made this bargain and I must suffer the consequences.

But suffering was far from her mind as Kilian continued his caresses. Her body sang with his touch. As if embodied of their own will, her fingers wandered up his chest, and wound their way around his neck.

"Ah, my mistress," he murmured as her fingers intertwined in his hair. "For weeks I have thought of nothing but this, of nothing but you."

Her raging thoughts of defiance swirled and muddled in her mind. She had forgotten how powerful he was. She had suppressed all the memories of their one night of lovemak-

ing after she had left Normandy. They returned to her now,
in a great rush, and the remnants of her will dissolved. Her
dress loosened around her. He pushed a sleeve off her
shoulders and caressed the exposed skin.

I can't resist, she thought languidly as she felt the
smooth leather of the seat against her back. I am his mistress. He lay on her heavily, awkwardly, for the carriage
was not made for lovemaking. He peeled off his waistcoat,
folded it, and placed it beneath her head as a pillow.

She opened her eyes. He tore off his cravat and hovered
over her. His white linen shirt was open to the waist and
Aimee could see the gleam of his hard chest between the
edges. She wanted to touch it, to trace the strange, sculpted
lines so different from her own body, but as her gaze met
his she stopped.

He wanted her. His eyes devoured her with need, but
there was something in the raw, unfettered gaze that reminded her of where she was and how she arrived here. He
stared at her as if she were a meal for a starving man.

Part of her, something buried deep inside, responded to
his gaze. She wanted him, too, in the same way he took
her in Normandy. Her blood pounded for him. Yet even as
this alien, primitive urge raged in her body, her mind took
control of her thoughts again.

This was Kilian de Laclos. The man who betrayed her.
The man who stole her virginity and her castle within a
week. She could not succumb to him without a fight.

"No!" she cried as he leaned down to kiss her.

"You are my mistress now, *a stor*." His voice was
ragged. "You cannot say no."

The carriage stopped suddenly. Cursing, he pulled the
leather curtain away from the window and glanced out.
Bereft of his hold, she struggled to a sitting position and
clutched her bodice.

"We're home." He unrolled his waistcoat. He glanced at
her and noticed that her gray bodice sagged enticingly

away from her bosom. "It seems I've lost control of myself. Put this on for now."

For now. Aimee had the distinct feeling that she would not need his waistcoat, or any type of clothing, later. She fumbled with her hair, which had tumbled down her back. Kilian tossed his cravat over his shoulder and opened the carriage door. He jumped to the street and unhooked the stairs.

"Come, Aimee." He lifted his hand. Struggling with her hair, her unhooked dress, and her wide panniers, she had no choice but to take it. As she reached the street he did not let her go. She glanced, dazed, at the building in front of them. A wide stone fence surrounded the land, but above the fence his house rose to two stories. Several candles burned in the upper windows.

Kilian led her to an iron gate, opened it, and let her pass through. She smelled the sweet scent of wisteria as he led her along the cobbled path to the front entrance. The carved door opened as they approached.

"Jeanne, this is Madame de Chacontier. She will be staying with us for a while."

Aimee flushed hotly as the small woman nodded, expressionless, and stepped away to allow them to pass. Aimee pulled Kilian's waistcoat more tightly around her as she entered the foyer. The room was dark except for the candelabrum that the servant carried.

"Come this way, madame," she said, leading Aimee to a set of stairs. Still dazed from Kilian's touch, she mutely followed the servant's trim back. The stairs curved around to the second floor. Jeanne, dressed in a simple black dress with a white, unembroidered apron, led her to the end of the hall and opened a narrow door. "This is the only room prepared for a guest," she explained. "If it does not please you, I can prepare another one tomorrow."

She nodded, wondering how often Kilian brought women to his house for his servant to be so casual. Jeanne observed her without the slightest expression of condemnation or approval. She took one of the tapers out of the candelabrum and began to light several around the room.

"I can help you undress, madame."

She started. Of course she would need help. She was tempted to stay in her clothes, but she sensed, especially after the incident in the carriage, that Kilian would only ruin them by ripping them off her body. He would want her naked tonight, pliant and willing in his bed, and she had few enough dresses to worry about their care.

She slipped his satin waistcoat off her shoulders and pulled her arms from the sleeves of her dress. "I could use some help with this corset," she said quietly. "Then I can take care of the rest myself."

Jeanne said nothing as Aimee turned and showed her the half-unhooked dress. She finished the job and then unlaced Aimee's corset. "Will there be anything else, madame?"

She shook her head. The servant left and quietly closed the door behind her.

Déjà vu. Once before she had entered a man's room suspecting she was about to become his mistress. How different this room was from the glorious white and gray room that the duke had designed for her at Montchamp. This room was as sparse and sterile as a garret.

She closed her eyes and sank on the bed. This time, she feared, she would not be able to escape her fate. Kilian had won her fairly and she either had to give him what she anted, or forever hide from Parisian society and the court of Versailles for going back on a bargain.

Men had been killed in duels for less than that.

Her stomach trembled beneath her loosened corset. Her bewilderment gave way to the heat of passion. She pressed her hands against her lips, remembering in a feverish rush the taste of Kilian's kisses. She must stop! How could she battle him in spirit if she could not control her body? She fought to stifle this primitive passion that surged in her blood.

What was it about Kilian that made her so weak? After all that had happened in Normandy she should hate him with every fiber of her being, but each time she saw him she could not help watching him, wondering about him, thinking about him. Now, living in his own house, how could she fight him?

She *must* fight him. She could not let him hurt her as he hurt her before. The quicker the thing was done, she reasoned, the quicker he would leave her alone and she could struggle with the feelings that fermented in her body. Resolutely, she rose from the bed and shrugged out of her dress, her panniers, and her corset. Lifting her chemise she unrolled her stockings and tossed them with the rest. Clad only in a gossamer chemise, she wrapped her arms around her midriff and glanced around the room.

The servant had left the armoire open. A slip of silk hung from a hook inside.

A peignoir.

Her throat burned with fury. Aimee welcomed the anger, for it gave her strength. Kilian was exceptionally prepared for a mistress. She glanced at the bed and wondered how many other women had slept in it, and then wondered, with a pang, how many more would sleep here after her. Her eyes narrowed. Well, she would not wear that silk peignoir. She would submit to Kilian's lovemaking because she had to, but she would do nothing to encourage it.

She shivered in her thin cambric chemise. Embers flickered weakly in the fireplace. She gathered a wool blanket around her shoulders and hid her near nakedness. Settling in a cushioned chair near the fire, she reached for a poker and toyed with the embers until she could feel their heat on her skin.

She heard his steps in the hallway. She listened until they stopped right in front of her door. He scratched twice.

She stiffened beneath the woolen blanket. What did he expect her to do, invite him in?

He hesitated a moment and then entered. He still wore his breeches, his linen shirt, and his boots. He closed the door behind him. He approached her but stopped on the other side of the fireplace. His gaze grew far too warm on her swaddled body.

"Is the room to your satisfaction?"

She shrugged. She had barely noticed her surroundings. "It's fine."

"Tomorrow, when you see more of the house, you can choose another room if you wish."

What did it matter, she thought shrewishly, as long as the room had a bed for *his* pleasure?

"One of the benefits of being my mistress is that you now are also the mistress of this house. I think you'll find that it's sadly in need of care."

"Haven't your other women seen to it?"

Kilian lifted his brows. "Other women?"

"Yes." She gestured to the armoire. "The women who so thoughtfully left their clothes here."

He glanced at the peignoir and a light of understanding brightened his eyes. To her dismay, he laughed and leaned more comfortably against the hearth. "Ah, I see. Are you jealous, *a stor?*"

"Of course not."

"You have no reason to be." He walked across the room and took the peignoir off its hook. Returning, he tossed it in her lap. "Look at it, Aimee. You may recognize it."

She lifted the straps and flushed wildly. It was her own silk peignoir, her wedding peignoir, the one she had worn the night she and Kilian made love. Shocked, she rolled it into a ball between her hands.

"Don't—" He took the slip of silk from her and straightened it. "You'll ruin it and I want to see you in it again."

"Not now," she hissed huskily, still reeling from the

sight of the intimate garment. The faint odor of gardenias rose from its folds. "Please, not now."

"Nay." He lifted the silk to his face and breathed the lingering scent. "When you wear this again, Aimee, you'll wear it willingly."

She lifted her hand to her brow. The peignoir was too brutal a reminder of their single evening in Normandy. Did he hope to crush her defenses by reminding her of her weaknesses? Why, why, didn't he just take her in his arms now and have his way with her instead of playing cat and mouse? Her brows lowered crossly as he carefully hung the peignoir back in the armoire. He was acting more like a contrite lover than a man who had just won a woman in a card game.

But that was foolish, Aimee thought, for he had never loved her. He had betrayed her. He did not want her to wear it because he wanted her bared to his gaze and his touch. She closed her eyes as the heat of her memories rushed in her blood.

"I brought a few other things from Château Bocage," he said, returning to stand behind her chair. She stiffened as he toyed with her hair. "I wanted you to be comfortable."

"So you have been planning this."

"Of course. I've wanted you for my mistress for a long time, *a stor*. I never thought I'd win you in a card game." He pulled a few pins from the black tresses. "Your hair is tangled. Let me brush it."

Aimee sat up in the chair and pulled her hair out of his hand. "I'm quite able to comb it myself."

"I want to do it. I've always wanted to do it." He rose and fumbled in one of the drawers of the dressing table that stood beside the bed. "I've got you trapped, my sweet. Relax. I'm going to brush your hair whether you want me to or not."

Aimee tightened the blanket around her and frantically

ran her fingers through her hair. Relax, indeed. She felt as relaxed as a deer in the king's forest.

"Up," he commanded, wielding a silver-handled brush. "Sit on the footstool. It'll be closer to the heat, and you are shivering as if it were December, not June."

Her eyes flashed defiance, but she knew she would not win any fight with him—in body or of words. Tightening the wool around her shoulders, she settled on the small footstool in front of the chair. Laughing, he settled behind her. "I've obviously got you at a disadvantage. You used to rage like a tigress when I spoke to you like that."

"Fighting with you will only provoke you more," she muttered as his knees rose on either side of her body. She wrapped herself tighter to avoid touching him. His fingers entwined in her hair. His hands were warm against her scalp, gentle as they removed the silver pins that remained and let them fall to the floor.

"I suppose I should apologize for attacking you in the carriage this evening," he said softly.

"I am your mistress. I expect to be attacked."

"You did not protest too much."

"Would it have made a difference? You've won my favors, Kilian. Protesting will not change that."

"No, it won't."

His fingers felt soothing in her hair and she closed her eyes, trying not to let his touch lull her into security. He traced her nape and stopped on her shoulders. "You are tense, *a stor*."

"Did you expect me to be pliant at your touch?"

His laugh rumbled in his chest. "I had hoped as much."

His fingers kneaded the tight knot of muscles in her shoulders and she bit her lower lip. He knew how to touch her far too well. He seemed to press the tension out of her upper body. She felt her resistance quiver. "You're very good at this."

"At what?"

"Seduction."

"Good." He lifted her hair and placed a kiss on the back of her neck. He stopped his kneading and returned to the task of pulling pins from her hair. "Tell me if I hurt you."

Yes, Kilian, you hurt me. You hurt me more than anyone has ever hurt me before. Aimee winced as he pulled a strand of her hair. "Don't I always?"

"Yes." His voice held a note of dismay. "Sometimes you tell me all too brutally." Having found all the pins, he ran his fingers through the black waves, separating the tresses and smoothing them down the length of her back. Though the wool blanket separated her skin from his fingers, Aimee could feel every stroke of his hands as if they lay on her naked back. Her body throbbed. If he continued, she knew she would fall into his arms like a willing servant girl. Her heart twisted in her body.

This gentle seduction was far more dangerous than the attack in the carriage. If he were violent, or if he overpowered her, she could at least blame her submission on his brutality. But this . . . This seduction crushed her resistance, and there was no excuse for succumbing except the weakness of her will.

She felt the brush against her back as he combed through her hair, starting at the ends. He followed each stroke with a warm hand to smooth her tresses. The rhythmic motion made her languid, almost sleepy, and completely submissive to his touch. She relaxed her grip on the wool blanket and it slipped off her shoulders. The heat radiating from the red embers in the hearth felt good on her skin.

The brush reached her neck. She felt the bristles weave their way through her tresses to scrape her nape. Kilian gathered her hair in his hand and lifted it to his nose.

"You smell like apple blossoms, still." He caressed the length of her hair. "Just like in Normandy."

She wanted to tell him that she brought the scented lye from Normandy, and she had not yet used it up. She felt like falling back against the chair and nestling between his thighs. She felt like nuzzling against his warm body and sleeping with his heart beating beneath her ear.

"You're sleepy, *a stor*."

She bit her lip. Yes, she was sleepy, but to admit it was to admit she wanted to go to bed. She glanced at the bed. She was not prepared for this. He had destroyed her defenses in a matter of an hour.

"Come." Kilian rose from the chair and left the brush on it. He leaned down over her.

"No! I mean . . . I'm not sleepy, not yet."

He slipped an arm beneath her legs, and another behind her back. With one lunge he lifted her against his chest. Aimee stared into his eyes, and watched as the edges crinkled in laughter. "You are sleepy. And you are going to bed whether you like it or not."

He whirled around and laid her down on the embroidered spread. His sun-speckled gaze brought the blood to her cheeks. He released her, reluctantly, and sat on the edge of the bed.

His linen shirt gaped open and she forced her gaze away. She realized again how handsome he was, how his eyes glowed beneath the dark slash of his brows, how the gold and the white-blond and the butter-colored strands of his hair wove against his nape. Any woman would be proud to be this man's mistress, she thought, and she would, too, if she didn't know how duplicitous he was. She tried to summon anger or pain, but his power was too strong. He had cast a spell over her, and until he left her side she would not have the power to struggle against it.

He brushed her hair off her temple. "Do you want anything? Something to drink?"

She wondered if she could delay the inevitable, then wondered if she wanted to. "No. No, I'm fine." She should not feel like this, she told herself. She should not want him to kiss her so much.

He leaned over her. She sucked in her breath. He hovered for a moment, above her face, then he kissed her softly. Her lids fluttered shut and she knew she was lost.

He released her.

"You'll be warmer if you get under the linens," he murmured, rising from the bed. "I'll send Jeanne up to stoke the fire."

With that, Kilian turned around and left her alone in the room.

Aimee woke the next morning to the sound of two women yelling in the hall. She glanced around, completely disoriented. Seeing her hope chest from Château Bocage at the end of the bed, she wondered if she was home, but the sounds and smells of Paris rose distinctly from the street below.

As she sat up the memories returned in full force. She lifted her hands to her heated cheeks.

"I don't care how many titles that blackguard has—he cannot hide behind his nobility this time. He has hurt Aimee de Chacontier for the last time."

The Comtesse de Vierzon lunged into her room. "Oh, Aimee!" Rushing across the space that separated them, Marie gathered her in her plump arms and pressed her head against her ample bosom. "What did that beast do to you, my poor country cousin?"

Aimee glanced over Marie's shoulder to see the distorted face of Jeanne, the servant who had led her up here the evening before. The servant whirled in a rush of taffeta skirts and marched down the hall.

"Did he beat you? I swear if he touched you at all I will summon all the power I can to have him exiled from court."

"He didn't touch me, Marie," she murmured, still disoriented. She shook her head. The lilac scent of Marie's powder tickled her nose and she pressed away. "I'm quite all right, I think."

"Ah, my poor Aimee!" Marie glanced about the room. "Look where he has put you—it's as bare as a cell in the Bastille in here! That man has done his last to hurt you, I swear it. I've already sent word to the Marquise de Pompadour and she won't be pleased to hear what the Chevalier de Bourg-en-Bresse has done now."

"Marie, please." She closed her eyes. She felt the first twinge of a headache in the middle of her forehead. "Really, he didn't touch me."

Marie stopped her tirade and searched her friend's face. A white feather in her hat quivered in surprise. "He didn't—"

"No, he didn't. Though I don't know why. Probably just to torture me more."

"I'm sure that's it." She rose from the bed. Aimee gaped as the comtesse, in uncharacteristic fervor, began to pick up her scattered clothes. "You *must* come back with me. The chevalier has had his fun for the evening, and now you have fulfilled your end of that ridiculous bargain."

"I don't understand." Aimee struggled out of the covers and reached sleepily for one of her silk stockings. The comtesse shook out her dress and laid it on the bed.

"You agreed to become the chevalier's titled mistress, but he did not specify a length of time. As far as I am concerned, you fulfilled that bargain last night."

"No, madame, she hasn't."

Both women started and turned to the door. Kilian leaned against the frame and filled the portal. He wore only his breeches. His bare chest gleamed in the morning sun pouring through the front windows. Aimee struggled under the linens again, hiding her near naked body from his perusal.

The comtesse puffed up like a mating bird. *"You!"* She

put her hands on her hips and blocked Aimee from his sight. "You are a despicable excuse for an aristocrat, monsieur! Taking advantage of a young, innocent widow from the country and forcing her into an ignoble arrangement for the sole purpose of wreaking your vengeance against the Duc de Montchamp!"

"I hardly think that becoming my titled mistress is an ignoble arrangement," he interrupted, his lips curving in a smile. "And as for the Duc de Montchamp—"

"The Duc de Montchamp shall hear of it," the comtesse interrupted. "And the Marquise de Pompadour. And the king. You have disgraced this woman—"

"I shall remind you that she is far from disgraced. She's my titled mistress and the lady of this house."

The comtesse flushed an angry red from the mounds of her breasts to her low hairline. "Against her will."

"She initiated the bargain, not I. And the game was won fairly. Do you doubt that?"

"Whatever the arrangement," Marie continued, "she has fulfilled her side of the bargain. She was your mistress for one evening." She lifted her chins. "Come, Aimee. Get dressed. My carriage is waiting outside. I shall take you home."

"Aimee is going nowhere," he said quietly. "This is her new home, for as long as she is my mistress. When we made the bargain last night, I said nothing about when it would end." His gaze traveled over Marie's body. "It will end when I say it is over, unless Aimee chooses to go back on her agreement."

"You are despicable!"

He shrugged and his smile widened. "I have been called worse."

"The king shall hear of it."

"I suppose he shall."

Marie's eyes narrowed. "You are already in disfavor,

Chevalier. An incident such as this could cause you to be exiled."

"I doubt it." He walked deeper into the room. "Jeanne, bring up some chocolate for Madame de Chacontier." He glanced at Marie. "I suppose you won't be having breakfast with us, Comtesse?"

Marie, exasperated, whirled to Aimee. "Aimee, come with me. What can he do, chain you to the bed?"

One of his brows lifted. "What an interesting idea."

"Beast! Come, *mon amie*. You'll be under my protection and he won't be able to hurt you."

"She will be going back on a bargain made and won, fairly, at a card game." Kilian settled in the chair by the hearth. "Men have dueled over far less than that. Who will invite Aimee to salons after such an incident? She will be unofficially exiled from court."

Aimee glanced at him, and then the pleading eyes of the comtesse. "He is right, isn't he?"

Marie frowned and nodded. "Unfortunately, he is. But what does it matter? You never wanted to be a part of court, anyway, and I was a fool to push you into it. I had forgotten that men like *that* existed and that you are so innocent."

"It is not leaving court that bothers me," she said as she leaned back in the bed. "But I shan't have anyone thinking I go back on a bargain. I'm a woman of my word."

"He knows you too well," Marie snapped in frustration. "He has captured you as firmly as a fox catches a hen. Now that you are trapped you're afraid to fly."

"If you don't mind, Comtesse, it is quite early and I would like to break the fast with my mistress." Kilian smiled with all the grace of a courtier. "I am sure Aimee would like you to visit sometime in the future, at a far more reasonable hour, of course."

"Come with me, Aimee. Don't let pride or some misguided sense of honor stand in your way."

Aimee frowned and stared at Kilian through narrowed eyes. "I am afraid I cannot leave, Marie. Kilian is right. If I leave he can spread word that I did not fulfill my end of the bargain, and I shall never be invited to play cards again. Then I'll have nothing to live on—"

"The Duc de Montchamp will get you a pension from the king, I am sure of it," Marie insisted.

Aimee reached for Marie's hand. "Don't worry, Marie. He'll tire of me in a few days and I shall be released from the bargain."

"Don't count on it, *a stor,*" Kilian said softly. "I don't intend to let you go for some time."

Aimee's brows drew together. She pressed the comtesse's hand. "Come visit me later."

"Indeed I will." She sneered at Kilian. "Perhaps after a day with this man you'll reconsider." She gathered her gold and green skirts in one hand and turned her fiery gaze one last time on Kilian. "I warn you, Chevalier, if you hurt her you'll have my wrath to contend with, and I assure you it is considerable."

"Obviously."

"Hmph!" The comtesse lifted her chin as Kilian bowed and she stomped out the door.

He turned to face Aimee as the comtesse rustled down the stairs. "You've got a very loyal friend. That's rare in court."

Her gaze dropped from his bare chest. "We've been friends since childhood. She used to come over to the castle during hunting parties, in younger days when the vicomte was well."

"I see."

"You will allow me to see her periodically, won't you?"

He frowned at her question. "Of course. You are not my prisoner, Aimee. You are my mistress. I see that I will have to explain to you the full meaning of the position."

Aimee toyed with the knitting of the wool comforter and

kept her eyes lowered from his. The chemise she wore did little to hide her figure, especially with the bright light of the morning pouring through the windows. She couldn't possibly rise from beneath the covers with Kilian in the room. She was not yet ready for the first lesson in the meaning of the position of mistress.

"Is the light too much? I remembered how you liked mornings, so I thought this room would be best for you."

"No, no. It's quite all right." She wondered why he insisted on being so nice to her.

Jeanne knocked on the door and he barked for her to enter. She bore a silver platter with a large silver pot and several pastries. Settling it on a small table Kilian had pulled in front of the fire, she left as quietly as she had come.

"Will you join me in breakfast?"

Aimee lifted the comforter higher on her shoulders. "No. I'll just rest here. You can eat."

Kilian glanced at her and walked to the armoire. Rifling through the clothes, he pulled out a long swath of red silk and tossed it on the bed.

"What is it?"

"A robe. From East India." He bent over the silver service with his back to her. "Put it on. Stop squirming beneath the covers like a virgin and join me."

The command had entered his voice again. She fingered the rich scarlet silk. Her stomach growled. Shrugging, she lowered the comforter and slipped her arms into the long sleeves. As she swung her legs out from under the linens she glanced toward him. He had not yet turned around.

She needed a good, strong cup of chocolate, she thought as she settled in the chair opposite him. He was treating her more like an honored guest than a woman whose services he had just won in a card game. She wondered how long his favor, and his patience, would last.

He poured. "Do you have any plans for the day?"

"Plans? If I had any plans I would certainly cancel them after last night."

"I don't want you to do that." He handed her a cup of chocolate and met her gaze. "Lesson number two on being my mistress. I want you to continue your life as if nothing has changed—except for one thing." His chin hardened. "I don't want you seeing the Duc de Montchamp."

The porcelain warmed her cold fingers. "I thought as much."

"That is the only thing I will deny you, and I don't think I have to explain the reasons."

"Not to me."

Kilian settled in the chair opposite her, a frown marring his face. He sipped his chocolate and reached for a pastry. His green gold gaze caressed her. "You didn't answer my question, Aimee. Do you have any plans?"

She shook her head. "No. And, as I said, if I did I would cancel them all. I have no desire to go back into society."

"You have no choice."

Her gray eyes flashed. "And what does that mean?"

"That means you shall go into society with me, whether you like it or not."

"In that case, I shall go out only with you. I shan't be seen otherwise."

"If that is what pleases you." He finished the pastry. "We shall attend court today."

Aimee stiffened in her chair. *Court!* The last place she wanted to be seen, the morning after this bargain, was in court. The queen would look at her in disgust for so easily bartering her virtue, and the Marquise de Pompadour, after so graciously having had her introduced to court, would be embarrassed at her presence. She could not bear court— she could bear anything but court. "Please, Kilian." She lifted her gaze to him. "Not court. I shall go anywhere with you, but don't make me go to court."

"You must face these people."

"Please." She put her chocolate down and lowered her head. "I'll go anywhere else—salons, the *Française*, the Bois de Boulogne—I'll even walk through the streets of Paris—but please, don't make me face the royal family."

She heard his cup rattle on the silver tray. "You must understand, Aimee, that being my mistress is not a thing of shame."

"It is a thing of shame to me." She shook her head until her hair screened her face from his perusal. Her voice grew husky. "I'll do anything, Kilian. Just don't make me attend court."

He pushed the table out of his way and leaned toward her. His fingers brushed her hair away from her face, then traced her cheek. Slowly, she lifted her gaze to his.

"You'll do anything?" His gaze was as soft as candlelight. He saw the fear jump in her eyes. "Aye, you shouldn't say such things, *a stor,* if you don't really mean them." He sighed and released her cheek. "But I shall honor your wish, under one condition."

Her eyes narrowed. "And what is that?"

"You'll come for a walk with me in the Bois de Boulogne, right now."

Aimee glanced down at her robe. "But—"

"After you dress, of course." He reached beside the hearth and pulled a tasseled cord. "Though that robe flatters you, I don't want all of Paris seeing you in it."

"I have nothing to wear."

"I've taken the liberty of having your things moved here." His eyes sparkled. "I think that is what roused your comtesse from her toilette this morning. My servants arrived at the break of day. Everything should be hung by now, in that closet." He gestured to a door on the far side of the room.

Aimee struggled between anger and gratitude. At least he wasn't trying to deck her in clothes bought with his own money, but still, she felt as if she were about to be shown off like a prize. She twisted the tie of her robe in her hands.

"Ah, Jeanne," he said as the servant entered. "Help Madame de Chacontier dress, would you? She's going on a walk through the Bois de Boulogne."

Kilian bent over and chucked up her chin. "Come now, Aimee. It won't be all that bad."

"Yes, it will. You are going to strut me around like a prize Arabian."

"Yes, I am," he agreed. "A very lovely, very intelligent, and very hard-won prize, too. I am going to enjoy every minute of it."

CHAPTER

15

A prize, indeed, Aimee thought as she descended the narrow stairs to the bottom floor of Kilian's town house. He waited in the bare foyer, his tricorn beneath his arm, with a slow smile spreading across his face.

"Much better, madame." His gaze roved over the salmon silk dress trimmed with rose-colored ribbons. A single red rose, plucked from one of the bushes in the front garden, accented her simple coiffure. "I thought you would put on another somber dress and I'd be forced to send you upstairs again."

She frowned. She hated to wear such an attractive gown, for it was cut low in the front and held a richly embroidered stomacher that did not quite cover the curve of her breasts. But Kilian would have none of her sedate dark blues and browns, which she had worn first. She had fought, but he had threatened to come up and change her himself.

"Don't frown, Aimee. It ruins the effect."

She tilted her chin. "What will you do to prevent me from frowning? Put wire in my mouth?"

"It's a thought." He reached for her arm, but she snapped it away. "You might consider *not* looking so indignant. After all, not long ago I was considered quite a catch, with all my heroics in the Netherlands."

"You should have found a mistress who could appreciate you, then."

"But I wanted you, *a stor*." He laughed as she avoided his touch. He opened the door and waited for her to pass. "Don't you think it would be a far better idea to act as if you had planned to snare me all along?"

"What a conceited oaf you are! You'd love to have me simpering all over you, wouldn't you?"

"Yes."

"Well, I shan't." She lifted her skirts. "You'll just have to live with the fact that *I* do not want *you*, Laclos."

"We'll see." Despite her protests, Kilian helped her into his carriage and sat directly across from her. He tapped the roof and the carriage lurched forward.

She turned her gaze stubbornly away. He looked exceptionally handsome today, decked in dove white breeches and a dark blue waistcoat. He dressed more starkly than his contemporaries, but the starkness complimented him. Kilian de Laclos, she thought, was devilishly attractive enough and didn't need the trappings of fashion.

Her mood darkened as she watched the streets narrow. As they entered the heart of Paris the noise became louder and so did the stench. The June day promised to be hot and decidedly uncomfortable. She hoped that a breeze would linger in the Bois de Boulogne.

Not that it would matter, she thought. Kilian would parade her around the entire park and make sure all of Paris knew he had made her his mistress, no matter how hot and uncomfortable it became. Last night, in her weakness, she had forgotten who he was and what he had done to her. She suspected that today he forced her into society for one reason: a confrontation with the Duc de Montchamp. Aimee closed her eyes. She did not know what would happen when the duke discovered this predicament.

"What are you thinking that makes you so angry and silent?"

"I am remembering why I dislike you."

"Had you forgotten?" He shifted his weight. "I thought it would take weeks, months, for you to forget."

"Years."

"Aye, perhaps years." He shrugged. "That's all right. I am a patient man."

A crease marred her brow. He acted as if he wanted more from her than just an opportunity to anger the Duc de Montchamp. She could not let herself believe that. If he had wanted more . . . She turned away. He would have made love to her last night, instead of leaving her alone in that bed.

Not that she wanted him to make love to her, she thought quickly, knowing her thoughts to be lies. She did want him. God help her, she still wanted Kilian de Laclos as a lover. She must resist him until her last breath.

"Please, Aimee." He touched her brow. "You're working yourself up into a rage."

"Don't—" She pushed his arm away. "Please."

He clutched both her hands in his. "You're my mistress and I don't want to see you unhappy."

"Since when?"

"Since Château Bocage," he said quietly, placing a finger on her lips as she stiffened into fury. "Though you don't believe it now, and may never believe it, I wanted only your happiness."

She wrenched her hands away from his grip and rubbed them, though they did not hurt. He sighed and sat back against the leather upholstery. He leaned his elbow on the window edge and gazed out past the gates of Paris.

She wished he would yell at her, clutch her, do something violent so she could hate him more. This new, patient, undemanding Kilian was a man she did not understand. She did not know how to fight his calm—she knew only how to fight his anger.

"You are a liar. And a debaucher of innocent women. And a thief."

"Aye, I've been all that."

She sighed in exasperation. "You are using me now, as you used me in Normandy."

"Nay, *a stor*, I'm not."

"You are no better than the Duc de Montchamp—he took your sister and made her his mistress, and you are doing the same to me."

He flinched slightly and she knew that her arrow had hit home.

"The Duc de Montchamp never claimed my sister. You are my titled mistress."

"Against my will."

A muscle twitched in his jaw. "It was your bargain. You took your chances. You had an opportunity to leave this morning, Aimee. You can still leave. I shall not lock you away in my town house."

"You know very well that if I leave I shall be shunned from all salons. I will never be invited to a card party and that is the only way I have been making my living." She settled back in the seat and looked out the window. "I am forced to stay until you ask me to leave."

To her surprise, a smile curved his lips. "And no matter what you say or do to me, *a stor*, I shan't let you go."

She stared at him in utter, frustrated confusion. He leaned over and touched her cheek.

"Come, it won't be so bad. You may find that you enjoy being my mistress. There are certain advantages."

"Indeed?" She crossed her arms. "Like what?"

"Well, first of all, you have full access to my finances.

All you have to do is tell Jeanne what you want and she will arrange it all. You can buy yourself an entire wardrobe for all I care. Hire a cook for the house, set up a salon—"

"You don't have a cook?"

He shook his head. "I've no need for one. Until now, I have always eaten out."

"What about Jeanne?"

"Jeanne is everything but a cook." He glanced at her. "And now, it seems, she is a lady's maid. You'll find that the furnishings in the house are worn and out of date. My father lived in it when he was alive, but he's been dead for ten years. Then, my brother used it, but he gambled away so much of the Bourg-en-Bresse money that the creditors took most of the furniture."

Aimee's eyes widened. Her own room was sparse— consisting of a bed, an armoire, two chairs, and a small dressing table—but she had thought that was because it was only a guest room.

"You see now that there is another reason for me to make you my mistress. I need someone to take care of the house."

"And what makes you think I will want to play the lady of the house?"

"I don't know." He toyed with the ruffles of his cravat. "Call it intuition, if you like. In any case, you don't have to do anything if you don't want to. You can live in your room and we can eat at the *hôtels* of my friends, if you wish."

She winced and he laughed. "I thought that would change your mind."

The carriage slowed down as it approached the most populated part of the Bois de Boulogne. Aimee lifted her face to the air that flooded through the window. On the outskirts of the city, the Boulogne forest had none of the stink or heat of the streets but still had all the people. It seemed that the entire teeming population of Paris strolled its tree-lined paths.

Kilian tapped on the roof for the driver to stop. The carriage lurched as the driver climbed down and released the steps. Kilian descended first and reached for her hand.

She breathed in the fresh air as she descended. She had not realized how hot it was inside the cabin. He took her hand and wedged it in his elbow tightly.

"Come, Aimee. You'll not deny me your hand, at least." He tossed a coin to his driver. "Go have an orange, George. We shall be a while." The carriage driver tipped his hat and drew the horses into the shade.

Heads turned their way. First, only a few, but as they walked deeper into the center of the promenade they received more attention. Her cheeks burned and she wished she had brought a parasol, or at the very least, a hat with a wider brim. Kilian continued to walk in his maddeningly slow pace.

"*Bonjour*, Madame de Tencin," he called as they approached a finely dressed older woman. The woman's eyes sparkled with vivacity.

"*Bonjour*, Chevalier." She turned to Aimee. "This, I assume, is Madame de Chacontier."

Aimee inclined her head a fraction to the sister of one of the king's ministers. "*Enchantée*," she lied.

"I have heard quite a bit about you, madame," the woman persisted, her gaze fluttering between Kilian and her. "Congratulations on your introduction to court."

She murmured a word of gratitude and Kilian skillfully led her onward. She took a deep breath as she noticed several men from the previous night's salon in their path.

"*Bonjour, messieurs*," Kilian said, eyeing each one as he crossed their path. Their gazes rested with cupidity on Aimee's bent head but slipped away when they met Kilian's glare. She could hear their whispers in their wake.

He steered her with determination toward the Abbé de

Bernis and the Marechale de Mirepoix. The day was young and many courtiers still had not emerged from their toilettes, yet Aimee felt as if the entire world marched through the well-kept paths.

"You're doing quite well," he whispered as they finished their greetings to the Abbé. He pushed a strand of hair off her cheek. "I especially like the way you cling to me each time someone approaches."

"You would," she murmured beneath her breath as she espied two men heading in their direction. "Kilian." She turned the full power of her gaze on him. "How much longer—"

"Ah, Messieurs de Duverney. A pleasure. Have you met Madame de Chacontier?"

She smiled stiffly as the men kissed her hand in sequence. Kilian spoke for a while on financial matters, then made his excuses. He headed her toward the other side of the field.

"I shouldn't flatter myself that you want to be alone with me, I suppose," he said as he led her toward a darker path.

"No, you shouldn't."

"Well, if you want to avoid these Parisians, you'll just have to wander into the darkness of the woods with me."

"The lesser of two evils." She released his arm and stepped away as soon as she could see that the path was clear of pedestrians. Under the rich shade of elms, the air was cool and fresh. She lifted her head to the breeze and let it chill her cheeks.

"That wasn't so bad."

"It was horrible." She wiped the perspiration off her brow with her hand. "And we didn't even see most of the courtiers."

"They're still abed. Eleven is too early for them to be up and dressed."

"I know."

Kilian pulled a crisp white linen from his waistcoat

pocket and pulled her to a stop in the middle of the path. He lifted her face by the chin. Her gaze fluttered to his as he wiped her forehead with the cool cloth. "There, that's better."

Her eyes narrowed. "What are you going to do when the Duc de Montchamp discovers this situation?"

His gaze hardened and he released her. He walked farther down the path. "What makes you think that the Duc de Montchamp will care about this?" he snapped, turning to glare at her. "Unless he had the honors before me?"

She lowered her gaze. Let him think the duke and I were lovers, she thought. Let him wonder. It seemed the only way she could anger him. "The entire court knew I was the duke's protégée," she said carefully, lifting her skirts over some refuse. "He won't take kindly to this."

"You are my mistress of your own doing. I won the honors in a fair game of cards. Even the duke understands that that cannot be challenged, unless he wishes to risk his life at the end of my sword." He pulled on the lace that hung from his wrists. "But you need not worry about the interference of the duke, at least not yet. He was called away on urgent business to Normandy."

She started. "Normandy?"

"Yes. A fire in his château or something."

Fire! She wondered how dry the land was, for in June it could be parched enough for fires to rage through the forests for miles. If that were the case, then all her tenants' homes and Château Bocage itself were in danger—

Kilian took her arm. "Don't worry, *a stor*. I heard it was a small fire, in the château itself. I'm sure it hasn't spread."

"But if the land is dry—"

"When I was last there, the land was quite wet. Too wet, in fact. Half the crops were ruined because of it."

She began to speak but stopped herself. She wanted to ask if the first crop of grain had been harvested, if the garden had been tended, if the ledgers had been kept up and the day-workers paid. She wanted to know if the next vintage of calvados tasted as piquant as the last, and if the apple cider fermenting in the great barrel had been checked this month.

"You need not worry about Château Bocage. Gustave is overseeing everything."

"He couldn't possibly! There's far too much for him to do already." She turned away. These things no longer concerned her and it was cruel of him to remind her of her lost estate. Lifting her chin, she shrugged one bared shoulder and headed farther down the path. "It doesn't matter."

The bushes rustled beside her. As she turned, a huge man dressed in common clothes leapt from the undergrowth and his large, dirty hand clamped over her face.

"Aye, a filly, we have," the man bellowed. "And a fancy man with her—Come clean his pockets of gold."

She struggled in the man's grip until she could see above the dirt-encrusted fingers. Kilian stood with a point of a dagger beneath his chin. His assailant wore a linen across his face and his tricorn low over his eyes. His breeches hung in tatters about his knees. "Spit up the gold," Kilian's assailant said, the light glinting off the blade of the dagger.

Thieves! Her heart thumped hard in her breast. Never had she heard of them in the Bois de Boulogne in the bright of day. She and Kilian had walked deep into the forest, but she could still see the skirts and waistcoats of other walkers just at the end of the path. Bold and desperate thieves, she thought with a tremor. A dozen stories flashed through her mind. She wondered if she would leave alive or if her throat would be cut by the man who held her firmly against him.

She watched Kilian as he reached slowly into his waistcoat in search of his gold. His eyes never left his assailant's face. Aimee realized that though Kilian had a dagger pointed at his neck, the man behind her held no weapon, for both his hands held her. In a dizzy second of hysteria, she opened her mouth and bit down—hard—on one of the dirty fingers.

Her assailant yelped, and Kilian took advantage of the distraction to knock the dagger out of the thief's grip. Unarmed, the smaller man crouched as Kilian leapt on him. Aimee twisted and kicked her assailant in the shin with the tip of her heel. He bent in pain and she took advantage of his loosened grip to slip from beneath his fingers. She ran —as fast as she could in her wide skirts—but the man caught her easily by the dress and hauled her back into his arms. Enraged, he tightened his grip around her middle until spots swam before her eyes and she slumped in his arms.

She heard the sounds of a scuffle. She heard grunts and the hard crush of fist against bone. She struggled to regain some semblance of consciousness. As she lifted her head she saw Kilian's white linen shirt exposed beneath a tear in the satin of his waistcoat. He lifted his assailant in the air and tossed him toward the grass. When he turned to Aimee, his eyes were fiery with anger.

"Let the woman go and fight like a man," he sneered at her assailant.

"If you want your woman, throw me your gold," he growled. He shifted her under one arm, which dug unmercifully into her waist. He spread the other hand out to Kilian. "Give me the gold."

Kilian's glance flickered to her. He reached inside his waistcoat and pulled out several gold *louis*. Defiantly, he tossed them on the ground in front of the large man. "Let her go," Kilian said, his voice low and icy, "and the gold is yours."

She struggled in his grip as she gasped for air. The man that held her was huge—nearly as tall as Kilian but twice as wide. His arm bulged with muscles.

"Fool 'ristocrat," he bellowed. "You think you're a match for the likes of me?"

The man tossed her to the ground. She lay in the litter and struggled to catch her breath. Kilian's boots scraped against the pebbled path. She rose to her elbows and winced. Squinting, she watched in horror as the huge man lifted Kilian and tightened his arms. Ignoring the pain that speared through her upper body, she stood up and found a stick near the base of an elm tree. She rushed to the man and hit the assailant on the back—as high as she could reach. More surprised than stunned, he dropped Kilian and whirled on her. She ran away as Kilian began raining punches on the man's soft belly.

The assailant's tricorn fell off in the scuffle, revealing a lion's mane of red hair. Kilian increased his assault until the man bent over in pain. Aimee turned away as she heard the sickening crack of Kilian's fist on the giant's cheek, followed by another, and another, until the man fell to his knees. She turned and watched as he gathered his tricorn, snarled at Kilian, and lumbered off into the woods.

Kilian rushed to her side and lifted her chin. "Did he hurt you?" Her eyes fluttered shut as she began to feel the pain of the bruises that marred her waist, her ribs, and her arms. Vaguely, she gestured to her middle and then sank into his embrace.

"Pauvre petite," he murmured, pressing her carefully, but close to his body. "We shouldn't have wandered so far." Her hat had fallen off and her hair tumbled in tangled curls down her back. Kilian combed his fingers through it as she leaned heavily on him.

"Are you hurt?" she asked.

"Nay, nothing but a few bruises. I've seen much worse in battle." He leaned over her shoulder "The fiend ripped and soiled your skirts."

"I tried to get away."

"You fought quite well for an untried soldier, *a stor.*"

She pressed her cheek against his chest. Her head pounded, first lightly, then more insistently. She knew she shouldn't be leaning on him. Kilian, too, was a beast, as much of a beast as the thieves who had attacked them. As she felt her knees buckle beneath her she had no choice but to admit her weakness. "I'm not feeling very well, Kilian."

He forced her to face him and his gold-flecked eyes scanned her pale, drawn face. "You look like the devil." Gently, he settled her weight in his arms and lifted her. Her panniers stuck out in strange directions, but she did not care. He placed her at the foot of an elm very close to the main promenade.

"Rest here for a moment. I'll have the carriage brought to us. I don't want Paris seeing you like this." His eyes twinkled. "They'll think I dragged you out into the woods and had my way with you."

She smiled weakly, but the movement increased the pain in her head. Her side ached where the giant had crushed her ribs. She watched Kilian through a haze as he hailed a young boy and gave him a coin to fetch the carriage.

She felt exceedingly silly. The giant had tossed her around, but he had not harmed her seriously. She wondered why she was having such a "fit of the vapors," as the comtesse would call it. As Kilian returned with her hat in his hand, she struggled to shake off the dizziness.

"Don't move, you'll just make it worse." He bent beside her and watched her face. A light of concern deepened in his eyes. "You're really hurt, aren't you?"

She blinked twice and stared at him. "It's nothing but a few bruises and the shock, I think." She rubbed her temple. "My head hurts and my waist, and my arms."

Kilian took her forearm and turned it over. A livid yellow bruise grew on the underside. "That idiot!" His lips tightened over his teeth. "I should have beat him to—" he cut his own sentence off as he glanced at her. "Are there other bruises like this?"

"My waist—I could barely breathe in his grip."

"Your head aches?"

"Yes."

He pressed her head against his chest and ran a hand down her back. "We'll be home soon, *a stor*." He rubbed his lips in her hair and kissed her temple. He ran his fingers along her nape and loosened her dress. She murmured a feeble "no," but he paid it no heed. "You need to breathe freely and this damned dress is suffocating you."

The carriage rumbled to a stop beside them. He rolled his torn waistcoat off his shoulders and draped it across hers. Lifting her in his arms, he maneuvered her into the coach and closed the door behind them.

Aimee sank into the soft leather seat, but Kilian jolted her from her drowsiness. "Let me loosen that damned corset, Aimee."

She flushed despite her weakened condition. "It can wait until we get back to your town house—I am not that hurt."

His dark brows lowered and left his eyes in shadow. "We shall see about that. Come." She had no strength to battle him. He twisted her limp body so he could unhook the rest of her dress and loosen the silk ties of her corset.

"Please, Kilian." Though the looseness of her dress eased the pounding in her head, his probing pained her. "You're hurting me."

"Aye, and I'm sorry." He released a rattled sigh. "That brute left bruises the size of apples on your side."

"I could have told you that."

He drew her back against his chest. She did not protest. He brushed hair from her forehead. "At least now you won't have to face any more aristocrats for a day or two."

"Does that mean you are not going to force me out into society?"

"I never want to force you into anything."

She turned her head until she could hear the slow, steady beating of his heart beneath his linen shirt. She closed her eyes. What did it matter if she leaned on him? What did it matter if she extracted some comfort from the strength of his arms? This was only temporary, after all. Soon he would metamorphose back into the vengeful, angry thief who had betrayed her. Until then, she thought, sighing into slumber, she would make the best of the situation.

She woke as the carriage came to an abrupt stop. Kilian hugged her close to his body, but his arms loosened as she stirred.

"Awake?"

She blinked up into his eyes. Slowly, she realized that during her sleep she had twisted until her body lay across his in tangled intimacy. As she tried to straighten, her skirts rumpled around her legs and her dress nearly fell off her shoulders.

"Easy." He eased his legs from beneath her body and untangled her skirts. "Here, put on my waistcoat."

Mute, she took the satin waistcoat and draped it over her shoulders. He stepped out of the carriage and reached for her. He told George, the carriage driver, to fetch a doctor as he led her to the house.

"That won't be necessary," she said sharply, stopping inside the iron gates. She turned to the carriage driver. "Don't bother with the doctor, George. I'm quite fine."

"Aimee—"

"Kilian, really." She shrugged deeper into his waistcoat. "I'm feeling much better. And all that doctor will do is take your gold and bleed me to death. I'll do much better on my own, with a little sleep."

He smiled and waved the carriage driver off. "The lady has spoken, George. Give the horses a good lather."

She entered the town house and walked up the narrow stairs. Jeanne met her in her room a few minutes later and helped her undress. She thought vaguely that this was the second time she had entered the town house, and both times she had entered half-dressed. Jeanne must think her a complete tart.

When she was bare to her chemise, she lay down atop the woolen coverlet and closed her eyes, but sleep would not come. Jeanne left to boil water for a cup of tea. Though the room did not collect afternoon sun, the air was as hot and still as in the thickest parts of Paris. She rose and opened a window. She watched the throstles fly about in the tangled front garden.

That garden needs cleaning, she thought idly. She looked down at her hands, white and soft from weeks of nonuse. She wondered if Kilian would care if her hands became callused from digging in the Parisian soil, and then, just as suddenly, remembered that he had not cared while they were in Normandy.

While they were in Normandy. . . . She closed her eyes as a breeze moved the thin curtains and brushed over her legs. The scent of dying roses drifted to her from below, and suddenly she remembered the violets Kilian had plaited for her on May Day. With that memory came another from the same day—the memory of his smile as he greeted her, bold and upright on his stallion. She remembered his kiss on top of the knoll while they waited for Manon and Gustave to round the bend in that rickety old cart.

She sucked in her breath as more memories stirred. She hid her face in her hands as the images tore through her mind: his strong, naked shoulders, his body as it moved on hers, the crackle of the hearth fire as his kisses lingered on her neck. Her heart lurched anew and she wondered why he had betrayed her, and why, now, he held her as his captive mistress.

Revenge, she thought. It could be nothing else. He still carried the flame of vengeance for the Duc de Montchamp. He would not rest until he was dead, and he did not care if she was caught in the middle.

Her brows drew together. He had fought like a wolf this afternoon to save her. He had tossed his gold on the ground to ransom her safety. He had held her in his arms like a porcelain doll and let her sleep peacefully on his chest. And last night, he had seduced her without touching her, and left her aching for more.

"*A stor?*"

She started and twisted toward the door. Kilian carried in his hand a tray with a steaming porcelain cup. His gaze fell to her body, thinly veiled in the sheer chemise.

"*Ar ghrá Dé.*" He settled the tray on a small table by the hearth. Stomping over to the armoire, he pulled out the red silk robe and tossed it behind him. "Put something on."

Aimee caught the silk and struggled into the sleeves. She winced as she tied it too tight about her waist. Kilian sat heavily in the chair by the hearth. She stayed on the bed until he peered over the upholstered back.

"Join me." His voice was strained.

She shook her head and curled up on the bed. "I'm tired, Kilian. I . . . I think I'll try to sleep."

"It's impossible to sleep in this heat." She heard him rise and pick up the tray. He rounded the bed and placed it on the nearby dressing table. "Drink this tea. It might help."

She leaned on an elbow and reached for the tepid liquid. Obediently, she finished it and returned the empty cup. She could not meet his gaze. It seemed to melt her clothes from her body.

"You are feeling better?"

She nodded. "I have a few bruises on my side, but that's it. I don't know what happened to me this afternoon. I felt as faint as an over-corseted dowager."

"It was the shock, I think." He sat on the bed in the curve of her body. "Would you mind if . . ." He faltered.

She met his gaze. The light from the windows lit the tawny streaks in his hair. His eyes emanated their own light beneath the darkness of his brows. She waited for him to continue, but he seemed to have forgotten what he wanted to say. "Do I mind if what?" she asked huskily.

"I want to make sure that you are only bruised. That thief was strong. He could have broken your ribs."

Aimee knew that her ribs were intact. She knew, too, that his touch would be a heady, dangerous thing. "No," she murmured. "No, I don't mind."

The silk of the robe and the cambric of her chemise were no match against the heat of his hands. As his fingers curled around her hip she knew she was as good as naked beneath him. He laid his other hand flat against her belly.

"Tell me when it hurts."

His hands moved slowly over the curve of her hip, pressed into her waist, then lifted to her side. He rolled her gently onto her back and began to probe the lower rib. His fingers hesitated as they traced up toward her heart and the lift of her breast. Then they returned once again to her side.

"You're too thin."

She could not open her eyes. She felt him hovering over her. His gaze stripped her naked and suddenly she wanted, more than anything, to be naked beneath him. She winced as he probed the center of the bruise on her side.

"That's the bruise."

"Mmm." He traced the rib. "Does it hurt here?"

She shook her head. "Only on the side."

He probed another rib, his fingers pressing with insistent but gentle pressure through the length of the bone. Aimee arched instinctively as his fingers brushed the underside of her breast. Her eyes flickered open.

He leaned over her, far too close. His body cast a shadow over her own. Their gazes met.

"Did I hurt you?"

"No."

"Then there's nothing broken," he whispered. He

touched the hollow between her breasts. "Except, perhaps, your heart."

His lips captured hers and she did not resist. He stopped his probing and wound his arms beneath her body. Aimee's hands rose to his chest until she could feel his heart racing beneath her fingers. He shifted his weight on top of her.

She struggled for breath as sparks exploded in her blood. How could she have forgotten this ecstasy? He teased her pliant lips with his tongue and she acquiesced to his silent demand. All pain, all soreness, all resistance disappeared under his touch. She wanted Kilian de Laclos with all the ferocity of a woman starved of love.

He yanked the silk robe apart and his fingers slipped underneath to cup her breast. Her hardened nipples swelled beneath the cambric chemise and he teased the nub with trembling fingers. She broke their kiss at this heady touch and threw her head back to gasp for breath. He shifted his weight until she could feel his passion pressing against her thigh.

She was lost, completely and utterly lost. Vaguely, she felt him lift her up and remove the robe from her body, leaving her exposed beneath his gaze. She tugged at his linen shirt until the tails came out of his breeches and her fingers felt the light spray of hair that covered his abdomen.

Suddenly, he pulled himself off her. He stared down into her eyes, and she noticed that the gold flecks were nearly obscured by the emerald green of his irises. He swung his legs off the bed and held his head in his hands.

"I'm no better than a rutting bull," he snapped, rising and walking away from her. She stared at him in dazed confusion, but he avoided her eye. "You've had quite a shock this afternoon, Aimee, and I am deeply sorry for taking advantage of your condition."

She lifted herself to her elbows, wanting to tell him that it was all right, that she wanted him, that all she wanted was for him to love her as he loved her in Normandy. But the fire of passion began to cool and she realized that she lay, half-naked, upon the tousled bed. Kilian ran fingers through his tawny hair and turned to look at her from the door.

"Sleep, *a stor*. When you regain your strength you'll thank me for leaving you alone."

CHAPTER

16

"The Treaty of Aix-la-Chapelle is already signed, by every party but Austria and Spain. There is nothing I can do to change its terms now." Kilian eyed the two Scotsmen who sat across the great wooden trencher. "The best we can do for the prince is raise money and guns before the last two powers sign and King Louis is bound, by its terms, to remove the prince from France."

Though the tavern was gloomy, he saw the flashing light of defiance in the Scots' blue eyes. Their fingers stiffened on their earthenware mugs.

"'Twould be different had you gone to Aix-la-Chapelle in April, when you should," Ian MacDonald scolded in his Scottish bray. "Then we wouldn't be in this muddle."

"Hush, you disrespectful dog," Eamon roared, rising to his full height. The frightened tavern keeper dropped a mug at the sound. "Laclos had a dead sister to avenge—"

"He's not a Scot," Ian said in a dangerously soft tone.

"And neither are you. You can't understand what a Stuart prince on the throne of England would mean to a Scot."

"My grandfather was in the Battle of the Boyne, Mac-Donald. As was Kilian's." Eamon lifted his meaty arms to his hips, nearly knocking over the tavern keeper in the process. "Our families have fought for the Stuarts for fifty years, since William of Orange stole the throne from James II. Kilian and I both fought in the Scottish campaign, and have the wounds to show it. Do you question our loyalty to the Stuart cause?"

"Sit down, Eamon," Kilian warned, gesturing to the tavern keeper for another round. The Irishman quieted, but his anger flushed his face as red as his hair. "MacDonald is thinking only of the prince."

Eamon settled uneasily on the bench. The Irishman and the Scotsman watched each other with wary eyes. Nothing had changed since the glorious battles of 1745 and 1746; the inner circle of the prince's advisers battled among themselves with ferocious constancy. The Irish versus the Scots, the MacLeods versus the Campbells. It was a wonder that a coalition still existed in Paris.

"I will talk to the king one more time," Kilian said. "But I guarantee you nothing. The prince has become an embarrassment to the monarch."

"Ach, he's no friend of the prince then, to so quickly turn on a royal guest." MacLeod, the second Scot, pushed away his ale. "What will he do when the prince refuses to leave?"

Kilian lifted his brows. "I wouldn't advise the prince to refuse. The king will treat him no better than any other royal prisoner. You must remember that the king will soon be bound to the terms of the treaty. He will have no choice but to exile him. It would be best if the prince left of his own accord."

Ian shook his blond head. "The prince'll not be running out of France like a dog with its tail between its legs."

. "Then he'll be escorted out by the French army. King Louis wants peace above all else—even above the friendship of the young pretender."

Ian MacDonald's blue eyes narrowed. Dressed defiantly in his tartan, the Scot sneered, showing gaps where he had lost teeth in battles. "And so you'll petition this back-stabbing king, for money and arms?"

"Aye."

"I've heard, Laclos, that the king's mistress is displeased with you for taking the Norman lass as your mistress."

Kilian's eyes hardened. Aimee was not a subject he cared to discuss casually, especially not in a tavern with two men who were acting more like adversaries than comrades-at-arms. "Make your point, MacDonald."

"How can you expect to receive any favors from the king? He doesn't want to promote the prince's cause, nor does he wish to give favors to a man who is stained in the eyes of his mistress." Ian toyed with his tartan sash. "A lost cause is yours."

"Nay, not lost." He sipped the bitter ale. "The court is a different country, MacDonald. It runs by different rules. Granted, the Marquise de Pompadour is powerful and she wants me out of court. I want arms and money for the prince." He shrugged a shoulder. "I intend to convince her to advise the king to give me what I want, and I will promise to leave court if I receive my demands. The king will not object to giving arms if it is done in secrecy—and if the prince leaves voluntarily and causes no scandal. All parties will be appeased."

Eamon twisted to face Kilian. "Then you'll be coming with us? For the next attack on England?"

"Nay, my friend. I've got one battle already on my hands." He frowned briefly as he thought of Aimee. "I'll leave court when I receive the money and the arms, but I shan't leave France." His lips twisted. "The marquise, I suspect, will not be pleased when she finds out that Madame de Chacontier will leave court with me."

"You are risking your favor with the king," Eamon said, glancing at the Scots. "You shouldn't do that for the likes of them."

"I am not doing it for them, but for the prince." He turned to the Scots. "But I shan't try this at all unless the prince voluntarily leaves France, in disguise and secretly. If the king is forced to publicly exile him then the cause is lost, and he will give no assistance at all. The prince must be in Scotland before the arms, and before his absence is noticed. Is that understood?"

The Scots thundered and frowned, but in the end promised to speak to the prince. Kilian and Eamon finished their ales in one draught and paid their *livres*. Outside, on the edge of the Faubourg St. Germain, carriages rumbled over the cobbled streets, delivering their riders to *hôtels* across the city for dinner, and the hot June sun heated the stones beneath their booted feet.

Eamon fell into step beside him. "Do you think they will talk to the prince?"

"Yes, but all they'll do is talk. They don't want the prince to leave France, and they've got too damned much pride to realize the consequences."

Eamon shook his great head. "A pity, it is, to watch the prince's cause die here in Paris. And after so many generations of battles. My dear father is rumbling in his grave."

"Aye." He glanced sidelong at Eamon. "But there's another matter I'd rather discuss, Eamon O'Sullivan, now that we're finally alone."

The great giant glanced away and flushed a vibrant red. "I'd figured you'd want a piece of me for that incident in the Bois de Boulogne."

"Aye, more than a piece of you. You were supposed to hold her, not beat her."

"I didn't mean to, Kilian, and to that I'll swear." He

lifted his massive shoulders. "The lass has sharp teeth and a vicious kick. I've still got a welt on my leg from her—"

"And she's got bruises on her waist the size of my fist," he interrupted as he remembered all too vividly the marks on her fair skin. "Why couldn't you just hold her still, as I told you?"

"On my mother's grave, I meant the lass no harm." He spread his hands before him. *"Ar ghrá Dé*, Kilian, don't you know that?"

He sighed. "Aye. I know you meant no harm, but to see her so bruised I nearly lost my mind. If she ever finds out that that whole attack was planned, she'll never forgive me."

"Aye, she will. I'll apologize to her on my knees, if necessary, and tell her your true motives. It was not your fault I don't know how to hold a lady properly," Eamon ribbed Kilian. "Besides, if and when she does find out about it, she'll know you did it only to get her to trust you again."

Kilian's face darkened. His plan had not worked as he had wanted it to work. Although Aimee and he had come to a wary truce, she still regarded him with suspicion. If she hadn't responded to him so passionately the afternoon after the attack, he would have given up all hope. Since then, she had been as cold and aloof as a princess of the blood. And since then, he had done everything in his power not to be alone with her in a room with a bed.

When he was alone with her he felt like a boy of seventeen rather than a man of thirty. He quickened his pace and Eamon followed in amiable silence. He thought about her constantly. She would walk into a room and he would completely lose his thought. He found himself staring at the curve of her breast, at the graceful arch of her throat. He found himself probing her gaze, trying to read a glimmer of love in the shadowed gray depths of her eyes.

At least she had taken to being the lady of the house, he

thought, a wry smile curving his lips. In a single week she had hired a cook, furnished a sitting room, and aired out all the rooms that had remained closed since the days of his father's residence. She missed Château Bocage. He knew she would respond to such a situation as his neglected town house with vigor, once she got used to the idea of being his mistress. That part of his plan had worked to perfection.

It had only been a week and a half since she had officially become his mistress. He expected too much too fast. In deference to her wishes, they had only gone out into society one more time since the card game. She preferred receiving the Comtesse de Vierzon in the newly furnished sitting room, rather than attending the Française or the Opera, or any other salons. That would change soon, he mused, waving absently to Eamon as the Irishman headed down a narrow, winding alley toward his lodgings, that and this frustrating game of abstinence.

He loved her. He wanted to wrap his arms around her and whisper the words in her ear, over and over, until she believed him. He wanted to make love to her until the wall she had built between them crumbled down and he could see her feelings bright and luminous in her lovely gray eyes.

He could not attack her. He would lose her that way. He had discovered that Aimee could battle his anger and his physical strength, but she could not battle his kindness. As long as he treated her as he wanted to treat her for the rest of her life—with respect and gentility—then he could wear down her defenses. Unfortunately, his patience and control hung on a thin, frayed rope. He wanted her, too, and if her own body's signals were any indication, she wanted him as well. He did not know how much longer he could follow his own well-laid plans.

Kilian sighed and hailed a fiacre as he approached a small square. He would win this battle, he thought, climbing into the vehicle. It was, after all, the most important

battle he had ever waged, and the reward was the heart and
hand of Aimee de Chacontier.

Aimee dug deep into the rich soil and turned it over to
the sun. The black earth clung to her hands and lodged
deep beneath her fingernails. She had found a pair of rusty
scissors in the cellar of the town house, but they were so
dulled she could barely cut the high, thin blades of grass
that obscured the edge of the pathway. She used them,
instead, to turn over the earth in this far corner of the front
garden, in preparation for another rosebush. Later, when
she worked up the courage to go into Paris, she would
deliver the scissors to a knife sharpener.

A carriage rumbled down the cobbled street and stopped
in front of the town house. Aimee glanced at her calico
cotton dress and smeared arms in dismay. Kilian was not
due back for at least a half hour, she thought, glancing up
at the position of the sun. She stepped behind a hedge as a
liveried carriage driver opened the creaking iron gate.

"Marie-Celeste!" She tossed the scissors to the ground
and crossed the wild grass to greet her. The comtesse drew
back when she saw her filthy arms.

"That's quite all right, Aimee," she said, dropping her
parasol in front of her for protection. "We can forgo the
embraces until later, when you've washed."

She wiped her hands on her skirt and smiled. "I didn't
expect you, Marie. I would have dressed for the occasion."

"Is *he* here?"

"No." Her smile faded. "He's due soon, for dinner."

"Well, I'll be sure to be gone by then." The comtesse
lifted her parasol over her head and twirled it. "I am glad
you are alone. I have a few things to tell you."

"Indeed?" Her brows arched. Undoubtedly the comtesse
had more gossip from court. More gossip about the "scan-

dal" of Madame de Chacontier and the "brashness" of the Chevalier de Bourg-en-Bresse. Truly, she did not want to hear any more of the stories, but the comtesse seemed to find some pleasure in telling her how displeased the court —especially Madame de Pompadour—was with Kilian. "Come in for some lemon-water," she said, turning toward the house. "You can see what I've done to the parlor."

"I cannot stay long. I was on my way to Versailles and had to pass by." She squinted into the sun. "Come, over here, under the shade of the elm for a while. Too much sun makes me as pink as a milkmaid."

Marie took her arm with two pristine fingers and led her into the cool shade of the elm that grew just outside the high stone fence.

"Well, what is it?"

The comtesse hesitated and searched her face. "You know that you're becoming as brown as a day-worker?" She pursed her reddened lips. "Somehow, it compliments you. Has he touched you yet?"

Aimee flushed full to the roots of her hair. Kilian had touched her, but not in the way Marie-Celeste thought. Each evening for the past seven nights he had walked her to her bedroom door. Each evening she wondered if he would kiss her like he had kissed her after the attack in the Bois de Boulogne. He never did. And as each evening passed she wanted, more and more, for him to make love to her.

"No," she stammered, glancing away. "He hasn't done more than kiss my hand since last week."

"You say that with reluctance, *mon amie*. Could it be that you are succumbing to the charm of the handsome chevalier?" Marie's bright blue eyes sparkled beneath the saucy brim of her wide, feather-bedecked hat. "It would please me if you finally took a lover, even one as corrupt as the chevalier."

"He broke my heart once, Marie. I shan't give him a second opportunity."

"Yes." She shrugged a plump, bare shoulder. "Have you ever thought that perhaps the man has more than just a passing attraction to you?"

"Marie!"

"Think, Aimee. He could have had any woman in all of Paris as his mistress—as his willing mistress. Yet he chose you, and then, doesn't touch you."

"He did not choose me. He *won* me in a card game."

"Mmm. Curious." Marie tilted her head. "The chevalier also won a card game with the young pretender that night, didn't he?"

"Yes. He had bartered Château Bocage, and that is what drew me into my own folly."

"Do you remember what Prince Charles anted in that game, Aimee?"

She shrugged her shoulders. "I don't know. Gold plate or something."

"He anted a set of gold plate that he bought from the king's goldsmith, worth over a hundred thousand *livres*," the comtesse corrected. "The same gold plate that I ate off of last night, at the Princesse de Talmond's salon."

"The same plate?" Her brows drew together. "Perhaps . . . perhaps Kilian has not yet had time to pick it up."

"I thought nothing of the plate until this afternoon," Marie continued. "As I was riding through the city I saw your chevalier walk out of a tavern on the edge of the Faubourg St. Germain. He was with a huge bear of a man —the biggest man I've ever seen—and the man had a mop of hair as red as flame!"

"What?"

"A giant, Aimee. A giant man with red hair. Talking amiably with the Chevalier de Bourg-en-Bresse." She searched Aimee's eyes. "There can't be two such men in all of Paris, and the way you described your assailant in the Bois de Boulogne—"

"Are you quite sure it was Kilian with this man?"

"Yes. Kilian wore white breeches, white hose, and a dark green waistcoat. The chevalier is certainly an easy figure to spot!"

She bit her lower lip as her thoughts whirled. "You don't think that . . ." She shook her head. "Why would Kilian set up the situation in the Bois de Boulogne? It makes no sense. I was *hurt!* The other assailant had a knife pointed at his throat, and the giant that held me would have choked Kilian to death if I hadn't hit him from behind."

"And the force of your blow was enough to distract him?" the comtesse asked suspiciously. "And whatever happened to the first thief? Why didn't he scramble for the gold Kilian had left on the ground and run while Kilian and the giant fought? And the entire incident, happening in the brightness of the day, not far from the main promenade— It seems to me, Aimee, that this explains everything."

"But why? Why would Kilian set that up?"

"Why hasn't Kilian picked up the proceeds of his bet with the young pretender? He insisted on receiving your ante immediately. Why did he not send for the plate the next day? Or, moreover, why didn't the prince, who is a man of honor, not send it to the chevalier himself?" The comtesse flushed with discovery. "I think the entire situation has been arranged for the sole purpose of entrapping you. But why the chevalier would go to such lengths to drive you into his arms is another matter."

Aimee's head swam. She felt like a blindwoman who had suddenly been given sight. All of Kilian's actions, from the night of the card game, to last night when he had kissed her on the palm, were suspect. He toyed with her. He had manipulated her. She had thought the tiger had changed his stripes. Anger began like a fire in the pit of her belly, and with it, pain. "I'd wager my pension that he cheated at our card game."

"I wouldn't be surprised," Marie agreed. "But the question I asked after I saw him with the giant, is *why?* Why would he go to such lengths?"

"Kilian de Laclos went to greater lengths in Normandy to wreak his vengeance on the Duc de Montchamp," she said angrily. "This is just part of a greater plot, and I'll not be a part of it."

"The Duc de Montchamp has been in Paris for four days. He knows what has happened to you. Yet Kilian has done nothing to flaunt you in front of him. In fact, he has avoided the court functions to which the duke has been invited."

"He's biding his time."

Marie wrinkled her pert nose and shook her head. "I think you are being exceptionally blind, *mon amie.*"

"I know him better than you. He is capable of anything."

Marie reached for Aimee's arm, despite the dirt, and pulled her close to her. "He's also capable of loving. And it seems to me that he is doing his best to win your heart."

"For what purpose? To break it?"

"Non." She tilted her head and the feathers fluttered in a light breeze. "The Chevalier de Bourg-en-Bresse is in love with you. I'm convinced of it now. He set up the incident at the Princesse de Talmond's salon because he knew you would play against him if Château Bocage were the stakes. The prince and the chevalier have been friends for some time, so they must have agreed to arrange the game so the chevalier would win. Then, you would challenge him and he would make you offer yourself as his mistress—no, his *titled* mistress, thus removing all signs of disrespectability." The comtesse grew more and more animated. "Then, once he won—and he may have cheated on that game, as well—he took you here and proceeded to barrage you with kindness. He doesn't touch you, except, of course, when

he can't resist"—her eyes sparkled on Aimee—"and then
he sets up a situation where he protects you from thieves so
you will trust him more."

"You are ridiculous!" she snapped. "That story is utterly
preposterous, Marie. You are letting your imagination get
the best of you."

"No, I'm not. Don't you see? This explains everything."

She shook her head and wiped her hands on her calico
dress. "I shan't talk about it anymore."

"Shan't talk about what?"

Aimee and Marie started. They turned simultaneously as
Kilian walked through the iron gate. In the heat of their
discussion, neither of them had heard the fiacre stop before
the house or the squeaking of the iron door. Aimee realized
in a flash that Kilian wore white breeches, hose, and a dark
green waistcoat—just as the comtesse had described.

"Nothing," she said, suddenly conscious of her disheveled state. "I didn't realize how quickly the time passed.
I'm sure dinner must be ready." She turned to the comtesse. "Will you be joining us, Marie?"

"No, no. Not today." She smiled and gathered her skirts.
"I shall leave you two alone."

Aimee blushed at the innuendo. "I insist, Marie-
Celeste." She took the comtesse's arm and stared at her
meaningfully. "I'll need your advice and recommendations
on the town house."

Marie's brows lowered over her eyes, but she knew there
was no way she could gracefully exit. Aimee's fingers
tightened on her upper arm. "Very well, then," she said
breathlessly. "I shall be more than happy to join you. Let
me send my driver to make my excuses at the Princesse de
Talmond's."

Kilian watched the exchange with a strange expression
on his face. Aimee headed toward the town house as the
comtesse gave her driver the orders. He followed close
behind her.

"You should have let the comtesse go," he murmured as the cool air of the foyer engulfed them. "I prefer eating with you alone, especially now, when you smell like sunshine."

"You are the one that wants me to go out into society," she snapped, bristling at the compliment. "This is the first step." Lifting her calico skirts, she hurried up the stairs and did not look back. "Entertain the comtesse, would you? I must wash and change before dinner."

She slammed her bedroom door behind her and stomped to the bowl of water on her dresser. She scrubbed her hands pink then tossed the dirty water out the window to the garden below. Pouring more from a pitcher, she sank her arms in to her elbows and splashed the fresh water over her face.

She lifted her head and let the droplets slither down her neck and between her breasts. What a fool she had been. She should have known from the start that Kilian had manipulated everything. He had told her, long ago, that he wanted her as his mistress. The Duc de Montchamp had warned her. And here she was, Kilian's titled mistress. He had won his prize.

She waited for the fury, but she felt only pain. Her heart ached. Tears mingled with the water that dripped over her face. She patted her skin dry with a thick towel and tore the pins from her hair. She had been played the fool, again. She struggled out of her clothes and searched in the armoire for her most dangerous dress. She would turn the tables on Kilian de Laclos today, she thought. She could not bear this pain anymore.

She walked down the stairs a half hour later, powdered, rouged, and perfumed as the comtesse had taught her. Her scarlet dress was a shade short of impropriety, but she needed the color to bolster her confidence. When she entered the sitting room and Kilian turned to her, she knew she had chosen the correct dress.

"It looks like I shall have the honor of dining with two beautiful women," he said as he crossed the room. She stared at his tawny hair, held back with a crisp black bow, as he bent over her hand. She turned before he could meet her eyes.

"Come, Marie, monsieur. I am sure dinner is quite done." She glanced over her shoulder at his admiring stare. "I am sorry I took so long. I was quite dirty from gardening."

"Worth the wait." He came to her side and put her hand in the crook of his elbow. His green eyes danced on the exposed width of her bosom and he made no effort to hide his gaze. "I've not seen this dress before, madame."

"No, you haven't." She opened the doors to the sparse dining room and gestured to the table. "I bought it on a whim after I won quite a bit at a card game." She stared at him significantly. "A reward for my *honest* labor."

She searched his gold-flecked eyes, hoping to see some trace of guilt, but he seemed oblivious to her innuendo. His gaze probed hers in return and she turned away.

Jeanne hovered like a dark shadow in the far doorway. Aimee nodded in her direction as Kilian pulled out a chair for Marie and then for her. They faced each other on either side of the old dining table. She ran her fingers over the neat lace of a tablecloth she had found in the cellar.

"You've done wonders for the house," Marie said, the strain of the situation evident in her voice. "Each time I visit it looks better."

"You're flattering me, Marie." Aimee nodded at Jeanne and the servant filled her glass with a deep burgundy wine. "This dining room is as sparse as a boarding house. It is next on my list to refurbish." She lifted her gaze to Kilian. "That is, if monsieur does not mind."

"This house is your house, Aimee," he said, using her first name unconsciously. "You do what pleases you."

The comtesse lifted a brow and tilted her head at Aimee,

but she ignored her glance. Jeanne brought out a simple soup of sorrel and leeks and ladled it in each bowl. Aimee toyed with it while she watched Kilian eat. "I think first we should get a decent setting," she said as she stirred her soup with a bent spoon. "This set is dreadful."

Kilian glanced around the table and shrugged. "I agree." He looked at Marie. "I apologize for the humble surroundings, Comtesse. I assure you that I don't intend to keep Aimee in such a condition for long. She has free access to my finances and can decorate as she chooses."

"So I've heard."

"Didn't you win a set of gold plate from Prince Charles, monsieur?" Aimee asked calmly. "The same night that you won me?"

The comtesse dropped her spoon into her soup and the liquid splattered over the front of her gown. Aimee rose to call for Jeanne, but Marie waved her back in her seat. "It is nothing, *mon amie*. Don't trouble yourself."

She looked at Kilian and waited, attentively, for an answer. He settled his spoon next to his bowl and sat back in the chair. "It seems to me that I did win just that from the prince." One straight brow lifted. "Remarkable memory, Aimee."

"It was a very unusual evening."

"Indeed." He shrugged one shoulder and attacked his soup again. "If it is the prince's plate you desire, I shall see that he delivers the setting to me tomorrow. He does, after all, owe it to me."

She lowered her gaze and rang for Jeanne. Marie fumbled with her linen and leaned toward Kilian. "You know the prince quite well, don't you, monsieur?"

"Yes." His gaze grew curious, but shuttered, upon Aimee's stiff features. "My grandfather fought for the Stuart cause in 1715, in the hopes of receiving religious freedom for Ireland. When I found out that the grandson of the man with whom my grandfather fought was actively seeking men to join him in retrieving the stolen throne, I decided to join. I accompanied the prince on the Scottish campaign several years ago. Right before I went to India."

"I've heard such wondrous stories of his adventures," Marie continued, warming to her subject. "Were you with him when he was hiding from the English, after the battles were lost?"

"No, by that time the prince was alone but for a few Scotsmen. The army was dispersed by then. But I was with him on the retreat, with the English at our heels."

Marie straightened in her chair and began to recite the dozens of stories she had heard about the prince, demanding more details from Kilian. Jeanne arrived with the entrée and the *rôti*, but Aimee had no appetite. In a break between stories, he glanced at her plate.

"You're not eating, *a stor*. Is something wrong?"

She hated when he used that endearment, especially in front of guests. She picked up her fork and pushed the meat around in the thick brown sauce. "There's nothing wrong," she assured him. "I'm simply not hungry right now."

Marie, ever sensitive to a lapse in conversation, turned once again to Kilian. To fill the silence she chatted about court until there was no more gossip to be told. Aimee listened, but she did not hear. She became intensely conscious of his gaze.

She toyed with her salad when the *rôti* was taken away. Marie's chatter faded into the background. Kilian's stare was like a physical thing, and she could no longer ignore it. She met his gaze across the long table.

Concern. His face bore the stamp of a man concerned about his woman. The anger rose until it nearly choked her and her cheeks heated with the rage. The concern on his face melted to confusion, and if she did not know him so well, she could swear he actually felt the emotions that flickered across his well-boned, well-trained features.

Ah, my handsome one, she thought, staring at the candlelight glowing off his hair. *I fell in love with you a long time ago and lived through the pain. It seems I will have to live through the pain again.*

She knew her eyes revealed her thoughts. She lowered her gaze to her well-tangled salad. The comtesse thought Kilian loved her. Foolish thoughts. Kilian didn't love her. He still played the hide-and-seek games he played in Normandy, only this time she was not sure why. She sensed that after he had succeeded in his new goal, she would understand everything. She struggled to cover her agony with anger. Kilian de Laclos toyed with a woman's heart as a cat toyed with its prey.

She speared a piece of radish. Very well. If Kilian chose to live with deceit, then the best thing she could do would be to beat him at his own game. He still had Château Bocage. She must think of a way to turn these games around so she would end up with her estate.

She would win in the end.

". . . and the marquise lost nearly six thousand *livres* at the salon of Madame de Tencin last night, bidding against the Baron d'Auteuil in a ridiculous game of *comète*—"

"Is the Baron d'Auteuil taking my place as the cardplayer to be feared?" Aimee interrupted suddenly. Marie stopped her endless chatter and stared at her with glassy eyes. "Yes, it seems so. Though it is only the first time I can remember that he won such a large bet."

"You shall win your title back quickly, Aimee, if you would come to salons with me," Kilian said.

"Yes, I would, wouldn't I?" she responded. "Perhaps then I should make the effort. After all, I haven't met any of your friends, Kilian."

Marie stiffened visibly.

"For instance, didn't you see Kilian this afternoon, Marie? In the Faubourg St. Germain?"

"Yes. As I was coming here." She turned to Kilian. "You were with a great giant of a man with flaming red hair."

"Yes," Aimee persisted, leaning on the table. She fixed Kilian with a stare. "I want to meet that friend in particular."

Silence blanketed the room as Kilian met her gaze. Marie looked back and forth between the two. Slowly, he pulled away from the table and stood up.

"Perhaps you should leave now, Comtesse." His gaze never left Aimee's stiff features. "Forgive the rudeness, but it seems Madame and I have several things to discuss."

She rose from her chair and rushed to Aimee's side. She looked frantically over her shoulder at the tall, broad-shouldered form of a very angry Kilian de Laclos. "I'll stay if you wish, or you can come with me—"

"It's all right, Marie." She patted her arm. "I shall speak with you later." Marie's hurried footsteps faded into the foyer.

Aimee lifted her chin defiantly. "Well? What is your explanation for this? Should I insist on it now, or do you need more time to think of one?"

"I don't need any time to make up a story, Aimee." He lifted his glass of wine and drained it of its contents. "The truth is strange enough."

She gripped the back of the dining room chair. "Truth! I don't think you know how to tell the truth. I wonder if anything you ever told me was true."

"At least one thing was." He rounded his chair and approached her. She stiffened and faced him with stormy gray eyes.

"What, Laclos?"

"I love you, Aimee de Chacontier. I always have, and I always will."

CHAPTER
17

Aimee reeled. The earth tilted and the only thing that held her upright was the feel of the hard oak chair between her fingers. She stepped back, dragging the chair with her, as Kilian stopped a few feet in front of her. His green eyes glowed with an emotion too tender for words and she wondered if he had lost his senses.

"Don't!" It was her voice that screamed, but she did not recognize it. Jeanne ran in from the kitchens and stared at them with wide eyes.

"Leave us alone," he snapped, as crisp and efficient as a general. He stepped toward Aimee, but she raised her arms against him. He lifted her half-empty glass of wine from the table and handed it to her. She snapped it from his hands.

She struggled between laughter and tears. He spoke so convincingly. His eyes held all the compassion and desire of a bridegroom, but she knew the duplicity of his heart. She had felt the sting of his betrayal not once, but twice.

He persisted, tortuous to the last, to win his game of hearts.

"Why do you do this?" Her voice broke. "Why don't you use someone else in your games—why don't you just go out and kill the Duc de Montchamp instead of using me to hurt him?"

"I did not want you as my mistress to hurt the duke. I want you as my mistress because I love you."

"Stop! Those words are vicious lies and I won't listen to them."

"They are the purest truth, Aimee. That is why they are so painful." He passed her and lifted her hand. "Come with me. I have much to tell you. I suppose the comtesse reminded you about the gold plate, just as she told you who I was with this afternoon, but the comtesse does not know the entire story."

Her eyes narrowed. "What web will you weave now, Kilian?"

A pang of pain fluttered over his features and he turned away. In the growing darkness, his silhouette was dark and slumped in the door frame. He sighed deeply. "You have every reason to distrust me. You believe I knew all along that I could have Château Bocage, with just a word to the king. You believe that I used you in Normandy simply to wreak my vengeance on the Duc de Montchamp, but all of that is wrong." He ran a hand through his hair until the bow disentangled and fluttered to the ground. "Now, I don't know what you think, for I don't know how much the comtesse has discovered. But I know, from the look in your eyes, that you believe I have betrayed your trust again. And that, my love, is exactly the opposite of what I intended."

She shook her head and some wine spilled on the hardwood floor. She could not listen to him. He was a master of lies. He would draw her back into his web and this time she would never be able to flee.

He was right. She felt betrayed, again. Over the past week she had softened to him. She had responded to his kindness, and this afternoon she discovered that his behavior was just another ruse.

"I know you feel I have no right to ask you this," he said, his voice soft. "But I want you to listen to *my* side of the story. Just for an hour. Then, if it is your wish, I will release you from your obligation to me."

Her heart beat erratically. "I . . . I won't be your mistress anymore?"

"Yes. I shall set you free."

She did not want to be free. He had captured her heart, the first time with strength, this time with kindness. She did not want to leave him now. Over the past week, she had made the fatal mistake of falling in love with her captor. Again.

What a fool she was! She should be furious for all his duplicity, but she felt no anger. Pain throbbed in her chest. She glanced at him. The expression on his face made her heart ache. His gaze pleaded for her acquiescence. Even if she had the will, she had not the heart to resist.

He approached her and took her wine from her hand. His other hand caressed her cheek. "Say yes. You shan't regret it."

I already do, she thought as she nodded and followed him into the sitting room. He took the half-full bottle of wine and filled her glass before he settled in the opposite chair. No fire burned in the grate, for the afternoon had been hot and humid. He stirred the gray embers idly with an iron poker.

His gaze lingered on the paleness of her cheeks as she twirled the stem of her wineglass. He sighed and turned to the hearth. "I cannot deny that I went to Normandy to seek vengeance on the Duc de Montchamp, Aimee. But I swear to you that I didn't have an elaborate plan to steal his mistress from his embrace. My motives were much simpler than that. I wanted him dead.

"You know what happened to my sister. I've killed men in battle with less reason. I had a right to challenge the duke." He ran a hand over his eyes as the rage heated his blood. "Unfortunately, the king summoned me before I had a chance to make the challenge. And, like a loyal soldier, I responded immediately. The king told me he did not want a scandal erupting from this situation. I told him that the duke's actions demanded immediate punishment and I would accept nothing less than exile. So the king suggested the duke leave court, for a while. But no writ of exile was made and the duke was free to return when he would.

"That was unacceptable. You must understand, Jolivette was the youngest of my family, my little sister. She was a gentle spirit who meant harm to no one, but she was not the great beauty my father wanted. I was always . . . very protective of her." His gaze slipped to Aimee. "As I am of you."

She stared into the burgundy waves of her wine but made no response.

"I planned my strategy as I have planned every battle of my life. First, I would scout the lands in and around his estate. I would find out when he ate, when he hunted, when he attended Mass—all the details of his existence. Once I knew his schedule well, I would use that information to strike when I would not be seen. I planned to kill him, then leave Normandy."

Kilian's gaze fluttered to hers. "It was all very simple. I did not expect to be caught in transit by a lovely Norman lady with eyes the color of silver. You stood in the way of my vengeance, and that, my sweet, was a dangerous thing. Soon eough I discovered that you needed scouts. What better disguise than to be in your employ? I could scout the duke's lands freely, strike, and several days later, escape from the Bocage estate.

"I had every intention of doing so. Until I discovered that you had a strange relationship with the duke, one that bore a disturbing similarity to the relationship between my sister and the same duke. I found myself wanting to protect you, but you spurned my protection. I knew I would have to earn your trust, but I couldn't do so without revealing my identity. To reveal my identity meant foregoing my vengeance."

He leaned forward in his chair and ran his fingers through his hair. He lifted his head to face her. "I fell in love with you. You were strong and honest and I admired your courage and convictions. You were unlike any woman I had ever known. The night when I scaled your castle wall I wanted to sweep you away and marry you. I wanted to tell you who I really was and make you mine. I thought you would trust me, despite the fact that I kept my true identity secret. You didn't. And the bitterness I felt at that lack of trust mixed with the hatred and anger I felt for the Duc de Montchamp until I could no longer distinguish the two.

"I went to the duke's that night and tried to kill him, but I was rash. I failed, but escaped. While I hid from his guards, I began to think of other ways I could destroy the duke—but my thoughts drifted to how I could save you from him instead. I knew that you would do anything to keep your estate. That is when I considered going to the king and asking for Château Bocage. The king had promised me a reward for my victories in the Netherlands, several years earlier, but I had thought nothing more of it. In a matter of days the thing was done.

"Vengeance was not sweet. It left a bitter taste in my mouth, *a stor*. In my haste I did not think of what my actions would do to you; I only thought of protecting you from the duke. Your hatred and anger haunted me for weeks, and still haunts me now. In my fury I had not only crushed the duke, but I had destroyed your life, and in the process my own. The castle echoed with your voice, exuded your scent, whispered with the rustle of your skirts. I was losing my mind." He sighed raggedly. "I had to win you back."

Aimee sat motionless in the overstuffed chair, her fingers curled around the stem of her wineglass. She was afraid to breathe, to blink, to think—she was afraid that if she spoke she would somehow shock Kilian back into the laughing, flirtatious, secretive man she had come to know. His voice wavered and cracked and he sank his head into his hands.

"I feared you entered a convent and were forever lost to me. Then I received word that you were in Paris. I followed, hoping that time had eased your pain. It hadn't. But I found you just as lovely, just as hurt, just as defiant as I expected. And I vowed, with time, that I would win you back.

"I am not a patient man. I knew the duke was trying to rekindle that aborted relationship. I wanted to save you from him and force you to be by my side so I could prove to you that I am not the lying, deceiving thief you think I am. And so, once again, I planned my strategy.

"I have one thing that you want. Château Bocage. You swore to me that you would marry me for one reason only; to regain control of Château Bocage. I would have no wife that wanted only my possessions, not even you, my love. I set out to make you my mistress using your estate as bait.

"The prince agreed to help. The game of piquet played between us was nothing but a well-rehearsed play. I knew when you heard me ante Château Bocage you would rise in indignation, but I did not know if you would dare to barter yourself." He smiled slightly. "I took my chances, and you did not fail me. We played, I won, and you were my mistress."

"You cheated at our game, of course," Aimee said quietly.

"Nay, *a stor*. You are far too good a player. I could not cheat without risking being discovered."

"But, what if you had lost?"

"If I had lost, I had other plans." He straightened and pulled off his waistcoat. "I made plans for every contingency. If I had lost I would have followed you to Normandy and plagued you in much the same way I am plaguing you here."

"But. . . ." Her brows drew together and she shifted her weight in the chair. "Why this attack in the Bois de Boulogne?"

"I wanted you to see that I would defend you. I wanted you to realize that you could trust me." He smiled. "I wanted you to cling to me in gratitude."

"But that man tossed me around like a sack of grain!"

"Aye, and I've doubled his bruises for it." He gulped his wine. "He's already told me he'd come and beg forgiveness on his knees if you ever fell in love with me."

Aimee glanced down at her hands, now folded in her lap. Kilian's story rang all too true and her heart ached to believe it. She probed her memory for something—anything—to prove it wrong, but nothing surfaced. Her blood coursed through her veins. Perhaps he did love her, she wondered. Perhaps she had mistaken him all along.

"Well, *a stor?*"

Darkness had fallen and swathed the room in night black shadows. A branch of a tree tapped one of the leaded windows as an evening breeze swayed it against the house. She could feel his gaze on her in the darkness. She could feel her heart opening to him.

"Aimee . . ." His voice broke and he rose from the chair. His hands captured her head and his fingers entwined in her hair. He pulled her out of the seat and drew her head onto his shoulder. Her body trembled against his. "Believe me, Aimee, for I have just laid bare my soul to you. If you do not believe me now I shall never be able to convince you." He released her head and wrapped his arms around her body, holding her so tight she could barely breathe. "I love you, Aimee. I love you, I love you, I love you."

She closed her eyes as he whispered in her ear. The words echoed in her head. After so much, could it be possible that he did love her? Could it be that he did not mean to betray her? Or was this just another set of intricate lies meant to hold her forever bound to his side?

She leaned against him. His lips brushed her temple and kissed her earlobe. His breath warmed her hair and his fingers roamed her body. Aimee rubbed her cheek against the smooth linen of his shirt and felt the bristle of his chest beneath it. He smelled of oaky wine and male sweat. He smelled of Kilian and comfort. She turned her head and found the open part of his shirt. He tasted salty.

She heard his sharp intake of breath as she kissed his chest. His fingers curled into her sides.

"Aimee. . . ."

She lifted her arms and traced the long, knotted muscles of his back. Gently, he pulled her head away from his chest and stared her in the eyes.

"You will stay?"

Lit only by the dim light of the evening, his face was cast in stony planes. His lips hovered just over hers. She yearned to touch them, but he drew away at her hesitant approach.

"Tell me, *a stor.*"

"I will stay," she murmured, rising on her toes. "Kiss me, Kilian. Love me."

He touched her face and traced the curve of her lips as if he could not believe what she had said. He shook his head, as if he wanted to ask her something again, but he stopped himself. Drawing her close, he lowered his lips onto hers and kissed her until her knees melted into water.

He lifted her off her feet. In the darkness he made his

way through the room into the bare foyer, then up the narrow flight of stairs. Jeanne had lit the candles that flanked the walls and Aimee pressed her face against his chest. She did not want him to see her so soft with need, so pliant in love. She wanted him to cover her, join her, merge with her until she could no longer tell the difference between the two of them.

He kicked the door open, then kicked it shut behind him. With maddening slowness he set her on her feet and pulled the pins, one by one, from her hair. He unrolled each tress and set it upon her shoulders until the mass cascaded across her breasts. When the last pin had fallen with a tinkle to the hardwood floor, he buried his face in the warm depths of her curls.

Aimee's head fell back as his touch ignited her. His hands trembled on her waist, but they did not falter as they whirled her around and unhooked the scarlet satin dress. His fingers traced the slow curve of her back before he pushed the dress, panniers, and petticoats off the slight curve of her hips.

The corset loosened as Kilian pulled the silk ties out from the small eyelets. He tossed the garment with the others and ran his hands over the wrinkled cambric chemise. He drew her back against him and lifted his hands to cup both of her breasts.

"I never thought you'd let me touch you again."

"I've missed your touch," she said softly as his gentle hands massaged the small globes of her breasts. She quivered as his fingers captured the taut peaks that poked against the chemise. She wanted to twist in his arms and kiss him, but as she struggled he held her tighter.

"Easy, my love. We have this night, all nights, and I shall never stop loving you like this."

"I need you, Kilian."

He sucked in his breath, then laughed softly. "Aye, and I need you, too, my love."

He released her breasts. She twisted to face him. He kissed her and his patience crumbled. She felt small in his arms, tiny, breakable, cherished. He lifted her without effort and laid her on the bed, then covered her body with the length of his own. She tugged at his shirt. She needed to feel his bare, hot skin against her.

He pulled it over his head and tossed it to the far corner of the room. His tousled hair covered his face in shadows as he hovered above her. Aimee brushed it out of the way and watched the love grow in his eyes.

"You are so beautiful," he murmured, moving down to the end of the bed. She sat up and reached for him, but he eased her back down. "Lie back, my sweet. I have waited a long time to touch you. I want to savor this moment."

He started at her toes. His lips massaged the tender skin of the arch of her foot then the gentle hollow behind her ankle. The heat of his mouth traced the taut curve of her calf and lingered behind her knee. She arched her back as he pushed her chemise up to her thighs and continued his kisses until her legs trembled beneath each touch. Unconsciously, she pressed her legs together.

"Nay, *a stor*," he whispered, gently prying her open to his gaze. "There will be no more secrets between us."

She pressed her cheek against the pillow as he guided her legs. His lips descended to the quivering flesh of her inner thigh, then continued, relentlessly, to rise to the heart of her desire. When he captured it she nearly fainted from the pleasure.

His hands rose to caress her sides, resting, ultimately, on her hardened breasts. All lingering doubts fled with his intimate caresses and she arched beneath his touch. Her body sang, shivered, tightened. She wanted him as she had wanted nothing else before. She wanted to join him and make him hers.

He released her breasts and rose to kiss the indentation of her navel. He slipped one hand beneath her back and lifted her up to pull the tangled chemise over her head. Bared beneath him, she held out her arms.

"Come to me, Kilian."

His gold-flecked gaze branded her. He struggled with his breeches and hose. She watched his body emerge from the trappings of his clothes, wondering at the taut, flat lines of his abdomen, the strong, long muscles of his back. How beautiful he is, she thought. How fine and strong and handsome.

She lost all sense of self-consciousness as she lay naked on the bed. He hesitated as he stared at her, drinking in the sight of her body. Her eyes no longer held the light of suspicion, only the brilliant, blinding light of desire.

He had her body, he thought as he covered its long, sinuous curves. He may not yet own her soul. As his flesh touched hers, all thought fled and he knew only their need. His need. Her need. And the surging blood and searing flesh of a man for a woman.

He slipped inside her and listened to her sigh of pleasure. Her arms wound about his back. She lifted her legs instinctively in order to draw him deeper. He had waited for this woman for so long; how fiery and passionate she had grown. Clinging to some form of control, he buried his head in her hair and breathed deeply the tantalizing scent of apple blossoms.

Ah, Aimee, my sweet and lovely mistress! She cried out and her body quivered beneath his. He wanted to hold back his own pleasure—he wanted to spend the night giving her this sweet taste of ecstasy over and over again. But as she clung to him and murmured in his ear he knew he could more easily kill off an entire army than resist this woman's embrace.

The last thing he remembered before he drew her hard against him was the feeling of her lips on his shoulder blade and the sweet sound of his name on her lips.

Aimee woke slowly, languidly, and the hot sun warmed the linens that covered her body. As the sunlight slowly teased her awake she wondered why she felt so relaxed. She sighed deeply and rolled over onto her side.

A warm weight anchored her to the bed. Her arched brows drew together as she reached down to push it away. Her fingers contacted the lightly furred texture of a well-muscled arm.

She suddenly remembered why she slept so soundly. The memory tore her from sleep. Her gray eyes flew open in shock as her body shuddered with waves of blood-hot shame. Only inches from her, Kilian's body lay long and leonine, tangled in the linens, completely naked.

She started and drew back, reaching down to lift his arm from her body. Clutching the linens against her breasts, she swung her legs over the side of the bed and sought her chemise. Her cheeks flushed as she observed the scattering of their clothes on the hardwood floor. How could she have been so wanton! She looked over her shoulder at his sleeping form and understood.

Shaking her head, she rose from the bed and covered her breasts as she tiptoed to the armoire. She knew she would never find her chemise in the melee of garments that carpeted the floor, so she reached for the red silk robe Kilian had given her. She wrapped it around her body firmly.

"Good morning, *a stor.*"

She jumped and turned to find him staring at her from

the bed. His green eyes twinkled behind a netting of gold-tipped lashes.

"Did I wake you?"

"No. I've been half-awake for a while, watching your face in sleep." His gaze burned through the red silk. "And I watched you cross the room, with only the sun caressing your skin. Come back to bed with me."

"It's late," she said, toying with the tie of the robe. "Don't you think we should rise and dress? I'm expecting the comtesse this afternoon—"

"To the devil with the comtesse, my love." He sat upright. "I've waited too long for you. I want you."

His voice growled with desire and she felt the answering flutter of passion in her belly. But it was one thing to succumb to his seduction in the dark of the evening with a glass of red wine heating her blood; it was another thing entirely to give herself so willingly in the stark light of day.

"What's wrong, Aimee?"

She jumped at his voice. She felt as skittish as an untried Arabian. What was wrong, indeed? She had spent the night making love to a man she loved. Why did the doubt linger? Why, when she looked into his concerned eyes, did she still question his motives?

"Come here."

Aimee bristled at the commanding tone of his voice and turned away. "I may have slept with you last night, but that does not mean I shall come at your every summons."

"Come here, *please*."

She turned to find him smiling with both arms outstretched to her. With reluctance, she picked her way over their scattered clothing and sat on the bed.

She resisted the urge to lean against his broad, lightly furred chest. She fixed her gaze on his to prevent it from roaming to the ripples of his abdomen. But his gold-flecked eyes, heavy-lidded in sleep, made a mockery of her resistance. She sank into his embrace.

"You've got the glow of a bride the morning after her wedding night," he murmured as he ran his fingers through her hair. "You're as nervous as one, too."

"Is that the same glow of a milkmaid after she has frolicked in the hay with the stable boy?"

His fingers stopped their caresses. "Aye. I suppose."

"That's a more appropriate image."

He pulled her away from his chest. "And what, my love, is that supposed to mean?"

"Simply that I am your mistress, not your wife, and where I come from what occurred last night is called adultery."

One dark, straight brow lifted on his face. "You weren't complaining last night."

"*Non*," she admitted, flushing. She wriggled out of his embrace. "And I'll probably not complain if—I mean when—it happens again. I never have been able to resist you, Kilian."

She twisted her hands in her lap until he reached over and engulfed them in one hand. She bit her lower lip. She knew she sounded shrewish, but she was too confused and bewildered by all that had happened to properly sort out her thoughts.

The smile left his face. "Do you remember everything I said to you last night?"

"Of course."

"You don't have to stay here if you don't want to."

She closed her eyes. It was too late. She couldn't leave if she wanted to leave. Kilian held her heart in his strong hands. She was afraid he would crush it if he knew. The doubts still lingered in her mind.

"I love you, Aimee."

"Don't—"

"It's the truth." He forced her to look at him. "It's just as

true this morning as it was last night. I cannot keep you
here against your will anymore. If you wish to leave, then
just go."

"I don't want to leave."

He waited. Doubt and confusion flickered in her eyes.
He wanted to hear her say the words to him. Through the
night he had waited and wondered if she would tell him she
loved him, but even in the heat of passion she held back
those words. Now, as he watched her struggle with her
thoughts, he wondered if she had even believed his story.

She leaned on his chest. He wrapped his arms around
her thin body and sighed. He must be patient. She would
learn to trust him, little by little. He must try to be satisfied
that she chose to stay. As the weeks passed and they grew
closer, his mistress would fall in love with him.

As he ran his fingers through her hair, Kilian wondered
why she had emphasized that she was only his mistress,
not his wife. He wondered if she stayed only in the hope
that he would make her his wife.

Then he remembered Château Bocage.

His fingers faltered in her hair. Her skittishness, her reluctance to leave, her failure to tell him she loved him—
suddenly he understood. He still owned Château Bocage.
His heart began to twist in his chest. She had nearly become the Duc de Montchamp's mistress for the chance to
live at Château Bocage. She had bartered her charms in a
card game for the opportunity to win the estate. And now,
he suspected, she rested with him as his mistress in the
hope that he would marry her and let her control Château
Bocage.

He opened his eyes and stared blankly across the room.
Could he blame her? After all that he had done to her, after
all the misery he had started in her life, could he blame her
for trying to turn the tables?

She shifted in his embrace. He pulled her beside him
until her body lay half atop his. He could feel her breath

brushing his chest and the lingering, delicate scent of apple blossoms still emanated from her hair. He loved this woman, and last night, in her passion, he thought she loved him.

The doubts crowded in his mind. He could no longer live with this torment. He needed to know if Aimee loved him, or if she clung to him for Château Bocage. There was one last thing he could do to find out for sure.

"Come, Aimee." He eased her off his chest. "The day is already late and I've work to do."

"I, too," she said in relief as she rose from the bed and scurried away from Kilian's all-too-warm body. "I've got a merchant coming this afternoon to show me some draperies for the sitting room. And the comtesse is coming as well."

He rose from the bed and stretched, unabashed by his nakedness. She turned away from the sight of all that long, lean muscle. He riffled in the refuse on the floor for his undergarment, his breeches, and his hose. He glanced up at her.

"We made quite a mess last night."

She picked up her own garments. "You certainly did."

"Me?" He laced his breeches. "You've got to take some blame in this, my sweet. After all, it was you who enticed me into bed."

"Me!" Her eyes brightened in mock surprise. "I did nothing of the sort. You seduced me, Kilian de Laclos, and don't you forget it."

"Aye, I'll not forget it." He reached behind her and nuzzled her nape. "Though if you don't dress in something more substantial than this robe, I'll be tossing it on the floor with the rest of your clothes."

She sucked in her breath. How easily she succumbed to his seduction. She laughed quietly and escaped his embrace. "Later, my sweet."

He captured her as she stepped away. "How much later?"

His lips found the most sensitive skin of her throat. "After the merchant has left. And the comtesse."

"But then we must go to court." He lifted his head up and faced her. "You will be coming to court with me tonight, won't you?"

The smile left her face. "I don't wish to go to court, Kilian. Not yet."

Mustering her wavering will, she stepped away from him. She gathered the red satin dress in her arms, reached for her corset, and tugged her tangled chemise from the grip of the twisted linens.

Jeanne's clipped footsteps echoed down the hall and stopped in front of Aimee's door. She knocked with vigor.

"Monsieur de Laclos? *Pardonnez-moi* for the interruption, but I have just received a note with the king's seal."

Aimee felt a small tremor of fear. Kilian crossed the room and opened the door. He took the parchment from Jeanne's hand and pried open the dull yellow seal. He glanced at the contents then folded it quickly.

"The king has summoned me." He crossed the room and kissed Aimee on the cheek. "I must leave immediately. I shall be back, *a stor,* and then we shall talk."

CHAPTER

18

"**M**arie? I did not expect you for hours! Why did you rise so early in the day to visit me?"

The comtesse fluttered her fan frantically in front of her face. Though she wore a cool blue silk dress with tiny pink flowers, and few petticoats beneath, she was as flushed and heated as if she had walked the distance between the two town houses. Aimee descended the last few steps to the foyer and took her arm.

"Sit down. You look absolutely dreadful." She glanced over her shoulder. "Bring some orange-water, would you, Jeanne? The comtesse is quite heated."

Aimee led Marie into her sitting room, gathered the pale pink gossamer curtains she had bought earlier in the day, and tossed them carelessly to the floor. Marie sank into the chair and took a deep breath.

"I'm sorry, Aimee, but I nearly killed two horses and one carriage driver rushing to get here." Jeanne appeared at her side and gave her a tall glass of water. Marie took it and drank deeply, letting some of the fragrant liquid spill onto her ample, heaving bosom.

"Catch your breath." Aimee knelt at her feet. The fear she had felt since Kilian received the summons from the king grew, but she forced herself to remain calm. She sensed that whatever Marie had heard that drove her like a madwoman through the streets of Paris must indeed be serious. She knew it concerned Kilian.

"Listen to me, Aimee. Last night I heard rumors, but this morning I know it to be true." She lifted her blue eyes. "You know Madame de Pompadour has long been angry at Kilian because he made you his mistress. Now the Duc de Montchamp is back at court, and he, too, is furious about the situation. He has been working night and day since his arrival to have Kilian sent to the Bastille, or worse, exiled."

Aimee fell back against the other chair and lifted a hand to her mouth. "Exiled?"

"Yes." Marie took a deep breath. "Last night, at the Princesse de Talmond's, Prince Charles received a letter from the king's ministers insisting that he leave France. The prince refused, quite rudely, and the king was enraged. I found out this morning that earlier in the day, Kilian had asked the king to supply the prince with arms and money for another battle in Scotland. The duke and Madame de Pompadour have decided to use this, and the king's anger at the prince, to have Kilian sent away."

"He's been exiled?"

"No, no." The comtesse shook her head until her blond curls bounced in the high coiffure *à la dauphine*. "The chevalier is too popular a war hero for the king to exile him. The marquise has convinced the king to send Kilian to Aix-la-Chapelle until Austria and Spain sign the treaty. That way, Kilian can no longer interfere with the king's plans to exile the prince which, I have been told, he intends to do *immediately!* In addition, Kilian will be separated from you."

"Separated from me?" Aimee shook her head. "No, he won't. I will go with him to Aix-la-Chapelle."

"A man's mistress cannot go on a diplomatic mission with him. It's not done." Marie sat back in the chair and observed her friend through half-closed eyes. "And what has happened between yesterday and today to make you so eager to follow your benefactor to the provinces?"

She flushed and rose from the floor. "I am transparent, aren't I?"

"Only to me, *mon amie.* I've known you long enough." She laughed. "I must admit, I expected this to happen after last night. The chevalier is in love with you. He is more transparent than you. Since you are in love with him, anything that keeps you two apart is just pride."

"I don't want to discuss it."

"Ah, then he finally made you his *true* mistress."

"Marie!" She turned away. "There are times, my friend, when you probe too deeply."

"What? You'll tell me nothing of it? After all those mornings I entertained you with the antics of my lovers?"

"You remember, of course, that I wasn't a completely willing ear."

"I'm sure you benefited from the vicarious experiences, *mon amie,* when you were between the linens with the chevalier." The comtesse laughed heartily as Aimee flushed crimson. "Relax, Aimee. I'll not tell a soul, though I'd love to watch Madame de Sassenage cringe in envy! Has he proposed to you yet?"

"Proposed what?"

"Why, marriage, of course!"

Aimee frowned and sank into the opposite chair. She ran a hand over her simple coiffure. "No, he hasn't. I'm afraid, Marie, that he has no intention of marrying me.

Why should he when I seem perfectly happy to be his mistress?"

The comtesse's rounded features pursed. "I am surprised. I expected him to make you his wife as soon as he coerced you into bed."

"You were wrong."

"Perhaps he is just waiting for a more perfect time."

"What more perfect time than when I'm . . ." she stuttered and looked away. She pressed her fingers against her temples. "I don't understand. He told me he loved me last night. I don't know if I can believe him. He has lied to me for so long."

"Ah, Aimee . . ." The comtesse lifted her skirts and knelt beside her. She took her hands in her own. "I've had more experience with men than you, *mon amie*, and never have I seen a man more in love than your chevalier. But I understand that you are blind to it. You see only all the pain he has caused you." She squeezed Aimee's hands. "Look to a man's actions to see if he loves you. Not his words. I think you'll find your answer there."

"Perhaps sooner than I'd like," she murmured. "Do you know when the king's orders will go into effect? How long will it be before Kilian is sent to Aix-la-Chapelle?"

The comtesse rose from her cramped position. "Immediately, I fear. He'll be sent off as soon as he has gathered his things." Marie straightened her skirts and wiped her bosom. "And I'm afraid, Aimee, that I can stay no longer. I must find the prince and warn him about the king's plans." She sighed wistfully. "I should not raise my hopes that he will shower me with gratitude. He has eyes for no one but the Princesse de Talmond."

"I don't believe that," Aimee said, distracted. "You'll find a way to attract his attention."

"I've got little time. The writ of expulsion is already signed. The king is planning to take him as he goes to the Opera tomorrow." She flashed a smile and shook her rounded shoulders. "Ah, well. *C'est la vie*. There'll be another like him soon enough."

"I wonder what is taking Kilian so long in Versailles," Aimee mused, rising to her feet and following the comtesse to the door. "Certainly the audience with the king didn't last long." She gasped. "You don't think he and the duke. . . ."

"The duke has been ordered, by the king, not to cause any more trouble with the chevalier." The comtesse adjusted her hat in a small, distorted mirror that hung by the door. "As for your chevalier. . . ." She shrugged. "He seems to do what he pleases."

"Yes, he does."

"Au revoir, Aimee." The comtesse kissed her on both cheeks. "I shall return later this afternoon to see what has happened. Don't fuss, my friend. At least Kilian is not being exiled. He won't abandon you."

The comtesse opened the door and shrieked.

A dark shadow stretched across the foyer. A man as tall as Kilian but far wider filled the portal and blocked out the afternoon sun. The comtesse stepped back and then fainted in a pool of vivid blue silk.

Startled, Aimee stared as the giant glanced at the aristocrat on the floor. Shaking her head, she knelt next to Marie and tapped each of her cheeks.

"Jeanne! More orange-water! And smelling salts!" Conscious of the man's hovering shadow, Aimee rose to her full height and faced him. "Who are you? And what are you doing lurking in the doorway of my town house?"

The man snapped off his hat and mutilated it in his great hands. His hair caught the light of the sun and glowed like fire. Her eyes widened. This was the man who had attacked her in the Bois de Boulogne. This was Kilian's cohort in his scheme to entrap her.

"You!"

"Aye, I see you recognize me, lass. Before you scream and find Kilian's musket—"

"Eamon O'Sullivan!" Jeanne rushed into the room and stopped in front of the figure of the comtesse. "I should have known it was you. Whenever you come here you cause trouble."

Aimee turned to the normally taciturn servant in surprise. She had never heard Jeanne utter a word against anyone. As she stood in front of the lumbering giant her pale, freckled face distorted into anger.

"Do you know this man, Jeanne?"

"Yes, I do, madame. This man is my first cousin, though I'm ashamed to admit it." She crouched next to the comtesse and waved the salts beneath her pinched nose. "He's been nothing but trouble since he stepped foot on French soil. Fighting with those Scotsmen—"

"Ach, Jeanne. Not in front of the lady."

"Did you come to see your cousin, Monsieur O'Sullivan?" Aimee asked as Marie stirred at her feet.

"Nay, it's you I came to see, madame." He crushed his hat harder. "Kilian'll be knocking me around when he finds out, but I couldn't let this go any longer."

She lifted a brow. "Indeed?" She stepped back and gestured to the half-finished sitting room. "Come in and have some tea with me, Monsieur O'Sullivan. I have a few questions for you, as well."

The giant lumbered into the foyer and glanced around uncomfortably. "I'll not be drinking tea, madame, but a pint of ale would be much welcome."

She smiled behind her hand and glanced at a glowering Jeanne. "Jeanne, would you see if we have any ale in the back? I shall take care of the comtesse."

Aimee helped Marie to a sitting position as her eyes fluttered open. Her gaze focused with difficulty on Aimee's face. "What happened?"

"You've just met Kilian's red-haired friend," she murmured, collecting the comtesse's hat, gloves, and fan. "Rather abruptly, I may add."

Marie glanced into the sitting room where the man stood considering which chair he preferred. Her eyes widened. "He's a giant!" she exclaimed, gathering her wits. "Oh, and I fainted like an old woman in front of him."

"He enjoyed the view, I am sure." Aimee adjusted the comtesse's lurching bodice and handed her her things. "If you wish to meet him more properly, I can introduce him to you—"

"That's quite all right." Marie stumbled to her feet and tried to regain her air. "I think I have made enough of a fool of myself. I shall leave at once."

Aimee closed the door firmly behind her and waited until she heard the carriage rumble down the street. Taking a deep breath, she entered the sitting room and took the chair across from the man. Jeanne entered with a tea setting.

"No ale, Jeanne?"

Jeanne's face tightened. "There's no ale in this house. And certainly not at this hour of the day."

To Aimee's surprise, the giant flushed above the dark red beard. Aimee reached for the tea service and poured two cups. "Tea is the best I can do, monsieur." She added a small sugar cube to the porcelain cup and handed it to him. He engulfed it in his hand.

She sipped the tea and watched him. He did not dress like an aristocrat—his clothes were dark and common, worse for wear. She imagined it would be hard to find clothes for a man so large. In the Bois de Boulogne this man's immense size had scared her out of her wits. In the coolness of her sitting room, he suddenly seemed as harmless as a tamed bear.

"What did you wish to speak to me about, monsieur?"

"Eamon's my name, madame. I'm no 'ristocrat." His accent rolled over the words. Though his accent was far broader and thicker than Kilian's, she recognized it as that of an Irishman.

"Very well, Eamon. If you have nothing to say to me, I have a few things to ask you."

"Let me have my say first." He fumbled with the cup. Rather than holding the handle with two fingers, he palmed the blue and white porcelain and lifted it to his mouth, as if it were an apple. Finishing the tea in one draught, he winced and placed the cup on the service with a clatter. "I came about that attack in the Bois de Boulogne. I came to apologize for hurting you. Kilian told me you still have bruises."

She flushed. Those bruises lay on her waist, a far too intimate place for a man to discuss with another man.

"I didn't mean to harm you. Sometimes I forget how strong I am." He shifted his weight in the chair, which sagged beneath him. "A few weeks ago, Kilian came to me and asked me if I would help him win a lady's heart. Jeanne will tell you, it doesn't take more than a pint of ale to talk me into an escapade. I agreed and he told me exactly what to do, like in the old days in the Scottish battles. Except this time I wasn't battling an Englishman, I was battling a frail little thing like yourself."

She coughed into her tea. She would not call herself a frail little thing, but she let the comment pass.

"I didn't expect you to fight quite so hard, and I knew I had to keep you away from the 'ristocrats in the main walk, otherwise me and Ian would find ourselves with a ball in the back, or hanging at dawn. So I held a bit tighter than I should, and for that I'm truly sorry. Kilian dragged me out of a tavern that night and made sure I understood how angry he was."

"Did Kilian send you today?"

"Nay. He'll be madder than hell—excuse me, madame —when he finds out. He planned this whole thing as carefully as he planned the capture of Edinburgh."

"What whole thing?"

"Why, winning your heart, lass." His bright blue eyes widened. "Surely you know. I've never known a woman yet who didn't know a man in love. He's been mooning like a sick calf for a month."

She settled her cup on the saucer and stared at the giant. She knew, instinctively, that he did not have the finesse to lie so well. Her heart began pounding in her chest, but she forced herself to remain calm. "And how well do you know the chevalier, Eamon, that you can so easily tell he's in love?"

"Ach, there's no doubt about it. I've known him since the campaign with Bonnie Prince Charles in Scotland, and in wartime, lass, there's no hiding the soul of a man. He's been bitten, and hard, and if you don't mind me saying, he couldn't have found a more handsome lady."

She flushed, for this compliment from a coarse and blunt man meant more to her than a hundred flowery phrases from a French courtier. She found herself liking the man who sat across from her. She also found herself believing him.

Her heart pounded in her chest. Her doubts shimmered and melted away. Perhaps everything that Kilian had told her last night was true. Perhaps the comtesse was right, and it was only her pride that made her so blind. She believed the story of this rough-hewn soldier. He reminded her of Gustave. He did not have the heart to lie.

She loved Kilian. She loved him more than life now that she understood. She would hold back her feelings no longer. When he arrived back from court, she swore she would throw herself in his arms and tell him that she loved him too.

"Ach, I can see in your face that I've done the right thing," he said, smiling to show long, yellowed teeth. "Your cheeks are brightening like the dawn."

"You have done the right thing, Eamon." Impulsively,

she rose from her chair and threw her arms around the big man's neck. She hugged him as tightly as she could then kissed each reddened cheek. Her heart burst with joy and she felt like dancing across the room. Eamon rose and bumped the tea service, and the table crashed to the floor. Two of the porcelain teacups crashed in a dozen pieces.

He crushed his hat in his hand and apologized profusely. He knelt on the floor and tried to pick up the sharp ends with his great hands. Aimee laughed and drew him away from the mess. Jeanne arrived and scolded the giant until he hung his head in shame.

"Hush, Jeanne. He has performed a great service today. It was worth a few teacups."

"Always trouble, he is," she muttered beneath her breath as she collected the shining shards in her apron. "Should have a wife and children by now."

But Aimee wasn't listening. She heard the clatter of a carriage and she rushed to the window. Kilian, dressed in his finest blue waistcoat and breeches, entered through the iron gate. Her smile dimmed. He was not alone.

Eamon glanced over her shoulder. "He's back. He'll not be pleased to see me here."

"I won't let him yell at you," she assured him, gazing with curiosity at the bevy of bourgeois that followed Kilian up the cobbled path.

"No offense meant, madame, but I've never seen his rage stemmed by a man, much less a woman." He backed away from her. "If you don't mind, I'll be slipping out through the back. There'll be plenty of time when he's in a better mood to explain to him why I came here."

"Hiding like a coward, eh, Eamon?" Jeanne shrilled as the giant lumbered across the room and slipped into the kitchens. She followed his tall silhouette, scolding all the way.

Aimee curled her fingers in her skirts as Kilian entered through the front door. Oh, how she wished he had come

home alone! Her heart ached as he stopped in the foyer and
leaned his cane against the wall. He peered into the sitting
room until he noticed her thin form near the window.

"Madame?"

"Yes, Kilian?" She did not care if the strange men that
surrounded him heard her use his first name. A light flickered in his eyes as he gazed at her, but his face was set in
stony lines.

"Could you come into the library with me for a moment?
I would like to talk to you about something of great impor-
tance."

She started and approached him. "What has happened?
Is there something wrong?"

He touched her chin then released her, suddenly remembering that they had guests. "I'll tell you everything in a
moment. Come."

"The library is quite unfit for guests," she said as they
headed past the dining room down the hall to a far door. "I
have only just aired it out and have had no chance to
dust—"

"It'll do for now." The door squealed in protest as he
opened it. The light that filtered through several high windows showed a thick curtain of dust. Furnished with only a
single desk and several hard-backed chairs, the room
seemed as stark as her fear.

"Sit," he said, gesturing to a chair. He leaned on the
edge of the desk and she wondered if his breeches would
be stained by the dirt and oil that had collected over the
years on the oak surface.

"These men are *avocats*. They have all helped me in
drawing up a document that concerns you."

"A document?"

"Yes." He gestured to one of the lawyers who reached
into his inner waistcoat pocket and pulled out a single,
rolled sheet. Kilian unrolled it and glanced at the writing.

"I have considered doing this for some time. Here." He handed her the sheet. "Read it."

She leaned forward and took the parchment from his hand. She glanced at the other men. "Why are all these men here? You could have just given this to me."

"Read it, *a stor*. Then we shall talk."

She lowered her gaze to the paper. The lawyer wrote with a fine, rounded hand, and as she read the first sentence her eyes widened. She stumbled over her words, but Kilian quieted her with a finger against her lips. She stared, dazed, into his eyes.

"Don't talk yet, Aimee. Read the document."

She scanned the page, her amazement growing with each passing sentence. She lifted her hand to her heart as she read further and found, at the bottom of the parchment, Kilian's bold, straight signature, still slightly wet.

She could not believe the words. She reread it from the beginning and let it fall to her lap.

"I don't understand."

"That's why these men are here. To explain it all to you. Ask them any question you wish."

She shook her head. Confusion filled her luminous gray eyes. "It is to you that I must direct my question, Kilian. I don't understand why you are signing the Bocage estate over to me. It is yours, by decree of the king."

"Aye, and it is mine to use as I please." He leaned back against the desk. "I can live in it. I can barter it in a card game. Or, if I choose, I can sign it and its wealth over to whomever I please." His hair glowed where a patch of sunlight hit it. "And it pleases me, my love, to give it to you."

She pressed a finger against her temple and scanned the paper once again. She became intensely conscious of the lawyers that surrounded her.

"I could not give it to you outright because women aren't allowed to own land." He watched her with an unwavering gaze. "But I am allowed to sign its yearly *rentes* to you, and I'm allowed to let you live on it for the duration of your lifetime. I'm afraid I had to add a stipulation in case you married," he said quietly. "I can't allow you to keep it if you remarry."

Her fingers trembled on the parchment. She had battled for a document like this since the vicomte died. First, with the intendant of Normandy, then with the Duke de Montchamp, and then, with Kilian de Laclos. She could not believe that Kilian offered her the chance to live on Château Bocage again. She knew she should be ecstatic. She should fall to her knees and thank him from the bottom of her heart, for nothing had driven her more than the need to return to Normandy and the land of her youth. But as she fingered the document, a tear fell from her eye and darkened the paper.

"Aimee." His voice broke and he took the document from her hands. Kneeling before her, he stared up into her face. "Leave us now, gentlemen. Jeanne will show you out."

Their heels clicked as they scurried out of the library. The door closed quietly behind them. Kilian pulled a lace-edged linen from his waistcoat pocket and wiped a wet trail that lingered on her cheek.

"Why do you cry? Aren't you happy?"

The words lodged in her throat and she swallowed. In the dusty room his eyes glowed with an unearthly light. She lifted her hand to his cheek then lowered it. He was sending her away. Kilian had been summoned by the king, and now he was sending her away.

"What did the king want this morning, Kilian?"

He traced her palm with his thumb. "The king has decided to send me on a fool's errand to Aix-la-Chapelle," he said. "His mistress and the Duc de Montchamp want me out of court, out of Paris, and far, far away from you."

"I see." She twisted his linen in her hands. "When must you leave?"

He ran a hand over her hair. "Tomorrow, my love."

She bent over to pick up the discarded document. "So you had this written to send me away?"

She felt the surprise in his touch. "Send you away? Nay, Aimee. The king's summons and this document have nothing to do with one another. I am giving you your long-denied life estate on Château Bocage because I thought that would make you happy. Isn't that what you've always wanted, all along?"

"Yes. . . ." *But*. The excuses swam in her head. Yes, she always wanted Château Bocage, but now, she wanted something more. She wanted him. As she fingered the document she realized that she may not be able to have both.

He rose from her side and released her hands. He walked to the desk and turned his back to her. "I can arrange to have a carriage here tomorrow. I know you must be anxious to return to your lands."

"You won't be coming, then?" She glanced up at his straight back. His hair, combed neatly back and pugged in a blue bow, glowed in the light.

"Nay. The king's orders cannot be ignored, no matter how useless they may be."

Aimee struggled with her love and her pride. She loved him. He said he loved her. Why, why would he give her Château Bocage if he did not want to send her away from Paris and into the provinces?

"I still don't understand, Kilian." She swallowed her tears. "This is a great sacrifice. Why . . . why are you doing this?"

"Because I love you, Aimee." He lifted his face to the light that spilled through the high windows. "I want you to be happy. That is all I ever wanted. In a sense, I am trying to right all the wrongs I have committed against you in the past year. This was the only thing I could do."

Lifting her chin, she took the parchment in two hands. With a slow, deliberate motion, she tore it down the middle. He whirled around at the sound and she faced him with tears in her eyes.

"I'd rather *not* have Château Bocage, Kilian, if it means leaving you." She lifted her chin higher and tossed her pride to the winds. "I'd rather be your mistress, hiding in Aix-la-Chapelle, than be a lonely old widow in Normandy."

"Aimee. . . ." He stood before her and searched her eyes, until he saw the light of love in them. His smile burst full and white on his face.

"I love you, Kilian de Laclos." She rose from her seat and threw herself into his open arms. "All your careful strategy has succeeded, I'm afraid. I trust you. It will take more than a bribe to get rid of me now."

He whirled her around in circles. Her heart burst with love as he set her down on her feet and captured her lips with his own. He framed her face in his hands and stared into her eyes.

"You do love me, don't you, *a stor?*"

"Yes, Kilian. Yes, yes, yes—" He stopped her words with a kiss that left her breathless against him. His arms held her prisoner, but she did not mind the restriction. She wanted to spend the rest of her life locked in lovemaking with this man.

"I thought you didn't love me. I feared you agreed to stay with me only for Château Bocage and I couldn't bear the thought." He buried his face in her tumbling hair. "I would rather see you happy at Château Bocage than forever pretending to be happy with me."

"I doubted you, Kilian. I couldn't help myself. I loved you so much, but I was so afraid you would hurt me." She gasped for breath as Kilian unhooked her dress. "But

Eamon came by this afternoon and I knew that he could not lie—"

"Eamon? Eamon O'Sullivan?"

"Yes." She touched his face. "Don't be angry at him. He only wanted to apologize for hurting me."

"I'm not angry at him, if he convinced you of my honesty."

"He did, and more."

"Then I'll treat him to more ale than he could possibly drink, my love, and I assure you that is quite a bit." He nipped the curve of her shoulder as the dress loosened. "But later, much later, for now I've got another appetite to fill."

"Ah, Kilian . . ." Suddenly it did not matter that the afternoon sun spilled brightly through the dirty windows. It did not matter that the door to the library remained unlocked and Jeanne could enter at any moment. All that mattered was Kilian's potent touch, his insistent lips, his beautiful words. He lowered her gently to the faded Oriental rug. Their clothes scattered in a confused, passionate array across the length and breadth of the room.

Flushed with love, she ran her hands boldly over his hard body. She dared to touch him as he touched her, kiss him as he kissed her, love him with as much abandon as her passion allowed. Her hair tumbled over her breasts, but she pushed it away, proud for the first time in her life of her naked body. He lifted her atop him and showed her a new way to love and she followed his gentle instruction with urgency. She discovered the power and joy of giving pleasure and cried out as his body tightened in ecstasy beneath her own.

Much later, long after the light faded from the room and left them swathed in a gentle blanket of darkness, Kilian lifted his mistress from the floor and dressed her in her wrinkled and dusty clothes. He pulled her body close to his

and did what he had yearned to do since he first set eyes on
her in Paris.

"I love you, *a stor*. I love you, I love you, I love you."
He nuzzled her neck and repeated the tender words until
his tears mixed with hers. The empty room echoed with the
refrain until Aimee kissed him quiet, her heart aching with
the sweet tenderness of their love.

CHAPTER

19

The carriage rumbled over the potted Rue de Sevres on its way to Versailles. Aimee smiled as it lurched to one side, thrusting her bodily against Kilian. His laugh rumbled in his chest as he pulled her closer. His lips found hers in the darkness.

"You're insatiable, *a stor*." He breathed in the rich floral scent of apple blossoms that emanated from her skin. "If we don't arrive at Versailles soon I swear I shall ravish you in this carriage."

"You'll ruin my hair," she teased, nipping the warm skin of his throat. "And then the entire court will know that you've captured my heart as easily as you've captured Indian sepoys, English soldiers, and the cities of the Netherlands."

"Winning your heart, my love, was the hardest battle I ever fought." He slipped an arm around her waist. "But not even the king of France could bestow such wondrous rewards."

She sighed as he brushed the sensitive tip of her breast.

In the night they had spent together she had learned more about loving and being loved than she had in a lifetime. Instead of packing in preparation for the trip to Aix-la-Chapelle, they had spent the day talking, touching, loving in her bed. As she lay against his fully dressed body, she traced the lines of his muscular abdomen and remembered how it flexed and moved. Already the heat of passion rekindled in her blood.

"How long must we stay in court, Kilian?"

"Only long enough to satisfy the monarch that we are, indeed, leaving tomorrow morning, and that you are coming with me willingly." He traced her square, low-cut bodice, then ran his fingers over the texture of her embroidered stomacher. "Then, my love, I'm going to sweep you away from the avaricious gazes of all the lusty noblemen and prove to you how much I love you."

"Sounds wonderful."

"I am glad you decided to come to court with me."

"I may embarrass you, Kilian. I'll be fawning over you like an overanxious hunting dog." She shifted her weight in the darkness. "And if Madame de Sassenage comes within a league I swear I shall draw your sword from its sheath and challenge her to a duel."

"Just kick her in the shin. Eamon told me he still bears a bruise from that afternoon."

"It serves him right for agreeing to go along with your schemes."

"It was my schemes, madame, that brought us to this blissful state."

She pushed away from him in mock anger. "Your schemes! If it weren't for Eamon I'd probably be in Normandy right now. You had wrapped yourself in so much intrigue that I could no longer tell the deceit from the truth!"

"Ah, but you always understood this." He clutched her

waist. His lips descended to hers in passion and she laughed deep in her throat.

"Yes, I understood that." His lips trailed fire down the length of her arched neck as he drew her upon his lap. Her panniers rose like twin tables on either side of her waist. "I hated you for it, too. You could so easily turn me into a quivering, panting wanton."

"Mmm. Can I convince you to turn into one now?" He lowered his head to the exquisite arches of her breasts.

"Nay," she mimicked, her voice sighing through her teeth. "Not now, my love. Later, when we're alone and I don't have to worry so much about appearances."

Reluctantly, he raised his head from her cleavage and lifted her off his lap. He eased her to the seat beside him and pulled the gray satin skirts down over her silk-hosed legs. He lifted her hand to his lips and his eyes spoke volumes in the dimness.

"My beauty," he murmured. "I have a surprise for you tonight."

"A surprise?"

"Aye." He glanced out the carriage window as the golden walls of Versailles rose at the end of the long, straight boulevard. "And no matter how convincing you are, I shan't tell you a thing about it until we are in the middle of court."

"Kilian!"

"Sorry, my sweet. This secret I must hold just a little longer."

The carriage lurched to a stop just inside the iron gates of the king's château. Two liveried footmen rushed to open the door and lower the steps. Kilian descended and reached for her hand. She stepped down into the pebbled courtyard.

Versailles glowed with the light of hundreds of candles. She clutched his hand as they followed a footman to a side door that led to the Hercules room near the state apartments. The heady scent of cologne wafted down the hall and grew in intensity as they neared the ballroom ahead. He covered her hand with his own as she hesitated near the mass of aristocrats.

"I shall not leave your side, my love."

She met his gaze and her heart quivered. Dressed in a waistcoat of lightly embroidered blue satin, with his hair powdered and combed neatly away from his face, Kilian stood every inch the handsome aristocrat. She wondered how she, a simple country noblewoman, had ever had the fortune to win his heart.

While she stared he led her into the center of the great ballroom. The pink marbled walls glowed in the light of the candelabra scattered across the room, and the snarling face of Hercules looked down upon the dancers from the ceiling. She tore her attention away from the room and faced the curious gazes of the courtiers.

The king and queen had not yet arrived. The room hummed breathlessly as the courtiers whispered among themselves. Kilian drew her aside, nodding at the guests along the way. The humming increased in intensity as they passed each huddled group.

The comtesse suddenly appeared, all brilliant pink feathers and well-rouged cheeks. "Hello, Chevalier," she said, raising her beringed hand. "I did not expect you, or Madame de Chacontier, to appear at court tonight."

"Neither did most of the court."

"Are you feeling better, Aimee?" Her blue eyes sparkled mischievously. "I came to your town house yesterday afternoon, but your servant said you were indisposed."

"Indisposed?"

"Yes." Marie watched the color rise in her friend's face. "A touch of the choler, perhaps? You do look flushed."

"Yes, perhaps that was it," she conceded, realizing that Jeanne had not wanted to interrupt their lovemaking. "It has passed now and I am quite fine."

"Yes, well, it may come and go," Marie persisted, bait-ing Aimee until her gray eyes flashed in warning. "In the future, I shall make appointments to see you. Until you feel better, of course."

"That won't be necessary, comtesse, for tomorrow I am leaving the town house."

Marie's gaze grew serious and she glanced back and forth between Kilian and her friend. "Leaving?"

"Yes," Kilian concurred, tightening his grip on Aimee's hand. "It seems Madame de Chacontier has decided she wants to see the south of France. Since I am traveling there as well, I humbly agreed to be her escort."

"I see." Marie tapped her fan against her skirts and surreptitiously glanced about the room. A slow laugh gurgled in her throat. "The Marquise de Pompadour and the Duc de Montchamp will not be pleased about this. I think they already had plans to marry Aimee off to the Comte de Roquefeuil in your absence, Chevalier."

"They shall discover that those plans, like the others, will fail."

"Well, well. How quickly things change in a matter of a few days." Marie snapped open her fan and held it before her bosom. "I think I misjudged you, Chevalier. You understand, of course, that I always had Aimee's best interests in mind."

"Of course." His lips twitched. "Then perhaps you will help me ease the Marquise de Pompadour's ruffled feathers when she discovers that I've taken Aimee away from court."

"Marry Aimee and all is forgiven," the comtesse said, shrugging. "That seems simple enough to me."

"Marie-Celeste!"

"It's all right, Aimee." He touched her cheek. "The comtesse is right—"

"Take your hands off her, Laclos."

Aimee started at the sound of the low voice. She broke

away from Kilian's touch and stared at the stiff, angry form of the Duc de Montchamp.

The entire ballroom hushed. Each woman quieted the rustle of her skirts, each man leaned in their direction. The duke, resplendent in his court finery, watched Kilian with unwavering black eyes. His hand rested on the hilt of his ornamental sword. Aimee lifted her hand to her lips and watched Kilian's face harden into a stony mask.

No. . . . She knew what was going to happen. The duke's fingers flexed on his sword handle as he seared Kilian with his gaze. She glanced at Kilian and noticed with a sinking sense of dread that his face had tightened in fury.

"You have orders from the king, Chevalier." The duke glanced at Aimee. "I suggest you follow them and release Madame de Chacontier from the shameful bargain."

"My orders from the king say nothing about releasing Madame de Chacontier."

The duke's broad chest expanded in anger. "How dare you bring her here and flaunt her before the court like a woman off the streets of Paris!"

Kilian's eyes flared in fury. "Did you just compare my mistress to a street whore, Montchamp?"

"Madame is a woman of the highest breeding. It is you, Chevalier, who are common swine." The duke pulled off his white glove and tossed it at his feet. "I thought you would leave the court and release Madame de Chacontier, Laclos, but it seems you are a greater fool than I thought. Let's not hide anymore behind royal decrees and women's skirts. It is my blood that you want—it is my blood you've always wanted, since Jolivette's death. Very well, then. I challenge you for Madame's freedom."

"No!" Aimee's cry strangled in her throat and she rushed between the men. "Monsieur de Montchamp, you do not understand—"

"Hush, Aimee," Kilian said, pulling her away from the duke. "This does not concern you."

"Indeed, it does concern her. You've used her for months to wreak your vengeance on me. I intend to release her from that bond." He lifted his chin. "With my own blood, if necessary."

The comtesse drew Aimee away from the men. Aimee pressed her hand against her lips as tears spilled onto her cheeks. Kilian's face had turned into a mask of fury, hatred, and revenge, and she searched his cold gaze for some sign of the man she loved. He stared relentlessly at the duke and ignored her struggles.

She knew, as she looked at him, that he would not give up the opportunity to kill the duke. Kilian still hated the duke for what he thought he had done to his sister. The duke had just tossed an opportunity for revenge in his lap.

"Whenever and wherever you please, Montchamp."

"At the *Point du Jour*. At daybreak." The duke bowed in Aimee's direction. "Comtesse de Vierzon, I suggest you take Madame de Chacontier to your home until this disgusting affair is settled." The duke whirled on one foot and marched through the parting mass of courtiers.

Aimee rushed to Kilian's side. "Kilian, please!" He reluctantly dragged his gaze away from the duke's retreating back to face her. His eyes were as hard and unyielding as stone. "Don't fight him, Kilian. He is one of the best swordsmen in court—"

"I must fight him."

"Come, Aimee," the comtesse said gently. "We must leave now."

"No!" She shrugged off the comtesse's hand and glared at Kilian. "You will fight a duel *against* my honor—and spill an innocent man's blood?"

"This duel has nothing to do with you. It is between the duke and me." His eyes hardened. "And the duke is not an innocent man."

"Are you so sure of that?" she whispered as she clutched his arm, not caring that the whole of the French court watched them. "Are you so sure that he used your sister?" She continued recklessly as his eyes grew as hard as emeralds. "Listen to me. The duke told me he loved your sister —that he went to Italy to annul his own marriage so he could marry Jolivette—"

"Blasphemous lies!" he snapped, crushing her arms in his grip. "He told you these things to make *you* his mistress."

"No, no, he didn't." She winced as his fingers dug painfully into her upper arms. "He had no reason to lie—I had made it clear to him that I wanted nothing to do with him here in Paris."

He released her and stepped away. "Do you believe the duke's lies to my truth? After all that happened in Normandy?"

"He told me these things to help explain all that happened in Normandy." She searched his gaze for reason. The forces of vengeance and fury obscured the soul she had come to love. She had not seen him so convulsed with anger since he had found her and the duke together in Normandy. She had fooled herself that he had disposed of the crippling need for vengeance after he had stolen her estate away from the duke. Now she realized that his fury had lain latent in him, and needed only the urging of the Duc de Montchamp to awaken.

"Go to the Comtesse de Vierzon's, Aimee." He picked the duke's white glove off the floor. "Tomorrow all will be decided."

"You will fight him, then? After all I have told you?"

"Yes."

"You will duel with the duke tomorrow for what he did to your sister, but if you win, remember that I shall be dishonored before this entire court."

He met her steady gaze. The courtiers, who had watched the exchange with unerring concentration, suddenly turned to the royal entrance. The footmen stamped twice on the hardwood floor to announce the arrival of the king. In a flurry of activity, they rushed to their designated places and bowed their heads and bodies in reverence.

"Come, Aimee," the comtesse whispered hurriedly, dragging her away from Kilian and toward the back of the room. "We must leave before the king enters!" Marie pulled her out of the ballroom and rushed her down the hall to the side door. Hailing a footman, she ordered her carriage to be brought around, then took the trembling woman into her arms.

"He must not fight!" she cried, her body shaking uncontrollably. She breathed deep gulps of the fresh evening air. "Marie-Celeste, you must help me stop this duel!"

"I cannot, Aimee, and neither can you. Those two men have been enemies since Kilian returned from India and found his sister dead. They should have dueled then and settled the affair, but the king prevented them." She tapped her fan nervously against her skirts. "Both of them have caused so much grief since that day—and you have been caught in the middle, not once, but twice. Let them fight tomorrow, Aimee. Let them settle this anger between them or it will forever haunt the three of you."

"But it is wrong!" She buried her head in her hands. "You don't understand. The duke loved Jolivette, but Kilian doesn't believe me. He will kill an innocent man."

Marie's brows drew together in concern. "These duels don't always lead to death, *mon amie.*"

"He'll kill him. You don't understand how much he hates the duke."

"Yes, I do. Anyone with eyes could see that this evening. Your chevalier rose like a warrior when the duke looked your way."

"He has forgotten about me in his rage. I know it. Tomorrow, when his anger is slaked with the duke's blood, he may remember. But for now, he knows only the fury of his vengeance."

Marie helped her into her carriage. "Come, Aimee, we must leave before the courtiers come to eavesdrop. We'll rise early tomorrow and I'll send a messenger to the dueling grounds to bring us news."

Aimee lifted her tearstained face. "Do you know where they will fight?"

"The duke mentioned the Point du Jour, on the banks of the Seine."

"Then you know where it is?"

Marie's eyes narrowed. "Yes. But no lady is allowed on the field of honor."

Aimee tossed her head. "Then I, Marie-Celeste, am no lady. They will duel at daybreak. I want to be there before the first glimmer of sun."

An ominous gray mist rose from the choppy waters of the Seine and hung in heavy layers over the thinly wooded bank. In the still blue light of dawn, a single lark sang a mournful song high in the branches of an elm. Aimee pulled her dark cloak closer to her body. The cold seemed to emanate from her bones.

"Are you quite sure this is the place?" she asked, turning to the form that huddled on a tree-trunk beside her.

"Yes, I'm quite sure," Marie-Celeste snapped, shivering in her woolen cloak. "And I still cannot believe I allowed you to talk me into this. It's colder here than in the dampest winter in Normandy."

Aimee frowned and glanced to the sky. Soon the sun would rise, yet the men had not arrived for the duel. Her breath formed clouds of mist in front of her face. The past night had been the longest night of her life. She had watched the brass clock in the comtesse's sitting room, wondering if Kilian would come to his senses and seek her out. She wondered if he would abandon her after the duel.

She wondered if their love had grown strong enough to overcome this, and prayed to a dozen saints that it would. When the clock finally chimed four, she had roused Marie from her sleep, wrapped an old cloak around her shoulders, and demanded the carriage driver take her to this darkened field.

Here they had waited, while the stars faded and dimmed and the birds slowly wakened in their nests above them.

"I hear a carriage." She peered down the rugged path and strained her ears. Her heart thumped as the distinctive rhythm of horses' hooves filtered through the thick air. Her stiff fingers curled into the cloak as Kilian's black carriage turned the far corner of the road and approached the field.

"Stay back, Aimee, else they'll send you away."

"They mustn't fight."

"They'll fight whether you want them to or not." Marie-Celeste rose from her seat and pulled her deeper into the woods. "No matter how much you plead with Kilian, he cannot avoid the duke's challenge without being labeled a coward. I have told you that."

She bit her lip as the carriage came to a stop. George descended from the box and opened the door. Her heart leapt as Kilian descended to the grass.

"Kilian!" She could not help herself. Tearing away from the comtesse's grasp, she lifted her skirts and raced across the narrow field.

"Aimee! You shouldn't be here."

She rushed into his arms and pressed her cheek against his chest. He ran his hand over her damp hair, hesitated, then pulled her tight against him. She lifted her tearstained face. "Don't fight, Kilian. Please, just leave now, before the duke arrives."

"I cannot, *a stor*."

"To hell with honor," she cried, touching his cheek. He looked weary, and she noticed he still wore the brilliant blue satin waistcoat he had worn the evening before. "Just come, now."

"Nay. I'll not leave this field without fighting the duke. You should not have come. This is no place for a woman—"

"This damned duel is being fought over me. I have a right to be here."

He did not deny her words. He looked over his shoulder and glanced at Eamon who had followed him out of the carriage.

"He'll be here soon, Laclos," Eamon said quietly. "'Twould be best to prepare."

"Aye." Kilian touched her cheek, then lowered his lips to hers. The kiss was mournful and tender.

"What if he kills you?" she whispered. "He's the best swordsman in court."

"Trust me, my love." He captured her lips again. "I must fight the duke. I have burned with rage over what he did to Jolivette for too long. Trust me. Trust me as you would have in Normandy, long ago, if I had told you my true identity."

She stared at him with an aching heart. So many times he had asked for her trust. She swallowed her doubts. "I'll trust you, Kilian, but you must trust me, too. Remember what I told you last night. And remember..." She hesitated and touched his face. "Remember that I love you."

She turned away. Eamon took her by the arm and led her across the field, then released her at the comtesse's side. "You must stay here, madame. If you come forward you could be hurt."

"Eamon." Aimee could no longer stop the tears that streamed down her cheeks. "Can't you do anything to stop this?"

"Nay. Nor will I be wanting to. Kilian's got to fight for no other reason than to rid himself of the hate."

A second carriage rumbled to a stop close to the start of the field. Aimee sank next to the comtesse as the Duc de Montchamp stepped out onto the grass.

She watched in horror as the battle unfolded in front of her in all its age-worn pageantry. Kilian chose Eamon as his second; the Duc de Montchamp chose a courtier whom Aimee did not recognize. Kilian and the duke faced each other across a narrow gap, and as Eamon dropped a glove to the ground they clashed swords.

The ringing of steel against steel echoed in the empty woods, over and over, in sickening monotony as the two men battled, stroke by stroke. Aimee could not bear to watch, but neither could she endure covering her eyes and listening to the clamoring of their weapons. The deceptively thin épées strained against each other as each man tested his opponent's strength. The duke drew back and waved his sword in small circles.

Aimee clung to Marie and chewed on her lower lip until she tasted blood. Kilian stepped forward and met the duke's stroke and pushed him off balance. Kilian was easily the stronger of the two as he drove the duke closer and closer to the edge of the trees, but the duke parried each blow with surprising agility. While Kilian attacked with bold, long strokes, the duke sought to slash forth in short, terse attacks.

Anger distorted Kilian's face. A gleam of sweat broke out on the duke's forehead as Kilian wore down his endurance. His own body bore no mark of weakening as he slashed forward, relentlessly, forcing the duke to maneuver around trees and roots. The men flattened the grass in the clearing with their footsteps until it formed a slick floor beneath them.

Suddenly, the duke edged back and around, then slashed forward to nick Kilian's arm.

Kilian stilled. He glanced down at the white linen sleeve

and watched as a small stain of blood spread through the threads.

The duke postured, steady, waiting for him to attack.

"You drew the first blood, monsieur," Kilian said calmly, gesturing to the growing stain. "Do you consider honor done?"

The duke's face spasmed in disbelief. He straightened and pointed his sword to Aimee's huddled form. "Release her, Laclos, and honor will be done."

"The lady will never be released."

"Then this duel will be finished when one of us is dead."

Kilian lifted his épée but stepped away from the duke's thrust. "She doesn't want to be released, Montchamp."

"Then you've seduced her, Laclos. You've used her and shamed her—"

"As you did to Jolivette?"

"I loved Jolivette."

"I love Aimee."

"You know nothing of love. You only know hatred and vengeance. Fight me. I'll kill you for what you've done to her."

"You're a fool, Montchamp." He easily parried the duke's answering blow and forced him to retreat to the center of the field. "I gave you an opportunity to live. You tossed it to the winds and now I swear I shall cut you to ribbons for what you did to Jolivette."

Aimee rose from her seat and ran a few steps in their direction, but the comtesse pulled her down to the ground by her skirts. Struggling up from the slippery earth, she pushed her hair out of her eyes and watched in horror as Kilian let loose the full strength of his anger. The duke was no match against this soldier of many wars, and as he stumbled back farther and deeper into the treacherous woods, Aimee saw the realization on his face.

The result was inevitable from the moment the duke re-

fused to end the duel. Kilian pounded his épée against the
duke's until the older man's arm could no longer hold it
still against the blows. He stumbled over a log and righted
himself just in time to avoid Kilian's thrust, but as he
struggled to his feet Kilian knocked his sword out of his
hands and sent it flying across the field.

He placed his booted foot on the duke's waistcoat and
leveled the épée in the white, powdered folds of his throat.
The duke opened his hands.

Aimee struggled out of the comtesse's grip and raced
across the field. Eamon stepped in her path. She glanced at
him, dazed, and tried to run around him, but he clutched
her by the waist and held her motionless against his body.

"Let me go, Eamon! He'll kill him!"

"And that won't be a sight for your eyes."

She stared desperately over his massive shoulder. Kilian's back was to her, but she saw the gleam of the morning sun off the length of his poised épée.

"Why are you hesitating, Chevalier?" the duke said, tilting his chin. "Kill me. Wreak your vengeance. Finish this
and let me join Jolivette in a far better place."

At the sound of Jolivette's name Kilian twitched and
Aimee cried out as a thin trail of blood dripped from the
duke's throat. Kilian lifted his head and his shoulders
shuddered in a great sigh. Removing his foot from the
duke's stomach, he lifted his sword and tossed it far into
the brush.

"Honor is served, Montchamp." He turned around and
faced Aimee. "Let it be known that I gave you your life."

The duke rose to his feet and stared after Kilian in angry
bewilderment. "You gave me my life for what? To torment
Aimee and myself further?"

"You are the only one tormented. Aimee will stay with
me, and willingly." He approached her, his gaze steady and
warm on her face. Eamon released her from his grip and

she rushed into his arms. He ran his hands through her hair as she trembled against him.

The duke observed the scene and stepped back in weary surprise. He touched his throat and looked at the blood that stained his hands. He shook his head and his dark hair, which had become unbound during the battle, flew around his ears. "I don't understand."

"I love him, Jean-Jacques," she said as she pulled away from Kilian's embrace. "I have loved him for a very long time. This duel should never have taken place, for I never want to leave him."

"He is using you, Aimee." The duke stepped toward the couple, but Eamon stopped his approach. "He's using you, just as he used you in Normandy. To torment me."

"I thought so, too," she said quietly, wiping the small beads of sweat that had gathered on Kilian's brow. "We were wrong, Jean-Jacques. Both of us were wrong."

"Aye, and you have Aimee to thank for your life, Montchamp. Though I don't know if what she has told me about you and my sister is true, I trust her enough to grant you your life until I can prove or disprove the story."

Aimee's smile grew on her tearstained face. Kilian wiped her cheeks, then lowered himself to his knees in front of her. "I never did tell you your surprise, *a stor.*"

"What surprise?"

"I promised you a surprise last night, at court. Unfortunately, the duke interrupted it." Eamon pulled a small box out of the pocket of his coat. Kilian took it and gave it to Aimee. "Open it."

She caught her breath as the diamond glittered in the first rosy light of dawn. She lifted it and let the box fall to the ground.

"Be my wife, Aimee."

Wife. . . . The ring felt cold on her finger as Kilian slipped it on. Its sparkle rivaled the glow in his gold-flecked eyes. She touched his face. He had trusted her. He had let the duke live. He had released his hatred and his fury and all that was left in his eyes was the brilliant, unwavering light of love.

"Yes, Kilian." She threw herself in his arms. "Yes, yes, yes."

EPILOGUE

Aimee stood on the worn steps of Château Bocage, watching the procession of villagers climb the path to her courtyard. It was Johnsmas Eve, and the day-workers had already constructed the wooden *bûcher* on a small knoll beyond the red gold fields. She could see its silhouette against the blue haze of twilight. The curé, who led the tenants in his dark robes, carried a torch in preparation for the midsummer fires.

An evening wind brushed over the fertile land and lifted the fecund, musky scent of damp earth to her nose. She smiled and raised her chin to the breeze.

"Are you sure you want to go to the fires?" Kilian pulled her body against him. "It's a long walk to the hill."

"It is not so long," she murmured as he nuzzled her neck. "And the evening won't be the same if I don't light the *bûcher*. It is tradition, you know."

"Blast tradition. It is your health I worry about."

She smiled as he placed his hand on her swelling abdomen. The babe was not due for four months, but Kilian coddled her like a woman on the brink of labor. She did not mind. In the year that they had lived at Château Bocage they had precious little time to themselves. The king constantly summoned Kilian to help in affairs of state, and after a season of neglect the estate was in dire need of attention. She took shameful advantage of his concern whenever he was home.

"My health would improve if you wouldn't keep running off to Paris," she scolded lightly as she leaned against him. "When will the king stop summoning you?"

"When these constant arguments with England are over, I think." As the procession drew closer he released her and stood by her side. "The treaty of Aix-la-Chapelle only made the situation worse. I fear there will be another war, and soon."

Fear quivered in her stomach. "You won't fight, will you?"

"Nay, *a stor*. My warring days are over." His green gold eyes sparkled as he glanced at her belly. "I've got a wife and soon, a child to worry about."

"What will the king say to that?"

"The king won't like it. He thinks I am being terribly bourgeois to be in love with my wife."

"He will just have to get used to it," she said. "And he'll have to stop sending you on these endless diplomatic missions."

His smile spread over his face and she trembled, as she always did, when he looked at her like this. He had made love to her this afternoon, gently, as if he was afraid to hurt her and the life that grew within her body. They had made love hundreds of times, in hundreds of places, and each time it was a wondrous thing. Her heart swelled in her chest. She had never known that such happiness could exist.

"I think we can appease him, my love, if we both attended court for a season."

She lifted her brows. "Leave Château Bocage?"

"Just for the winter. There is little to be done here when the ground is frozen."

"There's cider to make! And sewing, and mending, and beasts to slaughter and meat to salt and fruit to preserve and grain to mill—"

"All things that Gustave and Manon are fully capable of doing," he interrupted. He took her rough hands and eased them open. "You are the wife of the Vicomte de Bocage, my love. You should be running this estate, not working on it."

Her eyes narrowed in speculation. She did miss Marie-Celeste, and the town house in the Faubourg St. Germain was in desperate need of work. She did not care much for the courtiers of Versailles, but if one season at court meant she could see Kilian through the entire winter, and keep him at Château Bocage through the rest of the year, it might be worth it.

"Just a single season?"

"That would appease the king, I think." He smiled. "And it would get you away from this blasted château so I can get some of your attention." Despite the villagers that neared the courtyard, he tenderly kissed her lips. "I worry about you, my love. You work far too hard."

Aimee threw her arms around his neck and pressed her face in his strong shoulder. "Very well, Kilian, I shall share you with the king. Nine months in Normandy for three months in Paris. It is not so high a price to pay."

"Nay." His laughter rumbled in his chest. "I think it may be quite pleasurable, *a stor*. The Parisian winters can be quite cold, and many a night will be spent in our town house rather than attending court."

"Indeed?" Her voice grew husky. "Now I know what we intend to do when we winter in Paris."

"I shall love you, *a stor*." He ran his finger along her cheek. "Winter in Paris, summer, spring, and fall in Normandy—it doesn't matter where we are. I shall just love you."

GET LOVESTRUCK!

AND GET STRIKING ROMANCES FROM POPULAR LIBRARY'S BELOVED AUTHORS

Watch for these exciting romances in the months to come:

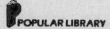